Praise for *Heiress in Love*

"Each scene is more sensual and passionate than the last."
—*Publishers Weekly* (starred review)

"Riveting tale of life, loss, convenience, and heart-wrenching love! Superbly written!" —*Fresh Fiction*

"With this delightful debut Brooke demonstrates her ability for creating a charming cast of characters who are the perfect players in the first of the Ministry of Marriage series. Marriage-of-convenience fans will rejoice and take pleasure in this enchanting read." —*RT Book Reviews*

"Clever, lush, and lovely—an amazing debut!"
—Suzanne Enoch, *New York Times* bestselling author

"A delightful confection of secrets and seduction, *Heiress in Love* will have readers craving more!"
—Tracy Anne Warren

"One of the most compelling heroes I've read in years."
—Anna Campbell

**St. Martin's Paperbacks Titles by
Christina Brooke**

Heiress in Love
Mad About the Earl

Mad About the Earl

CHRISTINA BROOKE

St. Martin's Paperbacks

This is a work of fiction. All of the characters, organizations, and events portrayed in this novel are either products of the author's imagination or are used fictitiously.

MAD ABOUT THE EARL

Copyright © 2012 by Christina Brooke.
Excerpt from *A Duchess to Remember* copyright © 2012 by Christina Brooke.

For information address St. Martin's Press, 175 Fifth Avenue, New York, NY 10010.

ISBN: 978-0-312-53413-4

Printed in the United States of America

St. Martin's Paperbacks edition / January 2012

St. Martin's Paperbacks are published by St. Martin's Press, 175 Fifth Avenue, New York, NY 10010.

10 9 8 7 6 5 4 3 2 1

Mad About the Earl

CHAPTER ONE

L ady Rosamund Westruther caught her first glimpse of Pendon Place from the carriage window and fell deeper in love with her destiny.

From this distance, the grand Elizabethan manor house loomed over the landscape, a massive expanse of gray stone with Gothic arched windows and crenellated turrets. Only the tendrils of deep green ivy climbing its walls softened the austerity of its aspect.

The house was gloomy, brooding, and utterly romantic.

A thrill of anticipation ran down Rosamund's spine. Today would seal her fate as the future mistress of this house.

She fingered the engraved surface of a large gold locket that hung by a chain around her neck. She resisted the urge to open it. Cecily would mock her mercilessly if she caught her mooning over the tiny portrait of Griffin deVere, a gentleman she'd never met. Besides, his features were now so familiar to her, she shouldn't need this keepsake for remembrance.

A giddy mix of delight, anticipation, and fear washed through Rosamund. Her guardian, the Duke of Montford, had chosen the heir to this fine Cornwall estate to be her husband. On this visit, she and Griffin deVere would pledge their troth, and she would set her slippered feet on the path she'd always been meant to tread.

She'd whirled in a flurry of excitement since the duke had proposed the journey, so eager to meet her intended husband she could have sprouted wings and flown to Cornwall, never mind the tedious carriage ride.

Would Griffin go down on bended knee when he paid his addresses? Surely he would. And give her a betrothal ring he'd designed especially for her. And perhaps even a posy of wildflowers he'd picked with his own hands. Or a poem, tied with a sprig of lavender . . .

Rosamund repressed a chuckle. The young gentlemen of her acquaintance wrote shockingly bad verse. But if Griffin should break into an ode to her left earlobe or some such thing, she'd keep a straight face, no matter what it cost her. For the thought was what counted, wasn't it?

Perhaps . . . She squeezed her eyes shut as a thrill skittered right down to her toes. Perhaps Griffin might even take her in his arms. And kiss her. A sweet, tender, cherishing kiss. Oh, wouldn't that be—

"Rosamund! Rosamund, I am *talking* to you."

Startled from her daydream, Rosamund glanced down at her fifteen-year-old cousin, Lady Cecily Westruther. "What is it, dear?"

Cecily rolled her eyes. "Look at you! You are being sold body and soul to a man you've never met, and all you do is sit there, looking cool and composed and utterly beautiful. As if you visited any old acquaintance."

"I'm glad I *look* cool and composed, for that's the last thing I feel inside." Rosamund gripped her cousin's mittened hand tightly. "Oh, Cecily! What if he doesn't like me?"

Cecily snorted. "Not like you? *Everyone* likes you, Rosamund. Even the duke holds you in affection, and his heart is as cold as an arctic winter." She patted Rosamund's arm. "Griffin deVere will fall desperately in love with you, just like every other gentleman you've ever met."

Cecily leaned forward to gaze out the window, her dark ringlets bobbing beneath her bonnet. "Do you think it's true this branch of the family descends from pirates? Perhaps there's treasure buried somewhere on the estate."

"I beg you not to mention pirates to the earl," said Rosamund. "He is extremely proud, by all accounts."

"I'm not afraid of any old earl," said Cecily. "I can handle the duke, can't I?"

Yes, Rosamund was forced to admit that even at fifteen, her precocious cousin seemed to sail without a care through the treacherous shoals of life as the Duke of Montford's ward. How Rosamund envied Cecily her odd mixture of charm and audacity. She'd have Griffin's grandfather eating out of her hand by teatime.

The clouds shifted, and a thick shaft of summer sunlight beamed down on Pendon Place. The pale gray stone of the manor house glittered with a silvery sheen. Suddenly the gloomy mansion sparkled with promise, transformed into a castle for a fairy-tale princess. Delight lit Rosamund from within. She could not wait to see inside her future home.

They rounded a bend in the drive, and the house was lost from view. The rich green landscape of a well-kept park opened up before them. A russet-colored doe lifted her head to gaze softly at the carriage as it rolled past. Rosamund recalled the charming legend about the herd of fallow deer that roamed the park at Pendon Place: If the herd ever died out, so would the deVere family.

The carriage finally crunched to a halt outside the front

door. Rosamund's breath stopped, most likely obstructed by her heart, which had jumped into her throat.

This was it.

The moment she'd been waiting for all her life.

Rosamund knew it was the height of bad manners to eavesdrop on someone else's conversation. In ordinary circumstances, upon hearing the low rumble of male voices in her host's library, she'd either make her presence known or leave.

But this time, extreme measures were called for. Upon their arrival at Pendon Place, none of the deVere family had greeted them. The Duke of Montford had ridden ahead of their carriage and must have arrived earlier, but he was nowhere to be seen. The housekeeper had shown Rosamund and Cecily to their respective bedchambers and asked them to wait.

Cecily had immediately disobeyed, slipping out for a ramble in the house and grounds, presumably to hunt for signs of buried treasure. A full hour passed before Rosamund gave in to impatience and made her own escape.

Rosamund sent a quick glance over her shoulder to sweep the empty corridor. Edging closer to the open library door, she pressed one hand to the green Spitalfields silk that papered the wall and canted her head to listen to the discussion within.

The drawling accents of her guardian, the Duke of Montford, met her ear. "Oliver, I realize the fellow is half-savage, but this is the outside of enough. Where the Devil is he?"

A deep grunt came from much closer to the door than she'd expected. Rosamund jumped and drew back, poised for flight. Then a voice she recognized as belonging to

Oliver, Lord deVere, said, "Down at the stables. But he'll come about."

Rosamund bit her lip. At the *stables*? When he ought to be here, proposing marriage to her! There must be some mistake.

"What?" The duke's tone could have frozen water. "Do you mean to tell me Griffin doesn't wish to pledge himself to my ward? Do we waste our time here?"

"Not a bit of it!" blustered Lord deVere. "He'll marry her, or by God, I'll know the reason why."

The implications of this speech had all the shock and sting of a slap in the face. Not only was he purposely absent, Griffin deVere didn't *want* to marry her. Rosamund turned cold. All her joy and anticipation shriveled like autumn leaves.

Montford spoke. "As I am sure you're aware, deVere, any number of candidates have been beating my door down for the right to wed Lady Rosamund Westruther. The Ministry—"

"To Hell with the Ministry! The boy is difficult, I'll not deny it. This is a show of bloody-mindedness, but he'll knuckle under. I'll see to it."

"*I* always found a thorough thrashing did wonders for disciplining Griffin as a lad."

This voice, Rosamund did not recognize. A breathy wheeze punctuated his speech, as if the speaker were old or ill. "But the boy grew to such an ungodly size, by the time he was thirteen, I was obliged to have three men hold him down to administer the whipping. Two years later, I'd have needed a regiment, so I had his younger brother thrashed instead while he watched. It answered." A long, weary sigh. "Shall I have my men bring them in?"

Rosamund gave a horrified gasp, then clamped her hand over her mouth. The duke had never favored corporal

punishment. Why resort to violence when his mere words
were such a powerful lash? But deVere might be of a different mind. Would she be obliged to intercede? Would
they heed her if she did?

The third gentleman must be the Earl of Tregarth,
Griffin's grandfather. What a horrid, cruel old man he
sounded. Pity filled her at the thought of Griffin's suffer-
ings, and those of his younger brother. Was that where
Griffin had come by the ugly scar over his eye?

There was a pause. "That will not be necessary," said
the duke. "No doubt, we'll see Griffin at dinner. In the
meantime, we might as well discuss other business."

"More matchmaking?" panted the earl, his tone laced
with disgust. A chair creaked. "I'll leave you two old women
to your scheming."

Rosamund turned on her heel and fled back down the
corridor, the skirts of her muslin gown flurrying around
her ankles. She'd changed into her best morning gown
upon her arrival, of course. Such an auspicious occasion
merited an exquisite ensemble. Purest white sprigged all
over with primroses and a wide sash in the same sunny
yellow.

She slowed to a more decorous pace when she reached
the wainscoted hall. Crushing disappointment made her
heart heavy as she climbed the stairs to the second floor.
Why had she hoped so hard for love in her marriage when
she'd been brought up from birth to expect nothing of the
kind? Clearly, Griffin didn't want her at all.

What an utter fool she was.

Ever since Montford had informed her of his choice of
a husband for her six months ago, she'd awaited this first
meeting in a fever of anticipation.

She'd even sent a miniature portrait of herself to Griffin.
After several promptings, he'd responded in kind. No

letter had accompanied the token. Not even a note of thanks for her own portrait, much less the poetic outpouring of devotion her romantic heart had hoped for.

A telling sign, but that had not daunted her, had it? She'd spent hours carefully transposing Griffin's likeness onto a small tablet of porcelain cut to fit her locket. Each stroke of that tiny brush seemed to bring him closer to her. Like a besotted fool, she'd spent an age mixing the precise shade of arctic gray for his eyes. Such dreams she'd woven in her head!

Gaining her bedchamber, Rosamund rang for her maid. As she'd done fifty times a day, Rosamund clicked open her locket and gazed down at Griffin's miniature.

She narrowed her eyes at her intended husband's face. Oh, hadn't she mooned and sighed over that portrait like a silly greenhead? As if it depicted an Adonis, rather than the fascinatingly ugly collection of features that stared out at her.

Griffin deVere was not handsome, not in the least. His large beak of a nose had obviously been broken, perhaps more than once; his jaw was uncompromising, bluntly square. The wild dark hair that grew thickly from his head moved beyond the fashionably windswept to the wildly cyclonic. A deep scar slashed his right temple, giving his eye a lazy, decadent cast.

Yet somehow, the very imperfection of his lineaments made them appear more striking.

He reminded her of the jagged cliff faces of the Cornwall coast, all weathered crags and treacherous angles. No softness to be seen, except in a shockingly sensual mouth.

No, Griffin deVere was not handsome. Decidedly not. But each time she gazed upon them, his looks pierced her to the core.

Was it only because she knew she was to wed him that

this likeness exercised such a powerful effect on her? Perhaps. The portrait had spawned a thousand imaginings, nonetheless.

She'd planned and plotted. She'd lain in her bedchamber late at night, dreaming of him. Such wicked dreams they'd been. So wicked, her cheeks heated at the thought of them. She'd spun a perfect imaginary world around this man.

All for nothing. He didn't want her. He hadn't even bestirred himself to *meet* her, much less beg for her hand in marriage.

The sense of bewildered hurt made tears smart behind her eyes. She shook her head and forced them down. Weeping achieved nothing. This was no time for maudlin theatrics. She needed to act.

Rosamund's hand clenched into an unladylike fist as latent anger flared. Regardless of wounded feelings, Griffin deVere's deliberate absence insulted her.

How *dared* he dismiss her with such disrespect? She ought not stand for this cavalier treatment. If he began so poorly, how would he go on once they were wed?

The assurances of both her mother and the duke echoed in her mind: *Marriage is a business arrangement between two families, no more.*

No. They were wrong. *Her* marriage would be far more than a dynastic transaction. She'd be the best wife Griffin deVere could wish for. And before she was finished with him, he'd be the best kind of husband, too. She refused to give up her dream of a happy home for some rude, ill-bred man who preferred hobnobbing with his horses to wooing her.

After all, she was a Westruther, wasn't she? *Au coeur valiant, rien est impossible:* "To a valiant heart, nothing is impossible." Griffin deVere would soon learn that Lady Rosamund Westruther might look like a Dresden china doll, but her heart was as valiant as any of her forebears'.

The door opened. Rosamund snapped the locket shut and composed her features into a serene expression.

"There you are, Meg." Rosamund smiled at her maid. "My riding habit, if you please."

Griffin deVere emerged from the horse barn for the first time in the past God-knew-how-many hours and squinted against the brightness of the sunlight that showered the stable yard. Wiping his grimy, sweaty face on the sleeve of his shirt, he headed for the pump.

He stank of linseed oil and other secretions he'd rather not think about. His favorite brood mare had died during a difficult birth two nights before. The loss of her had gutted him. He'd battled hard to haul her back from the brink of death, but nature gave him a sound thrashing for his impudence.

At least he'd managed to save her foal.

Griffin had paired the infant with another mare in milk, a difficult process that required patience, persistence, and a grand dose of sheer brute strength. The mare had to be restrained and tricked by scent into accepting the foal and letting her drink. He'd monitored the fostering progress closely so that the mare wouldn't hurt the foal as the infant suckled.

Now that the worst was over, he'd left the pair in his head groom's capable hands. Griffin was hungry, he was tired, and the message his bastard of a grandsire had sent demanding his presence up at the house had done nothing to smooth the rough edges of his temper.

He bent over to duck his head under the pump. The gush of water tingled icily on his skin as it sluiced over his neck and shoulders.

If it weren't for Jacks and Timothy, he'd have consigned his old Devil of a grandfather to Hell years ago.

He'd give anything to tell Lord Tregarth exactly where he could shove his marriage of convenience, but he had little choice there, either. His siblings always suffered for his misdemeanors; if he didn't knuckle under and betroth himself to Lady Rosamund Westruther, his brother Timothy would be yanked out of university and sent into the army. He couldn't let that happen. Education was the key to a younger son's future, as the old earl was well aware.

But even Griffin's compliance had its limits.

Or had it? Lord, he'd give a monkey to see the old gentleman's face if he appeared in the earl's library immediately, as ordered, muck clinging to his boots and his outer garments caked with filth. Ready to meet his intended bride.

Griffin ripped off his coat, which had probably suffered the worst of it, and flung it over a nearby rail. His cravat, waistcoat, and shirt followed. Then he set to work on the pump again, scrubbing at his torso as best he might.

Well, he wouldn't apologize for tardiness in a cause such as this. Dancing attendance on a spoiled Westruther heiress came a very poor second to his duty to a motherless foal. Besides, Lady Rosamund Westruther might as well learn now as later that Griffin deVere never danced, and certainly not to any female's tune.

He cupped his hands to catch more water and dashed it over his face. Briefly, he wondered about this girl he was supposed to marry. He'd deliberately closed his ears and his mind to his grandfather's lectures; he couldn't remember what, if anything, the old Devil had said about her.

Not that it mattered one way or the other. No gently bred lady would entertain the notion of marrying him for longer than it took to assimilate the full, spectacular extent of his ugliness. One glance at Griffin's monstrous bulk, and his delicate prospective fiancée would faint or fall into hysterics and beg the duke to take her home.

As soon as he'd heard of the scheme to bring them together, he warned his grandfather against it. Better for them to plight their troth by proxy if the union was truly the old man's wish.

But he needn't have bothered. The earl palpably anticipated Griffin's humiliation. Relished the prospect, in fact. He must be very sure of the girl to have agreed to this meeting.

Perhaps it was as his grandfather said: The Duke of Montford would never allow the chit to draw back from the union simply because her betrothed was a gargoyle.

Suddenly, Griffin noticed something . . . or the lack of it. The bustling stable yard had fallen silent. Only the *splat, splat, drip* of water on the ground could be heard.

He released the pump handle and straightened, wiping the water from his eyes. Glancing up, he saw at least three stable hands frozen in place, as if turned to stone. His eyes narrowed. Was that a hint of drool slipping from the corner of Billy Trotter's slackened mouth?

With a strong feeling he wouldn't like what he was about to see, Griffin turned around.

Sweet. Jesus.

He nearly shoved his head under the pump for another dousing. If the reaction of every other male in the vicinity hadn't told him his eyes didn't lie, he'd have believed her a vision conjured by exhaustion. But not even his imagination could have manufactured such a breathtaking piece of womanhood.

She wore a deep cobalt blue riding habit that fitted her form so precisely, his hands itched to shape themselves around those well-defined curves. The habit was in the military style, with elaborate silver lacing across her torso that drew the eye to a magnificent bosom and trim waist.

Griffin peeled his gaze from her mouthwatering form and forced it to her face. Eyes as blue as the heavens stared at him from beneath a sweep of thick black lashes and delicately arched brows. Rich golden ringlets escaped artfully from one side of her jaunty black hat.

The angle of that hat seemed unconscionably rakish. In fact, with her pearly skin and her adorable bow of a mouth, celestial eyes, and gilt curls, the set of that particular piece of millinery struck a jarringly saucy note. It was as if an angel stood before him, closing one eye in a sly, knowing wink.

Stunned as he was, moments passed before the truth crashed in on him, like Armageddon.

Lady Rosamund Westruther.

Bloody. Bloody. Hell.

Her lips moved, but he didn't hear what she said for the pounding in his ears. His heart pumped. His mouth dried. His hands grew clammy. Blood abandoned his brain like rats from a sinking ship.

She's not for you.

His skeptical, cynical mind fought for supremacy, but instinct, powerful and raw, drowned out the frantic messages from his brain. A low, animal hum swelled inside him.

I want her. Now.

The angel's brows snapped together, and for the first time, he noticed a distinctly militant sparkle in her eyes.

She put up her chin and said, "You, there! Didn't you hear what I said? Saddle me a horse, please. I wish to ride."

CHAPTER TWO

*B*eastly man!

Rosamund's first sight of Griffin deVere would have caused a maiden with a less valiant heart to quail. Shirtless, dirty, sodden, and glaring, he presented a spectacle to strike terror into any gently bred lady's soul.

His massive body gleamed wetly in the sunshine: acres of hairy muscled chest, miles of long, strong legs. Hands as big as plates shoved a shock of black hair from his eyes, plastering it back over his skull. The movement made the muscles in his biceps bulge with latent power.

Her fascinated gaze snagged on the tufts of dark hair beneath each armpit. Oddly, the sight was the opposite of repulsive. A hot shiver burned down her spine.

But it was the brooding, angry look in his eyes that made her insides melt and slide and sizzle, like butter in a sauté pan.

Rot the man! Why did he have to be even larger, more intensely alive, more masculine than her wildest imaginings had painted him? He was colossal, and not only in stature. The powerful life force within him seemed to blaze from those lightning-colored eyes.

She ought to be disgusted by the state she found him

in, particularly in the circumstances. The least he could do was make himself presentable on this, of all days!

Ah, how she wished she *were* disgusted. Her fury fired anew that he should have such a cataclysmic effect on her. He was rough and dirty and in a shocking state of undress, so far from the gallant prince of her imaginings, it would have been laughable had she not been consumed by disappointment.

Well. If he wanted to behave like a groom, she'd treat him like one.

But her heart obstructed her throat as she opened her mouth to teach him a lesson. Her voice wavered on the first attempt; she was obliged to repeat herself, and that only honed her temper to a sharper point.

Still, the brute made no answer.

"A horse, if you please," she said again. "I presume my saddle has been sent down by now."

A snicker sounded behind Griffin. His jaw hardened.

"Back to work." He tossed the command over his shoulder, not bothering to check whether it was followed. The men scattered, leaving Rosamund and her beastly betrothed alone in the stable yard.

He tilted his head, surveying her as keenly as a predator examines prey. She half expected him to sniff the air, bare his teeth . . . and pounce.

Instead, he crossed his massive arms in front of him. "Your mount hasn't arrived yet."

The deep rumble of his voice set parts of her to trembling. His pale, penetrating gaze traveled slowly over every inch of her, making those trembles multiply. If he *were* a servant, she'd reprimand him for such insolence.

More heat washed over her, wave after wave of it. "S-saddle me something from here, then."

Oh, she could have killed herself for that betraying stammer. Besides, she was never so autocratic as this in her dealings with servants. *He* put her all on end. She couldn't seem to come to grips with restraint.

He shrugged. "Nothing fit for a lady in these stables."

Her lips pressed together. "I'll be the judge of that." She nodded and started toward the stalls. "Show me."

She tried to sweep past him, but he caught her elbow and tugged her to a halt. "No, you don't."

Rosamund gasped. He wasn't rough, but his grip was firm enough to prevent her escape. She whipped her gaze up to meet his. "Let go of me."

"You can't ride the horses here. I forbid it."

She tried to pull away, knowing it was futile. His hold was as strong and uncompromising as a steel manacle. "*You* forbid it? And why should I obey your commands?"

He showed her his teeth in a grimace of a smile. "Ah, my sweet, innocent angel. Didn't you guess? I'm Griffin deVere."

Griffin waited, bristling with anticipation. *Now* she'd shriek and run away.

"But I know who you are," she answered, widening those impossibly blue eyes. "You sent me a miniature of yourself, don't you recall? Though you have a point. I should hardly recognize the grandson of an earl in such a guise." A twinge of impatience crossed her face. "Oh, do let go of me. You'll soil my riding habit, and it's new."

He dropped her arm as if it burned him. Astonishment was an inadequate word for what he felt. This . . . this slip of a girl stood up to him as if he weren't some ogre who ground children's bones for bread. No woman other than his sister had ever reacted to him like that before. And she *knew*? She knew that he . . . that they . . . And yet, she stood her ground.

Aware that his jaw had dropped, Griffin hastily shut it.

Wait. "Miniature?" he repeated, frowning. "What miniature?"

Her cool gaze flicked over him in a dispassionate inspection. How old was she? Seventeen? Eighteen? Yet she displayed all the poise of a matron in her prime.

Her lips quivered with impatience. "The portrait you gave me. I sent you my likeness and you sent me yours."

He felt himself redden around the gills. Damn his sadistic grandfather! Gruffly, he cleared his throat. "The earl must have sent it. I would never—"

He broke off. He'd almost said he'd never voluntarily inflict the sight of his face on anyone.

The lady's features relaxed. "Oh, I see. The earl appears to have kept you in the dark about all this." She tilted her head, her gaze softening. "Do you not know why I'm here today?"

Griffin gave a clipped nod. "I know."

His answer didn't please her. Coldly, she said, "Then why, might I ask, do I find you thus? Any gentleman with an ounce of courtesy would have awaited my arrival." Her gaze wandered over him. "And dressed appropriately for the occasion."

He snorted. "I had more important things to do."

"More *important*? What could be more important than meeting the person you're going to spend the rest of your life with?"

Griffin nearly laughed. She didn't seriously expect they'd go through with the betrothal? What a travesty that would be. Though every cell of his body urged him to take this perfect, virginal sacrifice, drag her back to his lair, and defile her in every way known to man, he knew better. Such an act would be a desecration.

This bright angel was so far above his touch, she might as well have dwelled in Heaven itself. How could the Duke of Montford even consider someone like Griffin an appropriate match for such a delicate maid? Lady Rosamund Westruther ought to take a handsome knight to husband, not a monster like Griffin deVere.

He reached for his shirt and used it to towel off his body in large, efficient swipes. "You needn't worry. I'll explain to the duke that we won't suit. Come on."

Snatching up the rest of his garments, he strode out of the stable yard, leaving her no choice but to follow.

Refusing to match his strides to hers, he obliged her to run to keep up with him. Even then, she soon fell behind. Rounding the rose garden wall, he heard her cry.

"Wait!"

With a curse beneath his breath, he halted. Turning, he watched her hurry toward him up the lawn. Despite her haste, she still looked unruffled and elegant. It made him want to muss her up good and proper.

Hell, he needed to nip those kinds of thoughts in the bud.

She finally caught up to him, and he noticed that the exertion had made a slight alteration in her appearance, after all. A flush pinked her cheeks, and her eyes glowed like sapphires. If anything, her beauty deepened with exercise. It made him wonder what she'd look like after a prolonged bout of lovemaking.

He dragged in a shaky breath.

"Do you mean to say you don't wish to marry me?" Her surprisingly low voice betrayed no emotion.

A harsh bark of a laugh burst from him. "Oh, come now, my lady. You cannot pretend *you* want to wed someone like *me*."

He refused to spell it out for her. If she chose to maintain the polite fiction that she didn't find the idea repulsive, more fool she. He ought not to marvel at how well disciplined she was. He knew something of her guardian, the Duke of Montford, after all. The man was famed for his ruthlessness and his insistence on the paramount importance of duty to one's family.

Were Griffin's prospects of wealth and position so attractive to Rosamund that she'd refuse to be swayed by his ugliness? Rich, heartbreakingly beautiful, well connected . . . Surely this girl had her pick of titles and estates the length and breadth of England. She didn't need him.

She swallowed hard. "I don't follow you, sir. Before we undertook this journey, the earl gave us to understand all was settled. Is—" She faltered and bit her lip. "—is there something about me that does not please you?"

Oh, for God's sake!

Pairing such an exquisite creature with him must be someone's idea of a joke—his grandsire's, most probably. The question was, why the Hell did she play along with it?

He stared hard at her. "Do *you* wish for the marriage, then? You are prepared to obey your guardian in this?"

She averted her gaze. "I—I never thought . . . I never considered doing otherwise."

Fury burned through him, the same kind of frustrated anger that ultimately crashed in after an encounter with a willing bit of muslin. Those women never cared what he looked like as long as he paid handsomely for their favors. This marriage was no less a business transaction than a punter taking a whore, though it was dressed up in the trappings of wealth and respectability.

Did Lady Rosamund have the slightest inkling of what she'd be called upon to do as his wife? He'd wager if she did, she'd turn tail and run. He couldn't imagine this cool goddess *accepting,* much less *enjoying* his touch.

Yes, he wanted her so much, he was near crazed with it. But he hated the feeling. The hurt and resentment of it tangled inside him until he couldn't see straight.

And that same impulse that made schoolboys pull pretty girls' hair made him step toward her, boxing her in between his body and the stone wall behind her.

She didn't shrink back or cry out or weep. She simply looked up into his face. Her eyes were wide, pink lips slightly parted.

What the Devil was wrong with the chit? Why wasn't she screaming?

His breath quickened. Brutally, he said, "There'd be no ordinary marriage of convenience between us, you understand? I'd want you in my bed. In mine alone."

Her color flared. When she spoke, however, her voice was even. "Naturally," she said.

Naturally? Was she touched in the head? Did she not understand what he meant? He sucked air through his teeth. "You don't know what you're talking about."

With a frown of impatience, she said, "I'm not a simpleton, Mr. deVere. I know what marriage entails."

The directness of her gaze threw down a decided challenge. Images of her tumbled naked on his bed flooded his brain, strangled the breath in his lungs.

No. No, she couldn't mean she'd willingly suffer his advances. It was all a ploy to get him to the altar. She'd do her duty and marry him, then wait until the wedding night to reveal her revulsion.

The tangles in his belly drew into tight knots. Were his prospects so attractive to her? No other woman had been willing to risk herself in pursuit of his worldly expectations.

As he stared down at her, a smile trembled on those plump, pink lips. Gently, as if speaking to a child, Rosamund said, "I'm not afraid of you."

The bottom seemed to fall out of his stomach. Apart from Jacks, he scared the living daylights out of every female he met.

Unreasoning anger filled him. Suddenly, he wanted to scare her, to make her admit her fear. Otherwise, what chance did he have against her?

With a strangled groan, Griffin gripped her waist and lifted her up and planted his mouth on hers.

Fire surged through his veins at the first touch of those soft, warm lips. He ravished her mouth, hardly registering her reaction. He wanted to punish her, to show her how much she'd loathe suffering the intentions of a man like him. To strip away her veneer of acceptance and make her admit her disgust.

But her soft, fragrant femininity called to him, a siren's song that drew him, not only stirring his body but shaking him down to his soul. With a hoarse groan, he wrapped his arms around her waist and angled his head to delve farther into her mouth.

Instinctively, Rosamund knew this kiss was punitive and full of anger. She'd not the least idea what Griffin thought she'd done to deserve such treatment. Her mere presence seemed to ignite his wrath.

His lips devoured hers with bruising force. One arm lashed about her waist, bringing her flush against his hard body. His other hand tipped the hat from her head and his fingers dragged through her hair. Pins scattered as her curls slipped free and tumbled about her shoulders in disarray.

No man had ever tried to kiss her before, much less handled her with such furious mastery. Overpowered but not cowed by this giant of a man, she yielded in a way that would have shocked anyone who knew her. Treacherous thrills chased one another down her spine. A strange, melting warmth began low in her belly.

He was immensely strong; his mouth gave her no quarter. Confusion, longing, and sheer curiosity warred within her. She'd dreamed of his kiss for so long, but she'd always imagined a careful, searching tenderness. Not the hard, domineering passion he showed her now.

Rosamund put her hands on his shoulders with some vague notion of restraining him, but the powerful muscles that shifted beneath her palms made her forget her purpose. She knew a sharp regret that she wore gloves and couldn't feel the texture of his skin beneath her fingertips.

Griffin smelled of the stables, of earthy masculine musk and sweat and something more pungent, like varnish. Strangely, it didn't bother her in the least.

He set her on the low wall behind her so that her head was level with his. Then, he slanted his mouth and slid his tongue against hers in the most shocking, lascivious move. Rosamund gasped deep in her throat, choking on her own answering surge of desire. She could barely catch her breath for the way his firm lips plundered hers.

A hot thread snapped inside her, unraveling, then coiling tight in the pit of her belly. Against her will, for a few heated seconds, she teetered on the verge of responding with equally fierce abandon.

Oh, God, what was happening to her? Was she so lacking in pride that this assault—for it could not be termed a gesture of affection—stirred her passions?

But it wasn't the wildness of his kiss that moved her. It was the pain she sensed buried deep beneath the savagery. What must it have been like to grow up at the mercy of his cruel monster of a grandfather? No wonder he couldn't believe she truly wanted to marry him.

But she did. Oh, yes, she did.

A wave of tenderness swept over her. With a soft sigh, she kissed him back, clumsily, eagerly. Her hands left his shoulders to frame his face and stroke through his thick, dark hair. Experimentally, she ran her tongue over his.

Griffin froze. Then, with a harsh gasp, he wrenched his mouth from hers.

She whispered his name, but he didn't seem to hear her. His head was bowed; his big chest heaved. She felt the warmth of his ragged breath against her neck.

After a long, tense moment, Griffin raised his head. Without looking at her or speaking, he lifted her from the wall and set her gently on the ground.

She brought up a hand to touch her lips, to feel the imprint of his kiss upon them. "Griffin?"

His gaze met hers. The baffled fury in those icy gray eyes made her hold out her hand to him. He stared at it as if she held a poisonous snake.

Gathering her courage, she stepped forward gingerly, as if he were a wild stallion she sought to tame. Lightly, she brushed her fingertips over his arm. The muscles there tensed, granite hard, unyielding beneath her hand.

"Shall we go to your grandfather now?" she said in a soft, gentle voice.

His nostrils flared as he inhaled deeply. The scar that slashed his temple glowed white. Then he shook his head in disbelief. "This is madness," he muttered.

Without waiting for her answer, he turned on his heel and strode away.

CHAPTER THREE

The rap of the chairman's gavel called the meeting to order. The Duke of Montford lifted his gaze from the agenda he'd been perusing and turned his attention to the collection of aristocrats assembled around the vast, polished mahogany table.

The winter meeting of the Ministry of Marriage was in session.

Inwardly, Montford sighed. These gatherings seemed to come closer and closer together as the years wore on.

There was Lady Arden, with that sparkle in her eye that always spelled trouble for someone—usually for him. Oliver, Lord deVere, appeared to labor under some sort of frustrated fury. But then, didn't he always?

DeVere slid a glance at Montford, then looked away, scratching his whiskered face. Like his warrior forebears, deVere was big, fierce, and dark. A remarkably hirsute man, he needed to shave twice daily to avoid looking like a ruffian. He seldom shaved more than once, however.

The chairman cleared his throat. "We have a lot to get through this afternoon." He glanced at the agenda in his hand. "The first item concerns the betrothal of Lady Rosamund Westruther to Griffin deVere, Earl of Tregarth."

The elderly Lord Ponsonby started from his customary abstraction. In his thread of a voice, he said, "*Eh?* What's that you say? Never tell me the old earl is dead? Well, well," he added placidly, "I make no doubt he is burning in Hell."

Unable to resist, Montford met Lady Arden's gaze. Her eyes danced with suppressed mirth.

Montford responded, "The fourth earl has been dead for more than a year, Lord Ponsonby. As to his current whereabouts, I would not venture to guess."

"Your Grace," said Lady Arden in her clear, cool voice, "are we to believe that this engagement between Griffin, Lord Tregarth, and Lady Rosamund Westruther still stands? Lady Rosamund has been out these two years and might have expected to be a married lady by now. If Lord Tregarth cannot see his way clear to tying the knot, then I propose we—"

"He will tie the knot, damn you!" Lord deVere leaned forward, shooting a furious glare at her from beneath bushy brows.

DeVere didn't heed the shocked gasps from the ladies, or the chairman's admonishment to mind his language. With a pugnacious thrust of his chin, he added, "The wedding date is set." He smacked the table with his fist as if it were a gavel. "Next item."

Unabashed by deVere's bullishness, Lady Arden turned her wide brown eyes on Montford. "Is that true, Your Grace?"

Montford's gaze locked with deVere's in a silent communication. DeVere's expression was fierce, but was there also a hint of a plea in those black eyes? Not that a plea

from deVere would move Montford to help him. The duke
had his own reasons for wishing the alliance to go ahead
without further interference from either Arden or the Ministry itself.

"That's right," Montford said coolly. He did not say precisely *which* date had been set and trusted no one would
ask.

Now all they needed was for the parties to the match to
agree.

Musing further on this subject, Montford took little interest in the proceedings until they came to another item on
the agenda that touched Rosamund, if only tangentially.

The marriage of Griffin's sister, Lady Jacqueline de-
Vere.

The Countess of Warrington spoke up. "*That* affair is
well in hand, I assure you. Since Lady Jacqueline came to
live with us in Bath, she and my son have formed an attachment. I expect an announcement at any moment."

Montford's brows drew together over Lady Warrington's disclosure. Marriage between cousins occurred all
the time, but it was a practice of which he did not approve. Just look at her ladyship's rodent-like features. A
clear advertisement against inbreeding if ever there was
one.

Besides, Lady Jacqueline deVere had been betrothed
to Lord Malby from the cradle, if his memory served correctly. The Ministry had not been notified of any alteration
to that plan.

"Am I to gather from this that the longstanding betrothal
between Lady Jacqueline and Lord Malby is at an end?"
he inquired with a glance at deVere.

"Oh!" scoffed Lady Warrington. "*That* abomination
was the old earl's doing. My nephew will not be guided by
his grandsire's wishes, you may be sure."

"But I am the girl's guardian, not Griffin," rumbled

Oliver, Lord deVere. "*I* say whom she marries, madam. And it will not be your namby-pamby son!"

Lady Warrington stared at deVere, openmouthed with astonishment.

Montford intervened. "Perhaps we should adjourn this discussion until the parties can come up with a more . . . cogent proposal to put to the meeting."

He glanced at the chairman, who obediently took his cue. The meeting proceeded to a close without further incident. Afterward, the duke accompanied Lord deVere down to his carriage.

"One wonders how you propose to bring off Tregarth's marriage to my ward, deVere," Montford murmured, drawing on his gloves. His words made puffs of steam in the crisp wintry air. "Clearly, now that the old earl is dead, your protégé has developed cold feet."

DeVere jammed his hat on his head. "Cold feet be damned! The boy's promised to your Lady Rosamund. And a damned lucky Devil he is."

DeVere's eyes warmed, presumably in appreciation of Rosamund's beauty. Montford hoped he would not have the appalling taste to express his admiration.

A vain hope. "Never set eyes on a tastier filly," rumbled deVere. "Not in all my days. If I weren't leg-shackled myself—"

Repressing a shudder, Montford held up a hand. "We will leave Lady Rosamund's indisputable charms out of this discussion. The question is, can you bring young Griffin up to scratch? I'm aware of the difficulties he faces, but enough is enough, deVere. If you don't deliver me a groom by next meeting, I shall be obliged to bow to Arden's importunities and put Lady Rosamund back on the Marriage Mart."

DeVere scowled. "That bloody woman!"

Montford shrugged. "If not Arden, it would be someone else. This betrothal has dragged on for far too long." He cocked his head. "What ails the fellow?"

DeVere grunted. "You heard about that business with the music master?"

"Yes, but hasn't that been laid to rest? Besides, it's hardly an excuse for not marrying Rosamund." Montford raised his brows. "Oh, you're not implying he has refrained from matrimony out of some misguided sense of honor, are you?"

DeVere rumbled a denial, then struck his palm with his fist. "Ah, blister it! Who knows? That music master's death caused him no end of trouble. Besides, there was no love lost between Griffin and the old earl. Maybe he's reluctant to bend to the old man's wishes now that he's cocked up his toes."

Montford considered. If the marriage of Tregarth's sister were also up for discussion, that could prove a valuable bargaining chip to use against Griffin.

He raised his hand to dismiss the waiting carriage. "My dear sir. Walk with me, if you will. I have a notion that I think might answer."

Lord deVere burst into Griffin's library at Pendon Place. "Dammit, Griffin, you must marry that Westruther chit, once and for all."

Griffin put his pen back in its stand and sat back from his desk. Almost any interruption of his attempts to wrestle his accounts books into submission was a welcome respite. But not if it meant discussing Lady Rosamund Westruther.

The mere thought of her still simmered his blood, even after all these years.

"Must I?" He grunted. "Why?"

"If you don't marry her by the end of this month, the Ministry will give her to someone else, that's why!"

DeVere threw down a document that skimmed across Griffin's desk. "You'll need that."

Griffin glanced down at the paper. A special license with his and Rosamund's name on it. A strange, disorienting feeling swept through him, like wind across an icy wasteland. He raised his gaze and watched his kinsman stride about the room.

Lord deVere was a big man, accustomed to using his size and his bullish bluster to get him what he wanted. However, Griffin was even larger than his relative, so he counted among the few deVere failed to intimidate.

Griffin forced out the words. "They may marry her to someone else with my goodwill." He sighed and rubbed his palm over his face in a gesture of resignation. "It's about time."

"*What?*" thundered deVere. "You have the audacity to be pleased by this? After all the scheming and scraping and bowing to Montford I had to do to arrange that bloody alliance? You'll stand by while they give your betrothed to another man?"

"It's what I hoped they'd do," Griffin muttered.

Even he knew an honorable man didn't throw a lady over. But who could blame Rosamund for turning elsewhere when he didn't claim her? Or the Ministry for giving up on a marriage that would never happen and choosing her another mate? Now Griffin could cut ties with Lady Rosamund Westruther once and for all.

And go to the Devil his own way.

He put his index fingertip on the special license and pushed it away from him. "They'll have another candidate in mind. They always do."

DeVere snorted. "Well, it won't be young Lauderdale,

mark my words, though the two of them have been going around smelling of April and May."

Ah, yes, he knew all about Captain Lauderdale squiring Rosamund around Town. Despite his determination not to care, he hadn't liked that news one bit. But what right did he have to like or dislike what Lady Rosamund did? None at all. He was finished with her. He ought to be happy, or at least relieved.

He didn't feel either of those things. He felt as if something inside him had ripped from its moorings and been cast adrift.

"There's also the matter of your sister," said deVere abruptly.

Griffin's head jerked up at that. Something stuck in his throat. He swallowed, trying to dislodge it. "She is well?"

"Yes, yes, or at least, I haven't heard anything to the contrary. It's Malby, d'ye see."

Griffin's brows drew together. "Malby? One of my grandfather's cronies, wasn't he? What has he to do with Jacks?"

Astonishment showed on deVere's face. "You mean you don't know? How can this be?"

Know what? Griffin held himself very still.

"The girl's been promised to Malby since she was in swaddling bands. Thought you knew." DeVere pulled at his lower lip, deep in thought. "But Lady Warrington, now. *She* is all for marrying the gel to her boy instead. I don't deny it's a good match, but—"

Anger washed over Griffin. Anger laced with desperation. "I won't have it," he said through gritted teeth. "I won't let you sell Jacks off to the highest bidder."

His brow lowering, Lord deVere braced his hands wide apart on the desk and leaned in. "And just how do you propose to stop me? Your grandfather made *me* the girl's guardian, not you."

Griffin forced himself to be calm. DeVere might be full of bluster, but he wasn't completely heartless. Of course, Jacks must marry, as every woman of her situation did. But that did not mean she must wed some degenerate roué old enough to be her grandsire.

Stalling, Griffin said, "Give her a season, at least. Can you not grant her some choice in the matter, even if it's only among a select few?"

DeVere took a seat on the other side of the desk and fingered his chin. "Malby will kick up the Devil of a fuss. He won't let go of her fortune too easily."

He shook his head. "No, I'm inclined to agree to Malby's demands. Can't be too long before the old goat kicks the bucket; then your sister will be free." He shifted in his chair to unfob his snuffbox. "Of course, if you could see your way clear to wedding Lady Rosamund . . ."

That took only a moment to sink in. Griffin shot to his feet. "You bastard," he said in a low, dangerous voice. "You are blackmailing me."

DeVere rose also and met his gaze squarely. "Blackmail? I am reminding you of your obligations to a gently bred lady, sir! That *I* should have to enforce those obligations makes *you* the bastard, not me. But mark me well, Griffin, it will be no skin off my nose to get your sister off my hands and into Malby's bed. Indeed, it would put me to a vast deal of trouble to renege on the arrangement. But I'll do it if it means you'll take Lady Rosamund to wife."

He paused. "So. Which is it to be?"

Griffin clenched his jaw so hard, he thought it might crack. DeVere wasn't cruel, but he *was* bloody-minded, sometimes to the point of cutting off his nose to spite his face.

Damn the old earl for not making Griffin Jacks's guardian! DeVere was only a distant cousin, and he didn't give a fig about the girl. He didn't care about anyone in this benighted family, did he? All he cared about was increasing the wealth and standing of the deVeres.

It was a profound source of disgruntlement to Oliver, Lord deVere, that his branch of the family hadn't advanced beyond the title of baron. Like so many of his hot-tempered ancestors, deVere could never stay on the right side of the reigning sovereign long enough to climb any higher in the peerage.

After a prolonged pause, Griffin spoke. "Let me understand you. If I agree to marry Lady Rosamund as soon as may be, you will set my sister free of that nauseating betrothal?"

DeVere grunted. "That's right."

"I want Jacks to have a season," said Griffin. "I want full approval of a list of candidates, and she will have her pick among them. My sister must marry, but she will not be made miserable. Not if I have any say in it."

DeVere held up a warning finger. "There'll be no silly romantical notions planted in the chit's head, d'ye hear me?"

"Wouldn't dream of it," said Griffin grimly.

His chest eased a little at the prospect of seeing Jacks again. "I'll open the town house. Do the thing properly. I won't have that Warrington witch playing chaperone, mind. And that chinless whelp of a son of hers will not go near my sister again."

If he let Lady Warrington chaperone Jacks, the grasping harridan would do her best to scuttle the girl's prospects with the ton.

Come to think of it, Jacks might not need any help in that direction. . . .

"From what I've seen of her, the chit is likely to be recalcitrant," said deVere, as if echoing Griffin's thoughts. "And she's a graceless wench, besides." He shook his head.

"The season doesn't start for a couple of months yet. You have a lot of work to do in the meantime."

DeVere didn't know the half of it. He could just imagine what his sister would have to say about the prospect of a London debut.

But if he could see her settled and content, he would be well pleased.

Of course, the price he would pay for his sister's happiness was his own abject humiliation, but she would never know that. No one would ever know how much it cost him to take Lady Rosamund Westruther as wife.

Truly, it amazed him that the Westruthers had let matters get this far. Despite his and Rosamund's disastrous first meeting three years ago, Lady Rosamund had not fled Pendon Place then and there. The formal betrothal had proceeded, regardless of Griffin's objections.

His grandfather had been mightily amused at the disparity between Griffin's brutish form and the poised, delicious confection Griffin's fiancée presented. The shame of suffering his grandsire's open ridicule in front of Rosamund herself still burned like acid in Griffin's gut.

Then the old earl's health had taken an abrupt turn for the worse, postponing the wedding as he lingered for months on the brink of death. His demise had required a suitable mourning period. Besides, Griffin had been far too occupied in bringing the estate into order to trouble himself with a bride.

And now, there was that damnable business with Allbright.

But he had to admit the truth, if only to himself. For almost three years, he had seized every possible excuse to avoid actually tying the knot with Lady Rosamund Westruther.

He'd never forget the way she made him feel that first day they met. Overgrown and hideous, undeserving and *furious* at his own inadequacy. He'd fallen ludicrously short of her expectations, but she'd been so damned plucky, so gladly determined to make the best of it.

It was her cursed cheerful dauntlessness that rankled the most. At least if she'd behaved like a spoiled heiress, he could have some basis on which to despise her.

If only he hadn't let his animal instincts overcome him and kissed her. He'd passed countless nights since that day consumed with a longing to repeat that incandescent experience. He couldn't sleep for thinking of her sweet, fragrant softness. If—*when*—they married, he'd have to live and breathe every day beside that delicious temptation, knowing she must hold him in aversion and contempt.

Griffin closed his eyes. His grandfather still had the power to torture him, even from the grave.

But he couldn't consider his own stupid pride. His sister must come first.

And he needed to get Jacks away from Pendon Place for good. For a lady of Jacqueline's station, that meant one thing: marriage.

"I'll trust you to come up with a list of eligibles," he told deVere. "*Young* men, mind, honorable, pox free, and in possession of all their teeth."

"She's a difficult gel," said deVere. "I can draw up a list of possibilities. I can't promise they'll agree."

Griffin eyed his kinsman shrewdly. "Make it known that I shall settle a generous dowry on her. The Berkshire property, too."

At this, deVere's scowl lightened. He rubbed his big hands together. "That'll set 'em by the ears!"

"No doubt."

DeVere cocked an eyebrow. "She must have a chaperone who is up to snuff. Not only that, you'll need someone to school the girl in the ways of society. You'd best wed Lady Rosamund without delay."

The sudden urgency of it punched the breath from Griffin's lungs, made his heart pound in his chest.

He hoped to God Lady Rosamund would agree.

And what about this Captain Lauderdale fellow? Her tendre for him complicated matters, didn't it?

That some other man showed serious interest in Rosamund was no surprise. She'd caused a sensation when she debuted; Griffin knew all about that. How could it be otherwise? But if his sources were correct, she'd never shown a marked preference for any of the gentlemen who courted her.

This Lauderdale fellow was a different kettle of fish. Rosamund did, it seemed, display a decided partiality for him. And who could blame the chit for her infatuation? By all accounts, the man possessed wit, charm, and audacity, not to mention a head like a Greek coin. On the battlefield, it was said his bravery was second to none.

The bastard.

Still, Lady Rosamund had not openly repudiated her engagement to Griffin. That must mean one of two things: She was biding her time, waiting to secure the duke's approval to switch grooms; or she intended to take Lauderdale as her lover after she was wed. That's what ladies in their circle did, wasn't it?

A growl formed in his chest. *Over his dead body.* If he was going to subject himself to the torture of marriage to Lady Rosamund Westruther, he was damned if he'd be cuckolded, too.

He looked up at deVere. "I'll send for her today."

DeVere scoffed. "You're a fool not to have snapped her up when you had the chance. Who knows whether she'll have you now?" He shook his head. "I might not know much about women, but if you take my advice, *you'll* go to *her.* She's in London, you know."

Griffin would rather be boiled in oil than grovel to Lady Rosamund Westruther, particularly if that meant dancing attendance on her in fashionable London. He ground his teeth at the mere notion.

Besides, it was as well that Lady Rosamund knew from the start who would be master in their household.

He tapped a broad fingertip on the special license. "No. I'll send for her. We might as well get married here. Pendon Place will be her home, after all. I'll send for Jacks, too. We ought to begin preparing her for the season as soon as we can."

A creeping feeling of unease stole over him. How could he bring Rosamund here? The house was a shambles. Those servants he hadn't dismissed after his grandfather died had deserted him upon the music master's untimely demise, leaving one family to do the necessary labor in the house. The gloomy old pile was airless, dank, and full of dust. As unappealing as its master, in fact.

"That's settled, then," said deVere. "You'll marry Lady Rosamund. She'll give Jacks a season, and we'll get the chit riveted all right and tight."

"Send me that list of eligibles, will you?" said Griffin. "I want to know all about them in advance."

"Odd filly, your sister," remarked deVere. "Think she's up to the task?"

"Of course she is."

DeVere grunted. "You'd best win Lady Rosamund to your side as soon as may be." He regarded Griffin with a sapient eye. "You've got your work cut out for you there."

As his relative took his leave, Griffin wondered whether he referred to Jacqueline or to Griffin's beautiful betrothed.

Either way, deVere would be right.

* * *

Madam,

It is high time we were wed. I shall expect you at
Pendon Place next week.

Yours, etc.,

Tregarth

P.S. Bring your riding habit. The blue one.

Sir,

I confess I find myself Bewildered at this Summons, arriving as it does Out of the Blue. You must
forgive me if I say that at first I was at a Loss to
recall who you were.

I have obligations in Town which I cannot break.
Even were that not so, I should never answer such a
Peremptory Command, and certainly not from You.

You may, if you choose, call on me at Montford
House.

Yours, etc.,

Lady Rosamund Westruther

P.S. I do not know to which riding habit you refer.

"Another year, another collection of broken hearts."

Lady Cecily Westruther inspected the bower of floral
arrangements that typically arrived for her cousin each day
she spent in London. Though the season had not yet begun,
enough of the ton had returned to the metropolis to fill
Rosamund's calendar with social engagements. "Rosamund,
I vow you single-handedly keep London florists in business."

"Mmm?" Rosamund had been listening with half an

ear while perusing an elegantly worded card attached to a posy of violets.

"How very kind," she murmured.

She handed the posy to a maid and took up the next offering. She must endeavor to keep who gave her what straight in her head so that she could thank them properly when next she met them.

Men, she'd discovered, were surprisingly sensitive souls underneath all that muscle and swagger. She took great care not to wound them, and a tricky time she had of it, too. Sometimes she longed to tuck herself away in the country during the season, but that would be poor-spirited. She'd rather die than wear the willow for Griffin deVere.

The Earl of Tregarth, he was now. But she was not his countess.

Yet.

Rosamund buried her face in a creamy, ruffled bouquet, breathing in the musk-sweet scent of roses. She repressed a sigh. How ungrateful of her to feel a thorny stab of pain in her heart each time a gentleman sent her a tribute such as this. The gesture only reinforced the fact that Griffin had never given her so much as a dandelion to mark his regard.

Not that she cared about flowers so much; the occasional letter would have sufficed. At least by such communications, her betrothed might acknowledge she existed.

But in almost three years, he hadn't made a single attempt to further his acquaintance with her.

And now, all of a sudden, Griffin ordered her to marry him, posthaste! Even more galling, he sent her a rude, peremptory summons, as if she were a servant, not his future countess.

Well, she'd learned something since the age of eighteen. Men never valued what they won too easily. If Griffin wanted her, he'd have to work much harder than this.

"Another letter arrived yesterday," she murmured, handing on the rose bouquet.

Cecily looked up from a bunch of lilies she was arranging in a vase. "What did it say?"

Rosamund made a face. "More bluster, I'm afraid."

"The man is an oaf!" Cecily's strongly marked brows drew together. "You will not give in to him."

"Of course not," said Rosamund.

Yet, how she wished he'd hand her the smallest excuse to do so. One tiny sop to her pride, one small compliment, the slightest glimmer of affection, and she'd race down to Cornwall like a shot.

She lifted her chin. "I've told him if he wishes our wedding to go forward, he'll come here and court me properly."

But Griffin deVere was as stubborn as a rock.

"Let him but show his face," grumbled Cecily. "I'd have some words to say to him."

"No doubt." Rosamund smiled at Cecily's vehemence. "You are the most fearsome creature. Even I quake in my shoes when you frown like that."

Cecily's scowl deepened. "If I were a man, I'd run him through. Do you think Captain Lauderdale will challenge him to a duel? I'd like to see that."

Rosamund bit her lip. Like everyone else, Cecily thought Rosamund was in love with Philip Lauderdale. Guiltily, she acknowledged the misunderstanding was all her fault.

Despite her whirlwind success in her first season, when another year passed leaving her unwed, there'd been a constant, underlying question in everyone's gaze. Why didn't her betrothed claim her? Was there something amiss with Lady Rosamund that others couldn't see?

The Westruther ladies commiserated that she should be landed with such an uncouth beast for a fiancé; her male relatives had proposed several increasingly violent ways of bringing Griffin to heel.

Even her brother had offered to fix the matter. She'd no doubt Xavier would do it, too, in a manner so subtle and diabolically clever as to be worthy of the duke himself. Of course, one word to her former guardian, the Duke of Montford, and all would be settled.

But Rosamund didn't wish her family to intercede for her with Griffin.

She wanted Griffin to *want* her.

And then along came Philip Lauderdale, a dashing cavalry officer. The most honorable, handsome gallant any girl's heart could hope for. He adored her. Everyone said so. Not only that, he was intelligent, amusing company, the kind of man who cast all others into the shade.

Despite Rosamund's longstanding engagement and her insistence that she could give him no hope, Philip remained flatteringly persistent. He was so ingenious at cutting out his rivals that it soon appeared to everyone that Rosamund favored him.

That had not been her intention. She'd tried to show no preference for any gentleman, for the last thing she desired was to be labeled a flirt. But by the time she realized how particular her friendship with Philip must appear to the world, the damage was done.

Far from dubbing her a flighty miss, the ton had been captivated by these star-crossed lovers. Everyone murmured what a pity it was that the Duke of Montford remained adamant, a travesty that the exquisite Rosamund must be paired with the boorish Tregarth.

Rosamund—vain, stubborn fool that she was—made no real attempt to correct society's assumption. It was pleasant to be wanted by a gentleman whom all the other ladies fawned over. Philip's determined attentions were so soothing to her pride.

Pleasant. Soothing.

Hmm . . .

With all his myriad stellar qualities, she *ought* to be in love with Philip Lauderdale.

There was just one giant, rude, infuriating reason why she was not.

CHAPTER FOUR

The Duke of Montford paused on the threshold and raised his quizzing glass to examine the motley assortment of relatives ranged around his breakfast table.

Rosamund and Cecily were there, of course. And he'd rather expected Xavier, Rosamund's brother, to join them this spring. Understandable in the circumstances, if not altogether welcome at this delicate juncture.

Andrew, on the other hand . . .

"Good God," said Montford faintly. "You here, Lydgate?"

Andrew Westruther, Viscount Lydgate, smiled at him, sleek and self-satisfied as a cat. "Delighted to see you, too, Your Grace."

Xavier, Marquis of Steyne, said nothing, either by way of greeting or explanation. One side of his mouth twitched at his cousin's facile pleasantry, but his blue eyes remained hard and bright.

Had Montford wished to needle Xavier, he might have quizzed him about the reasons for his presence. It happened that Montford saw no benefit in doing so. At least, not this morning. The marquis could remain at Montford House as long as he wished, provided he didn't interfere with Montford's plans for his sister.

With a glance at Rosamund, Montford took his plate from the head of the table and moved to the sideboard to make his selection.

He decided to tackle Andrew first. "To what do we owe this pleasure, Lydgate? Pockets-to-let?" Andrew had yet to reach his twenty-fifth year, upon which he would inherit the full sum of his fortune. Until then, Montford held his purse strings.

Not too tightly, however. It disturbed him just how enterprising Andrew could become when in need of ready cash.

"How can you think it, sir?" returned the young viscount, his tone a mixture of amusement and indignation. "You know the business that has occupied me these past months."

Ah. Yes, indeed. Montford knew all about Andrew's latest scheme. Or one of them. They would not discuss it in front of the others, however.

He gave a slight smile. "Then what can I say but that I am honored?"

The duke returned to the table with a full plate and a sense of anticipation. One might find the presence of one's extended family a little trying at times. One could not complain, however, that life was uneventful with them around.

"If only Beckenham and Jane were here, we'd be one big happy family," said Cecily, clasping her hands at her breast with mock soulfulness.

Xavier looked up at that. "Bucolic bliss must have kept them at their respective estates this spring." He sipped from a tankard, his eyes glittering. "But then, Beckenham lost his taste for London, didn't he?"

An infelicitous remark that no one cared to answer.

Montford reflected that Xavier had always possessed the curious talent of halting a conversation in its tracks.

Andrew carved himself some ham and transferred it to his plate. "I doubt we'll see dear Cousin Jane before her confinement."

Rosamund turned her head to frown at him. "What is this? Jane's not increasing."

Andrew snorted. "She will be."

A general snicker greeted this statement. Montford was aware that such ribald talk ought not to be encouraged in front of Rosamund and Cecily. He let it pass, however. He'd never believed in sheltering young ladies from every stray innuendo.

He didn't doubt that Andrew was correct. The excessive passion between Jane and her new husband would probably bear fruit before too long. Montford wasn't entirely certain how he felt about that.

The answer came to him: *old.* But then, the guardianship and care of six children tended to age a man, didn't it? Regardless, he absolutely refused to act the role of grandfather to Jane and Constantine's progeny. Damn it all, he was in his forties, not his dotage.

Montford's correspondence awaited him at the table, as did a crisp, pressed copy of *The Morning Post.*

He leafed through the large stack of letters and cards. "Hmm. I wonder what threats I shall receive from Tregarth today."

The earl's demands that Rosamund marry him forthwith had become a running joke in the family. All eyes fixed upon Rosamund.

"We are out of chocolate," she said, lifting the lid of the silver pot to peer inside. "I'll ring for more."

Before she could rise, Lydgate demanded, "Tregarth? What's the fellow got to say for himself now?"

Sinking down again, Rosamund sighed. "He commands

me to travel down to Cornwall so that we can be married."

Montford observed her keenly. Rosamund's face, however, remained a beautiful blank.

"*Commands* you?" Xavier's sleek black brows rose. "One might suppose the man to be deranged."

"Not deranged," said Montford. "Rather . . . lacking in polish, perhaps."

"Which is quite as bad in its own way," murmured Xavier.

"No matter," said Rosamund. "I have told the earl he must come to Town and court me properly or I shall have nothing to say to him."

"Quite right, my dear." Montford was in no hurry to lose Rosamund. Certainly, it would be to everyone's practical advantage for her marriage to proceed, but until Rosamund had schooled her affianced husband to her liking, Montford was prepared to wait. He'd rattled deVere's cage to see if he might move the process forward. However, he had no intention of terminating this betrothal if Rosamund was content to have the Earl of Tregarth.

It rather baffled him that the new earl had remained recalcitrant when every other red-blooded male in Rosamund's vicinity tumbled over one another to worship at her feet. Yet Tregarth had ignored her for nearly three years.

Montford didn't believe in love within marriage, but he did believe in loyalty and respect between spouses. Until Griffin could show Rosamund those things, Montford would not countenance their alliance. He was not unduly concerned, however. He did not doubt Rosamund's ability to bring Griffin to heel.

The duke leafed through the various invitations and some correspondence to do with the Ministry of Marriage, which he set aside for later.

He sniffed one elegantly addressed missive, grimaced

at the cloying sweetness of its scent, then handed it to Lydgate. "Do you mind telling me why your billets-doux are addressed care of my house?"

With a flashing grin, the young man took the note and tossed it down beside his plate without so much as glancing at it. "Oh, didn't Rundle tell you? I'm moving back in." He shrugged. "Why keep rooms in Town when I'm never there? Dashed expensive practice."

"I see," said Montford. "Instead, you intend to live at my expense."

"Well, you did tell him he should economize," said Xavier.

Montford's lips twitched. "I have only myself to blame, in fact."

Truthfully, he welcomed Lydgate's company. But that was something he preferred to keep to himself. Lydgate's conceit was part of his charm, but Montford saw no cause to inflate that quality further.

Montford turned his attention to Rosamund. "My dear, are you at liberty this afternoon?"

"I am promised to Mama," said Rosamund. "Do you wish me to send my apologies?"

He could imagine the marchioness's reaction. "No, no. You must not disappoint Lady Steyne." He glanced over at Xavier, who looked more like a satyr than ever. "Do you accompany your sister to Steyne House?"

"No." Xavier's face—never expressive at the best of times—seemed to slam shut.

"I myself am engaged this afternoon." Montford pursed his lips. "Someone ought to go with Rosamund."

"I would, but I am not out yet," said Cecily.

"Thank Heaven for small mercies," Xavier murmured, earning a gurgle of laughter from her.

Montford looked pointedly at Lydgate. "That leaves you."

"Eh?" Lydgate sat up straighter, alarm written across his classically handsome features. "Now, look here, sir. . . ."

"Tibby will accompany me," said Rosamund quietly, touching her napkin to her lips. "You needn't put yourself into a stew, Andy."

Tibby was formerly the girls' governess, now their companion. A quiet yet strong-minded woman who was more than a match for Lady Steyne. Montford nodded. "Very well. That's settled, then."

Cecily's dark eyes challenged Lydgate. "Coward."

Between his teeth, Lydgate said, "I have another engagement."

"*I* know why he won't escort Rosamund to see her mama," pursued Cecily, her black ringlets bobbing with certainty. "It's because Lady Steyne makes love to him with her eyes."

"Nonsense, Cecily," snapped Andrew. "I'm practically her nephew."

"Only through several marriages," she countered.

Abruptly, Xavier rose, threw down his napkin, and strode to the door.

"Damn it, Cecily!" hissed Andrew as he pushed back his chair, his mouth turned down in disgust. "That's his mama you're talking about, and Rosamund's, too."

With a stricken glance at Montford, Cecily said, "I—I'm sorry! I didn't mean—"

"No, that's quite all right, dear," said Rosamund. She gave Cecily's hand a quick squeeze, but her gaze was fixed on the door through which her brother had left. With a forced smile, she added, "Mama is . . . incorrigible. I've always known it."

Montford said, "Lydgate's right. You go beyond the line of what is pleasing, Cecily."

Cecily bit her lip. "Yes, Your Grace. I'll apologize to Xavier."

"No," said Lydgate. "Leave him be."

Silence reigned, punctuated only by the clink of cutlery on china, while Montford perused the rest of his post and the others pretended to eat their breakfast. Finally, he came to a missive that made his eyebrows climb.

"Ah," he murmured. His gaze flickered to Rosamund. "It seems you have won the first skirmish, my dear. Your betrothed is on his way to London."

Rosamund choked on a morsel of toast and hastily grabbed Cecily's coffee to wash it down. Her hand shook as she replaced the cup on its saucer.

He was coming for her? Apprehension seized her, mushrooming into fully blown panic.

Oh, how foolish! She'd demanded Griffin's presence in London, hadn't she? But she hadn't thought he'd give in so soon—or at all! Despite her ridiculous longing for him, she was totally discomposed by his sudden capitulation.

"He's coming?" she managed. "Here?"

"Yes." Montford fixed his penetrating gaze upon her. "It's what you wanted, isn't it?"

"I've rather been looking forward to making the earl's acquaintance myself," drawled Lydgate. His words were idle, but the steel in his eyes belied the studied nonchalance.

That snapped Rosamund out of her panic. In a warning tone, she said, *"Andy."*

Her cousin blinked at her innocently. "What, my dearest?"

She bit her lip against a smile. "I want him alive, do you hear me? Promise me you won't *do* anything to him. Unless I give you leave, of course."

His eyes narrowed. "Define *anything.*"

"He's a big man," put in Cecily. "Quite monstrous, in fact. I doubt even you could beat him if it came to fisticuffs, Andy."

"That shows how much you know about the noble art of boxing," said Lydgate, an anticipatory gleam in his eye. "The bigger they are, the harder they fall, eh, Your Grace?"

Montford inclined his head in assent. "Though I wonder a little at your describing your, er, *novel* mode of pugilism as either noble or an art, Lydgate. Regardless, you will not exercise your talents upon Rosamund's fiancé."

"No, indeed," said Rosamund, adding a hint of steel to her own smile. "You may safely leave him to my tender mercies."

By the time she was finished with him, Griffin would beg her to marry him on bended knee. And it would all be for the best in the end, for she meant to be the most excellent wife any man could wish for.

But first she would punish him a little. It was no less than he deserved for leaving her on the shelf so long.

Suddenly, exhilaration swept over her, drowning out her nervous panic. A bubble of laughter expanded in her chest.

Griffin was coming for her.

At last!

Later that day, the Westruther gentlemen were gathered on a matter of business in Montford's library when the discussion turned once again to Rosamund's betrothed.

"He had the nerve to ask me to intercede with Rosamund for him," said Montford pensively. "I'm to command her to the altar, if you please."

Xavier snorted. "The man doesn't know whom he's dealing with."

Lydgate's brow furrowed. "Strange that neither of them has pressed the matter until now." He shrugged. "Oh, I suppose in Rosamund's case, it's understandable that she wouldn't wish to rush into wedded bliss with a fellow like that. But she hasn't cried off, either."

"A most dutiful little lamb," murmured Xavier, setting his sherry glass down with a click.

A lamb to the slaughter was the allusion, of course. No prizes for guessing whom Xavier cast in the role of shepherd. Montford tensed, then cursed himself for reacting to Xavier's provocation.

"Let her go, Your Grace," said Xavier, ruthlessly exploiting his advantage. "You know she'd be happier with Lauderdale."

Montford held on to his temper. "No. I don't know that."

Captain Lauderdale was not the man for Rosamund. Even if Montford believed in romantic love—and he didn't—he would not permit Rosamund to marry her cavalry officer. The very fact she hadn't so much as mentioned the possibility to him told its own tale.

Surely if Rosamund believed herself deep in love with another man, she would not have waited for Tregarth all these years? Tregarth's neglect had given her the perfect excuse to break the engagement. And yet, she had not once sought Montford's permission to do so.

As for Tregarth himself, well, the duke knew something of the difficulties the earl had faced since his grandfather died. Montford was willing to overlook the delay that in other circumstances he would deem insulting. Particularly as this rare alliance between a Westruther and a deVere would consolidate the Westruthers' influence in the southwest.

"But what has Tregarth been about, to leave her on the shelf for years?" demanded Lydgate.

"You needn't look so indignant," commented Xavier. "You've not lifted a finger to help her in all that time."

"I haven't precisely been at leisure these past few years, have I?" said Lydgate silkily. "Unlike some."

With a gleam of amusement, Montford scanned Lydgate

from the soles of his expensively shod feet to the top of his immaculately styled hair. "Live within your means, and you would have ample leisure to do with as you wish."

The butler entered then, announcing, "Lord Tregarth, Your Grace."

It was not often Montford was caught by surprise. "So soon?"

"The man of the hour," drawled Xavier, rising to his feet.

Tregarth strode into the room, looking large, belligerent, and decidedly unkempt.

"Good God!" said Lydgate in accents of horror, looking him up and down. "Did you come directly from your horse barn or did you take a great roll in a cow byre for good measure?"

Tregarth flicked his glowering gaze Lydgate's way. "Don't try my patience, sir." His attention returned to Montford. "Where's my bride?"

Lydgate's expression of disgust turned to astonishment, then outrage. "You cannot mean you intend to call upon my cousin—your *affianced wife*—looking like a cursed farm laborer!"

Curling his lip, Tregarth ran a cursory, contemptuous glance over Lydgate's splendor. "Better that than a damned fop."

In three strides, Lydgate was across the room. Without warning, his fist connected with Tregarth's jaw.

Montford watched with interest, lifting a finger to stay Xavier, who had taken one step toward the two men.

Lydgate might look like a fashion plate, but he boxed regularly with the first pugilists of the day. Besides that, he was more acquainted with gutter fighting than any gentleman ought to be. Rather unfairly, he'd caught Tregarth unawares.

The big man reeled back, but somehow he managed

to keep his footing. A great red welt bloomed across his jaw.

His brow lowered; his fists clenched.

"Ah. Tregarth," said Montford, letting his voice slice through the violence-thickened air. He smiled. "Welcome to the family."

CHAPTER FIVE

Griffin faced the three Westruther men and tightened the stranglehold on his fury. He had not beaten a man in anger for a long time. He would not break that rule now.

His temper, far from complacent at the best of times, was threadbare from the long journey to Town. The roads had been bad, rutted by recent rains. While he'd usually ride, the expectation that he'd bring Rosamund back with him had made him take the carriage instead.

What with the tedium of the journey and the discomfort of the badly sprung chaise, his temper was in shreds by the time he'd arrived at the town house. Only to find, of course, that the house was draped in Holland covers. The retainers he paid to look after the place had no notion of his coming. The letter he'd sent heralding his arrival had failed to reach them in time.

He loathed hotels, but there didn't seem much point in setting the London household on its ears when he'd stay two nights at the most. How long could it take for Rosamund to pack her bags, after all?

He'd secured a room at Limmer's and come directly to

Montford House with the special license Lord deVere had procured for him burning a hole inside his waistcoat.

He'd put an end to Rosamund's shilly-shallying, once and for all.

But he ought to have known it wouldn't be that easy. He'd have to charge through this formidable phalanx of Westruther men first.

Of course, Griffin remembered the duke from Montford's visit to Pendon Place three years ago. The other two were clearly related, with that Westruther arrogance that seemed bred into their very bone structure. All three were different in coloring, build, and stature, but they shared the same high, sharp cheekbones and straight, patrician noses, with that telltale suspicion of a hawkish curve at the end.

"Where is she?" he repeated, refusing to be cowed by Montford's aristocratic hauteur.

"Not here," answered the golden young man who'd hit him, nursing his bruised knuckles. Griffin hoped that hand hurt as much as his jaw did. He doubted it.

"Won't you sit down?" Montford indicated a chair by the fire.

Griffin shook his head. "I've no time for your flummery, Your Grace. Tell me where she is, so we can get married once and for all."

"Rather a sudden interest you're taking in my sister, isn't it?" the sardonic-looking gentleman said. That must be Xavier, Lord Steyne. Rosamund's brother.

Yes, the difference in coloring might have fooled him, but now he saw the likeness. They had the same deep blue eyes, but the brother's hair was raven-wing black, whereas Rosamund's shone gold as newly minted guineas. And Rosamund's eyes were clear and true, unshadowed by the world-weary cynicism that hardened her sibling's gaze.

"You're her brother, are you?" Griffin nodded to Steyne. "Then perhaps you can make her see sense."

"Believe me, you wouldn't want that." Steyne looked contemptuous. "I doubt your idea of sense and mine coincide."

"Do sit down," Montford repeated. He waved a languid hand toward an array of decanters close by. "Let me pour you a drink. There is much to discuss."

"I don't want to sit. I don't want a drink," said Griffin in a soft, dangerous tone. "I want my betrothed."

Hell, but his jaw ached. That pretty-boy cousin of Rosamund's packed a powerful right hook. Nothing Griffin hadn't taken in the ring many times, but still.

Montford took his own chair and spread his hands. "Regrettably, Lady Rosamund is not here—," Montford began.

"She's at my house in Berkeley Square," interrupted Steyne with a quick, sidelong glance at the duke. "Calling on our mother."

The gesture was ostensibly helpful, but the malice in Steyne's mocking gaze did not escape Griffin. From years of living with his grandsire, he'd learned to judge when someone laid a trap for him.

But whatever deep game her brother played, Griffin needed to see Rosamund. Steyne had just handed him the means to do so.

Favoring Steyne with a curt nod, Griffin said, "Thank you. I'll see myself out."

Horror made Lydgate's jaw drop. "You can't call on the marchioness looking like that! My dear fellow, it simply isn't done!"

"I'm not paying a social call," snapped Griffin. "I'm going to claim my bride."

With a nod in farewell, he swung around on his heel and left the room.

On the way to the marbled entrance hall, he heard a penetrating whisper. "Lord Tregarth! Over here!"

He turned to see Lady Cecily Westruther beckon from a room to his right. Tempted though he was to ignore her and keep going, he recalled the fondness his prospective bride had for her incorrigible young cousin. Perhaps Cecily could give him information that would help his cause.

As he hesitated, her expressive face went through a series of contortions. She gestured again, more emphatically. "Come *on*!"

With a quick glance around the empty hall, he complied.

She caught his hand and drew him inside. The casual contact disconcerted him, but he followed her into the small cloakroom and waited as she shut the door behind her.

"You took your time getting here, didn't you?" Lady Cecily's hands were planted on her hips, her gamine features arranged into a scowl.

He scowled back at her, with interest. "That's no business of yours."

"Anything that affects Rosamund's happiness is my business," said the girl. "You have a *lot* of work to do."

"Work? What work?"

"To atone for your past boorishness, of course!" She threw up her hands. "Rosamund is the greatest catch on the Marriage Mart. She is exquisitely beautiful, for one thing. But far better than that—not that any of you *idiotic* men would notice—you would not find a more good-hearted, gentle girl in all of England."

She poked him in the chest. "And yet *you* have treated her abominably. Demanding she trot down to Cornwall to wed you! Why, would you respect her at all if she fell into your arms after you've left her on the shelf for *three years*?"

Griffin blinked, a trifle stunned at this tirade. All along, he'd assumed Rosamund would have been thanking Heaven for the reprieve. He'd certainly dismissed her recent correspondence as stalling tactics. Obviously, she wished to retain her freedom for as long as possible.

But this begged the question: Why *hadn't* Rosamund thrown him over by now?

Cecily shook her head, her dark, brilliant eyes fixed on him. "You must prove to her that you're worthy. You must court Rosamund in form and show the world you don't scorn her."

"*Scorn* her?" The girl rocks in her head.

"It's what all of London thinks!" said Cecily. "Everyone has badgered her to cry off from your engagement. Rosamund refused because she is too good, too honorable to serve you a trick like that. She would never go back on her word. But if you are wise, you'll play your cards carefully now. Try her any further, Lord Tregarth, and you will push her into the arms of *another.*"

The last word was uttered in a thrilling whisper and with the dart of a glance around them. So, the girl thought that was a secret, did she? More fool her. Griffin had no doubt exactly to whose arms Cecily referred.

Lauderdale. Something twisted in his gut whenever he thought of that damned paragon dancing attendance on Rosamund.

He burned to ask Lady Cecily for more information, but pride stopped him from doing so.

Instead, he fixed the saucy chit with a hard stare. "Let me get this straight: Even though we are already betrothed, even though I'm—" He gestured down at himself, powerless to put into words what he was. "—she wants me to *court* her?" He nearly choked on the last words.

"Yes," said Cecily. "And she won't marry you until you do. Oh, Rosamund might *look* like an angel, but she can be excessively stubborn. Besides, she has her pride, just as you do."

For the first time, Cecily looked him over, with a horror that almost matched her sartorially magnificent cousin's. "What in Heaven's name are you wearing?"

Not that again. "Look here, Lady Cecily, I don't have time to waste on fripperies, so if you're quite finished . . ."

But she wasn't listening to him. Cecily tapped a fingertip to her pointed chin. "We *must* do something about your wardrobe."

We? "No!" said Griffin. "I don't need to do anything with my wardrobe. I am here to take Lady Rosamund to wife, and that's an end to it."

She frowned. "Have you listened to a *word* I've said?"

It occurred to him that this little thing was the second lady, besides his sister, who had ever faced him down, unafraid. An interesting breed, these Westruther women.

Then he collected himself. "There is *no* way I am going to court Lady Rosamund. Not a chance in Hell."

He stomped past the girl and made for the door.

She called after him, "Then you might as well go back to your pigs and your cows, Lord Tregarth, for you will not win her consent to the marriage otherwise."

He swung back to face her, his teeth bared in a snarl, and finally, *finally,* she looked scared. With a gasp, Lady Cecily shrank back from him, her dark eyes wide, hands reflexively raised to protect herself.

Unreasonably angered by her reaction, he hissed a breath through his teeth. "We'll see about that."

Then he turned and slammed out of the room.

Why, oh, why do I let Mama talk me into these things?

Rosamund stood on a low plinth in the front drawing room of Steyne House, one arm curved around a pottery urn and one hand raised above her head in a graceful arc.

She was uncomfortably aware that the layers of filmy material her mother had insisted on draping about her did little to conceal the contours of her body. Particularly when the marchioness had not allowed her a corset, but only a gossamer-fine shift beneath.

"It is a pity you are so tall," mused Lady Steyne, narrowing her darkly lashed blue eyes. "Quite Amazonian, in fact." A frown flickered for an instant. "My dear, do I detect a little extra padding at your waist? A suspicion of fleshiness beneath the arms? François, do see if you can eliminate my daughter's *wobbles*." Her beautiful mouth turned down at the corners. "I am sure I never had *them* when I was her age."

Rosamund flushed and stared at the wall. *Ignore her. It doesn't matter what she thinks.*

The old mantra was stale, worn with use. She told herself there was nothing wrong with her body, that her mother's diet of air and champagne would keep anyone's figure fashionably waiflike.

She longed to demand of the marchioness why she wanted her daughter to pose for this painting if she found her form so unsatisfactory.

But that imaginary piece of defiance didn't help. The old, sick sense of self-loathing rose up within her like a murky tide.

Her sole comfort was that no one but Lady Steyne and the artist himself would know who the model for this work had been. Monsieur François would impose Mama's raven-black hair and classically beautiful features on the face of this sprite or nymph or whatever she was supposed to be.

Rosamund could see nothing amiss with her mother's figure, but gainsaying her parent when that lady had a fixed notion in her head was far more effort than giving way to it. Lady Steyne had sighed and muttered about taut, dewy young skin, an attribute all the marchioness's cosmetic aids could not entirely preserve or reclaim.

She ought to pity her mother. To Nerissa Westruther, Lady Steyne, her beauty was her sole personal asset, the one true measure of her worth. While others saw the marchioness as an exquisite woman, Rosamund knew Nerissa felt her former glory slipping through her slender fingers like water. This composite portrait was a desperate—and quite pathetic—attempt to recapture it.

The drawing room was chilly despite the soft, golden sunlight that streamed through the window beside her. Rosamund shivered, uncomfortably aware that she'd developed goose bumps on her arms and that her nipples had tightened to hard, embarrassing peaks.

Far from displaying any propensity to leer, the artist himself was all business. With a hint of impatience puckering his fine black brows, he spoke around a paintbrush he held wedged between his teeth. "Hold the urn a leetle higher, mademoiselle. Higher. Yes, that is it. I must work *vite, vite, vite,* before we lose the light."

Rosamund complied, reflecting that her mother's lovers were becoming increasingly less aristocratic, yet commensurately younger and more attractive as the years went on. The footman at the door had been staggeringly handsome. Did François know he had a rival? Or didn't he care?

But then, one might go mad speculating about the intricacies of her mother's *affaires.*

How much longer? The arm she'd raised ached, her nose itched, and the wreath of spring flowers and leaves Lady Steyne had set in her hair possessed malevolent protruding twigs that stuck into her scalp.

Rosamund had agreed to model today primarily to assuage her stinging conscience. Her mother's reproaches of neglect had merit; visiting Lady Steyne proved so emotionally draining that Rosamund seldom called in Berkeley Square at all if she could avoid it. Even then, she usually chose the marchioness's "at home" days to avoid a tête-à-tête.

Had she made good on her promise to Montford and brought her old governess, Tibby would have found some way of extricating Rosamund from this hideous obligation. But knowing that her bluestocking former governess secretly despised her mama, Rosamund hadn't brought her after all.

It was one thing to harbor her own misgivings about her errant parent. Quite another to see those misgivings mirrored in her respected companion's eyes. Instead, Rosamund's maid awaited her in the kitchens and knew nothing of what went on upstairs.

No doubt, Meg was even now enjoying a comfortable gossip with Lady Steyne's dresser. Rosamund shivered. She'd give her eyes for a hot cup of tea.

"My dear girl, you look like you're facing an execution!" drawled her mother. "You're supposed to be Arethusa, the water sprite. Ethereality, my dear! Lightness! *Esprit!*"

"I'm sorry, Mama." She forbore to point out that it would not be *her* expression on the portrait but Lady Steyne's. Obediently, Rosamund tried again.

When her mother wasn't looking, she sent a longing glance toward the clock on the mantel. Fifteen minutes—half an hour at the most—was all she'd intended to spend at Steyne House. No more than a formal morning call. Instead, she'd remained over two hours. She could only hope her mother's protégé would finish with her before she was due back at Montford House to dress for the evening.

With an effort, Rosamund pushed her thoughts beyond the humiliation she felt. How soon would Griffin come?

While she'd taken a proud stand over making him court

her before she agreed to tie the knot, she wasn't certain she'd have the strength to hold out against him if he insisted on wedding her straightaway. She was all too impatient for her married life to begin.

If he came to her now and displayed the least contrition, she would abandon her plan and marry him gladly.

Somehow, she doubted that large, angry young man ever apologized for anything.

Griffin had not made it halfway to Grosvenor Square before he felt a peremptory tap on his shoulder.

"I say, slow down, old chap. What's the hurry?"

"Damn it!" Griffin half turned to find Rosamund's cousin, Viscount Lydgate, dogging his steps.

Lydgate lowered his cane—with which he'd presumably tapped Griffin's shoulder—then used its silver knob to tip his beaver hat at a more rakish angle. "Thought you could do with some company," he explained.

"You were mistaken," said Griffin, walking faster.

Though he complained of the pace, Lydgate's long legs ate up the ground in step with Griffin's. "You'll be glad of me when we get there," he murmured.

Griffin grunted. "I don't need your help, my lord."

"Call me Lydgate," said his companion. "You're practically family, aren't you? And you do need me, if only to run interference."

That startled Griffin. "Interference?"

"Of course. How are you going to get Rosamund alone if I don't distract her mama?"

Griffin frowned. He hated being placed in the position of supplicant when he had every right to claim his affianced bride. "Just let her try and stop me."

Lydgate halted. Instinctively, Griffin stopped also.

His unwanted companion's eyes hardened; the mobile

mouth grew flat and tight at the edges. If Griffin hadn't received ample proof of the steel beneath Lydgate's affable
charm when he slammed him in the jaw, he saw it now.

"You have no idea what that woman is capable of," said
Lydgate grimly. "I'm coming with you. If it's any consola-
tion, I'm doing this for Rosamund's sake, not yours." His
eyes narrowed. "Do you think Xavier meant to do you a
favor by telling you where Rosamund is?"

No, Griffin didn't think Lord Steyne did anyone any
favors. He hadn't cared what his prospective brother-in-
law's motive might have been, either, as long as this business with Rosamund was resolved as soon as possible. He
didn't want to waste time dawdling in London when there
was so much work to be done.

For a few moments, Griffin met Lydgate's eyes squarely.
Then he shrugged and kept walking.

"If only you'd make yourself presentable first, it would
go a long way with Rosamund," said Lydgate with asper-
ity. "And with her mama as well."

Griffin ignored that. Fine clothes would serve only to
emphasize his unfashionable brawn and the startling ugliness of his face. He refused to make himself utterly ridiculous, even for Lady Rosamund Westruther.

Particularly for Lady Rosamund Westruther.

"This is it," said Lydgate, turning to climb the steps.
Again, his gaze flickered over Griffin's clothing. "You'd
best leave me to do the talking."

"Be damned to you," Griffin said. "I don't need you to
be my mouthpiece."

Before Andrew could rap on the door with his cane,
Griffin overtook him, pounding on it with his fist. The door
opened immediately, revealing an impassive footman in
deep blue livery.

Griffin never troubled to evaluate the appearance of
his fellow men, but even he was astonished. This was eas-

ily the most beautiful young man he had ever seen, like a dark angel or a Greek god or some such thing.

The footman seemed equally taken aback to see Griffin, though clearly for different reasons. A sudden ache in Griffin's jaw reminded him of the appearance he must present.

He scowled; the pretty footman blanched.

The door began to shut in Griffin's face.

He slammed his hand flat against the panel to stop it. Before he could move the footman bodily out of the way, Lydgate ducked through the opening and interposed himself between them.

Lydgate flicked out a card made of creamy stock and handed it to the bemused footman. "Might I suggest that instead of brangling on the doorstep, you ascertain whether Her Ladyship is receiving, my good man? Lords Tregarth and Lydgate to see the marchioness."

In taking the card, the footman relinquished his hold on the door. Griffin stepped inside as well.

Tossing his hat, gloves, and cane on the occasional table, Andrew walked into the hall as if he owned it.

Griffin followed. The damned fool of a footman remained rooted to the spot, goggling.

"Weren't hired for your brains, were you?" Griffin commented. "Do as Lord Lydgate says, and be quick about it."

With a wary eye on Griffin, the young man bowed. "I'll show you into the library, my lord."

"Never mind. I know the way," said Lydgate, waving him off. With a gleam in his eye that Griffin found hard to interpret, he added, "We'll drink my cousin's brandy while we wait."

CHAPTER SIX

They were kept kicking their heels far longer than Griffin would have stood for if Lydgate hadn't been with him.

But if he had to wait, he might as well find out more about the family he was marrying into. He glanced about him at their deeply masculine surroundings. "If this is Steyne's house, why doesn't he live in it?"

"He does. Usually," said Lydgate.

"Then why does he stay at Montford House?" said Griffin.

Lydgate eyed him coolly. "Why don't you ask him?"

The man was right. It was none of his business. Griffin was saved from making a reply by the rustle of silks heralding a female intruder into this male preserve.

Griffin looked up, rising to his feet.

She was dark where her daughter was fair. Yet in the lineaments of her oval face, in the fierce, arresting blue of her eyes, Griffin saw Rosamund. His heart gave a sharp pound of recognition.

The lady's expressive eyes widened. "Andrew! My dear." The marchioness spoke in a low, breathy voice.

"Nerissa." Lydgate bowed.

She put out both her hands to him. "What is the meaning of this? You *never* come to call on me anymore. . . ." Her fine eyes flickered over Griffin disdainfully. "Ah. But you are not alone, I see."

Lydgate barely touched Lady Steyne's hands before releasing them. His charming smile didn't reach his eyes, Griffin noticed. "As I don't doubt you have been informed, ma'am, this is Griffin deVere, Lord Tregarth."

When she tilted her head as if she'd never heard the name before, Lydgate gave an exasperated sigh. "Your daughter's betrothed, Nerissa." He indicated the lady with a wave of his hand. "Tregarth, Lady Steyne."

The lady did not return the courtesy of Griffin's bow. Her features stilled in an expression of surprise. "This? *This* is the man my daughter must marry? Good God, Andy. What can Montford be thinking of? I thought he was your groom."

Mildly, Lydgate replied, "No you didn't."

Griffin had known the likely reception he'd get. It didn't bother him one whit. "If you're quite finished, ma'am, I want to see my future wife." He grinned. "Why don't you trot back upstairs and find her for me?"

She gave a hissing inhale through her small white teeth. "You dare to order me about in my own house?"

"Not your house, Nerissa," said Lydgate, inspecting his fingernails. "As it happens."

"And also, as it happens," said Griffin, "your son, the marquis, bade me call."

"Oh, he did, did he?" Her features tightened for the fraction of an instant, then smoothed again.

Her gaze roamed over Griffin, but more slowly this time and with greater attention. A cat-in-the-cream-pot smile spread her lips. "Well, of *course* he did."

On a low laugh, she added, "You are quite, quite perfect as you are. Yes, I am a dunce not to have seen it at once."

She switched her focus to Lydgate. "And did darling Xavier send me you, too, Andy?" she breathed. "*What* a considerate boy he is. I must remember to thank him."

With her gaze fixed on Lydgate like a snake hypnotizing its prey, Lady Steyne flicked a careless hand in Griffin's general direction. "You may go up. And tell François he is to take himself off. I won't need him this afternoon."

"Who the Devil is François?" Griffin muttered.

But the lady had already dismissed both him and the unknown Frenchman from her mind.

She gave another of her slow, satisfied smiles. "Andrew will entertain me. Won't you, my dear?"

Rosamund wondered why her mother was taking so long. That unnaturally handsome young footman of hers had called her away, muttering to her in hushed tones, which Rosamund couldn't catch from her frozen position by the window.

Nor had her mama explained; she'd simply left the room. Knowing the marchioness, she could be gone minutes or hours. Rosamund's arm felt as if it might drop off if she held this urn any longer.

"I must leave now, Monsieur," she said. She turned her head. "I—"

Griffin deVere stood in the doorway.

The urn dropped to the floor with a crash.

"Oh!" Automatically, Rosamund reached out for the broken pottery, then realized how exposed she must be, the way the sheer swaths of muslin and gauze clung to her breasts and hips.

She snatched up her robe from the chair back next to her and clutched it to her chest.

With an irritated exclamation, Monsieur turned to see who had disrupted his work.

His gaze traveled up and up. *"Zut,"* he said.

"Out."

That one laconic word from Griffin set Monsieur in motion. In no time, he'd packed up his paints and easel and fled the room.

Coward, thought Rosamund bitterly. It just went to show one should never trust a Frenchman.

Oh, she supposed she ought to be grateful Monsieur's strong sense of self-preservation prevented him from leaping to her defense. She could imagine how *that* would turn out.

Her heart pounded as she dragged her arms through the sleeves of the robe her mother had provided. The celestial blue garment was sheer, soft as rose petals, flowing down to froth about her ankles in a frivolity of ribbons and lace. Not the most concealing garment, but it would have to do.

She narrowed her eyes at Griffin. Another gentleman— Philip Lauderdale, perhaps—would have offered to turn his back or leave until she'd made herself respectable.

Not her beast of a betrothed. He loomed there, watching her so intently, he might have been trying to memorize the number of stitches on her robe.

Then his gaze homed in on her chest. Rosamund darted a glance downward to see what the point of such concentrated interest could be, then flushed. Two points of interest, in fact; her nipples stood to attention like tiny tent poles propping up the layers of gauze and silk. How utterly mortifying!

She crossed her arms over her bosom. As coldly as she could, she said, "Well?"

"Yes, as a matter of fact, I am well," said Griffin affably, not at all quelled by her frigid welcome. Of course, one could only be so formidable when dressed in something approximating one's chemise. "All the better for seeing you, my dear Lady Rosamund."

Griffin sauntered into the room as if he owned it. His controlled, predatory assurance was a far cry from the wild fury of the young man she'd met at the stables all those years ago.

His glittering gaze made another slow pass over her body and settled at her bare feet. She resisted the urge to tuck them under something.

"What were you doing just now?" he asked, strolling toward her.

"I'd have thought that was obvious." She tried to sound unflustered and sophisticated and faintly amused, as her mother might in such a situation. She failed dismally.

"Monsieur François is a . . . protégé of my mother's. She asked me to model for a . . . portrait."

He cocked an eyebrow toward the door, then looked back at her. She thought he might take exception to her behavior—certainly *she* was conscious of the impropriety of it—but he said nothing.

Rosamund stood there, feeling awkward and unsure. She longed to escape his gaze and cover herself, but she was loath to admit she'd done anything wrong by posing thus. Everyone knew artists were like doctors; they didn't count as *men*.

She regarded him uncertainly. Perhaps Griffin was not so enlightened as to subscribe to such a view.

The plinth raised her many inches from the ground. Yet she had to look up into Griffin's storm-cloud eyes.

What she saw there made her hot and a little giddy. She was conscious of a strong pull of attraction, as if his sheer size created a gravitational force all its own. She stopped herself swaying into it and stepped down from the plinth.

And found herself quite overwhelmed by the man before her. She'd forgotten how very large he was.

As calmly as she could, she said, "Excuse me. I must dress."

He reached out to put his hand on her arm. He wore no gloves, and her arm was bare. Warmth tingled beneath his palm and flowed through her body. The memory of him picking her up and kissing her invaded her senses.

"Stay as you are," he said. "My business with you won't take long."

She stepped back, breaking the contact that raced up her arm like a flash of fire. "Very well. Pray, say your piece, my lord, and go."

It was only then that she noticed the way he was dressed, all thrown together anyhow. His hair was wild; in place of a cravat, he wore some approximation of a belcher handkerchief. He probably still had the dirt of Pendon beneath his fingernails, its mud on his boots. And he sported a great red welt covering his left jaw.

She winced in sympathy. In spite of all that lay between them, tenderness welled in her chest. Her hands itched to soothe that livid flesh.

With an inward struggle, Rosamund fought off the moment of weakness.

She'd be fooling herself to think he'd come by that bruise in some noble manner. He'd probably stopped for a taproom brawl along the way.

"My God, sir, who hit you?" she demanded.

"Your cousin Lydgate," he replied.

"Good!" The response broke from her without warning. Then a fear clutched her. Andy had probably come off the worse in that encounter. "What did *you* do to *him*?"

"Nothing at all. He's downstairs with your mama."

Oh, no! Poor Andy. That was worse punishment than anything Griffin could dish out with his fists.

Bewildered, she said, "But why—?"

He interrupted her. "My lady, I don't have time for explanations. You must prepare yourself at once for our marriage and a journey back to Cornwall."

She looked up at him in sudden consternation. "Why the rush? Has there been an accident?"

She could not imagine what—unless . . . "Your brother?" She knew his brother Timothy was fighting in the Americas. If Timothy had been killed, that might explain Griffin's sudden wish to marry and gain an heir.

His heavy brows contracted, stretching the scar that slashed so close to one eye. "What? No, no, nothing like that. I'm here to marry you, that's all."

"I see." Relief swelled to anger. "And after my stipulation that you must court me in form, you come to me in *this* guise?"

His gaze meandered down her form and back to her face, with a blatant linger at her breasts. "If we are to talk of *guises* . . ."

Heat flared in her cheeks. Of course, he would refer to her embarrassing costume, even play upon it to set her at a disadvantage. She couldn't count on him to act the gentleman.

Her face must be as red as a poppy, but she refused to show any other sign of discomfiture. Instead, she lifted her chin and stared blandly back at him.

Griffin gave a curt shake of his head, as if to dislodge something inside it. After a pause, he said, "You will return to Pendon with me, where we'll get married. That's the end of it. Pack your bags, bring some female or other with you if you prefer, but we'll be on the road in two days, ma'am."

She gave an incredulous laugh at his audacity. "And that's the full sum of your eloquence on the subject? I've never even had a decent proposal from you, you know."

He ground his teeth in impatience, making the color in his jaw shift and deepen. The scar beside his eye stood out, stark white against his tanned skin. "If you recall, my lady, we were betrothed years ago. Will you break your oath?"

"Of course not. A Westruther always keeps her word. But, my dear Lord Tregarth, you have kept me dangling these three years, not knowing whether I'd be a maid for the rest of my days. I think some measure of openly expressed contrition—or at least, *enthusiasm*—is called for. If you want me to marry you, you must submit to my conditions."

He let out a frustrated growl. Despite his assurance that there was no dire emergency, his manner was urgent. She eyed him with suspicion. "Just why are you in such a hurry to marry me now?"

There were many correct answers to this question:

Oh, dearest Rosamund, I struggled in vain. I couldn't go on any longer without you.

Or:

My darling, I contracted a wasting disease, which laid me low these past years. I could not ask you to share in my misery. But now that I have recovered, we can be together at last.

"My sister," he said bluntly. "She's to make her comeout this spring. She needs a chaperone. You're it."

Rosamund's heart plummeted, even as her ire rose. She might have counted on the reason being a prosaic one, grossly unflattering to her vanity. How could she be so stupid as to keep hoping for more?

She masked her anger and disappointment with an icy smile. "I see."

She had a vague recollection of the lanky, awkward girl she'd glimpsed on her sole visit to Pendon Place. Poor little thing, growing up under Griffin's harsh, ham-fisted rule. Of course, Rosamund would see to it that Griffin's sister had a magical debut.

But first, she'd make Griffin pay handsomely for it.

"So . . ." Rosamund took a step toward him. "Am I right in saying you need me?"

He looked even more ferocious when he gritted his teeth. "Yes, I do. Damn it."

She ignored his shocking language. "Well, then. You will simply have to play by my rules. You must do as I requested at the outset and court me in form."

He made as if to interrupt, but she overrode him. "Ah, but let us be more specific, shall we?" She counted off on her fingers. "A drive in the park, two routs, a musicale, a picnic, and one ball. I shall see that you get the requisite invitations. You will squire me about and make it clear to the ton that although you neglected me shamefully for three years, you are now *ecstatic* to take me as a bride. *I* shall display similar devotion—"

The words burst from him. "Damn it! No!"

"Oh, I assure you," she said sweetly, "I am very good at acting a part."

"What?" He looked as if steam would shoot from his nostrils at any second. She began to feel quite cheerful.

"You will do this," she continued, "or I will not marry you at all. Not now. Not ever."

His entire frame tensed. He turned away from her. "I can have the duke command you, you know," he said in a low voice.

Rosamund shrugged. "You can try."

Montford would never coerce her into marriage, particularly not when her prospective groom had hitherto shown himself so reluctant.

Yet, the tension in Griffin's massive shoulders told her his unwillingness to join in the festivities of the season ran deeper than mere reluctance. Rosamund realized that from his perspective she seemed frivolous and selfish. But he was wrong. She fought for her happiness. And ultimately for his happiness, too.

After that disastrous first meeting with Griffin, she'd made up her mind. She could never be content with a man who didn't respect her. She no longer required love—his behavior had brought home to her how unlikely that was. But civility and respect? Those were not negotiable.

Surely it was not too much to ask that Griffin show himself to be a willing suitor, and not a put-upon groom. Raised without a mother in a household dominated by males, he had no earthly idea of how to treat any female, much less a wife. She pitied his poor sister.

Well, she could take it upon herself to train Griffin to the task, but she needed some sign that he was willing to meet her at least partway.

For good measure, she added, "You must see to a new wardrobe if you are to enter society. My cousin Lydgate will advise you."

He turned at that. "Ha! That man-milliner."

She raised her eyebrows. "You are mistaken. Andy has excellent taste. Oh, he might favor the exquisite in *his* dress, but he won't force that on you. You must choose exceedingly plain styles, of course. Find a coat to set off those magnificent shoulders of yours. You won't be sorry you did."

A startled look passed over his face. Then he scowled. "You speak as if this is already settled, but let me tell you—"

She put up her hands, palms out, in an arresting gesture. "Don't bother, for I'm not interested. Those are my terms. You may take them or leave them."

Ah, Hell. Griffin had been on the verge of unleashing his pent-up frustration when Rosamund had uncrossed her arms from her chest and put out her hands, causing those glorious breasts to give a small bounce.

He swallowed hard. Not only could he see the shadow of her nipples through those outrageous layers of gossamer-fine covering, but he could clearly make out the precise, mouthwatering contours of those lush, creamy mounds. For such a slender woman, she had a stunning bosom.

His head swam. A fierce hunger and a driving need to

assuage it burned inside him. His brain disconnected from the rest of his body. At that moment, any wish to deny this heavenly, luscious creature every little thing her heart desired fizzled and died.

He groped for one last grain of sense. Hoarsely, he said, "No balls."

"What?" she said faintly. Hope dawned in her face.

"I'll do those other things, but I'm not going to any blasted balls."

He eyed her belligerently. "Don't try to gammon me that the rest isn't enough for your purpose. If I take you about London a bit and we announce our engagement, and I appear suitably—" He waved a hand as words failed him. "—*pleased* with the arrangement, the news will be all over town in the blink of an eye. There's no need for me to caper about at some damned ball."

Stupid bloody idiot! This was going to be pure purgatory for them both. But how could he resist her when she'd looked at him with that roguish, calculating gaze?

"But I do so love to dance," she said, staring up at him with those china-blue eyes. "Wouldn't you like to dance with me?"

Even the mighty pull of attraction between them couldn't overcome his horror at the mere mention of it. "No."

She must have accepted that his word on this was final, for her shoulders dropped and she emitted a little "Humph!"

Then her pretty mouth firmed with resolve. "Two rout parties, one musicale, one picnic, and one drive in the park," she said. "*And* a new wardrobe. For you, I mean."

She dared to bargain with him over this? He stared at her, struck dumb by the way the mulish determination on her face sat so oddly with her dazzling beauty.

The combination completely undid him. "Done," he heard himself say.

Oh, Hell.

Her face flooded with happiness. She was incandescent with it. The temptation to reach for her and claim some of that glowing delight for his own became almost unbearable.

He managed to resist the promptings of his baser self by thinking about all the gallivanting she had in store for him.

With a groan, he said, "It's going to be Hell on a man, all this gadding about."

Clearly delighted with her victory, she made a teasing and quite voluptuous little pout. "Ohh, the poor bear will have to come out of his cave and dance."

"Ha! And you're the bear-leader, I suppose."

She laughed. "Yes, something like that. How unromantic. But you will do this for me, Griffin?"

"I'll do it. I won't like it."

She tilted her head. "Oh, you never know what you might like until you try."

"No, I'm pretty certain I won't."

A notion occurred to him, so outrageous yet so potentially satisfying, that his mind briefly drifted into fiery fantasy. Griffin hesitated. If she'd met him in any other costume, he might never have dared to suggest it. If she'd had less backbone, if she'd been more meek and compliant, he wouldn't have dreamed of demanding something in return. But . . .

He took one step toward her, closing in. "And now, my pretty, I have a condition of my own to make."

Her eyes widened, but not, he thought, with terror. Aye, he admired her pluck. Come to think of it, unlike most females, she'd shown no inclination to shrink from him at all.

"What is it?" she breathed.

Could he do this? According to the pounding pressure in his groin, most assuredly, he could. With a rasp in his voice, he said, "As a reward for my good behavior, *I* get something from *you.*"

"Something?" Her gaze drifted to his mouth, and his lips heated under her regard. The memory of the one time he'd kissed her surged back, vivid and hot.

"Yes." Oh, but not just kisses. He cast about for a way to express what he wanted without making it sound coarse or, worse, desperate. "Intimacies. My choosing."

Those heavenly blue eyes grew so huge and deep, he could drown in them.

He'd shocked her and it made him feel a brute. Unaccountably annoyed, he said, "We are to be husband and wife. You ought to get accustomed to the fact."

The soft light died from her gaze. "Of course," she said in a subdued voice, her lashes modestly lowered, her color rosy. "I agree to your terms, Lord Tregarth."

She stuck out her hand like a man offering to shake on a wager. He took it in his big paw, feeling an almost overwhelming urge to raise that delicate appendage to his lips and cover it in passionate kisses, to fall down at her remarkably pretty feet and promise her the moon.

But he had his pride. So he merely gave her hand a businesslike shake and released it. He bowed to her; she curtsied with a queenly dignity not many ladies could assume in such a costume.

His final view of Lady Rosamund Westruther was of a goddess standing there in a slanted shard of pale sunshine, the lines of her body clearly delineated beneath that gauzy material, her tumbled golden hair burnished in the light.

And a speculative expression in those heavenly blue eyes.

Griffin had been tempted to leave Lydgate to Lady Steyne's tender mercies, but what Rosamund said was true: If he was to squire her about in London, he'd require the right wardrobe. For that, he needed Lydgate.

Griffin knew nothing at all of fashion or where to buy clothes. He'd visited London only once before. On that occasion, he hadn't wasted his time shopping.

He didn't want to waste time shopping now. Lydgate might be rather too fine for Griffin's plain tastes, but surely he could find him a good tailor. Despite Griffin's mammoth proportions, he didn't expect ordering a couple of coats would be too onerous. They could probably knock it over in an hour that afternoon.

He found his own way down to the library and took care to make a deal of noise outside, stomping down the corridor, clearing his throat, fumbling with the door handle for an age before letting himself in.

He needn't have bothered with all that nonsense. Lydgate stood alone, staring into the empty grate with an indecipherable expression on his face.

"Ah! I was about to come up." The fair-haired man straightened and moved toward him. "You were gone so long, I thought Rosamund might have slain you with a fire iron or some such thing."

Griffin grinned. "Partial to violence, is she?"

"No, but women tend to get a trifle tetchy when their fiancé ignores them for years on end."

They left the library. "Well, she's getting her revenge," said Griffin. "I'm to dance attendance on her in society, if you please."

"Good for her," said Lydgate. After a pause, he said, "You'll need dressing, of course."

"Before or after she roasts me?" Griffin said glumly. "I feel like a great fat goose, so I suppose that's appropriate."

They received their accoutrements from the beautiful footman, whose sullen scowl showed he hadn't forgiven Griffin's earlier behavior.

As they went down the front steps, Lydgate set his beaver hat on his head. "Where are you staying?"

"At Limmer's."

Lydgate shook his head. "You can't possibly put up at Limmer's for more than a night or so. Dashed rowdy place. All the bucks of the town gather there of an evening to carouse."

The fellow had a point. Griffin hadn't intended to stay more than one or two nights, but now . . .

"If you're moving anyway, you might as well come to Montford House," said Lydgate. "Don't know why the duke didn't invite you in the first place."

"He did." Montford had written a month ago. The invitation had smacked of appeasement or perhaps some deep scheme to set him at a disadvantage.

Griffin remembered the duke very well from his visit to Pendon Place, and he also knew him by reputation. But now that Griffin had seen Rosamund, he no longer cared what plans Montford had for him. There were many tactical advantages to living under the same roof with his chosen bride.

"You're right," he said. "I'll do it."

Lydgate picked up the pace. "I'll inform His Grace. I believe there's some jaunt planned for tonight." Again, Lydgate's gaze swept over Griffin's form. Yet again, he shuddered. "But perhaps you'd prefer a quiet evening instead."

"Until I get togged out, I can't go anywhere respectable, I suppose," said Griffin, far from displeased by this.

"Never fear. Tomorrow, we shall see to your wardrobe."

"Hmph. I was hoping we could knock it over in an hour this afternoon."

Lydgate laughed gently. "My dear Tregarth. How much you have to learn."

Griffin rolled his eyes heavenward. Was it all worth it? Making a fool of himself for a woman?

Not just any woman, by God. Merely thinking of her made his heart race.

While Lydgate expatiated on gentlemen's fashions, Griffin's thoughts slid into lust-fueled daydreams. Rosamund had granted him carte blanche with her body that afternoon. Did she know it? Perhaps she counted on him stopping at kisses as he had all those years ago.

But he hadn't *said* kisses, now, had he? And the flare of shock in her eyes told him she sensed his meaning, even if she had no specific knowledge of what those intimacies might be.

He wondered if Rosamund guessed just how wild his imagination could run.

CHAPTER SEVEN

Rosamund trembled every time she thought of the way Griffin had looked at her that afternoon. She knew enough about men from the seasons she'd already spent in London to recognize when a man desired her.

She almost laughed to recall the way he'd pressed her for "intimacies" in return for his dancing attendance on her. As if she would deny him!

But of course, a gently bred lady could not admit to desires of her own. She could not inform him that she longed for him to commit whatever intimacies he cared to name upon her person. The mere thought of it made her insides shimmer with heat.

The impropriety and embarrassment of such a frank confession had stopped her. But there was no denying that tactically, she'd been wise to appear reluctant. Now Griffin thought she'd made a costly concession in return for his compliance, whereas in fact, she was getting everything she wanted.

Almost.

No matter how often she told herself that an amicable, respectful marriage would be enough to satisfy her, she couldn't seem to subdue a twinge of longing for the kind of passionate love her cousin Jane enjoyed with her husband, Constantine, Lord Roxdale.

While preserving their privacy to some degree, Jane had confided to Rosamund about the many and varied delights of the marriage bed. "I want you to know how it can be, darling. How it ought to be. Think what you will miss if you go ahead with this arrangement. If you love Captain Lauderdale, it would be criminal to take Tregarth."

But she *didn't* love Lauderdale. And while she might not love Griffin deVere—why, she hardly knew him!—the savage, hungry way he looked at her excited her more than all the respectful admiration of her gentler beaux put together.

Her mother came in as Rosamund finished dressing. "Rosamund, my dear, you poor, poor darling." The words were spoken without feeling or inflection. Sometimes, Rosamund wondered if her mother possessed emotions at all.

"I suppose that means you've met Lord Tregarth," Rosamund said.

"Good gracious, yes. The man is impossible." In an elegant gesture, Nerissa threw up her hands. "What on earth are you going to do with him?"

She was going to turn him into a model husband and breed beloved children with him and make a warm, happy home for them all. That's what she was going to do.

Instead, she said, "Andy will take care of making him more presentable. Lord Tregarth will do the pretty in Town for a while, and then I daresay we shall wed."

"And then you will send him off to the country while you enjoy yourself in London," said her mother, nodding as if they'd discussed her intentions already. "An excellent plan. And have you already chosen your cicisbeo? Can I guess who it might be?"

Rosamund wanted to repudiate the suggestion immediately, but with caution born of experience, she hesitated.

She needed to tread warily. If she flew to Griffin's defense as her nature urged her to do, she risked alerting her mother to her true feelings. The past had taught her it was better that her mother remained ignorant of emotions of any kind on the part of her children. Indeed, the more Rosamund wanted something, the closer she kept that longing to her chest.

Instead of rebutting her mother's assumption, she wiped all expression from her face. "I don't know what you mean, Mama. Surely, it is too early to be thinking of setting up a flirt. We are not even married yet."

"My darling, what else is a young girl's season for but to audition lovers?" asked Nerissa, blinking in surprise. "Clearly you have wasted your time these past years." She smiled. "Ah, but then, *of course* you haven't. You think you are discreet, but the whole world knows Lauderdale is just waiting for the chance to snap you up."

"Captain Lauderdale is an honorable man," Rosamund began.

Her mother laughed. "He might be as honorable as the day is long and still wish to warm your bed once that ghastly ogre has done his duty upon you." She shrugged her slender shoulders. "There's no crime in it, you know. The one benefit we ladies receive when our marriages are arranged is that we need not be faithful to our husbands. Pity those poor wretches who marry for love! Tied to one man for life?" The lady shuddered delicately.

Rosamund said nothing. Of course, she knew all about her mother's proclivities. The marchioness moved from lover to lover in a seemingly endless, intricate dance.

Rosamund had experienced firsthand the destruction such conduct wreaked and vowed long ago never to follow in Nerissa's dainty footsteps. Once she married Griffin, she would make a secure home and a content and peaceful family.

Nothing was going to stop her achieving her dream. Not her mother. Not even her future husband.

"Will you be at Lady Bigglesworth's rout tonight, Mama?" she inquired, changing the subject. "The duke has made up a family party."

Too late, she realized her mention of a family party to which her mother had not been invited was hardly felicitous. It was just that she considered the duke, her brother, and her cousins more her family than the marchioness had ever been.

Nerissa seemed unperturbed. "No, I have another engagement. I daresay it will be a little livelier than yours, darling." She licked her lips. "Have you never tired of living with that dull dog of a duke of yours?"

Montford and Lady Steyne had never been friendly, but a special animosity sprang up between them when Montford took Nerissa's children away.

The duke claimed to have done it in accordance with the terms of their father's will. Rosamund suspected otherwise but had never sought to raise the matter with her guardian.

"I am content, thank you, ma'am," she said. "I'll not live with the duke much longer, in any event."

"Ah. Yes, of course. Well, do send me a card for the wedding, won't you, my dear?"

Guilt washed over Rosamund, as her mother had no doubt intended. Resolutely, she stemmed the flow. Hadn't she suffered enough at her mother's hands that afternoon?

She forced a cheerful smile. "Oh, I daresay we shall see one another before then."

Lady Steyne did not mention any need for Rosamund to return to have the portrait completed. Rosamund would not raise the matter if Nerissa forgot. With any luck, the painting would simply languish, unfinished, in an attic somewhere. She'd been foolish and weak to let her mother persuade her to pose. Next time she paid a call here, she would bring Tibby.

"*Au revoir,* my love," said her mother, dismissing her with a wave of her hand.

Rosamund knew better than to kiss her. Instead, she merely curtsied and rang the bell for her maid.

"You did not ask him to stay here!" Rosamund gasped, horrified. "Andy, you cannot be serious! For goodness' sake, why?"

They'd gathered before dinner in a small, cozy parlor that had been their retreat since they were children. This room, adjacent to the nursery, had a comfortable, homey feel to it, and contained only the slightest odor of dog.

The parlor's sole canine inhabitant at present was an ancient Great Dane with a black and white harlequin coat. Her black spots had faded to gray, and her movements were slow and lumbering. She looked well loved and worn, much like the overstuffed furnishings and outdated draperies in this room.

The Westruther cousins had refused to allow even the most minute change to this parlor since they'd taken possession of it years before. Their static surroundings only served to remind Rosamund of how much she'd changed since the day Montford brought her here. Then, she'd been bewildered, lost, her spirit as thin and hollow as a husk.

Now, she stood decked out in a robe of blue sarcenet over a white satin slip, perfectly matched pearls at her throat and ears and wrists, her hair elaborately arranged. A young woman confident in the love of her family.

Montford had done that for her. Montford and her beloved cousins.

Andrew inspected his fingernails. "I thought having Tregarth to stay might speed things up a little."

"But you don't want me to marry him," objected Rosamund.

Andrew took a seat by the fireplace and stretched his legs before him. "I didn't say that. I quite like the fellow, in fact."

"I wish I'd seen you hit him," said Cecily, plunking down on the rug next to Ophelia. The old dog lifted her head and rested it in Cecily's lap with a soulful expression, then closed her eyes.

Rosamund frowned. She'd forgotten to reproach him about that. "*Not* the friendliest overture, Andy."

"My dear girl, I've knocked down most of my friends at one time or another."

Cecily shook her head. "I'll never understand men."

Andrew narrowed his eyes, as if to bring Griffin's image into perspective. "He's determined to have you, Rosamund. If you mean to give him the go-by, you ought to do it cleanly and do it now and not string the fellow along, making a fool of him."

Rosamund lifted her chin. "When I want your advice on my affairs, I'll ask for it, Andy. Besides, the duke approves my strategy."

"Don't look down your nose at me," he retorted, unimpressed. "Just take care you don't send him running in the other direction with all these conditions of yours."

Rosamund's heart thumped in her chest. Her gaze flew to Andrew's. "H-he told you of our bargain?"

Intimacies, Griffin had said. She repressed a reminiscent shiver.

"Ha!" said Andrew. "Call that a bargain? Don't see what he gets out of it, dragged along to picnics and parties when it's clear the fellow's no more up to snuff than old Ophelia here."

At the mention of her name, the Dane's eyebrows lifted in inquiry and her eyes opened a fraction. Then she gave a cross between a moan and a sigh and went back to sleep, her looping jowls whiffling with each breath.

Thankful that Griffin had been discreet enough to keep the extremely improper aspect of their agreement to himself, Rosamund said, "I trust I can rely on you, Andy, to see that Lord Tregarth *is* up to snuff."

"Oh, I can rig him out in style. In fact, I mean to do so. But I can't change the man, can I? And why the Devil should he take direction from me? Damned impertinent thing to tell a fellow how to behave."

"And yet, I am positive you will find a way to do so without putting up his back," said Rosamund. She softened, gazing down at him imploringly. "For me, Andy."

"Don't try to gammon me with that look," said her cousin. "You might have the male half of London at your feet, but you don't have me."

She laughed. "As if I'd want you at my feet, Andy. You have a heart of stone, for all your charming ways."

A frown creased his brows before he smiled. "Oh, not of *stone,* m'dear," he said softly. "I'm reliably informed that I don't have a heart at all."

How comfortable that must be, she thought.

Rosamund blinked, surprised at herself. "Nonsense! Of course you have a heart, my dear. But sentiment aside, you *will* admit you owe me a favor after what happened last year."

"That's quite true," said Cecily. "Rosamund saved you from accidentally compromising that odious Lady Emma Howling. That puts you greatly in her debt, I should say."

Andy blanched at the memory. He never could resist damsels in distress. Even shrill, unprepossessing damsels who'd been on the shelf for ten years. If it weren't for

Rosamund's quick thinking last season, Andrew would be married to the lady now.

"There, you have me," he said, holding up a hand in defeat. "Very well. I shall do my poor best, dear Rosamund."

A complicated tattoo sounded on the door. The secret knock, known only to the Westruther cousins and certain other trusted individuals.

Cecily jumped up to unlock the door, and Andrew rose from his chair as Tibby walked in, pulling on her gloves.

"It is time to leave for the rout party, my dears," said their companion.

Rosamund smiled at her. "Thank you, Tibby."

She kissed Cecily and bade her farewell, taking Andrew's arm as they left the room. "I wish I could stay home with Cecily," she said. "I do not feel like going out tonight."

He cocked a brow and glanced down at her. "Mooning over your giant?"

She gave a self-conscious laugh. "*Mooning?* Good God, no! What nonsense you talk, Andrew, dear."

The rout party was a dreadful crush, as they might have expected from a gathering of Lady Bigglesworth's. The flounce of Tibby's gown tore as someone trod on it in the press of bodies flowing up the staircase to the drawing room. While Tibby retired to mend it, Rosamund made a beeline for the card room.

She found Andy, who had just sat down to whist with another gentleman and two ladies. She stood silently behind him, watching the play and wishing the night would end.

"Ah, you are in fine beauty tonight, my dear. As always." The murmur filled her ear before she'd fully registered the presence of a man beside her.

"Oh!" She jumped and put a hand to her breast, turning to see who had accosted her. "You startled me, Captain."

Philip, Captain Lauderdale, appeared so vividly gorgeous in his scarlet regimentals that it hurt the eye to look at him. Indeed, he was the most dazzling creature she'd ever seen, with his golden hair, soulful dark eyes, and a classical profile that would put any Greek statue to shame.

Not for the first time, Rosamund wondered what was wrong with her that she could remain unmoved by all this masculine glory, yet yearn for . . .

No. She did not *yearn* for Griffin deVere. She wanted him to marry her; that was all. She was tired of waiting for her life to begin.

Lauderdale drew her apart from the card tables, leading her to sit on a bergère couch against the wall. He was adept at finding appropriate places for an intimate conversation among a crowd of people.

She gave him an impersonal smile. "How do you do, sir?"

He looked beyond her with a faint, mocking smile curving his lips. "Not well, I confess. Not since I heard the most disturbing news this afternoon."

"News?"

"Your dreaded betrothed has arrived in Town. They tell me he has come for you, Rosamund." He hit her with a full blast of those melting brown eyes. "My dear, how could you? And not a word to me."

She glanced away from him, nodding to an acquaintance who had been trying to catch her eye.

"How could I not?" she said quietly, turning back. "I agreed to this betrothal, Captain. Indeed, I have no wish to repudiate it. And please refrain from addressing me so familiarly. I never gave you leave to do so."

His head tilted in an ironic bow. "Of course, *Lady*

Rosamund. I apologize if my . . . feelings for you led me to be overly familiar."

He sent her a sidelong glance. She raised her eyebrows in haughty inquiry.

"It is not a surprise to you," he said. "You knew Tregarth was in Town."

"I . . . Yes."

She wanted to protest at his questioning her thus, but guilt trickled through her. Had she encouraged him to believe she might welcome his suit? She had not meant to do so, but with some men, it did not take much to convince them the object of their attentions reciprocated their regard.

He registered her answer with a tightened jaw. "But Lord Tregarth is not here with you tonight?"

"He is not."

He laughed softly. "What a trusting fellow he is. If I were the earl, I would not let you out of my sight."

"His trust is certainly not misplaced," said Rosamund coolly. To steer the conversation to less personal waters, she added, "Tell me how you go on, sir. How is your wound?"

"Healed very nicely, or that's what the sawbones says, anyway," said Lauderdale. "I'm to return to active service immediately."

Fear for him clutched her. With Napoleon on the loose again and amassing forces at an alarming rate, war was inevitable. Oh, she didn't care for Lauderdale as a sweetheart might, but as a friend, she couldn't help a craven regret that his wound wasn't serious enough to keep him from duty. He, of course, would never see it that way.

"You will leave soon?" she said.

"Next week." Bitterness laced his voice. "Tregarth *has* come for you, hasn't he? After all this time. He ought to be horsewhipped for treating you so." He met her gaze and said softly, "And you, a diamond of the first water."

Her throat seemed to close over. "Forgive me, but that is not your concern. I do not wish to discuss—"

"But I am glad," he interrupted. "I'm glad that you're finally to be wed."

Glad? She blinked at him in surprise.

He edged closer, close enough that she could smell wine on his breath. "Do you know why, Lady Rosamund Westruther? Can't you guess?"

Shaking her head, she glanced away from him. "No, I cannot, and I can't imagine why you would—"

"Rosamund, darling, don't you see what this means? We can be together at last. In all the ways that truly matter."

Rosamund choked, her gaze snapping back to him. *"What?"* The word would have been a shriek if she'd had sufficient breath in her lungs. As it was, it came out as a hollow whisper.

"Oh, you must do your duty by him," said Lauderdale soothingly. "I loathe the very idea of you in the arms of another, but we both know it must be done. With any luck, by the time I return home from battle, you'll be with child. And then you and I, my very *dear* . . ."

He trailed off, his heated gaze fixing on her mouth before sliding down to linger at her breasts.

She stared back at him, so appalled she could not think clearly. Surely she'd misheard or misconstrued his words? But no, his meaning was far too plain to be mistaken.

Shock slammed into her like a fist. Nausea curdled her stomach. To her horror and disgust, tears pressed at the backs of her eyes.

On some level, she must have guessed his true intentions, mustn't she? It was too, too stupid of her to be sitting here getting propositioned and never have had an inkling that his intentions were so base. Her mother had been right.

Lauderdale raised her nerveless hand to his lips. He'd released her before she could rouse herself to react or snatch her hand away.

Conscious that they were in public, she lowered her voice, battling to keep the shock and dismay from showing on her face. "You assume far too much, Captain Lauderdale. I have no intention of entering into any kind of liaison with you."

He did not appear at all chastened. He merely gave her a smug, knowing smile. "We'll see about that, shall we? Lord, Rosamund, that oaf wouldn't know the first thing about pleasing a woman." Again, his dark gaze flicked over her body. "But I assure you, my dear, I do. By the time you've been married a few months, you'll be begging me to take you."

He must have seen the stark horror in her eyes because his brows snapped together. After a moment, he said, "Good God, are you asking me to believe you are shocked? A daughter of the great Lady Steyne? No, no, my dear. Doing it rather too brown, I fear."

Hysteria bubbled up inside her. She could laugh at how she'd fretted and fussed, terrified of hurting the captain's precious feelings. He had no feelings at all for her beyond physical desire. He was in love with her face and figure, just as the rest of them were.

She shot to her feet, betrayal and anger tumbling inside her.

Lauderdale rose, too, and was about to say more when Andrew materialized beside Rosamund and handed her a glass of champagne.

She could have thrown herself upon her cousin's chest and sobbed her thanks down his pristine waistcoat. *Thank God!* Thank God for Andy.

Rosamund took the champagne with a trembling hand and sipped, welcoming the cool tingle of bubbles on her tongue.

Andrew addressed Lauderdale. "I believe you have another appointment somewhere else, my friend." His manner was affable, but there was steel in that lazy, cultured drawl.

"Quite right, Lydgate." Easily, Lauderdale bowed to both of them, while contriving to send her a covert glance that was hot with desire. "I'll see you both at Lady Buckham's soiree."

I hope not, thought Rosamund.

She watched him stride away, so godlike in his regimentals, so invincible and perfect. A vain, self-centered coxcomb of a man. Inwardly, she shuddered at what a fool she'd been to believe he had any finer feelings toward her than mere lust.

"You are overset. What was that about?" Frowning, Andrew cocked his head in Lauderdale's direction.

"Nothing, nothing." Seeing another group of acquaintances, Rosamund plastered her society smile on her face.

But Andy persisted. "Did he press his attentions on you? Shall I call him out and kill him for you, m'dearest?" His words were flippant but the expression in his eyes was dangerous.

She shook her head. "Oh—but, Andy, I . . ." Her smile was so rigid, it cracked at the edges. She couldn't hold up her chin for the rest of the evening and pretend all was well. "Andy, will you please take me home?"

CHAPTER EIGHT

Lydgate had been right about the noise at Limmer's. Even the effects of his libations in the taproom had not allowed Griffin to sleep through the din. Tired and out of sorts, he paid his shot and left the hotel.

Lydgate had sent around a note saying he'd made all right with the duke and reiterated his invitation to stay at Montford House. Griffin could only trust that was truly the case as he followed the ancient butler up to his allotted chamber. He'd inquired after Montford, but the duke was not expected back until evening. Lydgate was still abed. No doubt he never rose from it before noon.

When he'd visited Montford House the previous day, Griffin had been too caught up in his quest to pay much attention to his surroundings. Now, as he followed the butler up the staircase, he had more leisure to observe.

Grandeur was the word that leaped to mind. This was no ordinary town house like the one he owned in Mayfair, but a free-standing mansion surrounded by its own park.

The entrance hall had the cold, lofty feel of a cathedral—airy and spacious and filled with echoes. Blind-eyed statues from the Greek pantheon stood spaced between columns surmounted by intricately carved capitals.

At the turn of the stair, Griffin glanced over the balustrade. Early spring sunshine shafted through a glass dome above to pool like melted butter on the black and white chessboard floor below. The marble tiles gleamed as clean and polished as a dinner plate. Indeed, one probably *could* eat one's dinner from it if one chose.

He grimaced. Only the rodent population would ever contemplate dining off the floors at Pendon Place.

In dire contrast to his ramshackle abode, *this* house exuded luxury like an expensive perfume. It was likely to choke him before the week was out.

When the butler showed him to his chamber, Griffin hesitated on the threshold. He couldn't remember ever having seen anything so fine. Except . . . A sudden rush of memory nearly unbalanced him. His mother. Silks, satins, velvets. The cool caress of her lovely hand, flashing with diamonds.

No. Not diamonds. Emeralds, to match her eyes. How could he have forgotten that?

Griffin swallowed hard, then became aware that the impassive butler still hovered, waiting for his approval.

He ought not to gape in front of a servant, even such a well-trained servant as this. A wealthy earl should be accustomed to such finery, not marveling at it.

He nodded. "This will do."

The butler bowed. "I trust you will be comfortable, my lord." He oversaw the footmen, who delivered Griffin's modest baggage. "Does your valet follow you, sir?"

"No," said Griffin baldly. Couldn't the man tell he didn't have a valet?

"Very good, my lord," said the butler. "I shall ask Lord Lydgate's man to assist you."

"No need." He would not dine here tonight or go anywhere that merited a valet's attentions to his dress. "Hot water in the morning is all I need." He glanced down at his mud-splashed footwear. "And someone to shine my boots."

The butler inclined his head. "I'll see to it, my lord."

With gruff thanks and a generous tip, Griffin dismissed him.

Griffin stared out the window at the pleasant vista of a garden studded with fountains and flower beds and surrounded by a high stone wall. At the foot of the garden stood a charming summer house, overgrown with purple wisteria. Griffin pictured Rosamund and her friends taking tea there, fluttering around inside it like a flock of butterflies.

The rarefied tranquility of that scene seemed to heighten his impatience. How long would it take to meet Rosamund's conditions and get her to the altar? He'd forgotten the exact extent of the frivolity she had in store for him. He frowned. Maybe he should have made her put it in writing so she wouldn't sneak in any extras.

He'd been an idiot to agree, of course, but how could he help it? The memory of her lush breasts and slender waist beneath that filmy material tantalized him.

All that could be mine.

Yesterday, the image of a vividly pretty girl in a blue riding habit that matched her eyes had been superseded by a stunning siren of a woman, confident in her manner and definite in her opinions. And far more dangerous to his peace—not to mention his sanity—than she'd ever been.

Instinctively, he knew Rosamund was still an innocent. She might dress in that scandalous costume for a painting, but Rosamund would not have granted any other gentleman her favors, certainly not before she married.

After she was wed—well, that was a different matter. Despite his insistence that theirs would not be a typical marriage of convenience, he knew how it was with Westruther women—and for that matter, how it was with deVere men. In their elevated circle, no one married to please themselves. Naturally, it followed that the participants in such bloodless alliances would look outside marriage for passion.

In the sophisticated set to which Rosamund's mother, Lady Steyne, belonged, fidelity was considered deeply unfashionable. A lady was expected to bear her husband the obligatory heir; then she might bed whomever she chose. Husbands were not expected to be faithful at all.

The notion of Rosamund following the same path as her mother made his stomach churn, made him want to smash his fist into the wall—or into her unknown lover's face.

He'd agreed to this marriage under duress while his grandfather lived, before he'd comprehended all the implications. His intended bride had scarcely crossed his mind before he'd met her. Why should she? He'd accepted the old earl's decree with the vague notion that she must be some kind of antidote for her parents to allow her to throw herself away on someone like him.

He'd never appreciated the true depths of his grandfather's malice until he set eyes on the exquisite loveliness that was Lady Rosamund Westruther.

Lord, to think he'd hoped for a docile, plain girl who'd be content to live out her days in quiet seclusion at Pendon Place! One who wouldn't interfere with him or demand his attention. One who wouldn't drive him nigh crazed with lust or make his gut roil with a mess of longings and fears he'd hoped never to experience again.

How deluded could he have been?

And now she had him dancing like a performing bear to her tune. Well, he'd go through with the business, if only to speed her to the altar. But he would exact every ounce of the payment she'd promised him in return.

* * *

"You cannot be serious," said Griffin.

Lydgate sighed. "Of course I am serious. I never joke about anything pertaining to fashion. Tregarth, meet your new valet."

Griffin gave the servant a cursory inspection. The man's height was average, his figure lean. His features were regular, and his manner might best be described as unassuming. He wore a dark coat and a plain waistcoat and blindingly white linen. Altogether, he was as neat as a pin and bland as cream.

"His name is Dearlove," said Lydgate.

"Dearlove?" Griffin stared. "As in 'Dearlove, where did you put my smalls?' Or 'Dearlove, I'll need a bath drawn in an hour.' Or—"

"Yes, yes, I take the point," said Lydgate testily. He turned to the valet. "What is your given name, my good man?"

The valet gave a self-deprecating cough. "If you don't mind, my lord, I'd prefer you didn't—"

"Damned if I'll go around calling him Dearlove," said Griffin. "Not that I need a valet, mind. But if I did, I'd find something else to call him."

Lydgate studied the valet with a gleam of curiosity in his blue eyes. "Your name, Dearlove. Out with it."

It might have been Griffin's imagination, but he thought the corners of the valet's dark eyes compressed in an infinitesimal wince. "It's . . . Ahem. Sweet William, my lord."

"Sweet—?" Griffin's mouth dropped open. He glanced at Lydgate, whose shoulders shook with suppressed mirth. "Hmm. Interesting."

"My mother's choice, my lord. God rest her soul." The valet assumed a mournful expression, fixing his gaze upon the ceiling.

After a short struggle, Lydgate mastered himself and

clapped his hands together. "Well, that's all right, isn't it? You can call him William."

"No, sir." Sweet William Dearlove shook his head, quietly adamant. "My mother would never allow it. She named all of her children for her favorite flowers, you see. I was the only son, and she insisted I was not to be left out. It would be disrespectful to her memory to shorten the name. And, er, I'd prefer Dearlove, if it's all the same to you."

Lydgate rolled his eyes at Griffin in comical dismay.

"Oh, the Devil!" muttered Griffin, helpless in the face of the servant's sainted mother. "Dearlove it is."

"You won't notice it after a few weeks, my lord," said Dearlove helpfully.

"Right. Well, then." Lydgate gave the valet's shoulder a heartening thump. "Come along, both of you. We have work to do."

Somehow, Griffin allowed himself to be carried along in Lydgate's enthusiasm. It wasn't until they were well on their way that he regrouped sufficiently to mount another protest.

"What the Hell am I supposed to do with him?" he muttered to Lydgate as they turned into New Bond Street.

He cut a glance over his shoulder at the soberly garbed individual following dutifully behind them. The fellow was so unobtrusive as to be almost invisible. Griffin found it highly unsettling.

Lydgate's lips twitched. "You look as if the bogeyman is at your heels. Dearlove is some sort of cousin to my own valet. He's a wizard by all accounts, and you're dashed lucky to get him. On short notice, too."

"Most honored, I'm sure," grunted Griffin. "But I repeat: I do not need a valet!"

With a put-upon sigh, Lydgate said, "Frankly, I never saw a fellow who stood *more* in need of one. If you are to dress as befits Lady Rosamund Westruther's betrothed, you will require assistance. A valet keeps your linen clean and starched, your coats pressed, and your boots shined to perfection. He helps you on with your coat, helps you off with your footwear. He'll even tie your cravat if you want."

Lydgate glanced at the knotted belcher handkerchief at Griffin's throat and briefly closed his eyes, as if pained by the sight. "I'd avail myself of his services in that direction if I were you."

Griffin snorted. "If you're ashamed to be seen with me in public—"

"Don't be absurd," snapped Lydgate. "If that were the case, I'd have sent you off alone with Dearlove. You're family now. Don't be more of a clodpole than you can help."

Perversely, his companion's insult made Griffin feel better. Grinning, he followed Lydgate into the first shop.

His good humor was short-lived. To his frustration and disgust, he discovered that one could not simply order several suits of clothes in one place and be done with it. According to Lydgate and the estimable Dearlove, the best breeches were made by Meyer, the most splendid waistcoats could be had at Weston's. It was Lock for hats, Hoby for boots.

The only cause of discord between these two princes of fashion was over coats.

Dearlove spoke without heat or inflection, but he was adamant. "My lord, I believe it must be Schweitzer and Davidson."

"No, no," said Lydgate. "Stultz is the man we want." He gestured at Griffin. "Lord Tregarth's sheer size ought to tell you that. Stultz makes coats for the military men. He's our best bet."

"If you will permit me to disagree, my lord," murmured

Dearlove. "A military cut is designed to make a figure even more . . . imposing. What we require is *elegance,* which, as Your Lordship knows, is all about proportion. And Mr. Schweitzer, you must agree, is a master of proportion when it comes to designing coats."

Dearlove went on to explain to Griffin the neoclassical principles of tailoring, which this excellent proponent of the art employed to such great effect.

Finally noticing that Griffin watched him open-mouthed with horror, Dearlove spread his hands with a self-deprecating smile. "It is not necessary for you to comprehend the intricacies of a perfectly fitting coat, my lord. But you may rest assured that Mr. Schweitzer *does*."

To Griffin's amazement, Lydgate considered this. "Do you know, Dearlove, I believe you're right."

"Yes, my lord."

"Schweitzer it is, then," said the viscount, redirecting his lazy saunter toward Cork Street.

Griffin raised his gaze to the heavens, shrugged, and followed.

Purchasing sufficient clothing, undergarments, and accoutrements to stock a gentleman's wardrobe to Lydgate's satisfaction took the better part of a week. Griffin suffered through measurings and fittings, traipsing hither and yon with Lydgate and Dearlove all over Town in search of the most superior example of every item any fashionable gentleman could possibly want or dream of.

His betrothed's cousin even insisted on helping him choose various decorative items such as fobs and seals and stickpins for his cravats. In a dazed kind of stupor, Griffin allowed it all. Besides, he'd need a well-stocked clothespress when he brought Jacks to London for the season, so he might as well get it all over and done with in one fell swoop.

He did, however, reserve the right to grumble.

After a stultifying interval spent poring over materials for waistcoats one afternoon, Lydgate finally agreed to call a halt. Their Lordships sent Dearlove home in the carriage with their parcels and elected to walk. Lydgate had a commission to perform, so they took a detour to Berkeley Square.

"Why don't you stop over at Gunter's?" suggested Lydgate. "They serve an excellent punch-water ice there. I won't be long."

Assuming from his failure to give an explanation of his mission that Lydgate's purpose was amorous, Griffin didn't inquire further. He ambled toward the confectioner's shop, which displayed the sign of a pineapple as advertisement of its trade.

The afternoon had grown uncomfortably warm, and he'd had a trying time of it that day. They'd poked and prodded and measured him until his hand itched to hit the next fool who attempted to fondle any part of his person. They'd discussed his physique and conformation with embarrassing depth and candor, as if he were a prize bull, not a man.

The tailor, Mr. Schweitzer, had been all admiration. He'd gone so far as to liken the proportions of Griffin's body to those of Gentleman Jackson, the famous boxer whose impressive form had been used as a model for a surprising number of aristocratic portraits.

Well, of course the tailors all spouted that rubbish, didn't they? It went with the territory, flattering vain aristocrats in the hope of extracting more business from them.

Yes, it had been a trying day. The idea of iced punch seemed very enticing.

The street outside Gunter's bustled with activity, for most of the shop's noble patrons did not take their refreshment within the establishment, but rather remained in their own vehicles. A gaggle of carriages collected under the shade of the ancient plane trees near the railed garden in the center of the square, while scurrying waiters wove in and out of passing traffic to ferry orders back and forth.

It was in one of these fashionable equipages that Griffin spied Rosamund.

Immediately, his pulse picked up pace. He'd scarcely seen her since that afternoon in her mother's parlor. He was out all day—shopping, for God's sake!—and she absent every evening, enjoying the social round.

She sat with her back to him in an open barouche, displaying her profile now and again as she turned to speak to one of her companions. The other occupants of the carriage were Lady Cecily and Miss Tibbs, their companion.

And beside the barouche stood a man in scarlet regimentals.

Lady Cecily ended some jest or other with an expressive roll of her dark eyes. The soldier laughed, his broad shoulders shaking with it.

That officer could have been anyone, but Griffin didn't think so. There was something overly familiar in the fellow's demeanor, in the way he leaned down to Rosamund to murmur something in her ear. The way he—oh so accidentally—let his hand brush hers where it rested on the doorsill of the open carriage.

Lauderdale.

Anger and betrayal snaked through Griffin, writhing in his guts, constricting his chest. While he'd suffered through hours of sartorial torture solely to please Rosamund, she'd been making eyes at her precious officer.

Resentment burned inside him, hot and dark. To Hell with her conditions, her parties, and her drives in the park! Why should he have to prove anything to her, anyway?

A waiter approached, distributing conical glasses filled

with pastel-colored ices among the ladies. While Cecily and the older lady were occupied with accepting their treats, Lauderdale surreptitiously laid his hand over Rosamund's and kept it there.

A blast of fury shot clean through Griffin's head. He started toward them, his brain seething with suspicion.

Then Rosamund withdrew her hand from beneath the captain's with some remark or other and pointedly turned her head away. Lauderdale let his hand drop to his side with the angry, baffled look of a man who had been unexpectedly rebuffed.

The tension drained from Griffin's body. He stood there in the middle of the crowded street for a full minute before he recovered equilibrium. Then he shook his head, astonished at the violence of his reactions.

He was a fool, all right, an idiot to jump to conclusions like some asinine schoolboy. Of course he didn't care where Rosamund bestowed her affections. He hadn't been *jealous*—he'd never give a woman that kind of power over him. But he did have strenuous objections to sharing what was his, and the sooner her tin soldier understood that, the better.

He'd hesitated too long with all this conjecture bubbling in his brain. Before he could decide whether to go or stay, Lady Cecily spied him and waved. Rosamund turned her head and saw him, too. Nothing for it but to grit his teeth and join them.

He suspected his teeth would be ground to stumps before his sojourn in London was over.

"Lord Tregarth. How delightful." Rosamund beamed at him and put out her hand.

Surprise at the cordiality of her greeting made him hesitate before taking her fingertips and bowing over them.

He met Rosamund's eyes and discerned a slight frown

in their blue depths. Did she suppose he'd brush a tender kiss over her knuckles? She ought to know better than to expect all that folderol from an oaf like him.

Instead, he released her fingers and greeted Lady Cecily and Miss Tibbs.

"Oh, and this is Captain Lauderdale," Rosamund added, confirming Griffin's suspicions.

Her voice was expressionless—carefully so—as if she were determined not to give any emotion away. That was perhaps more telling than any overt display of her feelings could ever be.

The captain turned, and for the first time, Griffin got a good look at the man's face.

Hell. If Griffin had needed any reminder of the chasm between him and his intended wife, there it was, embodied in scarlet regimentals. The fellow looked like a bloody prince from a fairy tale. How could a gargoyle like Griffin ever hope to compete with that?

Well, he'd go through with this charade because he'd given his word. But once it was over and Rosamund was his wife, she could forget about trying to change him into something he wasn't.

Lauderdale smiled, but his dark eyes were hard and bright. "A pleasure to make your acquaintance . . . at last."

Griffin ignored the implied criticism. "Isn't your lot stationed in Brussels now?"

"Yes. I'm about to join them." He glanced at Rosamund. "All the world flocks to the Continent, Lady Rosamund. You should ask the duke to take you."

"I can't imagine why," said Rosamund. "We'd be shockingly in the way."

"Oh, I don't know," Cecily said with a mischievous grin. "I expect we'd do our bit to keep up the soldiers' morale. And it would be an adventure, would it not?"

Miss Tibbs remarked, "Lady Cecily, as you are not yet

out, you would find Brussels just as tedious as London, I daresay."

"Rosamund is not going to Brussels," snapped Griffin.

The captain's sleek eyebrows shot up. Sculpted lips trembling with amusement, he slanted a glance at Rosamund. As if to say, *And this is the uncivilized brute you choose to marry?*

She held herself very still, clearly bracing for a confrontation.

"Perhaps you weren't aware, Captain," said Miss Tibbs in her soft, precise voice. "Lord Tregarth and Lady Rosamund are to be married. A happy event for us all."

The spring air hummed with tension. "Yes, indeed," returned Lauderdale with a significant glance at Rosamund. "Lady Rosamund informed me last night, ma'am. Might I be among the first to wish you both *extremely* happy?"

Rosamund's features froze. It seemed to cost her a great deal of effort to unclose her lips and say, "Thank you."

Then her gaze caught Griffin's, and she sent him another dazzling smile. Damned if it wasn't like being showered in diamonds, even if the smile didn't quite reach those Delft-blue eyes.

"I am sure we shall be," said Rosamund. "Very happy, indeed."

"Rosamund, dear, your ice is melting," said Miss Tibbs.

"Oh." Obediently, Rosamund lowered her gaze to her lemon-colored ice and licked delicately at the cool, swirling confection. An appreciative little murmur sounded in the back of her throat as she savored its sweetness; her pink lips glistened with moisture. She passed her tongue over them, innocently unaware of the effect she created.

Griffin sucked in a breath. For a searing instant, he felt light-headed. He longed to taste those cool, soft lips, to make them heat and move and part beneath his own, to feel her tongue stroking his, her mouth on his body. . . .

A soft groan came from Lauderdale. "You are a lucky dog, Tregarth."

Yes, he thought. *God, yes. I am.*

Then he scowled, realizing that Lauderdale's fantasies ran along the same lines as his own.

Rosamund's eyelashes fluttered a little as she raised her eyes to Griffin. Her gaze fused with his, her eyes soft and warm. She must have read the tenor of his thoughts in his face, for she blushed so adorably, he wanted to snatch her up in his arms.

Lauderdale's tone was sharp with annoyance. "What a shame you neglected Lady Rosamund all those years, Tregarth. Some ardent young buck might have stolen her away from you."

CHAPTER NINE

Rosamund dearly wished to knock Lauderdale's hat off and dump her ice over his guinea-gold head. Only her innate good breeding and years of practice in elegant restraint held her back.

Cecily was right: Sometimes being a well-bred lady was the very Devil.

"By the way, when is the, er . . . *happy* day?" the captain inquired.

Rosamund's fingers clenched around the handle of her glass. Lauderdale could laugh at her all he wanted, but it *would* be a happy marriage if she had anything to say about it.

The way Griffin had looked at her just now . . .

"The wedding is set for next week." Griffin shot the captain a challenging glare.

"Next week?" she repeated, doing her best to look flattered and amused. "You are impatient, sir! But I must insist we do the thing properly. Why, I've not yet had the chance to buy my bride clothes."

"Quite right, Rosamund," said Cecily. "One should never pass up an excuse to spend a lavish amount on one's appearance. The modistes are always at their busiest this season. There is no time to waste. We must plan our strategy."

Grateful that her cousin had helped steer the conversation to safer waters, Rosamund relaxed a little. "My thoughts exactly. Isn't it odd, Cecily, how often our cogitations coincide?"

"Great minds and all that," Cecily agreed. She bit into the rosy cloud of her raspberry ice. "Bride clothes. That reminds me. Where do you go on your bride tour?"

Rosamund choked.

"Bride tour?" Griffin looked as if his horrid old neckerchief strangled him.

"Well, of course!" Cecily considered. "Such a pity Paris is ineligible, now that Bonaparte is on the rampage. Perhaps you should go to the Lake District. Or even Scotland might be pleasant if you wait until summer. Constantine and Jane did that, although I don't believe they'd have cared where they were, they were so wrapped up in each other." She held up her ice. "This raspberry flavor is delicious. Would you like some, Rosamund?"

Slowly, Rosamund shook her head.

Cecily's mention of a bride tour conjured visions of days spent alone in Griffin's company. Many days . . . and a commensurate number of nights. Rosamund's heart thumped hard, and she felt her color rise. She couldn't even glance at her betrothed.

Her bergamot water ice had gone largely untouched and now began to melt in earnest. A single lemon-colored rivulet snaked down the side of the glass and pooled in the crook of her finger and thumb.

Resisting the urge to lick it off, she said, "Cecily, Lord Tregarth has only just arrived in Town. I am sure we shall sort out the details of our . . . married life later."

Abruptly, the captain took out his timepiece and glanced

at it. "Ladies, do forgive me," he said. "I've recalled a pressing engagement."

"Don't let us keep you," grunted Rosamund's betrothed.

Lauderdale met Rosamund's eyes. "I'll see you at Lady Buckham's soiree tomorrow night." He snapped a bow in their direction, nodded to Griffin, and strode away.

They all fell silent, watching him go.

When a waiter arrived, Rosamund gladly surrendered the sad remnants of her treat and hunted in her reticule for a handkerchief to wipe her sticky fingers. Her wits were a sad, melting mess, just like the ice. Her head ached; her heart felt strangely bruised.

Bruised? No, it wasn't her heart that was bruised, of course. It was her pride.

She'd never loved Captain Lauderdale. Yet, his unflagging devotion had been a balm to the wound Griffin inflicted three years ago, a wound Griffin's continued absence and other people's pity had rubbed raw. She'd never dreamed Lauderdale regarded her marriage with complacency, content to wait for the moment he could safely make her his mistress.

How galling to admit her mother had been right.

On impulse, Rosamund turned to Griffin. "Will you walk with me, my lord?"

He stared at her. "Walk?"

"Yes," she said, impatient all at once. "Promenade. Perambulate. I wish to stroll in the garden, and I require your escort."

He shrugged with exceedingly bad grace. "If I must."

Out of the corner of her eye, she saw Tibby and Cecily exchange significant glances. Rosamund put her chin up and pulled on her gloves. "Will you wait here, my dears? We shan't be long."

"Don't go out of sight, Rosamund," said Tibby.

"Of course not." Rosamund smiled, all compliance. She'd discovered that a habit of compliance tended to lull suspicion. The duke and Tibby watched Cecily like hawks, while allowing Rosamund far more freedom than they knew.

She picked up her parasol and stood and waited with a pointed look of expectation at Griffin.

There was a beat of silence before he took his cue, opening the low door to the barouche and letting down the steps. Without further prompting, he took her hand to help her down. She felt the immense strength in him even from that fleeting contact.

She snapped open her parasol, a frivolous tasseled shade made of sea green silk and white crêpe to match her gown.

"Let us go that way," she said, pointing. "I wish to pay my regards to the statue in the middle of the garden. Have you seen it? It's the king posed as Marcus Aurelius and remarkably ugly. I have a particular fondness for it."

Oh, dear, she was babbling.

With a slight shrug of his shoulders, Griffin tucked her hand through his arm and led her into the garden in the center of the square.

They walked in silence for a few moments while Rosamund absorbed Griffin's presence. She was no waif, as her mother was fond of telling her, but he was so much broader, taller, so much more solid than she. Larger in every sense. Her hand looked tiny nestled there in the crook of his arm.

The sea-foam froth of her skirts flirted with his shining black boots as she and Griffin meandered beneath the dappled shade of the ancient maples. Griffin's new valet must have gotten to those boots, she thought, for they had not gleamed like that when he arrived in Town.

Abruptly, Griffin spoke. "Are you in love with him?"

She did not need to ask to whom he referred, nor did she insult him by pretending ignorance. "No. Not at all."

She thought of the locket around her neck, which still held Griffin's portrait.

From the moment she'd seen that ill-painted miniature, only one man had occupied her dreams. Despite the success of her first season and Griffin's neglect, she'd never wanted another. Inexplicably, she'd set her heart on the great, recalcitrant colossus beside her, and no one else would do.

She caught the slip even as she thought it. No, not her heart. She'd staked her *future* on Griffin deVere. Her precious, fragile heart would never come into play. The odds of that gamble were not in her favor.

She thought he wouldn't reply, but after a few moments, he said, "I am glad. Not that I would have released you from our betrothal. He is unworthy of you, and besides, Montford would never let you throw yourself away on an army captain. Still . . . I am glad."

As an afterthought, he added, "For your sake, of course."

She digested this. "Did you think because my parents lived in separate establishments that I'd desire that sort of life?"

He turned his head to look at her. "I didn't know your parents lived separately."

She hid her relief behind an arch smile. "Not know about the epic battles between the Marquis of Steyne and his lady? My dear sir, where have you been living? Under a rock?"

"In Cornwall," he said, rubbing his jaw with the side of his thumb. "Which often amounts to the same thing."

She detected the suspicion of a grin and laughed. But she sighed, too. "My parents were so dreadfully incompatible, you see. Their marriage was arranged, of course. He was a cold, unemotional man for the most part, and he detested scenes. But when his temper was roused . . ." She shuddered. "And she—my mother—roused it whenever she could. She . . . she threw things. Tantrums, china. Once, she heaved up the ormolu clock from the mantel and hurled it at my father's head. Missed him by a mile, of course. But I do believe one of them would have ended up killing the other if Papa had not sent us away."

"Is that when you went to the duke?" said Griffin.

She shook her head, wondering how she had strayed so far from what she'd meant to say. "No, until Papa died, we remained in my mother's care. After that, the duke became our guardian. He took Xavier and me into his own household. That was much less . . . fraught."

"But still not like home."

"No. I don't suppose it was." Rosamund pushed her parasol back a little to rest the shaft on her shoulder and tilted her face to the sun. "But I had my brother and my cousins. I love them dearly. I wouldn't change that part for the world."

They came to a clearing at the center of the garden. "Ah, here it is," she said. "The statue."

Griffin grunted and tilted his head sideways. "A bit top-heavy, isn't it? Looks like it's going to keel over."

"I hope not. That would offend His Majesty's dignity, would it not? Poor man."

They contemplated the lugubrious statue in silence. Then Rosamund gestured to a path that led off to their right. "Let's go back a different way."

She took Griffin's arm again, quite naturally now, as they meandered. Griffin seemed in no hurry to return to the carriage, and nor was she.

After a pause, his low rumble broke the silence. "Do you? Want to live in separate establishments, I mean."

She shook her head. "No, that would not suit me at all. I want my family to live together in peace." Her voice rasped as a sudden rush of emotion overtook her. "That's all I've ever wanted."

"Never a cross word spoken?" He glanced down at her with the glimmer of his rare smile. "You might not have noticed, but I have something of a hasty temper."

"I shan't regard it, however." She put up her chin. She'd created a harmony of sorts from the chaos caused by far more difficult temperaments than Griffin's. Why, he was only an overgrown schoolboy when all was said and done.

A big, strong, powerful, quite *deliciously* overgrown schoolboy.

She gave a sigh that was part appreciation, part wistfulness. At this moment, she almost wished she'd agreed to wed Griffin immediately.

But how would they have come to the small measure of understanding they'd achieved today if she'd allowed him to ride roughshod over her? The key to taming this beast was to stand her ground, even when he was at his most ferocious. Particularly then.

Gathering her courage, she asked him the question that had nagged at her mind since his return. "Why did you never come for me?"

There was an arrested silence; then he exhaled a long breath. "Many reasons. None of them had anything to do with you."

Rosamund digested this in silence. Was she comforted by that or insulted? She couldn't decide. With all the upheaval of the previous two days, she was too confused and overwhelmed to puzzle it out. She would tuck his words away for later examination, like the miniature portrait in her locket.

She wanted to steal a covert look up at him, but his height and her parasol, not to mention the poke of her bonnet, prevented subtlety. She was obliged to crane her neck.

His expression was a stony blank, as if he'd slammed

the door on the fortress in which he imprisoned his deepest emotions.

She'd get nowhere with him when he looked like that, so she said, "Let us put the past behind us. You are here now, and the season is about to begin. We shall enjoy a little courtship. Yes—" She held up her hand to fend off the protest she anticipated. "—I *do* mean enjoy, my lord."

Once again, his expression altered. Those gray eyes held a rakish gleam. "I recall some parts I mean to enjoy very well."

She gasped. Could he actually mean—?

Amusement lightened his features in response to her confusion. He leaned toward her. "Starting tonight."

His voice was a low growl that vibrated through her body; his breath brushed her ear with tingling warmth. The implication caught fire in her brain, making her pulse jump and race. A hot flush swept over her breasts and up, into her cheeks.

Those intimacies she'd promised him . . .

Should she admit she anticipated those intimacies as eagerly as he did? Perhaps not. Something told her he'd want her more if she displayed a little reluctance.

"Oh!" she said. "But you've done nothing to earn any rewards yet."

A little grimly, he replied, "If you think spending an entire week at the tender mercies of your cousin and my new valet aren't enough to earn me a taste of you, let me remind you that I've been dancing attendance on you for the better part of an hour this afternoon." He threw out a hand as if to encompass their surrounds. "I'm *strolling*, for God's sake!"

She was enjoying this hugely. "That is true," she said, cocking her head as if to consider. "And yet, these were not the conditions of our agreement. I distinctly recall that I specifically listed various entertainments which— Oh!"

she exclaimed as he grabbed her hand and pulled her along with him. "What are you *doing,* sir?"

He yanked her off the path and whisked her behind a tree so that they were screened from the path, but not from any other chance passerby. In a flash, he'd captured the handle of her parasol, twisted it out of her fingers, and tossed it aside.

"That parasol cost me twenty guineas!"

"I'll buy you another." He maneuvered her so that her back was against the tree trunk and brought his palm flat against the trunk beside her head.

Leaning in, he said, "If you don't want me to kiss you here, now, in public, you'll agree to meet me somewhere in your house tonight."

"Oh, this is an outrage!" managed Rosamund, trying not to allow a delighted laugh to escape her. "I utterly refuse to agree to anything so improper." She turned her face away from him like a martyred virgin avoiding the flames licking upward from the pyre. Her heart thumped hard and fast in her breast.

But when he did not respond to this clear piece of encouragement, she breathed, "I should think you would treat your future wife with more respect, sir."

"Oh, I respect you, my dear." Griffin raised his hand and ran his fingertip gently over her lips. His breathing grew ragged. She closed her eyes and waited for his mouth to descend on hers.

It was scandalous behavior. They were in public, even if by some lucky circumstance, no one could see them now. Yet she longed for his kiss so much that she didn't care.

Voices. Coming closer. Now she really did panic, her bravado deserting her abruptly. "Oh, someone's coming! Let me go, I—"

"Not until you agree to meet me."

"Yes, yes, I agree! But let me g— Oh."

He stepped away from her just as a couple of small boys ran past, rolling a large wooden hoop.

She sagged back against the tree, limp with relief, giddy with exhilaration.

Griffin bent to pick up her parasol and handed it to her, and his gray eyes still held a devilish sparkle.

"When?" he said softly. "And where?"

CHAPTER TEN

"D earlove, I need your help." Now those were words
he'd never thought to say.

In fact, Griffin was quite bemused at the way
this consummate gentleman's gentleman had insinuated
himself into his life. Griffin had been so preoccupied with
thoughts of Rosamund that he had scarcely noticed the
quiet efficiencies of his new valet.

The French-milled soap the man provided for Griffin's
bath was doubtless contraband, but it smelled uncommonly
good. Fresh and clean, like pine needles and lemon. Griffin
didn't hold much with scents, but this one seemed appropriately masculine.

He needed to shave, but with his clandestine rendezvous looming, Griffin didn't trust his hands not to shake
at a critical moment. Accepting Dearlove's offer to wield
the wicked-looking razor instead of hacking at his throat
himself seemed like a sensible idea.

Before he knew it, Griffin was shaved, bathed, and
dressed, sitting by the fireplace in a comfortable armchair
with that morning's paper and a preprandial glass of Malaga
sherry at his elbow.

He could get used to this.

The valet bowed. "Help, my lord? Certainly. How may I assist?"

"It's this Lady Buckham's soiree tomorrow night." Griffin glanced again at the stiff engraved card in his hand, then gave it to Dearlove. "I want to go, but my evening dress won't be ready by then." He shook his head. "Oh, never mind. I know it can't be done."

Though Lydgate had called him a wizard, Dearlove was not truly a magician, after all. How could he be expected to conjure a tailcoat of ridiculous proportions from thin air? If Griffin had been a more reasonable size, then perhaps.

But Dearlove seemed undaunted by the task. With a slight smile, he said, "My lord, I shall endeavor."

Griffin looked up. "Really?"

"Oh, yes, my lord. You will go to the soiree."

Griffin nodded curtly. "My thanks," he said.

"Don't mention it, sir." There was a pause. "My lord?"

"Yes, Dearlove, what is it?"

"I understand Your Lordship is to be married. Might I be so bold as to wish you happy?"

A question that, a week ago, would have caused Griffin to bite his valet's head off. Of course, a week ago, Griffin would not have allowed Dearlove within ten miles of his person or his meager wardrobe.

Now, with the magnanimity of a man about to meet Lady Rosamund Westruther in a moonlit garden for the purpose of committing various unspecified intimacies upon her person, he said, "You may. Thank you, Dearlove. You are dismissed."

Once again, the Westruther family had all left for the evening to attend various entertainments. Griffin had considered a jaunt to his club, but he was too restless and preoccupied for company. He chose instead to eat a light supper alone in his rooms.

After picking at his plate and drinking three glasses of the duke's excellent Bordeaux, he hunted in the library for something to pass the time before his tryst with Rosamund.

Montford's collection was extensive, housed in awe-inspiring magnificence in a vast room with a gallery level and high, coffered ceilings. Books covered the walls from floor to ceiling. Griffin had never seen so many in his life. Not knowing how to begin to search for anything specific, Griffin chose at random a rather bland treatise on drainage systems.

Ah, who was he trying to fool with the pretense of reading? He couldn't possibly keep his mind on the page. His nerves were on edge. Anticipation hummed in his blood. Finally, he gave up on drainage and crossed to his window to peer out at the night sky.

He'd agreed to marry Rosamund to save his sister from marriage to a man old enough to be her grandfather. Or was that only what he'd told himself, the excuse he'd made for taking what he'd wanted all along? Regardless of the wishes of his betrothed.

But it seemed she did indeed wish for this union and always had. He couldn't wrap his mind around that part, so he set it aside.

Instead, he considered Jacks. Had she truly formed an attachment to young Warrington, as the fellow's mother asserted? Griffin hadn't seen Jacks for months, but it seemed unlikely that she'd developed a taste for chinless whelps in the meantime.

For the moment, however, Lady Jacqueline deVere was safe. She was still a minor, and that powerful tyrant Oliver, Lord deVere, stood her guardian. DeVere would not permit her to marry Warrington. A flight to the border was out of the question. Quite apart from the scandal that would ensue, Warrington must know that if he attempted it, Griffin would tear him limb from limb.

Once he and Rosamund were wed, he would send for Jacks to join them at his town house. Rosamund would school Jacks in what she needed to know, and then they'd launch her in society.

Tomorrow, he would see deVere and get that list of prospective suitors he'd promised. And then the vetting process would begin. It would take a certain kind of man to appreciate his sister's . . . *unique* qualities. Griffin intended to find that man if it was the last thing he did.

One thing was certain: Jacks could never return to Pendon Place.

Perhaps he ought to consult Rosamund about these fellows deVere was proposing as possible matches for his sister. After two seasons, Rosamund must know them all, at least by reputation.

He felt a twinge of guilt. She'd asked him that afternoon why he'd never come for her. As if she'd been some princess locked in a tower the past three years, waiting and dreaming of her white knight.

Didn't she know he was the ogre of this story? She seemed almost willfully blind to his ugliness, to his foul temper, and to his wish to be left well alone. He believed now that she was sincere in her indifference to his faults and that she did not regard the vast disparity in their situations.

Rosamund wasn't mercenary or in the market for a title, as he'd thought when he first met her. She was in love with the *idea* of marriage and a family to call her own. She refused to see the truth about him, but the reality of matrimony would rip the scales from her eyes all too soon.

Too restless to sit here festering in his rooms any longer, he took the small lantern he'd had the forethought to request from Dearlove and left his bedchamber.

* * *

Rosamund let herself out of the house, easing the French window of the conservatory until it was almost shut, but not quite.

Expectation danced along her nerves while the cool night air played over her skin. With a glance over her shoulder and a small, voluptuous shiver, she fled down the steps toward the small summerhouse that stood at the edge of the fountain.

The evening had seemed to stretch into eternity. Montford had escorted her to a dull musicale that necessitated sitting still for hours feigning interest in the sedate strains of a string quartet when she itched to be gone. Even worse, the principal entertainment of the night was canceled due to the soprano's indisposition.

The hostess threw her thin-voiced daughter into the breach, and sad work the girl had made of the program. Most of the audience chattered through the dismal performance. Montford had remained silent, contemplating the molded ceiling with an expression of pained endurance, but Rosamund felt so sorry for the poor young lady that she listened attentively and applauded at the end.

All the while, her nerves had screamed at her to flee.

Finally, they'd returned home. Rosamund had allowed Meg to undress her and brush out her hair and put her to bed, only to throw back the bedclothes and scramble out of bed again as soon as Meg left the room. Dressing herself hadn't been easy. Abandoning all hope of lacing a corset, she donned a chemise and chose a simple blue round gown and some dancing slippers and sat by her window to wait for the household to settle.

Andrew hadn't come in yet, and neither had Xavier, but they might not be back until daylight. She'd have to take the risk of one of them spotting her as she crept out to keep her tryst with Griffin.

He was her affianced husband, so she wasn't too

concerned that her behavior would rate serious censure. She simply didn't want to share what they did this night with anyone. Particularly not with her male cousins.

Now, finally, the moment had arrived. She hurried along the path, skirting the fountain and continuing on until she came to the place she'd proposed to meet him.

He loomed in the doorway of the summerhouse, a massive, muscled form in trousers and a loose white shirt. A frisson of fear shot through her, raising her senses to a pitch of heightened awareness. Every sight, every scent, every touch, every sound intensified to an almost unbearable degree.

The summerhouse dripped with wisteria and honeysuckle. Their delicate blooms shivered in the breeze, wafting a scent as wild and heady as her mood. The only sound was the gentle rush of soft night air whispering through the trees.

That, and the rasp of her quickened breathing.

"You came," he said.

His voice seemed to resonate deep inside her. "Did you think I wouldn't?"

His shoulders raised in a shrug. "I wondered if your scruples might overbear your courage. I'm glad they didn't."

Pleasurable anticipation had almost made her forget she'd protested vehemently against this rendezvous. She hardly knew why she continued the charade of reluctance. Some deeply feminine instinct seemed to dictate that she should.

She'd follow that instinct and see where it led her. It had brought her this far, after all.

"I honor my bargains, my lord," she said, making her voice prim.

"Is that so?" He reached out and touched her upturned face, feathering his knuckles gently down her cheek. "I trust you won't find this obligation too onerous."

The most onerous part was continuing to stand when her knees had softened to jelly.

"Come," he said, and led her into the darkness.

Inside the glass walls, the warmth of the day still lingered. A lantern burned low in the corner. He'd lit a few candles here and there to give the place ambient light. Ranged along one wall was a banquette covered in silk cushions. A wrought-iron table and chairs stood in the center of the room, and pot plants and hanging baskets dotted about gave the impression of the outdoors.

She'd been here countless times, yet now the place was an enchanted bower, full of moonlight and shadows and scents that were piercingly sweet.

But all she could focus on was Griffin and how much she longed for his kiss.

He turned and stood there, watching her, a bright-eyed predator of the night.

Seconds ticked by, and he did not move or speak. The tension built inside her until she could bear it no longer.

To goad him, she said, "We ought to set rules before we start."

He blinked. Then a muscle jumped in his jaw. "You're not serious."

"Of course," she said. "This is a bargain, is it not? Intimacies in exchange for social interaction. But I am not experienced in intimacies. I want to know what you mean to do."

Rosamund eyed him with the unnerving sensation that she'd just poked a tiger with a stick. His body seemed coiled, bunched with tension, as if at any moment he might spring.

She sucked in a breath, her hesitancy no longer feigned. "I don't wish to be taken by surprise."

He shook his head. "There's nothing left to agree upon.

The intimacies are whatever I want them to be." Then he tilted his head. "Unless," he purred, "you have suggestions."

Oh, Lord. She swallowed hard. "Not suggestions, no. But surely I have the power of veto."

He moved toward her. "You surrendered all power to me when you walked through that door."

His gaze ranged over her, lingering here and there, as if he were calculating which part of her to devour first. Suddenly, she was afraid she'd granted him license to do far more than she ever imagined he might.

When he looked at her like that, she felt as if a giant hand picked her up and shook her until her defenses fell away, leaving her vulnerable, exposed to the caress of his gaze.

Where had her courage gone? She'd expected to be more than a match for him, even in this arena. Too late to discover she'd been wrong.

Griffin's manner was intent and assured. He knew exactly what he was doing. She knew only what she'd been able to glean from snippets of conversation, hushed whispers about her mother, and the gems of information Jane had been willing to impart.

In other words, a mélange of theory and no practical experience at all.

Instinctively, Rosamund retreated. He followed, until the edge of a table stopped her and there were mere inches between them.

He smiled with a flash of white teeth, then closed in and planted his hands on the table on either side of her, caging her body with his.

She leaned back as far as she could, but there was no escape. He loomed over her, his ruined face stark in the moonlight.

Her breathing quickened, and she inhaled his scent. He smelled like a forest, mysterious and dark. Something inside her craved his touch, but she did not want to be overwhelmed by his darkness. She did not wish to lose herself in him and leave her heart behind.

"Frightened?" His tone mocked her. His breath held the faint sweet scent of wine.

"You are no gentleman, sir," she whispered.

"Just discovered that now, have you?" he murmured. Then his mouth descended to hers.

CHAPTER ELEVEN

To Rosamund's shock, his lips were gentle. They brushed against her mouth, caressing, teasing.

Once. Twice. She lost count of the times as their breaths mingled and their lips clung and molded and moved in opposition yet completely in concert. And she was falling, losing her grip on fear, abandoning herself to the darkness.

Tentative, but eager, she opened her mouth to the insistent press of his tongue. With a rumble of approval in his throat, he slid his arm around her waist, drawing her up against his big body. Her feet left the floor and she felt weightless, helpless, as he swung her into his arms.

He walked to the wide banquette and sat down with her draped over his lap. His strength surrounded her, and the renewed force of his kisses set her senses on fire.

Rosamund stroked her hands along his massive shoulders, exploring their contours, the great muscled expanse of his chest.

She needed to get closer still. She wanted more. Reaching up, she ran her fingers through his crisp dark hair and urged his mouth harder against hers.

That seemed to snap the last tether of his restraint.

With a groan, he caught her against him and plundered her, slanting his mouth over hers, delving into her with firm, suggestive strokes. She met him with all the passion and desperation he'd aroused in her.

As if spurred on by her response, he nipped her bottom lip and she shuddered at the welcome violence of it. How could she have known that sharp instant of pain would feel so sinfully pleasurable?

His mouth slid down to her neck, sending new thrills of sensation through her. She gasped and squirmed against him, gasped again when he grazed his teeth against the tender skin at her throat.

With a low hum of satisfaction, he raised his head and watched as he stroked a fingertip along her clavicle, then dipped beneath the gathered neckline of the gown. Ignoring her shocked denial, he slid the material away to bare her shoulder and the top of one breast.

His fingers delved lower. She gave a halfhearted whimper of protest, but he silenced it with his kiss and boldly tugged her bodice down. The cool night air tingled deliciously at her exposed nipple. The sensation was so illicit and thrilling, she could not bring herself to care about modesty anymore.

When he bit down on a sensitive tendon in her shoulder, she cried out and arched and melted against him; any vague notion that she should resist went up in flames.

His deep voice was hot in her ear. "I need to see the rest of you. Show me."

Moved by some wanton compulsion she didn't understand, she put a hand up to the side of her bodice that still covered her. With shaking fingers, she slid the capped sleeve from her shoulder, then hesitated.

"More."

Wicked with need, Rosamund slid her thumb between the layer of her chemise and her skin and slowly, slowly drew the material down. She reveled in the rasp of his breathing as she bared herself, inch by inch. The gathers of her bodice cinched the gown around her torso while the top hung down, leaving her breasts bare.

"Beautiful," he whispered. "Now stand up."

His awed approval made her bold. She did as he asked, though her knees shook. Her heart gave a sharp pound when she understood the reason for his demand. His head was now level with her naked breasts. From this position, he could look his fill.

The thought did not seem abhorrent or embarrassing as it might have before all this began. She was flooded with excitement. The vague, nagging sense that she might regret this loss of control later drowned in a king tide of passion.

Griffin settled back against the cushions, his eyes glittering. His gravel-rough voice abraded her nerves. "Cup your hands beneath them," he ordered. "Lift them up."

One part of her mind couldn't believe she was doing this, but all sense of shame and restraint had fled. She was a sensual, desirable creature, and Griffin would be her husband soon. He ordered and she must obey. She took the weight of her breasts in her hands and presented them to him.

Hunger ignited his eyes to a blaze. She didn't need to hear his hoarse murmur of approval to know that he was as aroused as she.

Leaning forward, he bent his head to one hard, puckered nipple and feasted. She threw her head back and swayed into him, relishing the rapturous torture. He set his hands to her waist to steady her against the workings of his mouth and lips and tongue, trapping her in an upward spiral of bliss.

His hand lifted her skirts. His quick fingers grazed her

thigh, then touched her in the place between her legs in delicious, sinful ways.

The shuddering sensations took her unawares. With a broken cry, she let her mind spin away as she surrendered to pleasure.

Wave after wave of rapture pounded through her until she felt wrung out with it. When she could stand it no longer, she drove her fingers through his hair and lifted his head so that he had to look up at her.

Tenderness welled inside her. "Griffin," she said. "Oh, Griffin, I—"

But there were no words, or at least she could not find them just then.

Instead, she bent to kiss him on the mouth.

The innocence of that kiss after the depravity he'd inflicted on her person threw Griffin off balance. His scattered wits slowly picked up and dusted themselves off and returned to assume their duties in his brain.

What had he been thinking?

The truth: After drawing her into the intimate ambience of the summerhouse, he had not been thinking at all. He'd challenged her, he'd aroused, worshipped, loved her . . . in a purely carnal way, of course.

This kiss was no prelude to ravishment but an end in itself, a burst of pure sweetness, like the heavenly rush of flavor from a ripe, warm strawberry that exploded on the tongue. That kiss aimed to seduce his heart even as he seduced her body.

He didn't mean to let it.

Her hands left his face to smooth over his shoulders; then her fingertips stroked into the deep V of his open shirt. He shuddered, fighting the urge to take her in all the ways he'd dreamed about. Her touch threatened to unman him, as if he were a callow youth fumbling in the dark with his first love. And wouldn't that just be the crowning glory of the night?

He broke the kiss and captured Rosamund's questing hands. With an inner groan at his own restraint, he rose to his feet.

She gave an instinctive, protesting cry.

Then she opened her eyes and saw his face. "Why, what is it?" she breathed.

He stole one final look at the delicious, rose-tipped delights before him, then regretfully drew her chemise and bodice up to cover them.

"I'm taking advantage of your innocence," he said, sounding, he knew, like the hero in a bad novel. "More of this, and you will no longer have a choice whether to wed me or no."

There was a pause while she digested his words. He saw reality return to her sky blue eyes as if a chill wind blew the mist away.

"Don't you know I've made my choice?" she said quietly. "I would not be here otherwise."

He thought she based important decisions on remarkably little. But it was not for him to do her thinking for her.

A smart man would follow up his advantage. He ought to secure her agreement to wed him straightaway. He had the special license already, thanks to deVere's interference. They could be man and wife in mere hours if he could find a willing parson.

He ought to take up where they'd left off, enjoy her body to the full. And in the morning, when the bitter taste of regret still lay on her tongue, he could present the matter to her as a fait accompli.

Then he wouldn't have to go through this damnable

charade squiring Rosamund to parties and whatnot. He wouldn't have to suffer the constant disapproval of her family. DeVere would be obliged to keep his side of the bargain and refuse to marry Jacks off until she'd had her season and made her own choice.

And finally, Griffin could have Rosamund as his bride.

All this whirled through his mind in the matter of one moment. It took him only one moment more to reject that reasoning as self-serving tripe.

With a beleaguered sigh, he said, "My lady, you deserve better than a quick tumble in such a place. I know that, even if you don't seem to. We'll wait."

Rosamund's eyebrows drew together in a frown. "So you've made the decision and I have to abide by it, is that it? Don't I get a say?"

"No," he said. "You don't."

"But I don't want to wait," she said simply. "I want to keep doing what we were doing. I may be an innocent, but I know there's more."

Christ Almighty! He jabbed a finger at her. "You are the female. It's your job to stop me, not push me to go on." Why should he be the one who held them both to standards of decency?

She laughed, a low, dirty, derisive sound that made his skin prickle and heat. "Why, Griffin, I'd no idea you were such a prude."

If she didn't stop this right now, he really would deflower her in her guardian's summerhouse, and then there'd be Hell to pay. "You are clearly befuddled and incapable of making rational judgments. Therefore, I'll make them for you. Let's go."

With a faint, knowing smile, she moved toward him with a sultry sway to her walk he'd never seen before. "Are you afraid I'll seduce you?" She trailed a fingertip over his lips. "But how on earth would I go about that?"

I'm sure you can think of something, screamed his eager male parts.

The struggle to beat down the demands of his lusty body cost him dearly, but there was too much at stake for him to mess this up now.

He grabbed Rosamund's wrist to stop her teasing explorations, then pulled her toward the door.

"Back to the house," he muttered. "Let's go."

"Rosamund, a word."

Her brother's voice flashed out from the shadows, steely and sharp as a rapier's blade. He startled her so much, she gave a cry of alarm.

She'd parted from Griffin before they reached the house. Thank Heaven he wasn't with her still, or there'd be trouble.

Rosamund pressed a hand to her chest as if to calm her pounding heart. "Xavier! You gave me a fright."

She peered through the gloom, but she couldn't make out her brother's expression.

How much did he guess? She loathed lying, but to keep the peace between her brother and her betrothed, she wouldn't hesitate. If Xavier discovered how close Griffin had come to anticipating his wedding night, he would make matters exceedingly unpleasant.

She didn't believe Cecily when she insisted Xavier could kill a man with his bare hands. Yet, Xavier had always been a law unto himself. Griffin might be a big man, but Xavier was ruthlessness personified. He was also insanely protective of her.

Whoever might win the encounter, no good could come of a clash between the two men.

"Come," Xavier said, turning his back on her and striding down the corridor.

Rosamund took a deep breath and followed her brother into the library. He gestured her to sit while he took the chair behind the mahogany desk. Only Xavier would ever dare to sit in Montford's place.

With an arrogant jerk of his head that sent the inky waves of his hair falling over his brow, he said, "Enlighten me."

She gazed back at him, her face impassive. "I don't know what you think there is to explain."

How much did he know, and how much was supposition? Had he actually seen them?

No, she thought that if he'd seen her and Griffin together, they would not be having this conversation.

He watched her with those blue eyes that were so very like her own, yet infinitely more jaded and cynical. "I confess, I am at a loss to even guess what game you think you're playing," he said. "The only solution that presents itself is one I cannot countenance."

"Will you please stop talking in riddles?" she said evenly. "Of what do I stand accused?" She made as if to rise. "Forgive me, Xavier, but I am tired and wish to go to bed."

"Sit down." He smiled unpleasantly. "Since you choose not to understand me, I'll make my meaning plain. Did you meet your lover in the garden tonight?"

"What?" She sank back into her chair. "No, of course I did not meet any lover." Technically, that was true. "I don't know why you should think it."

"What *am* I to think when my sister lets herself into the house alone at this hour of the night?"

Holding hard to her composure, she arched a brow. "You jump to prurient conclusions, my dear. It's not what it seems."

His features tautened to a harsh mask. "Damn you, Rosamund, it is exactly what it seems! Look at you! Your hair is down, you are flushed, your gown is in total disarray."

"I went for a walk in the garden," she said. "I am flushed from the exercise, and my hair is down and my gown is all anyhow because I had to dress myself."

"Good try, my dear, but it won't wash." With an impatient gesture, he said, "Do you think I don't know what a woman looks like when she's been thoroughly pleasured?"

She hit back. "I daresay you've seen quite a few in your time."

The look he threw her could have melted steel. "It's not the same for men, and you know it. If you won't acknowledge that, then you've abandoned your wits as well as your body."

Her voice shook. "You are insulting."

"If you wanted him, Rosamund, why didn't you say so? My God, you *begged* me not to interfere." His voice rasped. "Rosie, I could have gotten him for you. I could have made everything right."

Bewildered, she stammered, "But I—"

He dashed a hand through his hair. "*Damn* Montford and his bloody relentless matchmaking!" He jabbed his finger at her. "But you've been a willing accomplice in your own downfall, have you not, dear sister? And now you are doomed to a loveless marriage to that brute while you sneak around in gardens at night. Congratulations. You've managed the business to a nicety."

The truth fell on her like an anvil. He thought she'd met *Lauderdale* in the summerhouse.

She felt the blood drain from her face. "Xavier, no! It's not what you think. I was not with Captain Lauderdale, I swear it."

"Don't lie to me," he snarled. "If you insist on wedding Tregarth, the least you can do is wait until you give him an heir before you cuckold him."

She wanted to burst into tears so badly, her head throbbed with it. That he could think her so base!

Why did they all believe that because she had a pretty face, she must have a shallow heart? Why did they all assume someone like her could not possibly prefer Griffin to a flashy peacock like Lauderdale?

Fury at the slur Xavier cast on her character made her stiffen her spine. She'd have pleaded her case had he accused her of endangering her reputation by meeting Griffin before they were wed. She'd been prepared to defend Griffin on that score, too.

But her brother had no authority over her and no right to berate her like this. She refused to apologize for anything when she'd been so grossly misjudged.

"You are wrong, Xavier. Even if such behavior weren't abhorrent to me, don't you think our upbringing would have served as a grim warning?" With quiet vehemence, she said, "I am not like our mother. Not in any conceivable way."

Something flared in his eyes—shock, perhaps, and a dawning realization. Anger still simmered beneath the surface, but she suspected it was no longer directed at her.

He released a long breath and sat back in his chair.

After a tense silence, he said, "My apologies. If you say that you are innocent, I must take you at your word." He paused, watching her. "Of course you are not like her. Rosamund, you are quite the best person I know."

Which was why the conviction she'd become a sneaking, faithless baggage had affected him so powerfully, shaken him to the core of his cynical, arrogant soul.

She and Xavier both knew it was only by lucky chance—or perhaps by their clever mama's judicious management—that they both happened to be legitimate.

Thankfully, each of them resembled the late marquis in ways too marked to be denied.

Her own anger calmed enough to respond with forced lightness. "The best person you know? Your compliment would go to my head if it weren't for the company you keep."

His rare smile lifted the corners of his mouth. But he wouldn't allow her to distract him for long. After a moment, he tilted his head and pinned her with that keen, penetrating gaze. "What *have* you been doing, I wonder?"

"None of your business, dear brother."

His lips twisted. "I suppose I deserved that."

"Yes," she said. "You did."

"I *could* inform Montford of your doings tonight," he said, lowering his gaze to regard his long, elegant fingers as they toyed with the gold signet ring he wore on the third finger of his right hand.

"But you won't," she said gently. He sighed in silent acknowledgment that she was right. They'd always put loyalty to each other above their duty to anyone else. They'd had to stand together to survive.

Rosamund smiled sweetly and stood. "Now, dear brother, if the inquisition is over, I am for bed."

The next morning, Rosamund woke late from a restless slumber with exhilaration flooding her chest and lifting her heart. Her body felt tender and sated, yet there was a yearning deep inside her that she didn't fully understand.

After a few moments of sleepy confusion, her mind caught up with her body.

Griffin. The summerhouse. Last night.

She rolled over and drew a pillow to her chest, hugging

it tightly as her mind replayed the evening, dwelling on the most delicious parts.

Echoes of sensation swept through her, pleasurable but also tantalizing in their shadowy vagueness. She could not wait to relive the experience in the flesh.

Now she finally understood what all the fuss was about! Well, some of it, anyway. The challenge was to persuade Griffin to show her the rest.

She was cheerfully confident she would succeed at that. They'd have to be more discreet than they'd been last night, of course, but—

"Hallo, sleepyhead!" Cecily walked in, brandishing the latest issue of *La Belle Assemblée*. "Are you ready for a big fat *orgy* of shopping today?"

"Oh, yes! I'd forgotten," said Rosamund, stretching luxuriously and wiggling her toes. If anything had power to rouse her from sensual daydreams, it was the promise of new gowns. "I shall be ready in a trice."

Ophelia had lumbered in at Cecily's heels. With a sigh, the old dog collapsed on the hearth rug and propped her head between her paws. Her eyebrows lifted in turn as she looked from Cecily to Rosamund and back again, as if following their conversation.

Cecily maintained that Ophelia understood a smattering of English, even if Danish was her first language. The Great Dane seemed to find their topic of conversation too frivolous, however, because soon she fell asleep, emitting her habitual doggy snore.

Stifling a sympathetic yawn, Rosamund dragged herself out of bed. She bent for a quick scratch behind Ophelia's ear, then padded over to her washstand.

"Now, before we begin, I propose we make a list of what you'll need for your trousseau," said Cecily. With a mischievous grin, she added, "There is a modiste in Bond

Street who keeps special nightwear for her clients in the back room."

"I am not even going to ask how you know that," replied Rosamund, pouring water from a ewer into the basin.

"Jane told me," Cecily said. "She has become a veritable fount of information on the subject of dalliance since Constantine came along."

"He is a wicked, wicked man," said Rosamund with a chuckle.

"Yes, but quite deliciously so, don't you think? Although a little too intense *pour moi*."

"It is fortunate, then, that he fell in love with Jane." Rosamund splashed tepid water on her face.

"Oh, what's this?" said Cecily. "There's a letter on your mantelpiece. Aha! Do you think it's a love poem from your giant?"

"A letter?" Turning, Rosamund saw Cecily pluck a sealed envelope from the mantel.

Excitement clutched Rosamund's stomach. She took the letter from Cecily and ripped open the seal, not caring that her damp hands made splotches on the paper.

As she read the contents, her brows contracted. The final mists of sleep burned away as the bold, slashing words seared her brain.

Hardly aware of what she did, she crushed the letter in her hand and let it fall to the floor.

"What is it, Rosamund?" said Cecily. "What's wrong?"

She shook her head, her eyes blind.

"Rosamund?" Cecily's voice turned sharp. She bent to pick up the letter and smooth it out.

Rosamund put a trembling hand to her chest. "It's Griffin," she said. "He's gone."

CHAPTER TWELVE

. . . What have you been about in London, dear brother? Cutting a dash with your heiress? I know too well what my esteemed guardian Lord deVere has been up to: auctioning me off to the highest bidder, the horrid old Devil.

That must explain why Lady Warrington has suddenly become so insistent. She wants me to marry her son without deVere's consent, if you please! She plans to shepherd us all the way to Scotland!! Warrington, poor soul, has not the backbone to say boo to a goose, much less stand up to his mama. So it comes to this: I must leave here at once.

I miss Pendon and you and the horses and the sea and the dear pigs in the sty (in no particular order). I even miss Peggy's singular way with tripe. I cannot stomach stuffy old Bath nor the Warringtons any longer.

Don't be cross, will you, dear boy? By the time this reaches you, I shall be home.

Yours, etc.

Jacqueline deVere

"He said he has family business to take care of," said Rosamund, laying the badly creased letter aside. "He doesn't take me into his confidence."

Her gaze flickered to Montford and away again. "I do not count as family, it seems." Rosamund tried to keep the bitterness from her voice. She doubted she succeeded.

Griffin had left her. *Again*. And after the shattering, revelatory experience they'd shared, his abandonment seemed doubly hard to accept. He'd penned not one word of affection or reassurance to her in that brief note, of course. But then, she ought to have given up hope of gallantry from him by now.

Worst of all, he hadn't confided in her or asked her to share in whatever trouble took him back to Cornwall in such haste. That hurt more than she could have dreamed.

She thought—*hoped*—they'd reached some level of deeper understanding since that afternoon in Berkeley Square. He'd accepted that she wasn't his enemy.

But he didn't trust her, for all that.

Why couldn't he believe she had no hidden agenda in all this? He was her chosen mate, and she would stand by him through thick and thin, as any good wife should.

She knew Montford watched her closely, but even under his scrutiny, she couldn't summon the will to conceal her disappointment.

"All I want is to be a wife to him," she said with a helpless gesture. "Do you think I did the wrong thing setting those conditions? Perhaps I should have married him immediately, as he demanded."

I could be with him now if I hadn't been so puffed up with pride.

Montford's brows lifted. "I think that if a ward of mine displayed so little backbone, I'd wash my hands of her."

His cool rejoinder warmed her inside. The duke was not a demonstrative man. He would not give her the hug she so badly needed. Yet his unemotional support bolstered her courage as an embrace could not have done.

"What do you propose to do?" he inquired.

She blinked at Montford as the realization hit her. "I must follow him, mustn't I? It's the only thing I can do." She sat up as a sudden anger flared. "I'll—I'll be *damned* if I sit here and wait for him any longer."

"Such language," commented the duke. "I believe I am shocked. But I approve of the sentiment."

He eyed her for a few moments, pulling the feather of his quill through finger and thumb. Lowering his gaze, he said, "I am not a man who is fulsome in my praise or offers anyone mere flattery, so you may believe me when I say this. You had no hand in creating your beauty, so that is not to your credit. To some women, such beauty can be a curse."

Rosamund thought of her mother, growing more desperate as the years rolled past.

Montford lifted his gaze to hers. "But you, Rosamund, have qualities that are far more important than a dazzling form and face. Intelligence, grace, kindness, strength of character, and elegance of mind. I trust Tregarth is not such a fool that he cannot recognize them and value them as your husband should."

She was so overwhelmed by this speech, she didn't know what to say.

He regarded her with understanding in those dark, hooded eyes. "You will go to Cornwall and give Griffin one more chance." The corners of his mouth lifted in a slight smile. "And if he hurts you, I will cut out his heart and feed it to Ophelia."

His final words surprised a laugh from her, but she was obliged to blink away tears. "Thank you, Your Grace."

And because he had said exactly what she'd needed to hear at that moment, she took her courage in her hands and went to him.

He'd risen when she did, so she had to place a hand on his arm and reach up to press a kiss to his cheek. "Thank you," she whispered in his ear.

Drawing back, she searched his face, concerned that she'd overstepped some invisible boundary he'd erected between them long ago. The surprise in his expression was swiftly veiled, but the suspicion of a smile lingered on his lips and lit those dark eyes. A hint of color crested his sharp cheekbones.

Good God! Had she embarrassed him? The thought was as absurd as it was novel.

He cleared his throat. "Yes. Well. I'll make the arrangements for your journey."

"Thank you, Your Grace."

He tapped his lips with a finger. "Tibby will go with you, and your maid, of course."

She nodded. While she'd prefer to go alone, she had no desire to court scandal. She could work around Meg and Tibby if need be.

"Oh, and Dearlove must come, too." She gave a shaky laugh. "The poor fellow is utterly despondent because Griffin left him behind."

"I'll see to it." He paused. "You will put up at an inn, of course."

"Of course," murmured Rosamund.

Pendon Place was essentially a bachelor household, so it would be improper for her to visit Griffin there. She didn't intend to let that stop her, but she wouldn't tell Montford that.

The duke might well suspect her plans, but as long as she maintained the appearance of decorum, he would not complain—if her actions got him the results he wanted. She understood him rather well, she thought. Particularly after observing the way he'd handled Jane's romance with Constantine.

Besides, she would not need to remain at the inn for long. If she had to force Griffin to the altar at pistol point, she would do it.

One thing was certain: She would not leave Cornwall again until she was the Countess of Tregarth.

Griffin wiped his sweaty forehead on his shirtsleeve and took a swig from his water flask. It was hot, thirsty work, digging ditches.

He'd ridden home hell-for-leather upon receiving the tidings that she'd left Bath. He'd alternately cursed and feared for Jacks all the way from Town. Reckless, foolish chit! Why couldn't she have sent word to him and waited for him to come and get her?

Being Jacks, she'd challenged him over that. A little shamefaced, he admitted he hadn't acceded to her pleas to come for her thus far. But she ought to have known this was different. If the Warringtons were trying to coerce her into marriage, he would have rescued her from them without delay.

Typical of Jacks to take the matter out of his hands. Maddening little baggage!

Upon arriving back at Pendon Place and finding her there, unharmed and in lively spirits, he'd flown into a rage. She'd accepted his recriminations, patiently waiting for his fury to burn itself out.

He'd pictured all sorts of disasters befalling a young lady traveling by herself. She'd told him cheerfully not to mind it, for she'd been dressed as a boy.

Hell! Did she think that would set his mind at rest?

He still shuddered when he recalled her description of her journey home. Foolish, reckless chit! Thank God she was safe. But safety was a relative term where his sister was concerned.

His first inclination had been to whisk Jacks back to London immediately, but he hadn't prepared for an extended absence when he'd journeyed to town to fetch Rosamund. If he were to spend the season in London, he needed to attend to a number of crucial matters of estate business before he went.

Tossing the empty water flask down, he firmed his grip on the shovel and wedged it into the soil. His aching back muscles protested, but this ditch was needed for the new drainage system he was installing, and he was damned if he'd give up yet.

Of course, it wasn't *his* job to dig ditches anymore. He was the Earl of Tregarth now, owner of all he surveyed. His grandfather was no longer here to set him to menial, Herculean labors like this. The old earl had been fond of saying that mucking out stables was all a big brute like Griffin was fit for.

Despite his grandfather's malice, Griffin had taken a grim pleasure in manual tasks, in their usefulness and simplicity. He'd found a measure of peace in using his strength thus that he couldn't derive from any other source.

By the age of fifteen, his body had developed a hard muscularity that was profoundly satisfying in its effect on his bully of a grandfather. The earl had taken care never to call Griffin into his presence without a pair of sturdy footmen at hand.

The old bastard had been dead more than a year, and still Griffin dug ditches. Old habits were hard to break.

Truth was, he'd come out here to think. Separated from Rosamund's intoxicating influence, he saw things more clearly now. More objectively. He wondered whom he'd been trying to fool, seducing her in that summerhouse in the dark.

She was altogether too much for him to handle. So dazzlingly beautiful, vital and sensual and generous. He couldn't do it to her. He couldn't keep taking what she gave when he had nothing to offer her in return.

But he needed Rosamund, didn't he? DeVere had placed him in an impossible situation. The challenge was still to save Jacks from a horrible misalliance. He needed to get her married and away from Cornwall for good. Nothing had changed there.

Hoofbeats sounded on the trail that skirted the field. He looked up, squinting against the spring sunshine.

Two riders on cover hacks emerged from the copse and ambled toward him. A stranger might have mistaken the riders for two men, but he knew better.

Jacks was at it again.

Muttering a curse, he threw down his shovel and strode over to the equestrians. "Jacks!" he roared. "What in damnation do you think you're doing?"

"Don't yell at me like that. You'll spook Lady." Lady Jacqueline deVere dismounted from the demonstrably placid steed with more athleticism than grace. She wore old, worn breeches and a dun-colored coat that would have appeared proper on a young man, if a little shabby.

But Jacks was *not* a young man. She was his pestilential hoyden of a little sister.

He turned his fulminating gaze on her companion. "Maddox! I might have known."

Their neighbor looked the picture of the fashionable sportsman in buff breeches, a blue coat, and shining top boots. The whiteness of his linen was rivaled only by the gleam of his perfect teeth.

"Well, I suppose you might," he drawled. "Your sister's acquaintance in these parts is so small, it could hardly be anyone else, could it?"

Was that a gibe? If their good and worthy neighbors shunned them, it was hardly Griffin's fault. "You encourage her in this folly."

The dark eyes glinted. "What an odd notion you have of me that you should think so."

"You should have told her to go home and change," snapped Griffin.

"Ah, but that would argue a far more intimate relationship between us than you would allow, my friend."

"You needn't go on discussing me as if I'm not here," remarked Jacks. "Tony doesn't mind my breeches, do you, Tony? Besides, he's right. He has no authority over me, and I wouldn't heed him anyway, so I don't see why you should hold him responsible."

Maddox had shown singular interest in Jacks since her return from Bath. While his innocent sister seemed to think their neighbor offered nothing more than the friendship he'd always shown her, Griffin thought otherwise.

Maddox was Griffin's friend, too, but he was also possibly the last man on the planet Griffin wanted as a husband for his sister.

Besides, the fellow encouraged all her headstrong ways, including this mania the girl had for dressing in men's clothes. It was hoydenish, bordering on the scandalous. If news of her eccentric behavior traveled to London, he'd never marry her off.

No, Maddox could not be permitted to court Jacqueline. Besides, for a deVere, marriage was never a matter of personal choice. As none knew better than Griffin.

"Go home and change into a gown," he ordered her. "And tell Peggy to do something with your hair."

"Oh, very well," she grumbled, swinging herself up onto her horse without even a mounting block or a leg up. Griffin shook his head.

"She's no simpering miss, that one," said Maddox with a smile.

"What she is, is none of your concern!" flashed Griffin. "My sister is not for you, Maddox, so get that notion out of your mind once and for all."

"But as the dear girl so often points out, it's only nine hundred and forty-nine days until her twenty-first birthday," Maddox murmured. "And I am a very patient man."

The implication made hot blood rush to Griffin's face. "If she marries you, she won't get a penny from me."

Maddox's aristocratic mouth flattened. "You're a brute, deVere, but I've never heard you descend to vulgarity before. I don't give a damn about your money or hers, and you know it."

Griffin would not be fobbed off. Between his teeth, he said, "You'll not have her, do you hear me?" He'd let deVere marry her to the ancient Malby first!

"You always did possess an uncertain temper," said Maddox, leaning forward a little in the saddle. "Small wonder, the rumors that have sprung up about you. Even I begin to question if they're true." For a few heartbeats, his gaze locked with Griffin's.

No, no, not Maddox, too. Surely he'd believed Griffin's denial, even if no one else in the county had. Good God, they'd practically grown up together!

"The coroner entered a verdict of accidental death," he ground out. "The matter has been put to bed."

"Yes, but he can always reopen an inquest if new information comes to light, can't he?" said Maddox. He hesitated, and although his manner was customarily debonair, Griffin knew Maddox watched him like a hawk. "There are rumors of a witness."

White-hot terror shot through Griffin like a flare. He took a few moments to catch his breath. "A witness? Who?"

"That, I do not know. But I recommend you come out of your cave for a while and show the people you're not such an ogre as they think. Public opinion is stacked against you here." Grimly, he added, "They do try peers for murder these days, you know."

"Yes. I know it."

With a nod, Maddox touched his whip to the brim of his hat and urged his horse forward.

Griffin stood watching him go. For a few disorienting seconds, he felt as if every ounce of feeling had left his body. Then sensation returned in a surge of furious fear. Swearing viciously under his breath, he turned on his heel and strode off, back to his ditch.

But the work had lost the power to calm his jangling nerves. He'd delayed far too long and was about to reap the reward.

He needed to get Jacks away from Cornwall and safely married to a man who was not Anthony Maddox or the pox-ridden old degenerate their grandfather had chosen for her. To do that, he must give Jacks a season—immediately—and he needed Rosamund if he wanted Jacqueline's debut to be a success.

Maddox had implied he intended to offer for Jacqueline when she turned one and twenty, with or without a dowry.

But that marriage could never be. Jacqueline was out of her senses if she entertained the notion. Even mere friendship with the fellow was dangerous, if it came to that.

Griffin was no expert in such things, but it seemed to him that Jacks was not in love with Tony Maddox. The fellow was a Devil with the ladies, however. If he chose to *make* Jacks fall in love with him, she might do so. And what woman didn't unburden all her secrets to her lover?

That would be fatal. He needed to remove his sister from Maddox's vicinity and get her married off as soon as may be.

Time was running out.

CHAPTER THIRTEEN

W hen Rosamund and her companion arrived at Pendon Place, no one came out to greet them. Diccon the footman handed Rosamund and Tibby down from the carriage and preceded them up the stairs. He rapped on the door with a pristine, white-gloved hand.

While they waited for what seemed an inordinately long time for someone to answer, Rosamund gave Tibby a reassuring smile and looked about her.

What she saw daunted her somewhat. The exterior of the house showed clear signs of neglect, a sad contrast to her recollection of its immaculate grandeur three years before. The lawn hadn't been scythed for some time, and the graveled drive was dotted with weeds. On the house itself, the windows that weren't covered in ivy were in dire need of cleaning.

The place felt desolate, abandoned.

If the exterior of Griffin's lair looked like this, she shuddered to imagine the inside.

The massive door creaked open a short way, and a round-faced gimlet-eyed woman appeared. She had apple-red cheeks and mousy hair caught up in a straggling knot at her nape.

The woman jabbered something at them, which Rosamund found unintelligible but took as a demand to state their business.

Diccon the footman looked down his nose at the woman. "Lady Rosamund Westruther and Miss Tibbs to see Lord Tregarth."

"Strangers, you say?" The woman peered at Tibby, then at Rosamund. "We don't have no truck with them in these parts. The master, 'e don't see no one a'tall."

"He will see me," said Rosamund. "Fetch him and tell him his affianced wife is here." She smiled. "Would you be so kind as to show us in?"

She attempted to peer past the housekeeper, but the woman was a head taller than she and built like a sofa, so that was impossible.

The housekeeper eyed her narrowly, as if she suspected her of intending to steal the silverware. "He's not here and won't be back till nightfall, so there's no point in your waiting, is there? Affianced wife, did you say?"

"Yes. I did," said Rosamund. She took out her card and handed it to the housekeeper. "And you must be the housekeeper. Mrs. . . ."

"Peggy'll do, mistress." She thought for a moment. "You're that heiress." Her mouth turned down at the corners. "We don't have much truck with heiresses in these parts, neither."

Rosamund struggled against an absurd desire to laugh.

Diccon sniffed. "That, my good woman, is quite obvious. What are you about to keep my lady standing like this?"

Rosamund silenced Diccon with a glance. On impulse, she said, "Is any of the family at home?"

"Lady Jacqueline deVere is here, ma'am," the house-keeper said grudgingly.

"Will you send in my card and inquire if Lady Jacque-line will receive me?"

Rosamund wasn't sure whether Griffin's sister would remember her from her earlier visit, but perhaps she might at least recognize the name.

After another long wait, the housekeeper returned. "This way."

The woman sent a series of sharp-eyed looks at them over her shoulder as she led them through the bowels of the house.

Rosamund shot an amused glance at Tibby and called ahead, "When will your master be back?"

"Don't come home till dark most days," was the reply. "Thursday nights, he dines with the vicar, so it'll be even later than that tonight."

The vicar? Oblivious of Rosamund's surprise, the housekeeper halted and gestured toward an opened door. "Here we are, then."

Without another word, Peggy stumped away.

The housekeeper hadn't bothered to announce them. Rosamund and Tibby hesitated on the threshold.

A lady perhaps a year or two younger than Rosamund rose from the escritoire by the window and came for-ward to greet them. Her gown was drab and ill-fitted, and she had a strange, loping gait to her walk that made her appear all arms and legs. Her hair was jet black with a riotous curl to it, just like Griffin's. Her complexion was unfashionably brown.

Rosamund saw a clear challenge to dressing the girl and grooming her into a graceful debutante. That was all to the good. She relished a challenge.

On the positive side, despite her unconventional looks,

there was something very taking about Lady Jacqueline. The openness of her expression and the lanky vigor of her movements endeared her at once.

"Oh, Lady Rosamund, yes!" the girl said, throwing out a hand in an all-encompassing gesture of welcome. "Do come in. I remember you from that time you came to stay. You will laugh when I tell you that at first I thought that you were an angel walking among us. I was so frightened! I thought you'd come to take me up to Heaven to be with my mama. Which was rather optimistic of me, as it turns out. My brother calls me a Hell-born babe." She gave a low, throaty laugh. "How do you do?"

If she'd not been accustomed to dealing with Cecily's startling utterances, Rosamund might have been thrown into confusion by this. Instead, she said, "Please, call me Rosamund. I'm so happy to renew our acquaintance."

She introduced Tibby and noted with approval that Jacqueline was equally friendly toward her companion. Nothing set up Rosamund's hackles more than young ladies who thought their stations gave them license to be rude to people they considered beneath them.

Griffin's sister said, "Oh, and you must call me Jacks. Everyone does."

Rosamund regarded her thoughtfully. "Do you mind if I call you Jacqueline? It is such an elegant name."

"Doesn't suit me at all, does it?" said Jacqueline. "I'm no beauty like you."

"You are charming," said Rosamund. "You have just returned home, I take it?"

"Yes, thank goodness! I was staying in Bath with the Warringtons. Do you know them?" Jacqueline rolled her eyes. "The stuffiest people! And *Bath,* you know. You can't ride there—well, not properly. And the place crawls with invalids and fashionable ladies who are forever imagining they've contracted some mysterious complaint or other. And they want to tell you *all* the details. As if an illness makes them more interesting!"

Rosamund laughed. "How horrid for you. When you come to London, you will find far more to entertain you than in Bath, I assure you."

The girl's brow wrinkled. "London?"

Oh, dear. Griffin hadn't told her yet. Hurriedly, Rosamund said, "Perhaps I have it wrong. Do not regard it."

But Jacqueline wasn't listening. "So that's why! I *knew* there was something in the wind." Her heavy eyebrows drew together. "He's going to try to marry me off, isn't he?"

She spoke in a tone of such indignation that Rosamund was startled. "Is that such a bad thing?" She made a gesture of apology. "Forgive me, but most young ladies—"

"Griffin doesn't care for what most ladies do." Jacqueline shot to her feet. Her face was flushed—not with anger, as Rosamund had first thought. The sheen of tears glittered in those gray eyes, and her lips quivered slightly. "He wants to be rid of me. I am too much trouble and I've made a mess of everything and he wants me gone. Why do you think he packed me off to Bath?"

"That is not true!" Rosamund rose to her feet also, feeling like a witless wretch for upsetting the girl. "Pray, believe me. I *know* that is not true."

She didn't *know* anything of the kind, of course, but she couldn't let Jacqueline work herself up into this state. Good God, she'd never dreamed the news would upset Jacqueline so.

"But . . ." The girl's eyes widened. "He has told you about me?" The shocked betrayal in her tone confused Rosamund. What did she think Griffin had told her? A little bitterly, she reflected that Jacqueline need have no concerns in that quarter. Griffin never confided in her about anything.

"No, no, I give you my word, your brother has not betrayed any confidences to me. But I do know that he loves you dearly," said Rosamund.

Indeed, how could anyone fail to adore this funny, frank, awkward girl?

Rosamund held up her hand. "Now, please do not be hasty and fly out at Griffin for subjecting you to the Marriage Mart! I might have it all wrong. In fact, I probably do. Your brother is not the most communicative of men, in case you hadn't noticed! Besides, I am persuaded he will not force you to do anything you find distasteful."

"Oh, but—" Jacqueline made a helpless gesture. "Griffin is not my guardian, you see. He has no true authority over me. It is Lord deVere, you know. If *he* wants to parade me about the ballrooms of London like a prize heifer at a fair, Griffin could not stop him." Her shoulders drooped. "I'll have to run away again. But where would I go?"

"What is all this nonsense?" Rosamund took Jacqueline's hand and led her back to the sofa, where she urged her to sit down beside her. "Griffin would never abandon you, no matter who has legal power over you. No one can force you to get married if you don't want to."

Jacqueline gave a gusty sigh. "That is true, but it is horrendously upsetting and tiresome to defy them. You'd know that as well as anyone."

"I never even thought to defy my guardian," said Rosamund slowly. "But I suppose I know what you mean." Rosamund frowned. That she had not railed against her fate made her sound like rather a poor creature, but it hadn't been like that at all. "I am sorry to hear you do not wish for a season," she said. "But perhaps you will change your mind. When Griffin and I are married, I should be charmed to bring you out myself. I think you would make quite a hit."

Surprise and pleasure broke over Jacqueline's face. "You and Griffin are to be married at last? Well, that *is* good news." Her eyes went opaque. "Perhaps I haven't ruined quite everything, then." She glanced at Tibby, whose head was bent over her needlework, then looked back at Rosamund. Softly, she said, "You will be kind to my brother, I think?"

It was more of a question than a statement, perhaps with a hint of a warning thrown in. Clearly, Jacqueline felt protective toward her brother. Rosamund liked her even more.

"Yes," she assured her. "I mean to be *very* good to him." *If he'll let me.*

"Good!" said Jacqueline, throwing off her dark mood in an abrupt change of front. "What a pity he's not here. I expect he's fixing one of the tenants' roofs after the storm we had last night or some such thing. Have you set a date?"

"Not yet, no." Rosamund smiled. "Griffin doesn't know I've come. I hoped to surprise him, but no doubt he'll hear of my visit today."

"Oh, if you're putting up at the inn, the news of your arrival will be all over the village by now," said Jacqueline. "He'll hear of it before he sets foot in the house."

Well acquainted with village life, Rosamund didn't doubt this was true. She wondered if Griffin would be happy that she'd followed him. She feared he'd be angry with her for telling Jacqueline about the forthcoming season. And he'd be quite justified, too.

Hoping she'd allayed Jacqueline's immediate fears for her future, Rosamund took her leave.

"You will come back soon, won't you?" said Jacqueline, slipping an arm through Rosamund's as she escorted her to the door. "Do you ride? Perhaps you'd like to go for a hack about the estate tomorrow?"

"I do indeed ride. I'd be delighted. You can show me all your childhood haunts."

A shadow crossed the girl's face, but it was a look so fleeting, Rosamund might have imagined it, "Yes, of course," said Jacqueline brightly. "Are you staying at the inn? I'll call for you there at nine o'clock."

Jacqueline saw them to the door and gave a vigorous wave as the carriage rolled forward.

Rosamund sighed with a mixture of released tension and disappointment.

"An unusual girl," commented Tibby as they drove off.

"Fresh and unaffected," said Rosamund. "I liked her very much."

"She'll be a handful, I expect," said Tibby placidly. "But you will know how to manage her, Rosamund dear."

Rosamund hoped that Tibby judged her powers correctly.

Girls like Jacqueline needed constant activity to keep them out of mischief. She thought Griffin was right in wanting his sister to make her come-out. Even if she did not make a match, she would acquire a little polish, a touch of sophistication. Rosamund wouldn't want her to lose that winning freshness or tone down her lively personality. But the experience of a season would be good for her. She'd form friendships and connections that would last a lifetime. Once Rosamund and Griffin were married, she'd make sure Jacqueline had every opportunity to shine.

Rosamund sighed as the inn came into view and forbade herself to crane her neck to search the market square for any sign of Griffin. She'd given up hope of seeing him that day.

But there was always tonight.

The warm conviviality of an evening spent with the vicar almost washed away the worries of the day. But as Griffin climbed the stairs to his bedchamber, all his cares crowded in upon him again.

Maddox had been right. No one knew who'd started the rumor, but it was said someone had laid information over the death of Maddox's cousin, Mr. Allbright. Determined to know one way or the other, Griffin had called on the local justice of the peace, Sir William Drake, only to be told the gentleman knew nothing of any fresh information.

Griffin had come away even more confounded than before.

So if no one had laid new information, how had that devilish rumor sprung up? Had there truly been a witness to Allbright's murder?

Chasing down the source of the rumor was like clutching at shadows. The more interest he showed in the business, the guiltier he looked. Of course, Allbright had been in his employ, but everyone knew Griffin's interest was not that of a concerned master. They all thought he'd killed the man.

He only wished he had.

He turned into the corridor that held his bedchamber. The candle snapped and flickered as a sudden draft blew.

Damned uncomfortable barracks of a place! He'd always hated it. It was the house in which his grandfather reigned supreme, tyrannizing family and servants alike.

Even in his final days, the old earl had hunkered in the center of his web of minions and informants like a malevolent spider. Nothing had pleased him more than finding excuses to dish out corporal punishment to his grandsons. If the old Devil had but known it, for Griffin, the beatings had never been the worst part.

When his grandfather died, Griffin had entertained visions of a happier home. He'd dismissed the worst of the old earl's henchmen and hired new servants in their place.

But even those servants had left him when Allbright's body was found mangled and bloody at the foot of a nearby cliff.

All except Joshua and Peggy and their meek little Alice.

The door gave an eerie creak as he pushed it open. Damn Joshua! He'd told the man to oil it. Did he have to do every bloody thing himself? He'd be down in the kitchens cooking his own dinner next.

He fingered his jaw. Actually, he couldn't do a worse job of it than Peggy did.

At least Joshua had carried out his usual orders and drawn a bath and built up the fire beside it. Griffin thought of soap that smelled like a pine forest and sighed.

That led to more pleasurable recollections. The lush whiteness of Rosamund's breasts, the pink of her nipples, the intoxicating sweetness of her lips, the erotic promise in her sighs.

He pushed those memories away. Now that he was faced with a reprise of the ugliness surrounding Allbright's death, Rosamund seemed more out of reach than ever.

With a frustrated oath, he stripped off his clothes and climbed into the oversized bath.

The water had grown tepid, but he didn't mind that. After the day he'd had, the water calmed and soothed him. He washed his hair and scrubbed at his body, then reached for the ewer to sluice away the suds.

"Hello, Griffin," a soft female voice said.

CHAPTER FOURTEEN

J esus!" Griffin dropped the ewer into the bath and scrambled to his feet, his hand shooting out to snatch his towel. Water poured off him in sheets as he rose like some ancient sea god emerging from the ocean depths.

Rosamund tried to speak, but her mouth was curiously dry and the breath seemed to catch in her throat.

He was without doubt the most magnificent creature she'd ever laid eyes on. True, she'd never seen a naked man before, but surely they could not all be so breathtaking in their proportions?

She couldn't seem to drag her gaze from the fascinating collection of male apparatus at his groin.

To her disappointment, Griffin snapped out the towel and wrapped it tightly around his waist. "What the Hell are you doing here?" he demanded, tunneling his fingers through his thick, dark hair.

She lifted her gaze to his. "I—I came to see you."

"Well, you've seen me, all right." He stepped out of the tub, stalked to the dresser, and began to rummage through the drawers.

Rosamund bit her lip. She ought to feel guilty for

watching him like that, but too many other, more powerful emotions swamped her for any trace of guilt to survive.

"I've missed you, Griffin."

He stopped. For a few, breathless moments, she hoped
he'd rush to sweep her into his arms.

He didn't even turn around, but resumed his search
with renewed vigor. "How did you get in?" He tossed the
question over his shoulder as he yanked out a pair of
breeches.

"The secret staircase," she answered, mesmerized by
the play of muscles over his back. "Cecily found it when
we were here last."

He turned to stare at her.

Rosamund shrugged. "I believe she was searching for
buried treasure. She is a redoubtable girl."

"If we are to talk of redoubtable . . ."

"Oh, you mean me?" Slowly, she shook her head. "Not
redoubtable. Merely—" *Desperate.* She moved toward him
until she was within touching distance. "—determined."

She placed one hand on his shoulder. The skin there
was smooth and warm, damp from the bath. He sucked in
a breath, his big chest expanding with it.

That was not indifference. He couldn't deny this heat
between them. She refused to believe he truly wanted her
to leave.

As she slid her hand around to his nape, she removed
the breeches from his slackened grasp with her other
hand and dropped them to the floor.

For a few tantalizing seconds, she studied his face, the
taut, deep lines of strain about his mouth, the painful
puckered whiteness of his scar. And those storm-cloud
eyes of his, glowering with fury, blazing with desire.

Then she pulled him to her.

His mouth crushed down on hers in a kiss that was
wild and hungry and raw. All she could do was allow

herself to be swept along and match him as best she could.

With a guttural oath, he wrenched his mouth away and put her from him. "You shouldn't be here."

That's not what your kiss said. He wanted her, just as she wanted him.

Breathless with nerves and heat and desire, she licked her lips. "Griffin," she panted, "I admire your scruples, but—"

"You shouldn't be in my house," he ground out. "No, scratch that. What I mean is *I don't want you here.*"

Her confidence faltered. She stepped back, struggling to shore up her courage.

He put the heels of his hands to his temples as if to keep his head from exploding. "I told you in my note why I had to return. There was no call for you to post down as well. I'd planned to be back in a week."

"It has been a week already," she said.

He sighed. "I had business to attend to."

"And would that business have kept you another week?" she asked. "Another two? Three years, perhaps? Griffin, why don't you *trust* me?"

"It's not a question of trust. It's . . ." He turned away.

When he looked at her again, there was grim resignation in his face.

The fear that had dogged her since she read his note sank its teeth into her heart. "Do you not wish to marry me, after all?"

His features hardened to granite.

When he didn't answer, she fell back another step. "No. *No!* Griffin, you will not do this to me again. I won't let you leave me."

He dragged a hand down his face and inhaled deeply through his nose. "We might not have a choice in the matter."

She shook her head. "No, don't you see? Of course we have a choice. I made mine three years ago, and I stand by it, no matter what."

"No matter what," he repeated. To her astonishment, his features cracked in a ghastly parody of a smile. "I think you'll change your mind about that when you hear the truth about me."

He scared her, but she'd rather die than show it. It was a test, wasn't it? He was goading her to turn from him. If she didn't show that her allegiance was unswerving now, he would never believe in it.

"I don't care. I don't want to hear it now. Later you can tell me all the reasons we can't be together." She lowered her gaze. Then she took a deep breath and looked him in the eye.

"Now, I want you to take me to bed."

Dumbfounded at the direct, scandalous simplicity of her request, Griffin stood still and silent as one of those stuffed effigies on Guy Fawkes Night.

Rosamund picked up his hand and guided it to her breast. "Feel how fast my heart beats," she said. "Isn't that ridiculous?"

There was a smile in her eyes, inviting him to share her amusement in this phenomenon. But there was a sensual knowing in them, too.

Oh, yes, he thought. Ridiculous, the pair of them together. They could never be anything else. Yet he could feel her heart pound and race, it was true.

Though the firm, shapely globe felt like Heaven in his hand, for many moments, he didn't move.

Temptation pulled at him like some irresistible tide. His brain blanked. Reflexively, his fingers closed around her, giving her breast a gentle squeeze. He palmed her nipple, teased it gently with his fingertips, working it to a hard peak.

She tilted her head back and sighed. "Yes."

Oh, God. His member gave a sharp twitch, straining at the makeshift covering around his waist. He withdrew his hand to secure the towel, tucking it more firmly around him.

"Don't deny me," she whispered, pressing against him. "Not this time."

Deliberately vulgar, he said, "Woman, those pretty tits of yours would tempt a saint."

He kissed her, dragging his mouth roughly over hers and across her soft cheek, abrading it with his nascent beard. In her ear, he growled, "And the Lord knows I'm no saint."

She gave that low, wicked laugh that was his and his alone to hear, making his cock harden nearly to the point of explosion.

"Well." Her breath whispered over his cheek. "Contrary to popular opinion, it seems that I'm no angel, either."

He huffed out a shaky chuckle. His desire for her heightened to such a pitch, he could barely remember his own name, much less the reasons he should send her away.

He turned her and stripped the clothes from her body, ripping at tapes and laces in his impatience. When she was finally naked, he resisted the powerful urge to ravish her where they stood. He made himself wait.

Torture not to reach for her and commit all those sins upon her body that he'd fantasized about since the day they met. But he wouldn't have missed this first sight of her for the world.

She made as if to turn to face him, but he said, "No. Lie down on the bed."

His mouth watered as she complied with his command, walking away from him with a subtle, tantalizing sway to her hips. The globes of her bottom flexed and released in a riveting rhythm.

She was so graceful and seemingly unselfconscious in her nudity. Using the steps, she climbed onto the massive tester bed. Reclining on her side, she rested her head on one hand and watched him intently.

So shapely, so supple and smooth and soft. She ought to be painted like this. But no, he thought. She was a living work of art, and he was the only man with the right to a private viewing.

Lust ripped through him. But when he started toward her, she said, "Wait."

He halted, steaming with impatience. Oh, Christ, she wasn't going to tell him she wanted to stop now?

She pointed at his towel. "Take it off." She smiled, that dazzling, diamond-studded smile. "Please."

Insanity beckoned, but he couldn't help it. He decided to have a little fun with her. Scratching his chin, he drawled, "Well, I don't know about that. I might scare you, sweetheart."

She lifted her chin. "Ha! I've already seen you, anyway. I was watching you the whole time you were in the bath."

Yes, but his member hadn't been quite so rampant at that stage in the proceedings.

With a shrug and a flick of his fingers at his waist, he let the towel fall. He couldn't suppress a grin when he heard her gasp. "Heavens," she said a little faintly.

"Best not to think about it too much," he recommended, moving toward her at last.

Rosamund shifted over on the bed as he climbed onto it, then rolled toward him when his body made a deep depression in the mattress.

She put her hands on his biceps and looked into his eyes, her own gaze steady. In a clipped tone, she said, "This is going to hurt, isn't it? I've heard that it does."

"'Fraid so." He saw the apprehension beneath her bravado. An unaccustomed wave of tenderness washed over him.

He leaned over and nuzzled into her throat. "I'll make it good for you first, sweetheart. Perhaps then you won't mind so much what comes next. And it's only the first time that it hurts. After that . . ."

She stroked his hair. "I trust you," she whispered.

A heady kind of exhilaration filled him when she said those words. He knew she meant them, and he resolved then and there to prove himself worthy of that trust if it killed him.

As well it might.

He hoped to God he could leash his own selfish desires long enough to manage the business.

He didn't have an awful lot of experience with women, so he followed his instincts, paying close attention to her responses. In pleasing Rosamund, he discovered that his own pleasure doubled. That was something he'd never known before. He'd always been impatient with the preliminaries, eager to get to the good part. But then, he'd never done this with the woman he wanted to make his wife. He'd never done this with Rosamund.

On a mission to find all her most delicious points of pleasure, he kissed his way down her body, lingering at the tips of her breasts, which he already knew to be exquisitely sensitive.

He loved the helpless little sounds she made when he hit the perfect spot—the place behind her ear, the sweet little indent of her navel, the backs of her knees, her inner thigh . . .

The musky scent of her arousal made him a trifle smug and more than a little desperate. With shaking fingers, he parted her folds, opening her to his gaze.

Pink and intricate and mysterious, like the inside of

a shell. But she was all woman, warm flesh and glistening dew.

Yes.

She shifted restlessly beneath his hands, as if she wanted him to get on with it. He bent to her then, tasting her with his tongue.

She gave a soft shriek but she didn't protest when he clamped his hands on her thighs to hold her still and increased the pressure, working her with his mouth until she begged him for something—she didn't seem to know what.

He knew what she wanted, but he delayed, drawing out her need, building her anticipation until she writhed with it and thrashed her head from side to side. It was a vastly pleasant form of torture; she deserved it for the way she'd kept him in a constant lather since he'd first seen her again that day in her mother's drawing room.

Gently, he pushed one finger inside her as he swirled the flat of his tongue over her clitoris. Her hips bucked, and he pushed again, sliding into her. His body shuddered in hopeful sympathy. The hunger to possess her grew.

Pleasuring her this way aroused him more than he'd thought possible. He needed to bring this to an end or he'd disgrace himself.

Replacing his mouth with his thumb, he pressed firmly, rubbing her until she gave a surprised cry and her body jerked in hard, wrenching spasms. He bent to her once more, soothing, prolonging her release with his soft laps and swirls of his tongue.

She was still in the throes of orgasm when he moved over and touched the head of his penis to her entrance. With a harsh gasp, he guided himself inside her a little way.

She cried out—this time not with bliss—and he stopped, his jaw set with frustration. Though he knew better, it seemed an impossible fit. He'd never had a virgin before, and his fear of hurting her badly almost made him call a complete halt to the business.

But he was too selfish to do that, and besides, he couldn't put off the fatal moment indefinitely.

Still, he hesitated.

She gave a soft moan. "Best be quick," she breathed, shifting beneath him. "I can bear it. Just . . . do it quickly."

"Right."

He gripped her hips and tilted her up toward him, gritted his teeth and thrust.

The second he was buried inside her, his animal urges took control of his brain. He dimly heard her ragged gasp, felt her tighten about him, but he couldn't stop the driving need to surge into her again and again. She was hurting, but his pleasure was so deeply euphoric that in mere moments, he'd reached the brink.

One more thrust and his crisis exploded upon him, racking his body, blurring his vision. He gave a hoarse groan as his seed pumped into her.

Shuddering, he collapsed on top of Rosamund, crushing her to the mattress. When the spasms finally stopped, he barely gathered the strength to withdraw from her and roll to the side.

Fatigue claimed him instantly. His speech slurred, it was such an effort to get the words out. "Are you—? Did it hurt?"

Stupid question.

"Yes."

The waver in her tone made him cringe. *Oh, God.* He'd been such a brute, he'd turned her off bed-sport for life. But he was so exhausted, he couldn't find the words to reassure her. Not now. Now, all he wanted was sleep.

"But you were right." Her soft voice reached him through his weary haze. "After what you did beforehand, I—I didn't mind so much."

Good. That was good. Wonderful. "Ung," he mumbled into the pillow.

"Griffin?" She smoothed a hand over his shoulder, but for the life of him, he couldn't even turn his head to look at her.

That was the trouble with women. They wanted to talk afterwards and got their feelings hurt when he couldn't. He should have explained to Rosamund the soporific effects of a raging orgasm on the male of the species *before* he lost the power to speak in coherent sentences.

"Mm?" was all he could manage.

"We should get married. Tomorrow, if we can."

"Mm-hmm." He drifted away.

"Good," she said, planting a swift kiss on his cheek. "That is settled, then."

CHAPTER FIFTEEN

D iccon was waiting for Rosamund in the shadows beyond the inn's stable yard when she returned from Pendon Place.

"My lady." Relief colored the footman's tone. He lifted her down from her horse and took hold of the chestnut's bridle.

"Thank you, Diccon," she managed through gritted teeth.

Riding had been excruciating to her tender parts after the time she'd spent with Griffin. She ached in places she'd never known she possessed, and the jogging motion of her steed had exacerbated the pain considerably.

When Diccon set her down, her knees nearly buckled beneath her, but somehow she'd managed to remain upright. She didn't quite know how she'd manage to walk normally back to the inn.

Thank Heaven Diccon couldn't see her blushes in the darkness. Was the reason for her excursion as evident to him as she was certain it must be?

Thrusting that unwelcome idea from her mind, she pressed a handsome douceur into his hand. He appeared not to notice the gratuity, but quickly pocketed the coins nonetheless.

"I left a back door unlatched," he whispered. "It opens to a causeway between the inn and the laundry. Go up the back stairs and you'll not meet anyone at this time of night."

"Thank you, Diccon. Truly, you are a prince among footmen," said Rosamund. She hobbled in that direction, leaving him to return the mare to her stall.

She'd been fortunate that the duke chose Diccon to make one of her entourage on this occasion. She didn't know how she'd have managed her escape otherwise. The young footman had been suborned by Cecily the minute he arrived in the duke's household, years ago. Since then, he'd acted as Cecily's partner in crime on more occasions than Rosamund wanted to know about.

Perhaps it was unfair of her and Cecily to involve him in their adventures, but he seemed to be a man who enjoyed taking risks. And it *was* a substantial risk on his part to aid the Westruther ladies in such mad schemes as this. If the duke discovered Diccon's role in such an escapade, he'd dismiss the footman on the spot.

A twinge of guilt disturbed Rosamund's conscience as she limped around the side of the inn. Well, if Montford did find out about Diccon's role in this adventure, she would offer the footman a place in her and Griffin's household.

She savored the idea of living with Griffin at Pendon Place. Finally, she had everything she wanted. Well, almost.

A newfound tenacity had made her wait, restless and wakeful beside him, until Griffin could be roused enough to discuss wedding plans. Before she'd left, he'd undertaken to ask his friend the vicar to marry them the following day.

In mere hours, she would be his countess.

Despite her hurts, her body flooded with delight at the

thought of finally fulfilling the role she'd been destined for from birth. She only wished Jane and Cecily could be here so she could share the brilliance of her happiness with the two people in the world who would best understand.

Her mind flitted to Xavier and shied away. He'd only give that unpleasant, cynical smile of his and tell her she was fooling herself. Much he knew about it!

The sound of water splashing to the ground in a steady stream made her stop short. A beery voice rang out from the same direction, and she realized what the earlier sound had been. Two men stood with their backs to her, urinating against the inn wall.

Ugh. She whisked herself behind the nearest concealment, which happened to be the door to the laundry, if the smell of lye soap were any indication.

She listened, waiting for them to finish their business and go back inside. She didn't attend particularly to what they said until she heard the name Tregarth. Then she opened the laundry door an inch farther so she could hear better.

But the men were clearly drunk; their words slurred together, and that, on top of the thick Cornish accent, made them almost impossible to understand.

However, Rosamund did catch one word before the men pulled up their breeches and moved off. It clanged like a knell in her head.

Murderer.

When Griffin came in from his early-morning ride, he was astonished to find a bustle in his cavernous great hall.

Joshua and two footmen he'd never seen before carried two massive trunks upstairs and disappeared toward his bedchamber. Griffin went after them.

In his bedchamber, he found Dearlove standing in the midst of a sea of trunks and boxes, directing proceedings.

"What is all this?" Griffin snapped, though he knew very well what it was.

Dearlove permitted himself a smile. "Some items you left behind, my lord."

If Dearlove included himself in that statement, Griffin couldn't tell. He detected no reproach in his valet's expression, then wondered at himself for caring. Did he actually feel guilty for not bringing the man with him?

"Most of your commissions in London have been fulfilled, my lord. Knowing your immediate needs, I ventured to bring with me a few things more suited to country wear."

"You mean this isn't the full extent of it?" Griffin was horrified and a little awed at his own unwitting extravagance.

"Oh, no, my lord. The rest is in your rooms at Montford House."

He gazed about him. *Hell.* "When do you suppose I'm going to wear any of this?"

"If you will permit the impertinence, my lord, that is my concern." He spread his hands. "The advantage to having a valet is that Your Lordship is not obliged to think about clothing at all."

Griffin fingered his chin. He didn't give his garments more than a passing thought now. But however that might be, Dearlove was here. He might as well make use of him.

"I'm to be married today, Dearlove," he announced, and took a moment to enjoy the shock that passed over Dearlove's usually impassive features.

"Then we shall choose something special for the occasion, my lord. But first, a shave, perhaps? And a haircut. Joshua!" Dearlove addressed Griffin's sole manservant. "Bring hot water and towels. Quickly, now!"

As Griffin allowed himself to be primped and prodded, he mulled over the night before. Rosamund had seduced him quite effortlessly. He'd been putty in her hands, and now she must pay the price.

Oh, he knew things had gone too far for him to weasel out of a wedding now. On some level, he suspected he'd wanted to trap her just as much as she'd clearly set out to trap him with that shattering night of passion.

Finally, he would have Rosamund. Hot blood raced through his body at the thought.

But it was selfish of him to want her at the expense of her ultimate happiness. He was a bastard for letting her make the commitment before she knew the difficulties she was likely to face in becoming his wife.

If only he knew for certain whether there was a threat or not.

He was no closer to tracing the source of the rumor about new evidence in the murder of Simon Allbright. If old Sir William Drake, the justice of the peace, assured him no such evidence had been brought to his attention, he supposed he'd have to be content with that. He was not to be hauled off in irons just yet.

But the fact remained that in his neighbors' eyes, he was a murderer. It seemed there were those who had an interest in keeping that belief alive and fresh in people's minds.

Rosamund had said nothing else mattered to her, that she would marry him no matter what. Ought he to tell her the truth before the wedding? It might spoil the day—how could it not? But she should be given the choice. Few women would wish to marry a man who stood accused of murder by his neighbors, a man who could do nothing to prove his innocence.

The thought that even now she might carry the beginnings of their child in her womb made great cold waves of panic surge through him. If he knew Rosamund, she would prefer marriage to a murderer to the scandal of bearing a child out of wedlock.

Or perhaps she would choose a third option—a quick marriage to another man. Griffin's stomach lurched sickeningly at the thought. Lauderdale would take her in a heartbeat. So would a legion of other men, he didn't doubt.

Hell and the Devil confound it! He'd craved a simple life, and now look where he stood: his thoughts circling around like sharks around a dilemma that could have no good outcome whichever path he chose.

He didn't think he could live with himself if Rosamund despised him. He'd come to care far too much for her good opinion, it seemed. She would discover the truth of the situation soon enough if she lived at Pendon Place.

Yes, he ought to tell her. For her sake and his, he *would* tell her before they took their vows.

He sat to offer Dearlove his jaw for scraping with a sinking, horrible feeling of dread.

Rosamund could scarcely tell Jacqueline the true reason she'd changed her mind about riding that morning.

She was glad to know the pain of her first time would not be repeated. There'd been one, searing moment when panic nearly overwhelmed her. She'd wanted to throw Griffin off and yell at him not to come near her again.

It had been over quickly, however, and Jane had assured her the activity could be sublime if a lady's husband proved to be a considerate lover. She thought Griffin immensely considerate. What he'd done to her with his hands and mouth still sent twinges of pleasure through her body.

Rosamund suggested to Jacqueline that they walk down to the cliffs instead of riding and Jacqueline agreed willingly enough. The breeze whipped the skirts of their habits around them as they climbed to the top. Jacqueline had found a large branch and used it as a walking stick.

Now Rosamund said, "Tell me about the murder of Mr. Allbright."

The girl paled beneath her tan. "Who mentioned that to you?"

"I overheard some men talking," said Rosamund. "In fact, in the course of breakfast, I heard it mentioned three times. The subject is on everyone's lips, it seems."

This was what Griffin had tried to tell her last night.

"He didn't do it," said Jacqueline vehemently.

"Of course he didn't," agreed Rosamund. "Tell me."

Jacqueline stared out to sea. Her lips firmed and she turned her face to Rosamund, the wind whipping her hair from its pins and casting it about her face.

Pulling a strand from the corner of her mouth, Jacqueline said, "Come on."

They moved down the slope and took a path cut into the hill that was sheltered from the wind.

"Mr. Allbright was my music master," said Jacqueline, squinting against the wind. "An unnecessary extravagance. You can imagine my aptitude for the pianoforte." She rolled her eyes. "I can't guess why my grandfather hired him, except to subject me and the teacher to weekly misery. Allbright was some sort of cousin to our friend Tony Maddox. You will meet Tony. He lives at Trenoweth Hall. Over that way." She waved a hand to the east.

"Anyway, one day after Grandfather died, Griffin and Mr. Allbright had a row and Griffin dismissed Allbright, who then put it about the village that Griffin had threatened to kill him if he saw him in these parts ever again. We thought that was the end of him, but Allbright returned."

The girl's eyes grew hollow. "And then Allbright's lifeless body was discovered at the foot of the cliff."

Rosamund gasped. "How awful for you both!"

"Oh, it was . . . awful, yes. But the worst was when they took Griffin for questioning. No one believed him innocent—no one except for me and Tony and the vicar, that is—but there wasn't any evidence he'd done it, so the matter was allowed to rest."

"But the people around here won't let it rest, is that it?" said Rosamund.

Miserably, Jacqueline nodded. "Griffin sent me away to spare me the unpleasantness, but he doesn't understand! I want to stand by him. I don't care what they say—I know he didn't do it!"

Rosamund put her arm about her. "Your sentiments do you credit. But you cannot blame Griffin for wishing to protect you." She gave Jacqueline's shoulder a squeeze. "Shall we go back and take a glass of lemonade? Or perhaps some tea?"

And then she must get ready for her wedding.

CHAPTER SIXTEEN

Griffin strode through the village toward the inn where Rosamund stayed, ignoring the whispers that followed him like wind rustling the trees. He needed to talk to Rosamund before she took that final step.

He entered the vestibule and glanced toward the stair that led up to her rooms. On a sudden and admittedly craven impulse, he changed his course and ducked into the taproom.

If any occasion called for a drink, it was this one.

The taproom was empty, save for a shaggy old mongrel that lay by the empty hearth. That suited Griffin very well.

The barmaid, who'd been dusting with her back to the door, turned to face him. Her mouth dropped open. The dust cloth fell from her hands.

"Bessie, a tankard of your best ale, if you please," he said. The inn served only one kind of ale, of course, and the girl stared at him, confused.

He shook his head. "No, on second thought, I'll have a nip of that brandy you keep hidden behind the bar."

Despite the early hour, he felt in need of a strong stimulant. Not that he meant to make a habit of imbibing before noon, but if a man couldn't break with tradition on his wedding day, when could he?

Bessie's dark eyes were round with curiosity, but he was damned if he'd explain why he was rigged out like some dashed park saunterer. They'd all hear of his marriage soon enough. That was, if Rosamund still wanted to wed him after what he had to say.

"Well, well. If it isn't Master Griffin."

Griffin froze, the hairs at the back of his neck standing on end. That hoarse, hateful voice had stopped haunting his nightmares years ago. Yet hearing it now brought the past rushing back.

Crane.

He pretended he hadn't heard the remark, but of course, his tormentor wasn't discouraged by his seeming indifference.

"Ain't you fine today, my lord?" Crane rested one elbow on the bar beside him, swinging an expensive gold watch on a chain that hung from the vulgarly bright waistcoat he wore. He was a big man, perhaps fifteen years older than Griffin. Crane had held the position of steward at Pendon Place until the old earl's death. But steward had been only one of his functions.

"Too 'igh and mighty for the likes of me now, ain't you?" said Crane.

He leaned in to murmur in Griffin's ear, "But I remembers a day when you was no more than a worm beneath my heel."

Griffin's jaw hardened and his fist clenched at his side, but he knew a deliberate goad when he heard it. "Get away from me."

An avid light struck in the man's green eyes. He licked his lips and turned to the barmaid, saying loudly, "See that lovely scar the earl has there, Bessie love? That's my work, that is. I'm dead proud of that. Some men would have bungled it and got the eyeball itself, but not Barnabas Crane. The old gentleman would have sacked me if I'd gone and *blinded* his grandson, now, wouldn't he? Didn't mind me bloodying his back for him, though."

Blistering hot rage surged through Griffin like lava from a volcano. His hand shot out. He bunched Crane's shirt in his fist and hauled him up so they were eye to eye.

The frightened barmaid gave a cry of alarm. "Oh! Oh, please, me lord! Don't kill him!"

Griffin bared his teeth in a snarl. "You're not fit to lick the shit off my boots, Crane. You never were."

A smug look descended on Crane's features. The bastard thought Griffin couldn't afford to hurt him because he was still under suspicion over Allbright's murder. Crane took his shots in this public spot because he had no fear of serious reprisals. He knew Griffin didn't want to give fodder for any more speculation over the ungovernable violence of his beastly temper.

Crane tut-tutted. "Are you *threatening* me, Master Griffin? Like you threatened Allbright?"

Griffin tightened his grip. "Why do you ask?" he said. "Do you have any plans for getting thrown off a cliff that I should know about? In that case, I'll order champagne."

Crane couldn't have been comfortable with his collar tightening around his reddening neck, but the sneer on his face didn't slip. "You and that fool of a justice have sewn up that little business nicely, haven't you? All neat and tidy. But we know what you did, Master Griffin. Everyone hereabouts knows the truth."

Crane angled his head. "I wonder if that yaller-headed ladybird of yours has heard of it yet? I'd wager she hasn't. . . . But she will."

At the mention of Rosamund, a haze of red swam over his vision. With a roar, Griffin hauled back his fist, but it was caught from behind in a strong, restraining hold.

He pivoted, ready to pummel the newcomer for his interference, but then he saw who held him in an iron grip.

"Well, now, what do we have here, eh?" The vicar's hearty tones rang out in the quiet of the taproom as he hung on to Griffin's elbow with both hands. "Tregarth! I say, old fellow, let him go. You'll soil your gloves touching that."

Moments passed before Griffin grew calm enough to speak. With a short laugh, he said, "You're right. Hardly worth wrinkling my coat for." Griffin released Crane and stepped back.

"Go, now, Mr. Crane," said the vicar. "We don't want trouble in this fine establishment, now, do we?"

But Crane had achieved what he'd come for: He'd provoked Griffin to violence. With a wink at Bessie and a cocky smirk, he took himself off.

Griffin turned to the barmaid, who cowered behind the bar, holding an empty wine bottle like a club. She flinched when he stepped toward her.

"The brandy, if you please, Bessie," he said gently.

The girl set down her weapon and fumbled for the bottle of cognac stowed underneath the gleaming bar. She opened it and sloshed it into a glass.

Her hands shook, he noticed. Silently, he cursed Crane for forcing the quarrel and himself for rising to the bait.

He took the brandy with thanks and a handsome tip that did much to banish the fear from the barmaid's eyes.

Then he turned to address the vicar. "You're early."

Oliphant shrugged. "Parish business across the street. I happened to see Crane follow you in and thought there might be trouble. Ah!" Oliphant rubbed his hands together, eyeing Griffin's drink. "Dutch courage, eh? Capital idea."

The good vicar never passed up an opportunity to drink at someone else's expense, no matter what time of day. With a grin, Griffin turned to order a second brandy for his friend. They took their beverages to a corner table, well away from the bar and Bessie's ears.

"Well, well," said Oliphant, eyeing him. "You do scrub up nicely. Can it be the change that love hast wrought?"

Griffin hunched his shoulders. He'd complained bitterly to his valet that London ways simply wouldn't do here in Cornwall, but Dearlove had insisted on dressing him like some town beau on the strut.

He jerked his head toward the bar. "My thanks for the intervention."

"I've no cause to love the fellow," said Oliphant. "He lures all the younger men into that smuggling racket of his. Likely get them all hanged. That's if anyone hereabouts had the nerve to stand up to Crane and his gang." He hesitated. "You know, Tregarth, you could do something—"

"You'd best drink up," interrupted Griffin. "It won't do your standing any good to be seen with me."

"None at all," agreed the vicar, accepting the change of subject with equanimity. "But I have the excuse that I am about to marry you to your lovely heiress. What's she like?"

Griffin sipped his drink and hissed through his teeth as he felt the kick. The alcoholic warmth spread to his limbs, relaxing them a little. He needed that.

Yes, brandy had been an inspired idea. His nerves still jangled after that encounter with Crane. Besides, he had yet to see Rosamund, which was why he'd bought the bloody drink in the first place.

"Lady Rosamund?" He swirled his brandy, warming it with his hand. "She is without doubt the most exquisitely beautiful woman I have ever seen."

Oliphant laughed at his gloomy tone. "That's a bad thing?"

"It is if you look like me," he replied. "As for her character, she's good-natured, softhearted, but she's no fool. She has wit and intelligence and a little guile thrown in for good measure."

She'd wrapped him around her little finger from the start, hadn't she? And that had less to do with her spectacular face and form and more to do with her unique courage in standing up to him. She'd laughed at his ill-tempered rudeness, set her own price for complying with his wishes, then coaxed him to please her as if she were an experienced trainer breaking in a wild colt.

"She sounds like a paragon," said Oliphant.

"All sweetness and light, that's my lady." But he'd discovered a deliciously naughty side to his bright angel that he wasn't about to share with Oliphant. Rosamund's intimate, throaty laughter rang in his memory, heated his blood.

The vicar lowered his gaze, then looked up at him from beneath his brows. "Have you told her?"

Absorbed in Rosamund, for a moment, Griffin didn't take Oliphant's meaning. Then he held up his glass. "Why do you think I need the Dutch courage?"

An uncharacteristic flash of annoyance crossed the vicar's features. "If only you'd let me—"

"No." Griffin fixed him with a compelling stare. "No, my friend. Leave it be. Believe me, you would do far more harm than good."

"My dear, you are like a cat on hot bricks," said Tibby. "Stop fussing and fidgeting, or I shall make you read something to improve your mind."

Rosamund halted her pacing. "Mary Wollstonecraft? I've already read her. Cecily made me. Didn't she tell you?"

"Oh, not Mary Wollstonecraft," said Tibby, picking up a tract from the table by her side and holding it out. "Hannah More."

She said it in such accents of horror that Rosamund was obliged to laugh. "As if I could read such stuff. And at this of all moments!"

Tibby put down her tract. "You sent a message to Lord Tregarth, but that doesn't mean he'll drop everything and come running. Why, he could be from home all day, just as he was yesterday."

Rosamund knew he'd come because she'd prearranged it while lying naked in Griffin's bed last night, but she couldn't tell Tibby that.

"Why don't you take Meg and go for a walk?" Tibby suggested.

"No, no, that won't do." Fuming with impatience, Rosamund checked her reflection in the looking glass above the mantel once more.

She hadn't, of course, disclosed to Tibby any aspect of last night's adventure. For all her companion knew, she'd been tucked up safely in her own bed, not losing her maidenhead in Griffin's.

Did she look any different? Rosamund scrutinized her face for telltale signs of last night's debauchery as her mother might have searched her own face for wrinkles.

Rosamund frowned. Her cheeks might be a little pink and her eyes bright, but otherwise she detected no alteration. How could that be when she felt like a totally different person?

Someone scratched on the door, and Rosamund's pulse jumped. In as steady a voice as she could manage, she called, "Come."

The door opened and Griffin stood on the threshold.

Rosamund froze, staring up at him, her mouth ajar.

He was dressed immaculately, from the top of his neatly styled hair to the gleaming black of his boots. She'd been privileged to admire the strength and power of his form last night, but she'd never dreamed his big body could appear to such advantage in *clothes*.

And his face! He was clean-shaven, for one thing, but his hair had been trimmed in a style that revealed a pair of slashing cheekbones and seemed to emphasize those storm-cloud eyes. True, more of his cruel scar was visible without that unruly mane covering it, but she was so accustomed to the sight now, she hardly noticed it.

His eyes met hers, and some protective layer around her cracked and fell away. She quivered with it, this vulnerable, unprecedented feeling.

Suddenly it occurred to her that she'd given up more than her virginity last night.

He tilted his head a little, assessing her with those hot and cold eyes of his. That made her blush furiously. She couldn't help remembering all that they'd done together in his bed.

"Rosamund, dear," prompted Tibby.

"Oh." She groped about for her usual poise but failed to locate it anywhere. "How—how silly of me. Do come in, Griffin."

Tibby tugged the bellpull. "I'll ring for tea."

"W-won't you sit down?" Lord, it was like talking to a stranger. She'd been intimate with Griffin in ways she couldn't even begin to examine in the light of day, yet in those garments, she didn't know him at all. It was disorienting, as if she'd dismounted from a horse, only to discover the ground wasn't where she'd left it.

He made no effort to set her at her ease. In fact, he

seemed distracted. Didn't he recall that he was supposed to express surprise about her presence at the inn?

She took the initiative. "I suppose you are wondering why I am here, Griffin."

Confusion crossed his features. "What?"

Rosamund flared her eyes at him and glanced at Tibby. "I mean, you didn't expect me to follow you down here, did you?"

"Oh! Right. Yes. Yes, that's right. I didn't. Expect it, that is."

"And . . . ," prompted Rosamund.

She waited, but he merely stared at her in a baffled way.

"Since I am here anyway . . ."

He started. "Oh." He glanced at Tibby. "Yes, well. Perhaps we ought to . . ." He cleared his throat. "Rosamund, might I speak to you in private?"

Rosamund frowned at him. This was not part of the instructions she'd given him before she left the previous evening.

Despite her minatory look, he didn't amend his request, so she gave a small shrug and smiled at Tibby. "Would you mind giving us privacy, Tibby? Just for a few minutes?"

"Certainly, my dear," said Tibby, picking up her book. "I will return in *fifteen* minutes, to be precise."

Rosamund waited until Tibby closed the door behind her. Then she turned to Griffin and whispered, "What is it? What happened? I trust you have not changed your mind, for things have gone too far—"

"I haven't changed my mind!" Griffin's eyes blazed. "What kind of a bas—?"

"Hush! Keep your voice down!" She darted a look toward the door.

Lowering his voice, he said, "What kind of a blackguard

do you take me for? Of course I haven't changed my mind. But there's something you should know."

The gravity of his expression alarmed her at first. But then she remembered her conversation with Griffin's sister.

Rosamund decided to keep Jacqueline's disclosures to herself. She wanted to hear the story from Griffin.

Before he could begin, the maid came in with the tea.

They both fell silent, waiting for the serving girl to leave. China clattered together as the maid walked across the room with the tray and set it on the table between Griffin and Rosamund.

As the girl set out the tea things, Rosamund saw that the face under the mob cap displayed abject terror. She kept darting glances at Griffin, and nearly upset the sugar bowl in her nervous distraction.

"Leave it," said Rosamund with a snap in her voice. "Good God, girl, do you suppose he's going to eat you?"

The maid gave a whimper and wiped her hands down her apron, as if they'd grown clammy in her fear.

"Off you go. I shall pour." Rosamund waved a hand and the girl scampered.

Rosamund turned to look at Griffin. "My goodness, if that is what you must put up with around here, I don't wonder at your habitual ill temper."

"I am not ill tempered," growled Griffin.

"You are, but I am not going to argue with you over it. Tell me what you wanted to tell me. I am eaten up with curiosity."

Her light words seemed to relax him a little. Good.

He leaned forward to accept his cup from her. Absently, he took a sip. Then looked down, raising his brows. "How did you know how I like my tea?"

Strong, with a dash of milk and three lumps of sugar. Ugh!

"*Is* that how you like it?" she said innocently. "What a happy coincidence."

She would hardly admit that she'd memorized every scrap of detail about his likes and dislikes she could glean while she'd been at Pendon Place. So utterly mad for him, despite the horrid welcome he'd given her. So determined to be the perfect wife.

She fingered her locket, then snatched away her hand. She must stop doing that.

"Hmph," said Griffin.

"Pray, begin." Regally, she inclined her head.

And so he told her. About threatening Allbright, then finding him dead on the rocks beneath the cliff.

"I see," she said slowly. She saw the struggle he went through as he related what had happened that day. Had he told another living soul this tale?

"But that's not the worst of it," he said, rising, as if he could no longer keep a leash on his turbulent emotions. He paced to the window and looked out. "There are rumors of fresh evidence. A witness, perhaps. I am still the prime suspect, so of course, if they reopen the investigation it will embroil me."

"But you are innocent," she pointed out.

He looked at her strangely. "You believe me, then." He blew out a breath.

"Well, of course I do! That's why I don't understand your concern about a witness. Surely if there is a witness, he or she can clear your name."

He folded his arms; his expression grew tight. "What if there was no witness and this is a malicious attempt to finger me for the crime? No one has come forward with these accusations. But while the rumors persist, and while any investigation which comes out of that proceeds, Pendon Place will be a mighty unpleasant place to be. As my wife, you would have much to bear."

A sudden insight struck her. Why hadn't she seen it as soon as Jacks told her? "That was why you didn't come for me. Isn't it? First your grandfather died, and then this cloud of suspicion hung over your head."

He said nothing, but she knew she'd hit on the truth. Relief and exhilaration filled her—selfish emotions when he'd suffered so cruelly, but she couldn't help it. He had stayed away to protect her.

"You still want to marry me?" Griffin said hoarsely. For the first time since the business began, he felt hope.

"Of course I still want to marry you!"

She said it as if it *were* a matter of course. He could only stare at her, speechless as she fingered her lip in thought.

He longed to taste those lips, to kiss her senseless for her unquestioning trust, but there wasn't time for that. And he'd probably take it beyond the line of pleasing just as that infernal companion walked through the door.

"The only point against you is that you threatened him before he was killed," said Rosamund. "Why did you do that, Griffin?"

He hesitated. It made his blood boil even now to think of it. "Allbright had designs on my sister. He was her music master and a cousin of a family friend."

He didn't blame Maddox, of course. Maddox couldn't have known Allbright's propensities or he would never have recommended the man as a music master for Jacks.

He drew a tattered breath. "I trusted him. I left them alone together. And then I found him . . ." Rage at Allbright, at himself, suspended his power of speech. He wanted to put his fist through the wall.

Rosamund paled. "I assume his attentions were not welcome?"

Griffin shook his head. "She was such an innocent, she

didn't even know what he was trying to do to her." Another area in which he'd failed Jacks. A sensible female companion would have informed her of such dangers. "She certainly didn't like it. I came in because I heard the struggle."

"I wonder you didn't slay him on the spot!" said Rosamund, firing up. "In fact, if you *had* killed him, I would not blame you. In fact," she added, narrowing her eyes, "I should have killed him myself, if I were you. What a dastardly fellow to take advantage of a young girl."

That did it. He strode over and plucked her off the couch, hauled her up against him, and kissed her.

Emotions roiled inside him. Fury at Allbright's lechery and the trouble he continued to make long after his death, gratitude that one person on this earth understood. Jacks might understand, but what right had he to seek comfort from his sister when he'd failed her so miserably?

Relief flooded him so quickly and completely, he felt off balance, dizzy with it.

Rosamund's response to his kiss was gratifyingly eager. He devoured her and she matched him every step of the way. Thank God she believed in him, because he couldn't live without her.

When he finally raised his head, they both panted like hounds after a long run. Tenderly, she smoothed her hands through his hair, cradling his head. That gentle gesture nearly undid him. The blessed relief of her understanding and support flooded his body, weakened his knees.

"We must find a way to clear your name once and for all." Those impossibly blue eyes sparked with determination. "Griffin, we must find the real killer!"

His arms fell from about her waist, and he took a hasty step back. "*What?* Don't be a damned little fool!"

"It's not foolish. It's the only way to settle the matter."

Before he could reply, the door opened and Tibby walked in.

"Well, my dears?" Tibby said.

Rosamund glowed. "Oh, Tibby, you may be the first for wish us happy. Griffin and I are getting married today!"

CHAPTER SEVENTEEN

Rosamund hurried into the parlor to check her appearance in the looking glass over the mantel.

Griffin had taken himself off to fetch the vicar and to allow her the chance to dress more appropriately for the occasion. She'd chosen a white muslin gown sprigged all over with forget-me-nots.

"Aren't you being a trifle hasty, my dear?" Tibby looked up from her tambour frame with her soft gaze that saw far more than most people realized. "Surely you want Cecily with you, at least. And His Grace and Lord Steyne, too. On such a significant occasion—"

"The circumstances are hardly ideal," admitted Rosamund, fixing a gold earbob into her lobe with fingers that trembled from excitement. "But Tibby, you must understand how—how desperately impatient I am to begin my new life as a married lady. I've been on the shelf too long."

"Two seasons!" Tibby sniffed. "If you knew how many seasons I had, you would call me an ape-leader, my dear."

Rosamund regarded her with amusement. "I'd wager you didn't lack for offers, Tib."

"I couldn't possibly comment on that," said Miss Tibbs

primly, but with a sparkle in her eye. "But believe me, if I *had* accepted an offer, I would have made sure I was thoroughly acquainted with the man before I granted him ultimate power over me."

Rosamund widened her eyes. "Why, you speak as if men are monsters, Tibby. I'm persuaded that is not the case."

"Some of them *are* monsters, Rosamund. You have led a very sheltered existence in many ways, so you might not be aware of the way a husband can—can quite simply *crush* a wife. Then, too, no one speaks of it, so it is not likely you would hear of such things unless they happened to one of your nearest and dearest. But I have known more than one young lady who entered marriage starry-eyed and came out of it *black*-eyed." Tibby shuddered. "And worse."

"Griffin would never hurt me," said Rosamund, shocked at the mere suggestion. She sensed the innate gentleness in him that so few others perceived when confronted with that massive exterior.

"Physical harm is only one of the terrors that may be inflicted on ladies by their husbands," said Tibby, snipping a vermilion thread with her scissors. "I won't say more on that head, but before you proceed with this wedding, ask yourself if you are prepared to put yourself entirely at this man's mercy. Do you trust him that far, my dear?"

"Why, of course." Rosamund picked up the other earbob and fiddled with the hook, frowning. "I can manage him, Tibby. I won't let him tyrannize over me. And I *know* I can make him comfortable."

"I am sure you can," said Tibby. "But what about you? Is he truly the man you want, above all others, *forsaking* all others?"

By *others*, she presumed Tibby meant Philip Lauderdale. "Yes. Quite sure."

The small noise Tibby made in response was a cross

between a choke and a snort. "You might well change your mind about that one day."

Rosamund looked sharply at her. "Do you speak of *love,* Tibby? Do you really? For I thought you would have learned by now that we Westruthers do not ever marry for love. I accepted my duty at the age of seventeen, and I will fulfill my duty now. I will be content with Lord Tregarth. I will make a happy home with him and if God blesses us with children, I shall love *them* and—and care for them with all of my heart and soul."

Even as she said these things, a large sob seemed to stick in the region of her throat. She battled to force it down. She'd rather die than weep and show Tibby that her concerns might be justified.

Confound Tibby for ruining it! She'd been waiting for this day all her life.

"I see," said the companion at length. "And what of Lord Tregarth? Doesn't he deserve love?"

Pain stabbed Rosamund's chest. What could she say to that?

"How will you feel if he finds love with someone else?" pursued Tibby. "Such things happen, you know. More often than not in these arranged marriages, or so I'm told."

The thought of Griffin being unfaithful had simply never entered into Rosamund's visions of wedded bliss. *Why* hadn't it? As Tibby said, infidelity was more common than not among their set. Her own parents . . .

She shivered as a cold, cruel hand closed around her heart. The sob in her throat built and built.

Lifting her chin, she said, "I shall see to it that he doesn't stray."

She didn't need to see Tibby's skeptical look to know it was there.

Rosamund swallowed hard past the sob that threatened to burst from her at any moment. "Now," she said in a strained, brittle voice. "If you'll excuse me, I shall go to my bedchamber and finish getting ready."

Rosamund barely closed the door on the hired parlor before she burst into tears.

All that morning, Rosamund tried to resist, but it was like digging in her heels in the middle of a landslide. No use at all.

She couldn't deny the truth any longer. She was hopelessly in love with Griffin deVere.

She was in love with her husband.

Rosamund moved through the short marriage ceremony shrouded in a mist of shock. Jacqueline was there, in high spirits and seeming well pleased with the event. She was accompanied by a handsome, dark gentleman she introduced as Mr. Maddox. Peggy and Joshua and their silent daughter were there also. And of course Tibby, who seemed to have abandoned her former objections and now beamed on the proceedings with a lace-edged handkerchief in hand and sentimental tears in her eyes.

The vicar seemed like a friendly, amusing fellow, and she was pleased to see clear evidence of his regard for Griffin. But she couldn't find anything to say to Mr. Oliphant that wasn't vague or embarrassingly banal. Her new discovery possessed her thoughts.

Griffin appeared striking in his elegant, well-fitting clothes, but that was not the reason she couldn't stop looking at him. In fact, a small part of her resented that his new dress and careful grooming made him seem less fearsome, yet infinitely more unapproachable. The same part of her wanted him back the way he used to be, with that wild, unkempt veneer only she could penetrate.

But that was a selfish, unworthy impulse, one she quickly quashed.

If people saw Griffin as she always had, they might be better disposed to treat him with courtesy. Even in the short time she'd been in Cornwall, she'd been shocked at how the locals viewed him. That poor maid in the inn had nearly dropped the tea tray, she was shaking so hard.

When the vicar grinned broadly and urged him to kiss his bride, Griffin didn't hesitate. But it was a swift, chaste kiss, cognizant of their situation. His lips rested on hers, warmed them for a fleeting instant, and were gone. In that moment when their lips pressed together, Rosamund felt as if her love rushed upward to greet him. How foolishly sentimental!

She gazed up into his face. For the first time since she'd known him, Griffin seemed happy.

The smile she offered him in return was a forced one. She wished she could recapture her own joy in wedding him. That had been overtaken by a sense of utter despair.

What was the point of that? she chastised herself. Why realize *now* how greatly she endangered her own peace with this union? All she'd wanted was to create a stable, contented family to make up for the one she'd never had.

Yet how could she bear to live with him in a cold marriage of convenience? How could she have been so stupid not to realize before?

Of course, he'd shown her quite unequivocally that it would not be a cold marriage. But wouldn't such hot passion make it worse when she knew that despite it, he didn't love her? She'd seen too many men leave her mother without a backward glance to believe that passion was the same as love. Her mind knew that, even if her heart had a difficult time acknowledging it.

She raised her hand to finger her locket. In the past, the gesture had been a comfort, the locket a kind of talisman. Now it was a grim reminder of the enduring hopelessness of her love.

In no time, Rosamund had kissed Tibby, handed her pretty bouquet to Jacqueline, received the others' congratulations and good wishes, and driven off in Griffin's rattling old landau.

Griffin sat opposite her, his long legs stretched out in front of him. "That's a very fetching bonnet you're wearing, my dear," he said. "Take it off and come here."

Her eyes widened. "What, you mean *here*?"

"There is no harm in taking off your bonnet, is there?" inquired Griffin innocently. "Is it a crime to wish to look upon my wife's face without obstruction?"

"You know very well what I mean," said Rosamund with a laugh in her voice. But she tugged on the ribbon of her bonnet and lifted the confection from her head. Laying it aside, she rose to cross the carriage.

As she did so, his boot hooked behind her ankle, toppling her off balance so that she all but sprawled over him. He caught her, and silenced her cry of surprise with the ravenous drag of his mouth over hers. He held her and kissed her until the impropriety of her situation faded from her mind.

His hand found the backs of her thighs, and he lifted her to sit sideways across his lap while he continued to kiss his way down her neck.

The decadence of such behavior made her hot and feverish and ashamed at once, but she didn't want him to stop.

Forceful and demanding as he was, the tenderness inside her grew. She put up her hand to caress his thick black hair. Shorter now than when she'd done this last. She was surprised to find she missed the luxuriant length, the bushy texture of it.

Had it been only last night that she'd given herself to him? She seemed to have existed another lifetime since then.

The carriage halted, bringing Rosamund to her senses.

She sat up, scrambling to her own seat and diving for her bonnet, which had fallen to the floor during their frenzy.

The footman seemed a little slow in opening the door. She'd just retied her bonnet ribbons when Diccon appeared and let down the steps.

He shook his head. "Sorry, my lady. I shouted at the coachman to take you around to the front door, but he's deaf and, I fear, bent on having his own way."

Rosamund emerged from the dimness of the carriage to find they stood in the midst of the stable yard, where she'd first met Griffin those years ago.

She laughed. "No, no, Diccon. It is quite all right. Perfect, in fact."

Still smiling, she turned to Griffin as he emerged from the carriage. "The scene of our infamous first meeting, my lord. How rude you were."

He glanced down at her. "Pot calling the kettle black, my dear. You ordered me about like a groom, if I recall."

She sniffed. "That was to teach you a lesson. Anyway, you certainly *looked* like a groom." She felt a distinct pang when she glanced at his smooth elegance—perhaps a touch more disheveled now, after their tussle in the carriage.

"Do you want to see what I was doing that day?" he asked.

Curious, she nodded.

He jerked his head. "Come on."

He led her to an open pasture, where a gleaming black mare grazed.

"Oh, she's a beauty," said Rosamund. "What's her name?"

She glanced at Griffin. He was looking not at the horse, but at her. Then he seemed to snap out of his abstraction.

With a slight quiver to his voice, he said, "Her name is Black Rosie."

Surprise made her start and blurt out a laugh. "You named her for me?"

He nodded, his eyes dancing. "You and those black looks you gave me."

"Black looks? Did I really?" She blinked. "That was out of character."

"I liked it," said Griffin. "There aren't too many women who would stand up to me."

He leaned his elbows on the fence and clasped his hands together. "The filly was born a day or so before you came, but the mother died. I'd been struggling to get another mare to suckle her when my grandfather sent word of your arrival." He shrugged. "I couldn't leave her."

"Of course you couldn't." Rosamund shook her head in disbelief at her own behavior that day. "You must have thought me spoiled and juvenile."

He laughed, then shook his head. He turned to her, and the laughter lit his eyes as she'd never witnessed before. "I thought you . . . enchanting. Magical. Like a fairy-tale princess, far above the likes of me."

He drew closer, his gaze intent on her lips. Rosamund lifted her face to his.

Her soul shuddered as their lips met. They'd kissed many times, but those kisses had never been like this. So tentative, so sweet, so utterly new.

Gently drawing out her response, he cradled her face in his hands as if he held a precious gift. Their lips clung and brushed and sipped in a kiss that was almost innocent in its chaste restraint, filled with emotion and promise.

The tenderness of it nearly broke her heart.

Griffin raised his head and looked into her eyes. She saw pain reflected in his gaze. How could that be?

"Rosamund, I—" He started to speak when the mare, who had crept up on them unnoticed, gave him a forceful butt in the shoulder. "Hey, there!" He turned to rub his hand over the white blaze on the mare's nose. "Not so rough, sweetheart."

"She is jealous!" Rosamund laughed.

Stripping off her gloves, Rosamund joined him in fussing over the handsome steed. After a few minutes, gathering that no lump of sugar or apple was to be had, the mare loped off to lip at grass, her long tail swishing.

Griffin glanced up at the sky. "So. We are married."

"Yes," she said, with a shaky laugh. "Yes, we are."

"What would you like to do now?" He gestured around him. "I could give you a tour of the grounds."

She tilted her head and gazed at him from beneath her lashes. "Perhaps tomorrow. That would be pleasant."

"I could ask Peggy to show you the house," he said.

She'd seen quite enough of the house to know she was in no mood for that depressing excursion. "Thank you, but I am sure that can wait."

"Hmm," he said, tapping his chin. "We could go for a ride down to the sea."

At any other time, she would have jumped at that prospect. Now, she murmured, "I thought you said there weren't any horses fit for me to ride here."

"I only said that to be disagreeable," said Griffin.

"Aha, so you admit you were rude that day." She grinned up at him. "We make progress!"

He reached for her. "Listen, wife, if I have any more of your lip, I'll . . ."

Rosamund blinked up at him innocently. "You'll what?"

He exhaled an unsteady breath and brought his mouth within inches of hers.

Then he stopped and grabbed her hand. "Come on."

CHAPTER EIGHTEEN

The horse barn was sweet with the scent of clean hay. At the moment it stood empty, and Rosamund wondered why Griffin had brought her here.

She wasn't left in doubt for long.

He pushed her back into a bed of straw and swiftly followed to kneel down, straddling her legs.

Her heart raced and her breath came in rapid pants as he loomed over her. His eyes had lost their lurking humor as his gaze fixed on her mouth. Now his face was set with intent. He planted his hands on either side of her head and bent to kiss her.

He made her mindless with that kiss. She smoothed her hands over the fine broadcloth that encased his shoulders. Despite the thickness of his clothing, she felt his muscles shift beneath.

Stroking her tongue with his, he gathered up the muslin of her gown, shift, and petticoats until her legs were exposed to the air.

She had on stockings, of course, and she gasped as his finger traced the bare flesh above the garter that anchored them. He looked down as he fondled her, and the hunger on his face made her flush all over.

He spread her legs and changed his position to kneel between them, then set his fingers to her soft, sensitive flesh. He made her wild with his touch until she whimpered and begged. When it came, her release was swift and strong.

He moved up, over her once more. Resting on his elbow, he looked down into her face. "If you need me to stop, say so," he said. "You are probably still tender from last night."

She shook her head. She'd bear that pain gladly to return the bliss that he'd given her. But in the event, there was no pain. Only the odd and wonderful sensation of the inner walls of her body shifting to accept him, gripping the hard length of him as he eased deeper and deeper. With a guttural groan, he thrust all the way inside her.

He stopped, and she opened her eyes to see that his face bore marks of strain. Did it hurt him to hold himself in check?

"I am all right," she breathed. "It is lovely. There's no need to stop."

With his eyes squeezed shut, he stroked slowly, oh so slowly, in and out of her body.

Rosamund tried to move with him, but he held her in place, exactly where he wanted her, taking her as he wished, and it was strangely freeing to simply lie there and feel.

She'd expected more of that tearing pain in the place where they joined, but other than a slight burn when he'd first entered her, there was none.

She *hadn't* expected the sensations that now built in her body. They were distant yet, like an echo of the pleasure he'd already orchestrated within her. An echo that built and built, stronger and louder as he moved inside her.

Griffin slid his hand beneath her thigh, lifting it so that it hugged his waist. His buttocks flexed beneath her heel as he drove into her, and the change in angle took him deeper, striking a triumphal chord of bliss that resonated throughout her body.

Desperation made her whimper. She didn't know what she wanted or what to expect, but this steady, smooth slide of his body into hers drove her mad with longing for *something*.

"Rosamund," gasped Griffin. He demanded something of her, but she wasn't sure what she was supposed to do.

And then he pushed her leg even higher, pistoning into her with deep, hard thrusts, hitting something on the way that took her pleasure up another notch. Her body went taut as a violin string; her heart seemed to split open with sweetness. She convulsed around him. Ripples and shudders dragged her through wave after wave of bliss.

He remained hard inside her while the crescendo eventually died to a gentle harmony of aching tenderness and subtle sensation.

Her eyes fluttered open to see that his grim, almost pained expression had become fierce with triumph. She was so limp with satisfaction, she couldn't speak. But something in that smug look made her decide that next time she would not lie so passive in his arms.

For now, she would simply enjoy.

Griffin's release came with great, heaving shudders that racked his body and left him gasping for air. He rolled off her, his big chest heaving. Rosamund lay there in the midst of the soft, sweet-smelling hay, smiling and replete, as boneless as if she herself were made of straw.

After a moment, she saw that Griffin watched her with a hint of expectation in his eyes. She wondered if she was supposed to tell him what a wonderful lover he was. That felt awkward and forced. Besides, his smug expression told her he didn't need any reassurance on that point.

Instead, she said, "You are vastly pleased with yourself."

He tilted his head as he thought about it. "Yes," he said. "I do believe I am."

She laughed. "I am very pleased with you, too."

His expression was so open and unguarded that her heart turned over with longing. She leaned over to kiss him.

Then he said, "We'd best go into the house." He grinned and reached over to pluck a piece of straw from her hair. "With any luck, we'll make it to a bed next time."

In the following weeks, their nights were filled with sensual exploration, but Rosamund rarely saw Griffin throughout the day. He had much in the way of business to attend to around the estate.

Rosamund occupied herself with setting the house to rights, a gargantuan task, far too great for three women to tackle. She'd discovered that while the estate workers largely remained, Griffin had dismissed half the household staff after his grandfather died. The other half had left of their own accord over the business of Mr. Allbright. They might serve him in the stables or on the land, but no one wanted to sleep in the same house with such a monster as Griffin deVere.

"What nonsense!" she said to Jacqueline as they walked in the village. "I cannot abide such narrow-minded prejudice."

"Best keep your voice down, Rosie," murmured Jacqueline. "There goes Mrs. Simpkins. She's a neighbor of our friend Mr. Maddox, and the biggest gossip in the county."

"Really?" Rosamund's interest sparked. "My dear, come with me. I have an idea."

She took Jacqueline's arm, and they followed Mrs. Simpkins into the haberdasher's shop. This excellent establishment sold all manner of materials, buttons, ribbons, and threads. Rosamund had already patronized the shop on numerous occasions, and she smiled and nodded to Mrs. Thorne as she walked in.

Aware that the two other occupants of the shop were well within earshot, Rosamund spoke in a clear, carrying voice. "Yes, my dear Jacqueline, I'm afraid it will simply have to be London servants. A vast pity, but there is no help for it. Apart from a couple of daily maids I lured from the inn, there is no staff to be had in these parts."

Fortunately the girl took the lead quickly. "Very true, dear sister," said Jacqueline. "I think you must be right."

"I shall have to pay them double wages for coming so far, of course," said Rosamund. She made a little moue. "I detest the idea of London servants in the country. They are never content, and the locals do not like it."

"All of those handsome footmen making off with their pretty daughters, I expect," said Jacqueline, adding her mite.

"Oh, yes! And their odious way of looking down their noses at good, plain country folk," agreed Rosamund. She sighed. "I daresay I'd be prepared to pay double wages just to have some competent, honest local staff. But there's nothing for it; I must employ a London agency, no matter how distasteful I might find it. Pendon Place will not run itself."

With delight, Rosamund heard various gasps and mutters between the haberdasher and the county's greatest gossip. With any luck, she'd have a fully staffed house by the end of the week.

Rosamund picked up a length of raspberry-colored ribbon and held it flat on her palm. "Isn't this pretty? Too dark for me, perhaps, but not out of the question for you." She held the ribbon against Jacqueline's skin. "Hmm. It would look better if your skin were fair." She picked up a pale blue one. That brought out her sister-in-law's eyes and complemented her skin tone better.

"I don't see that it matters which color I choose," said Jacqueline, always impatient with what she termed *frippery and folderol*.

"I'll pretend I didn't hear you say that," said Rosamund calmly. "It would be far better for you, my dear Jacqueline, to stop fretting and fuming and *apply* yourself to the business. So many things become more enjoyable when you expend some effort on them."

Jacqueline slumped her shoulders, and her voice took on a tone that was a cross between self-deprecating laughter and a pained whine. "But I *loathe* dancing, Rosie dearest! You have no idea how much I detest it. I am all left feet—like a drunk giraffe, Griffin says. Poor Dearlove tries and tries to teach me, but it's no use. He tore his hair out the other day. Literally! I shall be solely responsible for turning the poor man bald."

"That won't do at all," said Rosamund. "What a pity my cousin Lydgate isn't here. He is an excellent dancer and a patient teacher, too."

She'd written to her family with her news, provoking a flurry of letters in return, filled with underlinings and exclamation points in Cecily's case and with restrained applause from the Duke of Montford.

Xavier, however, did not write at all.

She had asked them not to visit her until she set the house to rights. She, Jacqueline, and Griffin would no doubt return to London while the major work was carried out.

It could not be soon enough for her. She sighed. Surely Griffin must finish his estate business soon. Jacqueline was as ready for her debut as she was likely to be if she were not to miss the season altogether. Rosamund was eager to see her family again and share her happiness with them. Concern about Xavier's silence needled at the back of her mind, but she tried her best to ignore it. Most of the time, she succeeded.

Despite Jacqueline's restive demeanor, Rosamund took her time choosing all manner of laces, silks, ribbons, and floss. She couldn't imagine what she'd do with them all, as they were vastly inferior in quality to London wares, but that was beside the point.

She spent lavishly in the shop in the hope of ingratiating herself with its owner. As she paid for her purchases with coins, she wished she'd thought to bring Diccon with her to carry her parcels. Instead, she directed Mrs. Thorne to deliver them to Pendon Place.

The way Mrs. Thorne's round face had shone when Rosamund handed over coins rather than racking up the purchases on account gave Rosamund an idea. She followed that same practice over the next week or so, until she'd amassed all sorts of odd purchases.

"Would you care to explain to me why I now own no fewer than thirty monogrammed handkerchiefs?" Griffin asked.

"A lady in the village embroiders them," said Rosamund.

"Oh." He rubbed his chin. Then he shook his head. "No, that makes no sense to me."

She knew it would anger him if she told him she was trying to restore his standing with the locals, so she said, "An eccentric habit of mine. Why buy three when you can purchase thirty?"

With a kiss on his brow, she left him before he could question her further.

Tomorrow, she was due to interview a legion of potential servants. Hopefully, Griffin would be out of the way while she did so, but she couldn't help feeling on tenterhooks about it.

She would need to have Griffin's consent to doubling the wages, of course. It was unfortunate, but necessary, and it wasn't as if they couldn't afford it.

Some things were worth a premium, weren't they?

Somehow, she doubted Griffin would see it that way. However, she'd learned very early in their marriage that she would find him more malleable in the morning when he woke after a night of pleasure with her.

Yes, tomorrow morning it would have to be. For one thing, she did not think she could live in this house a week longer under such conditions. Besides the fact that Peggy and her family were neither skilled nor particularly hard-working, it wasn't fair to put the burden of a house the size of Pendon Place upon them.

Well, she would do her utmost to make Griffin so sated and happy that he'd deny her nothing. He might not admit it now, but he'd be so much more comfortable in a well-run home. And she would be that much closer to achieving her lifelong dream.

Briefly, she placed a hand over her flat stomach. Yet another reason to seduce Griffin thoroughly and often. She wanted a baby. Her arms ached with longing for a small bundle of soft skin and gummy smiles to call her own.

A grand, well-run house, content workers and tenants, cordial neighbors, and the light and color and diversion of London each spring. Children in the nursery, happy, healthy, and rambunctious. A husband who treated her with the gentleness and respect she demanded and fulfilled her physical needs with a passion and skill she'd never thought to ask for.

All those things were now within her grasp.

If only . . . oh, if only they were enough.

CHAPTER NINETEEN

Griffin couldn't find Rosamund anywhere. He'd searched all over the bloody inconvenient pile that was his inheritance, without success.

He often toyed with the idea of leaving Cornwall altogether and setting up residence on his Lincolnshire estate, but of course, that wasn't possible. Though he hated his grandfather and everything the old man stood for, duty was bred into Griffin's bones. Pendon Place had been his family's principal seat for centuries. He would not be the one to break with tradition. There was the estate to be run, and besides, he was stubborn enough to stay despite the swell of public opinion against him.

Music floating down the corridor alerted him to Rosamund's possible whereabouts. The old music room. Lord, he hadn't visited there in years.

Rosamund must have had the pianoforte tuned because the waltz she conjured from the instrument was pitch-perfect. Griffin loved music, but as neither he nor his siblings could play well and no one invited him anywhere, he'd not heard the pianoforte for a very long time.

Perhaps the last time was when his mother had played and sang for them when their nurse brought them down from the nursery for tea. An ache formed in his chest as it always did at the thought of her.

How foreign and tragic he would have thought it then to be without music for years on end. But at that time, he could not conceive of being without his mama, either.

Pushing those thoughts away, he stepped into the music room.

And caught sight of Jacks in a man's embrace.

"What the Hell are you doing with your hands on my sister?" he roared.

The music stopped. Jacks and Maddox turned their heads to stare.

Maddox lifted a brow. "Getting my feet trodden on, mostly. If you object, I'd be more than happy to hand the task over to you."

"I wish you would," said Jacks, dropping her hand from his shoulder with a huff. "Griffin wouldn't complain half as much." She tilted her head to survey her waltzing partner. "You're as cross as crabs today, Tony. What the Devil is wrong with you?"

"Not the Devil, Jacqueline, please." Unhurriedly, Rosamund got up from the pianoforte stool and came toward Griffin, holding out her hand. "My dear, your ire is unnecessary. My presence makes it all entirely proper. Your sister *must* master various patterns of dancing before she has her season. If she doesn't learn now, only imagine how excruciating it will be for her in a ballroom."

"Only imagine how excruciating for her poor partners' feet," murmured Maddox. He turned his attention to Griffin. "What is this nonsense about a season, Tregarth? Trying to steal a march on me, hmm?"

"I don't need to take you at a disadvantage, Maddox," said Griffin. "Your chances are absolute zero, in any case."

"What on earth are you talking about?" Jacks demanded.

Maddox glanced at her. "I'll explain it to you another time."

"There isn't going to be another time," Griffin said through gritted teeth. "Stay away from her."

"Or what?" said Maddox coolly. "You'll throw me off a cliff?"

Jacks gasped. A shocked silence fell over the room.

"Mr. Maddox, that was uncalled for," said Rosamund quietly. "I think you ought to leave us."

Was it his imagination or did Maddox's arrogance dim a little in the face of Rosamund's reproach?

"Tony!" Jacks said in a low, trembling voice. "Did you mean that? Do you mean to imply that *Griffin* . . ." She choked and sent an imploring glance Griffin's way.

Ever so slightly, Griffin shook his head at her.

Maddox held Griffin's eyes for a long moment. Then he said, "No, of course I do not. Do you think I'd darken his door if I thought that of him? Allbright was my cousin, after all." Stiffly, he added, "I beg your pardon, Tregarth."

Tears started to his sister's eyes. She cast a stricken look at Maddox. Griffin could not bear to see his gangly, cheerful sister seem so small and unhappy. He'd hoped that period of their lives was over, and now here was Maddox stirring the coals.

It would never be over, he realized now, not if she stayed in Cornwall. He needed to get Jacks away from here if she were to have any kind of normality to her life.

He addressed Maddox. "You heard my lady. Get out of here. Now."

"Griffin," said Rosamund in a placating tone. She fluttered a graceful hand toward Maddox. "Mr. Maddox apologized. Let us not alienate the few friends we do have."

Fury and fear twisted inside him. He knew he sounded unreasonable to her, but he had to get Maddox away from Jacks.

"I accept your apology," he told Maddox. "But I repeat what I said: Stay the Hell away from my sister!"

Jacks was crying in earnest now. "You can't stop me seeing Tony! He's my best—my only friend!"

"We are leaving for London tomorrow, so you'll have no opportunity to see him in any event," Griffin ground out. Lord, didn't she see the dangers? Why should he have to spell it out to her?

Maddox went to her and with one finger, tilted her chin. "There, now," he said softly, but with a dangerous note in his voice. "All this unpleasantness has made you cry, and you know that is not allowed."

He took out his handkerchief and carefully wiped the tears away.

Griffin would have objected to this if he hadn't seen a look on Maddox's face that . . . Oh, the Devil! This was getting more complicated than he could stand!

He glanced at Rosamund and saw surprise and consternation in her expression. She must have seen that fleeting, tender look, too.

"Well, it seems that is settled," said Rosamund. "Mr. Maddox, if you'll excuse us, there is much to do if we are to leave here at once."

"Of course." With a bow and a half smile for Jacks, he took his leave.

Jacks stared at Griffin with accusing eyes. "Why would you treat him so?" she demanded. "He is a friend, not one of those county people who shunned us when we were in trouble but now beat down our door because you've married a well-connected heiress. He was loyal to us from beginning to end!"

"Witness his earlier remark," said Griffin.

"He didn't mean that, and you know it," she said. "Griffin, it has been hard enough here after Mr. Allbright. Why would you take away the one true friend I have left?"

Because he wants more than friendship, you innocent little goose. Because it is dangerous for you to be with him.

Griffin folded his arms. "If you don't know the answer to that question, you're a fool."

"No, Griffin! It is you who are a fool. It is true what they say of you. You *are* a brute and a beast, and I hate you!"

Her voice cracking on the last words, Jacks fled the music room.

The music room fell silent with Jacqueline's departure, but the atmosphere still throbbed with the emotions that had played out there.

"Tell me about Mr. Maddox," invited Rosamund.

Griffin huffed a sigh. "There is no way Jacks will be permitted to marry him. Lord deVere, her guardian, has a list of possible suitors to choose from, and I can tell you it was hard work getting him to agree to that. If he had his way, he'd marry her off to Lord Malby."

Rosamund gasped. "Malby! That old lecher?"

"Aye, that's the one. Friend of my grandfather's. There was a longstanding arrangement."

This was all very troubling. Rosamund had observed Jacks and Maddox as they squabbled amiably over the dancing, trading quips and friendly insults. While Jacqueline displayed none of the self-conscious fluttering girls ordinarily engaged in when they fancied themselves in the throes of a grand *amour,* it seemed to Rosamund that the girl might very well love Maddox but simply didn't know it yet.

And there was a distinct look in *his* eyes. . . .

"But if they are in love," she said, "you ought not to separate them. It would be cruel."

He snorted. "Love? Jacks isn't in love. She's not at all missish, you know."

"That is abundantly clear," said Rosamund with a roll of her eyes. "I have had less success with her than I had hoped. But then the truth is I haven't tried very hard." She sighed. "I like her so very well just as she is."

She paused, then licked her lips, a frown furrowing her brow. "I think Maddox does, too. In fact, I believe that whatever her feelings might be, *he* is in love with *her*."

"Well, he can forget about marrying her," said Griffin.

"Is his birth not respectable?" Rosamund asked.

"Oh, it's more than respectable. Junior branch of a very old family, the Maddoxes."

"But not grand enough for the sister of an earl, I take it?" said Rosamund.

Why did the arrangements in place for Jacqueline make her at once so uneasy and . . . and angry, too? It was no different from her own situation. In fact, far more generous, because Jacqueline would have her pick amongst a number of eligible suitors.

Was it because *she* was in love that she wanted the same for everyone else around her?

"Jacqueline would be happy with Maddox, Griffin, I am sure of it."

"No! Can't you see how impossible it is?" He dragged a hand through his hair.

"Frankly, I can't. If you would only stand up to deVere—"

"It's not deVere," he said loudly. "*I* do not want her to marry Maddox!"

"But why?" said Rosamund. "You said yourself he is of good family and he clearly doesn't need her fortune. And she would be near us, Griffin. Don't you think that would be a wonderful thing for us all?"

"No, I don't! I want her as far away from here as possible."

She gasped. "So Jacqueline was right. You did send her to Bath to be rid of her."

"Damned right I did."

"And now you want to ruin her life by marrying her to one man when she is more than half in love with another! And he wholly in love with her! It is too cruel, Griffin."

He laughed. "Cruel, is it? Was it cruel of them to marry you to me?"

Her anger arrested, she said, "That was entirely different."

I loved you from the first, you thickheaded beast!

"Was it really?" purred Griffin, showing his teeth. He looked like a well-groomed bear now that Dearlove had taken him in hand, but the wildness was still caged inside that well-dressed form.

He said, "From the moment of your birth, you were taught to believe you had no other choice but to marry the man chosen for you. Even at eighteen, when any other girl might dream of a handsome prince to sweep her away, *you* accepted your duty to marry an ogre without a qualm. Vastly unpleasant though the thought must have been."

"If I had taken you in dislike, the duke would not have forced me to marry you," said Rosamund, striving for calm. She hated the groundless self-loathing that made him talk this way. She'd hoped to put a stop to that by lavishing physical affection upon him. It appeared she'd failed.

He used his forefinger to tip up her chin so she looked him in the eye. "But Montford would never have let you have your handsome soldier, would he?" Griffin said softly, his voice sounding like the crunch of gravel underfoot. "There's no need to deny it. Your high color betrays you, my dear."

She'd flushed with wrath, not guilt, but he clearly chose

to interpret her blushes in the harshest light. "You are offensive, sir." She jerked her head away from his hand.

He raised his eyebrows in cool skepticism, but his gray
eyes sparked with anger and his big body tensed as if he'd
spring. "The truth is so often offensive, don't you find?"

"You have no idea of the *truth*," snapped Rosamund.
"You make it up as you go along. There is no cause for you
to be jealous, my lord. I am sure I have never given you
one."

"I'm not jealous!"

"Yes! You *are* jealous or you wouldn't be so angry for
so little cause. I would never willingly do anything to injure you, or hurt you. Captain Lauderdale is nothing to
me. I don't care if I never see him again. Does that satisfy
you?"

His gaze dropped to the locket that hung about her
neck, the one she so often wore. She realized she'd been
fingering it again.

"I remember that locket," he said. "You had it on when
we first met. You wear it always." He took a deep, ragged
breath. "Show me what is inside."

She froze. It was *his* face in the locket, but she'd rather
die than admit she carried him with her like some foolish, love-struck chit. She might tell him one day, but he
didn't deserve such a confidence now. Not when he accused her of deceit.

"No," she said. "I am not going to show you."

The blaze of ire that crossed his face made her take a
hurried step back.

He wouldn't hurt her. She knew he wouldn't. But her
blood heated and pounded through her veins. She couldn't
let him see.

He advanced on her and she retreated, her hand laid
protectively over the locket.

Griffin's scowl deepened, if that were possible. "As your husband, I command you to show that thing to me."

She licked her lips. "No. It is not a keepsake from Lauderdale—of that, you may rest assured."

"Then why don't you want me to see it?"

"It's private," she said, halting as her back finally pressed against the wall. She lifted her chin. "I demand that you respect my wishes, Griffin. No true gentleman would do otherwise."

At her last words, his ferocity intensified. He lunged and made a grab for both her and the necklace. His arm lashed around her waist. His hand came up to grip the locket and tug.

She gave a shrill cry as the chain broke and the locket came away in his big hand.

"You brute!" She wished she knew a worse name to call him, for she'd never been so furious in her life as she was now. So angry, in fact, that she thought she might explode with it.

Before Griffin could step back and open the locket, she brought up her open hand and dealt him a ringing slap on the face.

The locket dropped to the floor with a dull thud. Griffin didn't even look to see where it went. Instead, he yanked her to him and kissed her, open-mouthed and hard.

She fought him at first, pummeling at his shoulders with her fists and stomping on his foot. But her fists made less impression on him than the beat of butterflies' wings might have done, and her feet were clad only in flimsy slippers. Still kissing her, he caught her flailing hands in his and pinned them to the wall on either side of her head.

Raising his head, he looked deep into her eyes for wordless seconds. In those moments, she saw all the pain he tried to hide. She saw hunger there, too, and hopeless longing. It was the expression of a starving man peering through a window at a feast he knew he could never eat.

Understanding hit her. Tenderness flooded her, tangling with her fury and hurt. They were all bound together inside her, like a living thing straining for expression. With an anguished little cry, Rosamund kissed him, fervently, sweetly, savagely.

Despite her understanding, anger still rode close to the surface. She gave it free rein and sank her teeth into his lower lip.

He groaned, a sound expressive of the deepest carnal pleasure that resonated down to her bones.

Like the flip of a coin, her ambivalence switched to pure, raging desire. She licked the injured lip, then tangled her tongue with his, gave back everything he dealt her. He still held her hands captive, and the feeling of being trapped, subject to the will of this big, strong man seemed to heighten her need.

The roughness of his jaw abraded her cheek as he trailed kisses away from her mouth and down her throat. Without warning, he bit her in the place where her neck met her shoulder. Spasms of the most exquisite mix of pleasure and pain scintillated down her body. She felt the place between her legs heat and moisten. Shamelessly, she rubbed herself against him.

He fumbled with his breeches, then lifted her so that her back was flat against the wall and they were at eye level. In one shocking, deep thrust, he was inside her, sheathed to the hilt, staring with those fierce, storm-cloud eyes into hers.

"Oh, God," she moaned.

He gripped her thighs and she wrapped her legs around him as he withdrew and surged up, into her, filling her, stretching her, stroking those intimate parts of her that he knew brought her the greatest pleasure.

They'd made love many times, but *this,* this was urgent and lusty and violent and raw. Their mutual anger had ignited a passion that caught them both up in its flames.

She sensed when the first flush of his ire faded. His lovemaking grew slower and more deliberate. He moved only the smallest amount, pulsing higher inside her, touching deep inside her, over and over again.

Ah, this was torture of the best and worst kind.

"Harder," she whispered in his ear, and he gasped and shook his head.

He didn't want to hurt her, but she knew what she wanted and it was him, all him, going harder and higher inside her. Experimentally, she licked his earlobe, then scraped it with her teeth.

He sucked in a breath and lost control, pounding up into her until she climaxed in a glorious conflagration of heat and light. She kissed him wantonly, communicating all her raw, elemental passion to him. In moments, his body arched and stiffened. With a primal cry of triumph and release, his body erupted into hers.

With an inward oath, Griffin relaxed his hold on Rosamund and slowly set her on her feet. While he adjusted his breeches, she slid down the wall a little way, watching him with glazed eyes, parted, bruised lips, and cheeks that were now flushed with neither guilt nor anger, but passion.

What the Hell had he been thinking, flying into a rage over Lauderdale? He knew she'd parted from the captain without a backward glance. If she had private longings for the man, she could hardly help that, could she? The marriage of the Earl and Countess of Tregarth had not been a love match. He had no right to demand her heart as well as her fidelity. And if she didn't act upon whatever feelings she might harbor for the captain, Griffin had no cause for complaint.

And yet, such reasoning seemed more than a little specious. While his mind knew he had no cause for such rage, pure reason could not cure him of this insanity. His was a damnably possessive nature. He wanted her—*needed* her—to think only of him.

All right, he was jealous! He admitted it. But that was his problem, not hers. He must keep telling himself that. Love had never been a part of their bargain. He couldn't command her to wrench Lauderdale out of her heart.

"I'm sorry," he said gruffly. "I don't know what came over me."

The hazy look vanished, and she glared at him. "If you dare apologize for taking me like that—"

"Oh, no, not for *that*," he said. "In fact, I fully intend to pick more fights with you so we can do *that* all over again." His gaze warmed as he looked at her. "Or some variation of it."

Her color heightened even further. Those bluer-than-blue eyes burned with desire. And with curiosity.

"You want to know what else I might do if roused to a temper?" he murmured. He tapped his chin with his finger, running his gaze over her in a leisurely fashion. "Hmm, let me think."

He paused as if to ponder the question, as if he hadn't already imagined every conceivable permutation of lovemaking in his many fantasies about her.

She licked her full, pink lips, and his mouth abruptly went dry. No, *that* was not a fantasy he would share with her. Not yet, anyway.

"Well?" she breathed. She still hadn't moved from where she stood, all but plastered against the wall.

Grinning, he said, "You'll just have to wait and see."

That made her brows twitch together and her lower lip stick out.

His grin grew wider. "You look like a sulky angel who wasn't allowed back in Heaven."

She laughed. "After what we just did, I shouldn't be at all surprised."

He bent to pick up her locket and, without hesitation, held it out to her. She took it, but their rapprochement didn't prompt her to show him what was inside it.

"I'll have the chain repaired," he said gruffly.

"That's quite all right," she said. "I'll attend to it. I have quite a knack with jewelry." The locket disappeared into the folds of her gown, where she must have had an inner pocket.

"Griffin?" she said.

"Yes?"

"I told you the truth about Lauderdale, you know. I never loved him. I don't love him now. I have not even thought of him since I saw him last."

Perhaps she believed the truth of that statement. It was too soon for him to tell what it meant that she believed it. Was it fact, or did she simply deny her feelings for Lauderdale because the truth did not fit with her design for a perfect marriage?

Ah, but he was thinking too much. He ought to be happy that she was wholly committed to him and to their union, to building a family together. A sudden vision of a golden-haired little girl made him catch his breath with fear and awe.

He touched Rosamund's cheek and bent to kiss her lips. "I am sorry for my outburst. It will not happen again."

"You are forgiven," she said, looking up into his eyes. "Yes, I would be *very* happy never to speak of Lauderdale anymore. As for the rest . . . I am not afraid of your temper, Griffin. In fact, I find it strangely . . . exciting."

Well, that was novel. He raised an eyebrow. "You do, do you?"

She nodded. "My parents' arguments culminated with the marchioness throwing things. My father would turn into a positive icicle, then leave, sometimes for weeks at a time. For myself," she said, "I like a good, honest exchange."

The exchange had not been honest. Not entirely. But he let that pass. "Particularly if it culminates in such an interesting manner."

With a laugh, she peeled herself away from the wainscoting, and he helped her put her gown to rights. He gathered up several pins that had scattered over the floor in the course of their frenzy and handed them to her.

She took them, crossed to the pier glass above the mantel, and began pinning up those shining tresses. Swiping some pins from where she'd dropped them on the mantel, he set to work, too. He hindered her more than helped her with this, he knew, but he liked to feel that silky mass slipping through his fingers.

Rosamund shifted her gaze to his reflection behind her. "And what about Jacqueline?" she said. As if he might have changed his mind about it.

His mouth hardened. "We leave for London immediately."

CHAPTER TWENTY

I know that you didn't kill Allbright.

Griffin crumpled the short note in his hand, staring out his window at the terraced gardens beyond. They'd been wild and overgrown for the past year because there was no gardener to tend them and Griffin could not spare the time from the estate.

Now, an army of gardeners worked around the flower beds and the park, setting all to rights. Soon, the garden would be in full bloom, bursting with color. If it was not entirely restored to its former beauty, it would be close enough.

How had she done it?

He shook his head. Better not to ask. That same efficiency and ruthless charm had brought servants inside the house, too. Slowly, the place began to look more like a home and less like a musty mausoleum.

He'd rather be dead than admit he wanted them all there, even though he did. Best to remain oblivious and pretend he didn't know she'd offered them double wages to return.

Gingerly, he spread the short note open again and studied it.

Had he seen that script somewhere before?

Oh, he'd received quite a few anonymous letters of accusation when the business of Allbright became known, most of them only halfway literate. But these had grown rare as the people of his village found new gossip to interest them and new victims upon whom to vent their spleen.

The persistent rumor of a witness to Allbright's murder still hounded his thoughts. In his dreams, he saw himself dragged away in chains while Rosamund turned from him in disgust and shame.

He'd roused to feel Rosamund's delicate hands smoothing over his chest, touching his face. She'd murmured softly to him, the reassuring utterances a mother might give to a child tormented by nightmares.

He'd gathered her into his arms and loved her with fervent urgency, desperately seeking the kind of comfort only her warm, giving body could provide.

Afterwards, she had not asked him about the dreams. Perhaps she knew their subject very well from his mutters and moans.

A jolt of fear gripped him. Had he given away too much in the unguarded state of slumber?

But no. Not even Rosamund would remain understandingly silent if she knew the truth.

Making love to her had kept the demons at bay for a time, but for once, sleep refused to overtake him. He lay there with her head on his shoulder, her arm draped over his chest, her slender legs tangled with his.

In the predawn silence, he rhythmically stroked her hair and tried very hard not to think about losing this. Losing *her*.

No one could prove he'd murdered Allbright. But then,

his innocence hadn't turned out to be quite the shield he'd thought it would be, had it? He didn't trust the locals. Who was to say but that one of them might be malicious enough to perjure themselves and say they'd seen him kill Allbright?

It would almost be a relief if that were the intent behind starting that rumor of a witness. He'd no doubt that a good defense counsel would tear such a false witness's testimony to shreds, if the case ever got to court.

The other alternative was far too dire to contemplate.

Rosamund had drifted in and out of sleep while he fretted silently in the semidarkness. Now, she stirred awake with a deep sigh.

"Griffin?" She raised herself and looked down at him, her golden hair a pale curtain across his arm.

"Yes?"

"You are still awake?" She smiled a little. "That is not like you."

He splayed his hand over her back. "I am . . . restless, I admit."

"Is there anything I can do?" The words, spoken in that husky, low voice that seemed to be natural to her in the bedchamber, made his body stir.

"Let me see if I can relax you," she said.

He held his breath as she toyed with him idly, touching him with soft, gentle fingertips, kissing him lightly, caressing his flesh delicately with her tongue.

Relax him? He groaned. More like tease him to an early grave.

She must have interpreted his impatience correctly, for she moved then. Her naked breasts brushed his chest as she straddled him and bent to kiss his throat, while she kneaded the muscles of his shoulders and arms with her hands.

He hissed in a breath. Impossible to feel his cock

harden again so soon after the last time, but she excited him as no other woman ever had.

He ran his palm down the sleek slope of her back and up.

"No," she said, capturing his wrists and pushing them down. She pinned his hands beside his head and bent to kiss him again.

The kiss was open-mouthed, long and slow and lascivious. Her breasts pressed against him as she breathed the words over his mouth. "Lie back and enjoy."

A ragged groan was all he could manage in reply. There *was* enjoyment, and heat, and passion. There was also torment as this goddess-turned-mortal-woman kissed him and touched him, and all the while, her wet, tight sheath hovered there above his straining member, tantalizing him.

The mere thought aroused him to such a pitch that the urge to plunge into her became unbearable.

"Let me inside you," he breathed. "Ah, God, I can't take any more."

There was a pause. Then she sat up, straddling him with her hands braced on his rib cage. He felt her wetness rub against him and gasped out a plea.

She adjusted her position and grasped his erection, then guided it into her moist warmth. She sank down, down until he was hard and deep inside her.

He gripped her hips to steady her, but he let her set the rhythm this time. Rosamund was an adept student of the art of making love. She was inventive and sensual and surprisingly earthy sometimes, with that low, dirty laugh she gave that never failed to set his blood racing.

Now, as she moved, he reached up to touch her breasts, rubbing her nipples with his thumbs. She gasped and he gave her breasts a gentle squeeze.

"Harder," she panted, moving faster now, grinding down on him, arching her back. She was glorious, unashamed, taking her own pleasure as she pleasured him. He'd never seen anything more magnificent in his life.

"Show me how hard you want it." He found her hands and pressed them over those full, luscious globes.

She was too deep in the throes of passion to demur at his request. He didn't know if she would have, anyway. She continually surprised him with the lengths she would go to please both him and herself.

The sight of her playing with her own breasts made him even harder, if that was possible. He gripped her hips and drove up into her again and again, making her give an agonized moan of pleasure.

Suddenly, her hips jerked and her body shuddered and spasmed beneath his hands. He gritted his teeth and held on until he could bear it no longer. He arched and thrust and thrust again, deep into her, touching every part of her he could.

And in that transcendent moment before climax, he knew with a clarity that was beyond mere thought: He would die before he lost this woman.

The pliers pinched Rosamund's thumb viciously for the third time. "Confound it!" She snatched back her hand and stuck her throbbing thumb in her mouth.

"Oh, not *confound* it, Rosamund dear." Jacqueline, who had entered the sitting room in time to hear Rosamund make that unladylike exclamation, arched one black brow.

"Damn and blast, then," said Rosamund around her throbbing thumb. She gave the pad of her thumb a last, soothing suck and removed it to inspect the damage. No blood, but it was puckered and turning a light purplish color.

"How shocking you are!" said Jacqueline with a grin.

She moved to peer over Rosamund's shoulder. "What are you doing?"

"Fixing my locket," said Rosamund. "But I don't have my usual tools with me. Diccon found some pliers and they are almost the right size, but not quite, so bending the links back in shape has been a tricky business. This link really needs to be soldered, I suppose, but for the moment . . ."

She bent over her work again. "I think . . . I have it. Yes!" She sat back, beaming with satisfaction.

Then she looked up at her companion. "Are you prepared for the journey tomorrow?"

Despite Griffin's urgency, it had taken more than a week to make all ready for their departure. Rosamund had promoted Diccon to butler as a reward for risking his position and quite possibly his hide as well on more than one occasion on her or Cecily's behalf.

She had also hired a housekeeper, a most excellent woman. Mrs. Faithful was the former vicar's widow, who wished to run a household and be paid for it, rather than doing the same for her more affluent relatives in exchange for bed, board, and daily condescension.

Rosamund liked her on sight and hired her instantly. With the redoubtable Diccon and Mrs. Faithful in charge, she felt she could return to London confident that all would be well at Pendon Place in their absence.

She was not so confident of Jacqueline's state of mind. The girl had a way of covering her emotions with laughter and funning. As Rosamund came to know her better, however, she grew more and more convinced that the girl hid great pain beneath her jolly mien.

Was she in love with Anthony Maddox, after all?

Now, in answer to Rosamund's inquiry, Jacqueline said, "Oh, I expect so, yes. I mean, there's no use complaining, is there? And it's so boring to sulk for extended periods, don't you find?" She sighed gustily. "I suppose I shall simply have to participate in this farce."

"A splendid attitude!" Rosamund picked up the locket and chain and held them out to Jacqueline. "Help me with this, will you, my dear?"

She sat still while Jacqueline clasped the cool metal around her neck. The locket dropped to nestle happily in her décolletage, where it belonged. "Thank you."

Jacqueline sighed again and took a restless turn about the room. She was like a caged animal when the squalling rain made it impossible even for an intrepid horsewoman such as she to venture out. She didn't seem able to amuse herself for very long indoors.

"Why don't you sit with me awhile?" suggested Rosamund, picking up her embroidery. "We haven't even begun planning for your stay in London. There must be many things you would enjoy seeing. London is full of diversion and interest, not just parties and balls."

"I *should* like to visit the Tower of London," Jacqueline conceded, sitting down on the window seat and staring out at the rain.

"There is Astley's Amphitheatre, too," said Rosamund, casting about for things that might entertain her sister-in-law. "I haven't been there since I was a child, but the horsemanship of the equestrians is held to be something spectacular, indeed."

Jacqueline wrinkled her nose. "Horses are noble, sensitive beasts. They should not be groomed for show and made to perform tricks." With a sidelong look at Rosamund, she added, "Speaking of grooming, my brother is very nearly resplendent these days. What a change you've wrought in him, Rosamund."

Rosamund paused in her work. Could Jacqueline possibly mean to liken Griffin to the horses at Astley's?

"I believe Griffin likes his new clothes," she said mildly. "I am sure he would let us all know about it if he did not."

With a slight, skeptical smile, Jacqueline turned her head and stared out the window again, as if the topic of conversation was no longer of interest to her.

Needled and uncomfortably conscious that there might be some spark of truth in what Jacqueline implied, Rosamund changed the subject. "I hear Mr. Maddox prepares for a sojourn in Town."

"Do you, indeed? I wouldn't know. I am not allowed to see him, and he is foolish enough to insist on abiding by Griffin's wishes, even if I couldn't give a fig about them."

But Rosamund caught the light that entered Jacqueline's eyes at the mention of her so-called friend following them to London.

"I tried to persuade Griffin to relent, you know," said Rosamund. "But he is adamant. What does he have against Mr. Maddox courting you? Do you know? I thought they were friends."

"Courting me? Tony? Don't be ridiculous, Rosie." An inelegant snort of a laugh issued from Jacqueline over that. "Tony is not a marrying man."

Rosamund stared. Could Jacqueline truly be so innocent? So oblivious?

She bit her lip. If Griffin wanted Jacqueline to marry someone on this infamous list of suitors, it was not for Rosamund to put ideas into the girl's head about Mr. Anthony Maddox.

"Would you not like to be married, Jacqueline?" she asked, watching the girl closely.

Jacqueline's face froze, just for an instant. Then she said, "I never thought about it much until you came here." She laughed softly. "I barely remember my own mother. I am not at all sure what a wife is supposed to do." She tilted her head. "You must wonder why I never took charge of the household here, made it more habitable."

"The thought hadn't occurred to me," said Rosamund. And it hadn't. Why hadn't it? Perhaps because she'd been so full of her own plans for Pendon Place?

"I didn't do it because I preferred to take charge of the stables instead. Humans can live with a bit of dust. Horses cannot fend for themselves, can they?" She hugged her knees tighter. "But I also knew that if I worked my fingers to the bone to make us comfortable here, I would end up a frustrated, angry shrew of a female and Griffin would have no incentive to change his reclusive ways."

Rosamund thought about that. "Your plan did not precisely work, though, did it?"

"Oh, I don't know." Jacqueline's grin flashed out. "He married you, didn't he?"

CHAPTER TWENTY-ONE

Rosamund arrived at Griffin's town house travel-weary but in hopeful spirits.

After she'd greeted the staff, Rosamund entered the hall and looked about her. "Oh, yes, this is most handsome indeed!"

Unlike Pendon Place, Griffin's Mayfair home appeared to be an exceedingly well-run establishment. With notice of the family's arrival and the time and authority to hire extra servants, the retainers of this house had done their master proud.

Every surface had been swept, dusted, polished, waxed, and shined. Scents of honey and lavender pervaded the air. The carpets were handsome, the rooms well-appointed and tastefully furnished. Now, *this* was more like it!

Receiving Rosamund's compliments with a beam of delight, the housekeeper took her up to her bedchamber, leaving Jacqueline to trail behind.

When Mrs. Minchin had taken herself off to order the tea tray, Rosamund turned to Jacqueline. "Tomorrow, we shall collect my cousin, Lady Cecily, and shop until we fall into dead faints of exhaustion."

Laughing at Jacqueline's expression of horror, Rosamund unpinned her bonnet and took off her pelisse. In a habitual gesture, she felt for her locket, but it wasn't there.

Dismay shot through her. "My locket. I've lost my locket!"

"Oh, no!" said Jacqueline. "Perhaps it dropped on the floor."

While Jacqueline got down to her hands and knees, Rosamund picked up her pelisse and shook it out, but nothing fell from its folds.

"I can't see it anywhere," said Jacqueline.

"I must find it," Rosamund said. "I simply must find it!"

She could not bear it if she lost that locket, not with Griffin's image inside. With tears filling her eyes, she left the bedchamber and retraced her steps, while Jacqueline directed someone to go and search the coach. Meg and Mrs. Minchin joined the search. They were all scrabbling about on hands and knees in the great hall when Griffin strode in.

"What's all this?" he said.

"It's Rosamund's locket. She has lost it," said Jacqueline.

Rosamund scarcely heard the exchange. "It must be here! Griffin, help us look."

There was a long, drawn-out pause. So long, in fact, that she looked up from what she was doing. "What's the m—?" *Oh.* She'd forgotten her necklace had been such a source of contention between them.

Anger burned in Griffin's eyes, but when he spoke, it was in a controlled tone. "I have business to attend to. Excuse me."

Rosamund gazed after him helplessly. He was angry. She ought to have known better than to think she'd put his jealousy over Lauderdale to rest.

Then she realized Jacqueline was talking to her.

She frowned. "I beg your pardon. What was it you said?"

"Do you remember putting it on this morning?" Jacqueline repeated.

Slowly, Rosamund shook her head. That's right. They'd had an early start. She had been half-asleep as she'd dressed at the inn. "No. But then I don't remember taking it off, either. In fact, I am almost sure I did not have it on the journey at all, because the day before, I wore my crucifix."

"So perhaps the locket didn't even leave Pendon Place?" said Jacqueline.

"That doesn't make sense. If I wasn't wearing it when we left, I'd have packed it in my jewel box." She turned her head. "Meg? Will you bring my jewel box, please?"

The maid hurried to comply. With feverish fingers, Rosamund rifled through the dainty velvet-lined drawers and compartments, but the locket was not inside.

"I shall write to Mrs. Faithful and request her to mount a search." She itched to fly home to Pendon Place to look for the locket herself, but that was silly. And besides, Griffin would never understand.

Well, that would serve her right for not telling him what was in the infernal locket in the first place, wouldn't it?

Thanking the staff for their efforts, Rosamund went to find her sulky bear.

"I have been thinking," she said, when she found him in his lair, "that we ought to give a party to launch Jacqueline in society."

"As long as I do not have to attend any blasted balls, you may do whatever you choose." He didn't look at her, but she sensed the tension that vibrated within him. She ought to have been more circumspect, more considerate of his feelings, but she'd been frantic about her locket.

She was still frantic, in fact. But now she'd regained sufficient control not to show it.

"So," she said softly, rounding the desk. "My big old bear will not dance for me at all?"

She trailed her fingertips over his shoulder, but instead of responding as he normally would, he took her hand in a firm clasp. His grip, she suspected, was not one of affection but designed to stop her trying to seduce him into a better frame of mind.

Had that become her sole strategy when dealing with him? She felt chastened at the thought.

She placed her other hand over his. "Why do you not like balls? You were presented by your grandfather upon your majority, were you not? You must have learned to dance and attended such entertainments then."

He looked at her for a moment. Then he said, "Oh, I have danced to your tune quite enough, I think, my lady. No balls. No dancing. That is my final word on it."

Contrary to her own predictions, Jacqueline enjoyed their shopping spree. She and Cecily, while polar opposites in fashion sense, were kindred spirits beneath the skin. Soon, Cecily had persuaded Jacqueline of the manifold benefits of being "out" in society.

"I envy you exceedingly!" said Cecily. "The duke is so stuffy, he refused to let me come out until I had grown a particle of common sense. Can you believe it?"

"I am surprised he is letting you make your debut next spring, then, Cecily," murmured Rosamund.

Jacqueline protested hotly in defense of her new friend, but Cecily broke into a peal of laughter. "No, no, she is quite right. The family lives in terror that I shall set the ton by the ears, and they are right of course, poor dears. I shall run amok. In the most genteel way possible, of course."

Cecily's plans to take the ton by storm lost nothing in the telling. By the end of her recital, even Jacqueline began to see how she might enjoy her own season.

By means of cajolery, persuasion, and outright coercion, they succeeded in ordering Jacqueline enough gowns and fripperies to complete her scant wardrobe.

Jacqueline's particular favorite was a cherry red riding habit that brought out her eyes and contrasted beautifully with her black hair.

"When you can look like that, why would you ever ride astride again?" murmured Rosamund into her ear.

"Oh, I don't know," said Cecily seriously. "We have been warned, have we not, about the danger in burning one's breeches?"

Jacqueline snorted a laugh at the bad pun. Rosamund rolled her eyes.

It put her in mind of something, however. "I am afraid you will be cross with me, Cecily," she said as they climbed into their carriage. "I have stolen Diccon from you."

"I had noticed he didn't make the return journey," said Cecily. "What have you done with him?"

"Appointed him our butler at Pendon Place," said Rosamund. "It was his life's ambition, so you must be pleased for him."

Cecily sighed. "How tiresome of you. But I *am* happy for him. Besides, poor Diccon was starting to look a bit ragged around the edges after all our adventures."

"No doubt," said Rosamund dryly. "And I don't doubt you will soon beguile some other unfortunate into assisting you on your escapades."

"Escapades?" said Jacqueline.

"Your escape from Bath was nothing to it," said Rosamund with an absurd touch of pride in her wayward cousin.

"Did I tell you about the time I almost got arrested?" said Cecily.

"What?" Rosamund shrieked.

Cecily settled back against the squabs with a smug smile. "I didn't think so."

The deVere ladies soon found that it did not take a party given by Rosamund to launch Jacqueline on the ton. Somehow, the matchmaking mamas of London had caught the scent of an heiress on the wind. They lost no time in tracking that scent to its source.

Preeminent among these denizens of the ton was Lady Arden, who bestowed the signal honor upon them of inviting them to tea. Rosamund was well acquainted with her, due to her ladyship's longstanding—what would one call it, *friendship*?—with the Duke of Montford.

Lady Arden was the designated matchmaker for the Black family, and had successfully assisted Montford in bringing about Rosamund's cousin Jane's marriage to Constantine Black, Lord Roxdale, the previous year.

Rosamund turned the list of suitors Lord deVere deemed acceptable over in her mind. With a little surprise, she recalled that not one of these had been a member of the Black clan.

Ah, of course! There was a centuries-old feud between the families, was there not?

Which made Lady Arden's enthusiasm for Jacqueline even more interesting.

Their hostess bent her clear-eyed gaze upon Jacqueline. "She is wholly unspoiled, is she not?"

So, Lady Arden approved of Jacqueline despite the odd abruptness of the girl's manners. Indeed, Rosamund suspected that her sister-in-law would need to take up prostitution or murder someone to rate any society matron's disapproval. Her merest utterance was interpreted as wit, her occasional awkwardness dubbed a pleasing freshness and lack of pretension.

She suspected Jacqueline's path had been eased considerably by the news of the enormous dowry Griffin would set aside for her.

For Jacqueline's sake, Rosamund was glad. The girl paid no attention to the toadies who gushed over her. Even so, the warmth with which she was received by haughty women like Lady Arden could not help but add to her confidence.

The door opened to admit another visitor.

"Ah!" said Lady Arden. "There you are, my dear boy. Do come in."

Rosamund had her back to the door and so did not see who entered, but Jacqueline did. Her sister-in-law's eyes widened, and she made a convulsive movement with her hands, as if she wished to stretch them out but couldn't.

The gentleman—for gentleman it was—rounded the sofa so that Rosamund could get a good look at him. "Mr. Maddox!" Rosamund said, rising to curtsy. "How delightful to see *you* here."

She said it quite as if she hadn't scribbled a note to him recommending that he follow them to Town. Well, but she *was* surprised. She'd no notion he was acquainted with Lady Arden.

Rosamund sent a glance toward Jacqueline, who hastily got up and bobbed a curtsy.

Maddox had been smiling, but at the sight of Jacqueline, he froze.

"A transformation, is it not?" said Rosamund softly.

The gown Jacqueline wore was white muslin embroidered all over with violets. The deep, vibrant color of the flowers somehow made Jacqueline's eyes appear blue rather than gray. Her hair had been cut and styled with a modish simplicity that was vastly becoming to her. A faint flush pinked her cheeks. She looked, Rosamund thought, very pretty indeed.

In a moment, the spell that seemed to bind Maddox broke. He bowed to her and Jacqueline and moved forward to kiss Lady Arden's cheek.

"Do sit down, Anthony," said Lady Arden. She smiled at them all impartially. "I believe you are acquainted?"

"We are," answered Maddox. "Or at least, we used to be."

A puzzled, hurt look crossed Jacqueline's face. She glanced at Rosamund, as if for support. "It was not so long ago that we were friends, Mr. Maddox. I hope that, at least, has not altered."

The fortnight they'd spent in London allowing Jacqueline to slowly become accustomed to the ton had altered her appearance. It had also taught her a modicum of restraint. So when Rosamund smoothly interceded to speak of neutral topics, Jacqueline did not burst out with some ill-considered remark but instead, followed Rosamund's lead.

Half an hour passed in meaningless social chitchat. During that time, Rosamund was pleased to observe that Mr. Maddox could barely take his eyes from Jacqueline, though he appeared to listen and respond to all that was said. Jacqueline was subdued, and her face retained its flush. When Rosamund signaled it was time to take their leave, Jacqueline leaped up with a trifle more alacrity than politeness.

As she stood to go, Rosamund said, "Mr. Maddox, I plan to give a ball in a fortnight. I trust you will still be in Town? I shall send you a card for it."

His brows drew together slightly. "Is that wise?"

Rosamund smiled. "I'll leave you to be the judge of that, Mr. Maddox."

When they were safely inside the carriage, Jacqueline put her hand on Rosamund's arm. "Oh, Rosie, Griffin will kill you! A ball *and* Mr. Maddox! You do believe in taking the bull by the horns, don't you?"

"I daresay he'll be in a towering rage when he finds out," she agreed. And she did not think that this time it would culminate in wild, vigorous lovemaking. "By then, it will be too late."

I can manage him, Tibby. Had she actually said those words? She wasn't at all certain she could manage *this*. At least, not without resorting to underhanded means that were completely unworthy of a Westruther.

But there had been that look in Maddox's eyes when they rested on Jacqueline. Rosamund shivered, closing her eyes as the most blatant and painful longing welled inside her. Not for Maddox to look at her that way, of course. But oh, she wished Griffin would!

Jacqueline said, "Did you think Tony had changed, Rosamund? He was so . . . guarded, so formal in his manners."

"You could hardly expect him to tease you the way he does at home," said Rosamund. "Not in Lady Arden's presence."

"Yes," said Jacqueline, brightening a little. "That must be it."

Rosamund hesitated. Then she said, "Perhaps it is you who have altered. Perhaps the change was unwelcome to Mr. Maddox."

Jacqueline frowned. "What on earth do you mean? You said I look a thousand times prettier in my new clothes. Though I am no judge, I *feel* prettier in them."

"You were always a very attractive girl," said Rosamund firmly. "The gowns and the hair merely show your looks to best advantage. I have a theory," she added, "that Mr. Maddox was content for you to remain home at Pendon Place and never spread your wings. He had you all to himself then, didn't he? Now he must compete with all the other young bucks vying for your favors."

"They only want my money," said Jacqueline.

"There are plenty of gentlemen among your admirers who do not give a fig about your money," said Rosamund, and it was true. "As Mr. Maddox will discover when he comes to our ball."

Doubtful, Jacqueline said, "So this is all a ploy to make Tony jealous?" She wrinkled her nose a little in distaste.

"Of course not. But it will show him how you are to be appreciated, my dear. I believe he cares for you a great deal, but he does tend to treat you as if you are another man on occasion. He will learn that he ought to have more care."

Jacqueline digested this. "You do not go to all this trouble for nothing, Rosie. Are you trying to make a match between me and Mr. Maddox? I—I wish you would not." Her voice trembled on the last words, and her gray eyes shimmered with tears.

"My dear, whatever is the matter?"

Jacqueline dashed moisture away from her eyes with the back of her hand. "Oh, you have no notion! It is so hopeless. Every time I see him, I forget. And later, it comes rushing back to me and I feel sick, Rosie. Rosamund, I *cannot* marry Tony. Griffin is perfectly right about that."

Shocked to her soul, Rosamund put her arms around Jacqueline and held her as close as she was able with their bonnets in the way. "But why, darling? Can't you tell me?"

Jacqueline shook her head and burst into sobs. Rosamund murmured reassurance and tried her best to soothe her.

The carriage halted, and Jacqueline made a heroic effort to compose herself.

"Go straight up," said Rosamund. "I'll be there in a minute."

"No, don't," said Jacqueline, trying to smile. "Truly, I am well. And I—I think I should like to be alone for a while."

Griffin arrived home late, a little jollier for the brandy he'd imbibed with Lydgate and his cronies at Lydgate's club. A trifle jollier but by no means intoxicated.

He went to his dressing room, where his valet awaited him. "Ah, there you are, Dearlove."

"Yes, my lord," said Dearlove, reaching up to ease the tight-fitting black coat from Griffin's shoulders. "A pleasant evening, my lord?"

"Yes," said Griffin. "It was."

Lydgate's friends had been far more congenial than he'd expected. Whether it was out of consideration for Rosamund or a liking for him, Griffin didn't know, but Lydgate had gone out of his way to introduce Griffin to the ton and to pave his way wherever possible.

Yes, the evening had been a pleasant one. And now he proposed to spend an even more pleasant interlude in the arms of his wife. "Lady Rosamund home yet?"

"I believe the countess and Lady Jacqueline returned an hour ago, my lord."

"Very good." Griffin sat in his comfortable wingback chair and extended his leg. Dearlove donned gloves to remove Griffin's boots, handling them with as much care as if they'd been a pair of infants rather than footwear. But Griffin had become accustomed to Dearlove's foibles and he forbore to scoff.

After a quick wash and a vigorous scrub of his teeth, Griffin dismissed his valet. He donned a dressing gown and went into the bedchamber he shared with Rosamund. Oh, she had her own apartments, of course, but she rarely slept anywhere but in his bed.

Tonight, however, there was no warm, willing woman waiting for him beneath the covers. He shrugged. Perhaps she hadn't finished undressing.

Impatient to see her, he crossed the bedchamber to the other side of his suite, continued through two sitting rooms and into the bedchamber that had been reserved for Rosamund's use.

Here, he found her standing before the full-length cheval glass, staring pensively at her own reflection.

And well she might stare. The breath left his lungs in an audible *whoosh*.

The garment was a simple robe in the Grecian style so popular earlier in the century. Low at the bosom, high at the waist. Very plain. Nothing startling in that.

But the material from which this particular garment was fashioned was so filmy as to be almost completely transparent.

Rosamund wore nothing underneath but her skin. Her firm, high buttocks and long legs showed clearly through that scandalous gown. In her reflection, he saw, with a surge of hunger, the shadows of her nipples, the contours of her breasts and hips, the slightly darker triangle of hair on her pubis.

She looked like a beautiful goddess. Aphrodite, perhaps? One of the saucier ones, anyway. Her bearing had that same mixture of regality and innocence and sinful knowing that never failed to send him wild.

"My God, woman," he said hoarsely. "Are you trying to give me a heart attack? Send me to an early grave?"

She turned her head. Then she smiled that siren's smile of hers, and he was lost.

They made love in one of their passionate frenzies,

falling into slumber almost instantly. In the morning, he woke, lying on his side with her body pressed against him, her backside snuggled into his groin.

A groin that was rock hard and aching for release.

He reached around and touched her, bringing her quickly to a long, muted, shivery orgasm.

"Mmm." She smiled sleepily. "That was a nice way to wake up."

Deliberately, she pressed back against him. "Do you have something else I might like?"

"Let me see," he said.

CHAPTER TWENTY-TWO

They had not left their bed yet when Rosamund finally broached the subject she'd been warming up to all night.

She had meant to raise it with him as soon as he came in, but he'd caught her trying on one of the scandalous garments she'd ordered from the back room of that clever modiste Jane had told Cecily about.

It had all gone downhill from there. Or at least, the lovemaking had been more than satisfactory, but it had made it impossible for her to mention Maddox. Nor was it the perfect time to speak of Jacqueline's suitor now. Griffin might well see such behavior as manipulative and dig in his heels.

But, well, she had to approach him about it sometime, didn't she? Perhaps it *was* manipulative of her, but she owed it to Jacqueline to tackle the issue when Griffin was in his mellowest mood.

And he was exceedingly pleased with himself today.

"I do not think I shall walk for a week," she murmured, stretching.

Griffin laid his hand on her breast. "That would be tragic. I might have to stay here and tend to your needs."

"How should we survive?" said Rosamund.

She sighed as he bent to lick her nipple. She caressed his hair, enjoying the exquisite sensations. Soon, however, she urged him to lift his head so that he looked in her eyes.

"Griffin, I need to talk to you about something."

His eyes took a moment to focus. Then he muttered what sounded like an oath under his breath and flung himself onto his back. "I knew it was too good to last. Talk away."

"I want to ask you about Jacqueline. And Mr. Maddox."

He muttered an oath but she held up a hand. "I am not going to pester you any more on the subject of his courting her—although I still cannot see the objection—but Griffin, Jacqueline was in tears yesterday afternoon, and I want to know why."

Griffin kneaded his temple with the heels of his hands. "How should I know? Females turn into watering pots at the drop of a hat, don't they?"

"Not Jacqueline," said Rosamund quietly. "In fact, the only other time I've seen her tearful was when you—" She broke off, realizing that what she'd been about to say would scarcely lighten his mood.

"When I what, my lady? I am quite accustomed to figuring as the ogre, so you needn't think to spare my feelings."

"All right, then. She thought you'd sent her to Bath because she was too much trouble and you didn't want her."

He sucked in a sharp breath, as if someone had punched him. "She didn't think that! She can't think that."

"It is probably illogical, but I am afraid that she does," said Rosamund. "I tried to reassure her, but I scarcely knew her then, and I am afraid it did little good."

"My God, what a mess," said Griffin in a hollow voice, staring up at the blue silk canopy above them.

"But that is not what I wanted to ask," said Rosamund. "Jacqueline told me she agrees with you that she must not marry Mr. Maddox."

His body relaxed a little. "I'm glad the girl has some sense, then."

"But why?" said Rosamund. "He is eligible in every way. He even lives close to Pendon Place, for goodness' sake. We would not even have to part with her."

He turned his head at that. "You would miss her if she went?"

"Oh, yes! Jacqueline is dear to me, Griffin. It is why I cannot bear to see her unhappy. And I don't think she *will* be happy unless she marries Mr. Maddox. Why can they not be together?"

"DeVere won't allow it."

"Oh, my dear Griffin, do but say the word, and I shall take care of deVere. The Duke of Montford has been running rings around the fellow for years. I daresay he could come up with a scheme to secure deVere's consent in the time it would take most people to add two and two together. Surely that cannot be the sole objection. And if it were, surely Jacqueline would not so wholeheartedly agree with it."

"Leave it be, Rosamund," said Griffin. He swung his legs over the side of the bed and sat up. Looking back at her, he said, "Just trust me."

"Trust you?" She sat up, too, clutching the sheet to her breasts in a really rather absurd attempt to cover herself. "Why should I trust you when you have absolutely *no* faith in me?"

His mouth was set in a grim line. "I cannot tell you, because it is not my secret to tell and knowing it could be dangerous. But the reason is a damned good one. Even Jacks thinks so. If you don't trust *me*, then at least respect her judgment!"

"Good enough to trump love, Griffin?" said Rosamund softly. "But how can that be? Surely nothing is more important or more powerful than love."

"Is that right?" Griffin yanked on his trousers and buttoned them. Then he reached for his shirt. "Did you put love before your duty when you married me?"

Oh, God. She'd walked straight into that trap, hadn't she?

"No," she said quietly. "I did not."

He looked at her then, and the stark pain on his features wrung her heart.

In that moment, she felt defiant and reckless and entirely without hope. But she would say it to him so that he would know. How it might change things between them she couldn't guess, but it was past time for her to be honest with him and remove all these doubts that seemed to fester inside him.

In a stronger voice, she continued. "I did not put duty above love, because in this case, they were one and the same." She met his gaze, hoping against hope that he would see all he needed to know right there in her eyes. "I love you, Griffin. I always have."

The magnitude and power of Rosamund's words hit him with such stunning force that he couldn't get his mind to take them in. They seemed to have bypassed his brain and driven straight through his heart.

But the feeling was less like the prick of Cupid's arrow and more like the plunge of a knife.

No one had ever told him they loved him before.

He didn't know how that could be, but it was. Surely his mother had loved him, but she'd never actually said it that he could recall. It was only now that he discovered how starved of love he had been since her death.

And it was cruel, so damnably cruel, that the first person ever to say those words to him should be so deluded. She was fooling herself, and she was killing him.

He stared at Rosamund, who sat up in bed, still clutching the sheet to her breast. She gazed up at him, clearly willing him to respond. As if it were a simple thing to comprehend, this love of hers for him.

"I don't know what to say." And he didn't, because she clearly believed what she'd said, even if he knew her love was the product of wishful thinking. She wanted, quite desperately, to love the man who was her husband. That just happened to be him.

If deVere and Montford's scheming had produced a different candidate, she would be saying those words to that fellow now, he was sure.

Rosamund tried desperately not to look crestfallen, but he knew she was. What woman wouldn't be? Or what man, for that matter? If he'd been so reckless and foolish as to express the depth of his feelings for her . . . He dragged his hands down the side of his face.

In a shaking voice, she said, "You don't have to say anything, Griffin. You simply have to believe it's true."

A tear spilled over and rolled down her cheek. He wanted to go to her, to hold her in his arms and kiss her tears away. But his own pain was so great that if he didn't leave, he might say something to hurt her even more.

There was nothing he could do. No genuine sentiment he could utter that would make her feel better. He could not even give her the satisfaction of believing in *her* love, much less tell her he loved her in return.

He could lie. Perhaps he would, when he could force the words beyond the lump of pain that obstructed his throat. He could say he believed her.

But he could not tell her he loved her, even as a kindly lie to stop her tears.

He could not say it back, because in *his* case, it would be true.

They dined with the family at Montford House that night. Rosamund did her best to appear in good spirits, but by the time the ladies left the gentlemen to their drinking and smoking, she was all but worn out with the effort.

Her worst fears had been confirmed that morning. Griffin didn't return her love. She wished she hadn't given in to the impulse to make that declaration herself. Now she knew his sentiments beyond doubt, when before she'd been at liberty to dream of a happy ending for them both. Against all common sense, she'd hoped Griffin's tenderness in the bedchamber signaled the depth of his feelings for her. How *could* a man be so considerate and passionate with a woman he didn't love? She didn't know. All she could do was hope his feelings for her would change.

She wished that tonight, of all nights, she hadn't agreed to dine with her uncomfortably perceptive family. A small measure of relief came when she could finally escape with the ladies to the drawing room. She trusted Cecily and Jacqueline would not quiz her in front of Tibby.

But before she could even lay her hands on a cup of tea, Xavier appeared and asked to speak with her.

"Is anything amiss?" she inquired as he ushered her to the library. Instead of taking Montford's seat behind the desk, her brother led her to a cozy grouping of chairs by the fireside.

Ah, so this was to be a *subtle* interrogation.

Her head began to ache.

Xavier crossed to the sideboard and plucked the stopper from a crystal decanter. Unusually, he chose two glasses and sloshed a finger of brandy in each.

"You look like you could use this," he said, handing it to her. "Or would you prefer me to ring for sherry?"

Rosamund took a small sip, choking as the liquor caught her throat. "My goodness, how can you drink that stuff?"

Then the burn turned to a pleasant warmth, and the tendons in her neck relaxed just a touch.

Xavier merely smiled and watched as she sipped again.

He asked her about Pendon Place and Cornwall and their journey back to London. Rosamund answered each question with a wary vigilance. He was lulling her into a false sense of security. At any moment, he would pounce.

Then it came. "Your wedding was very sudden," he observed. "I would have made the journey down to Cornwall for it, but I understand why you did not want to wait."

She wrinkled her brow. What was he getting at?

"The impatience of two people in love," he murmured on a note of explanation.

"Sarcasm doesn't become you, Xavier," said Rosamund lightly.

"On the contrary. It becomes me very well," he returned. "But that was not sarcasm, Rosamund. I saw the pair of you gazing at each other like moonlings this evening. A decided whiff of tragedy in the air, too. Something wrong in paradise?"

She forced a laugh. "My goodness, brother, you go too fast for me. One minute, you accuse me of cuckolding my husband before we are even married, and the next, you scent a lovers' quarrel between us!" Her voice had risen to an embarrassing pitch at the end of that speech.

Xavier stood and crossed to the couch where she sat and dropped his hand on her shoulder. "Tell your big brother all about it."

In other circumstances, she wouldn't have dreamed of confiding in her cold, unfeeling brother. But she was so very heartsick, and his usually clipped, cool voice was gentle and warm with understanding.

"Oh, Xavier!" she said on a sob. "I don't know what to do!"

He sat beside her and put an arm about her shoulders and let her weep the long, involved tale into his coat. The comfort that gesture gave her was immense.

"If only I'd never met that rotten Lauderdale," she said, wiping her eyes. "Oh, I am a mess."

"Never mind that." Xavier frowned. "Did Lauderdale offer you insult?"

"Oh, no!" She said it with every ounce of conviction she could muster. The captain would be a dead man twice over if Xavier found out about that dreadful proposition.

"Hmm." Xavier sat back, steepling his fingers together in a pose that reminded her of the duke.

Too late, Rosamund realized the error of confiding in Xavier. He always wanted to fix things for her. But she sensed this was a problem she had to solve alone.

"I'm sorry, I shouldn't have burdened you with my troubles. Please do not interfere, Xavier," she said. "I am sure that in these matters it is only worse when third parties get involved. I should not have told you at all."

He wasn't listening to her. "I shall contrive something. The Devil of it is that I must go out of town tomorrow for a week or so. I have a commitment I cannot break."

"With the added advantage that you will miss Mama's rout party next week," said Rosamund.

"That, too." Xavier frowned. "I wanted to speak with you about Lauderdale. Our mother has invited him to the party."

She gasped. "But he is on the Continent by now."

"That he is not. I heard he sold his commission and has returned to London. For what purpose, I wonder?"

He sipped his drink, eyeing her. Did he still suspect her of harboring tender feelings toward the captain?

On top of her troubles with Griffin, this seemed too much. "Oh, no! What on earth shall I do?"

"You must go, of course. If you stay away, you will cause people to talk, not least of all, Nerissa. But you must take Griffin with you and show the world—and Lauderdale— what a devoted couple you are."

"Good God, why did Lauderdale come back?" She would be conceited to believe it had anything to do with her. But, oh, confound Nerissa for her malicious med- dling! That her mother made mischief she did not doubt. Did she think throwing the captain in Rosamund's path would be enough for Rosamund to fall into his arms?

"Mama seems to delight in making me uncomfort- able." She smiled painfully. "I wish I did not have to go, but you're right. I must. If only to prevent her spreading lies about the reason for my absence."

"Our mother is a bitch of the first order," said Xavier grimly. "She is eaten up with jealousy of you."

Rosamund gasped, and he smiled rather evilly down at her. "That surprises you? Do but employ your intelligence a little, my dear. She has seen you as a rival for men's af- fections since the day you were born. What she never understood was that if she'd possessed one ounce of your sweet temperament, she would be able to keep the men she seduces. As it is, they use her body without emotion or sentiment. Once their desire for that commodity is sated, they leave her."

"Or she drives them away with her tantrums. It is a sad existence." Rosamund hesitated. "Was that how it was with our father?"

Xavier sighed. "Strangely, I think he loved her, or he wouldn't have stayed with her as long as he did." He was silent for a moment. "Our father doted on you."

Then why did he send us away?

She rested her head on her brother's shoulder. "He is fading from my memory, Xavier. All I seem to remember are the fights between them."

"He was not a demonstrative man. He did not show his affection in the way a little girl would understand," Xavier conceded. "But I was rather older, and I understood him. Better, I think, than our mother did. He adored you." He kissed her on the temple. "And so do I."

A quiet joy flooded her heart. Xavier was not a demonstrative man, either, but she knew he loved her. Perhaps only her. Suddenly that struck her as a terribly lonely existence.

"Promise me something," he said, closing his long fingers over hers.

"Yes? What is it?"

"Promise me you will be careful at that rout party," Xavier said. "I have a bad feeling about it."

Rosamund shivered. She had a bad feeling about it, too.

CHAPTER TWENTY-THREE

Y ou didn't tell me it was a damned ball," grumbled
Griffin as he escorted Rosamund down the stairs.
"I said no balls!"

"A few couples forming a set by the pianoforte does
not a ball make," murmured Rosamund, smiling and nodding to her acquaintances. "It is a rout party, Griffin. Do
try to smile and not look as if you are about to devour my
mother's guests."

They were late, which had been Rosamund's intention
in accepting two other invitations for the evening. She and
Jacqueline had already dined at Lady Barker's house and
danced a few sets at Mrs. Ashton's ball before collecting
Griffin in the carriage and proceeding to Steyne House.

It was as far as she dared go in order to avoid her mama.
That lady had lamented all over town that her daughter had
married in such a shabby way. Cornwall! With no relatives
or friends present. What, she asked plaintively, was wrong
with St. George's, Hanover Square?

They moved farther into the drawing room, and Griffin said out of the corner of his mouth, "Remind me. Why
are we here?"

"It would look odd if we were not," she said. "My mother would never let me hear the end of it."

She was at a loss to guess her mother's motives in inviting Lauderdale tonight. Perhaps she had no plan beyond getting Rosamund and Lauderdale in the one place, but Rosamund suspected there was more to it than that. She intended to stay very close to Griffin tonight.

Without warning, she spied Lauderdale and suffered a horrid jolt of mingled anxiety and fear. "Perhaps we should not stay too long," she said.

Griffin muttered a foul curse, and Rosamund turned to see that Mr. Maddox was making a beeline for them. Jacqueline hadn't seen him yet. She had her back to him, as her attention had been claimed by various other debutantes with whom she'd become friends over the past weeks.

As Maddox approached, Jacqueline turned as if sensing his presence. The intense, hungry look on his face, the banked longing in his dark eyes when he saw her made even Rosamund's heart flutter. She could only imagine what it did to Jacqueline's.

The girl appeared particularly lovely tonight in a deep rose-pink ball gown and long white gloves. She wore her hair piled high on her head, studded with tiny pearl pins. A matching pearl necklace encircled her slender throat.

A flush the same color as her gown swept over Jacqueline's face.

Maddox greeted them and bowed, failing to notice Griffin's glare. He was wholly absorbed in Jacqueline.

"My lady, would you care to dance?" Maddox's voice had lost its customary nonchalance. It sounded earnest, husky with suppressed emotion.

Jacqueline flushed a brighter pink. She glanced up at Griffin, whose face was now stony. She shook her head. "I regret, Mr. Maddox, that I do not dance this evening."

Rosamund could have killed Griffin for his steadfast refusal to bend!

"Nonsense!" she said. "Run along, my dear. You need not think you must eschew dancing simply because Griffin and I do."

"She doesn't wish to dance. Leave her be," said Griffin. "Maddox, you heard my sister."

Their neighbor hadn't taken his eyes from Jacqueline's. "Oh, yes," he said evenly. "I heard her. Most distinctly."

He made a brief bow, turned on his heel, and strode off in the direction of the card room.

With a fulminating look at Rosamund, Griffin said, "I'm going to get a drink."

Rosamund turned to Jacqueline, whose face had gone from flushed to stricken and pale.

"I am so sorry, my dear. I did try."

"Well, stop trying," said Jacqueline in a low, trembling voice. "I don't want your help. You are making it *worse,* do you hear me? Just . . . just leave me alone!"

Before Rosamund could react, Jacqueline broke from her and hurried away, leaving her standing alone, in the middle of the crowd.

Feeling distinctly shaky and a little sick as well, Rosamund started when a deep voice spoke behind her.

"Lady Rosamund."

She turned swiftly and looked up into Lauderdale's handsome face. Then her gaze shifted to the lady who clung to Lauderdale's arm.

The lady was her mother.

"Ah, but I believe it is Lady Tregarth now, is it not?" With an insufferably smug smile, Lauderdale took her hand and bowed over it. She snatched it away before he could raise it to his lips.

Her prior queasiness turned to full-blown nausea. "Good evening, Mama. Good evening, Captain." She let her gaze wander over his civilian garb. Then she opened her eyes wide. "Ah, but I hear you have sold out. So should I call you plain mister these days?"

He laughed easily, but her mother reproved her. "Once a captain, always a captain, my dear."

"Ah," said Rosamund. "Yes, I see."

Somehow, Lauderdale did not look as handsome as she had once thought him. It was not the lack of regimentals that lessened his appeal, however. It was the malice in his eyes.

"Will you excuse me?" said Rosamund. "I must find the duke." Montford would protect her, even if Griffin wouldn't.

"Oh, he was called away on some urgent matter of state or other." Lady Steyne waved a careless hand. "I daresay he won't be back tonight."

"What a pity," commented Lauderdale. "I was looking forward to renewing my acquaintance with His Grace. But come, my dear ladies. Let us adjourn to the long gallery and take a turn to refresh ourselves. It is a deuced crush in here."

Rosamund did not want to go to the long gallery with her mother and Lauderdale. They couldn't be . . . Were the two of them . . . *lovers* now? Rosamund shuddered even to think it, but she would not put anything past her mother. And why should Nerissa not take the captain as her cicisbeo? She was clearly the sort of woman Lauderdale wanted.

Rosamund couldn't believe she'd ever preened over his marked attentions to her, agonized about hurting his feelings.

"Rosamund, I insist you come upstairs at once! I wish to ask your opinion of something." Her mother exchanged a conspiratorial glance with Lauderdale, which could not possibly bode well for Rosamund.

"Really, Mama, I just arrived. I must . . . I must pay my respects to my acquaintances." She craned her neck. "Ah! I see Lady Arden over there, beckoning."

"Oh, pooh!" said Nerissa, gripping her arm with her talonlike fingers to prevent her from leaving them. "*That* is a weak excuse if I ever heard one. Who gives a fig for Lady Arden? I *demand* that you come with us, you disobedient wretch. Lauderdale, you must persuade her to come!"

Her mother's voice grew shrill. More than anything, Rosamund dreaded one of the marchioness's scenes. She'd do anything to avoid drawing attention to their conversation.

With a hurried assent, she went with them, searching the crowd for Andrew or Griffin, or even some other friend whom she might depend upon to come to her rescue.

There was no one. She followed her mother and her former admirer upstairs to the long gallery, the dread in the pit of her stomach compounding with each step.

When they reached the gallery, it was deserted. Rosamund didn't know whether to be thankful or sorry for that.

She felt the old helplessness swamp her. The same weakness that had overtaken her since she was a child and completely at her mother's capricious mercy—and at the mercy of the men with whom the marchioness associated. If it had not been for Xavier . . .

But Xavier wasn't here now, and she needed to protect herself from her mother's depredations on her confidence. Suddenly, she halted. Which alternative was worse? A scene at her brother's rout party, or the further erosion of her soul?

Giving in to her mother's demands had become an ingrained habit with her, only to avoid unpleasant scenes. No longer. Not after this.

"No," she said, turning to face her mother. "I'm not going to let you do this to me. Not again. *Never* again."

She wrenched herself from her mother's grip and turned to go.

That was when she saw it.

The painting.

But it was not a composite portrait of her body with her mother's face. It was *all* Rosamund! Form, features, a dreamy, sensual expression that belonged in the bedchamber, *in her and Griffin's bedchamber,* not on public display.

Hanging there, in the gallery of her brother's house, for all the world to see.

"A work of genius, is it not?" murmured Lauderdale. "I cannot wait to hang it in my own rooms. Somewhere private, I think. We don't want everyone to know what we are to each other."

"You are *nothing* to me!" flashed Rosamund. She turned to her mother. "My lady, this is too base, even for you."

Lady Steyne gave a tinkling laugh. "My dear, I thought you would thank me for bringing the two of you together so neatly. I shall leave you now, so that you may discuss your affairs in private."

She laid a slight emphasis on the word *affairs.*

With the sensation of swimming through the murky blackness of a nightmare, Rosamund managed to say, "Do you know something, Lady Steyne? I think I shall positively enjoy making you a grandmama."

She had the dubious satisfaction of seeing her mother's eyes flare with rage. Then the marchioness turned on her heel and walked away, leaving Rosamund with the captain.

Rosamund turned to Lauderdale. "I should warn you that my brother taught me various rather painful ways of defending myself against men like you."

Lauderdale laughed softly. "You think I would stoop to taking you by force? No, no, I shall merely enjoy my purchase in the privacy of my own rooms."

"My husband would kill you," she said contemptuously. "And then my cousins would carve you up like mincemeat and feed you to the dogs."

His face turned stark with pain. With a travesty of a smile, he shrugged and held out his arms. "Do you know something, Rosamund? I really don't care."

It was only then that she received an inkling of what was happening.

"You don't understand, do you?" said Lauderdale. "I *love* you, Rosamund. I always knew my case was hopeless— or thought I did. But that oaf of an earl of yours . . . *He* never came for you, did he? And so I fooled myself. . . ." He threw back his head and gave a crack of mirthless laughter. "After this campaign, I told myself, I shall put my fortune to the test. If I cover myself in glory on the battlefield and come home a hero, Rosamund's stuffy duke might agree to let us marry."

She put her palms to her scalding cheeks. She'd been afraid all along that he cared for her, that she might hurt him by going through with the marriage to Griffin. But then the captain had behaved like a scoundrel and laid those fears to rest.

"And then *he* came to London, didn't he?" whispered Lauderdale fiercely. "And you were all smiles at him. And all my hopes went to Hell."

"Those hopes . . . Captain Lauderdale, I was betrothed when you and I met. I told you over and over that I could not offer you more than friendship. True, the duke would not have permitted our marriage, but there is a more important reason: *I do not love you.* I love my husband." Her lips trembled. "I loved him before I even met you."

"*No!*" cried Lauderdale. "You only think you do because you are so good and honorable that the alternative to loving your husband is unthinkable. But how can you truly *love* a monster like the Earl of Tregarth? I refuse to believe it. My God, I can't bear the thought of his great dirty paws on you."

"It doesn't matter what you believe, Captain. I will never care for you. If you truly loved me, you would not treat me thus. And you would not have insulted me with a carte blanche, either."

He'd done that out of pique. He'd needed to hurt her as she had hurt him, she realized now.

"I came back for you," he said. "When a man has faced death, he realizes how little conventions like marriage truly matter. What matters is our love, Rosamund! Don't you see?"

With as much force as she could muster, she said, "I do not love you, Captain Lauderdale! I never shall!"

But he was beyond listening to reason, it seemed. The balance of his mind was so disturbed by whatever warped passion he'd conceived for her that he might indeed make good on his threats despite the dire consequences that would befall him afterwards.

Griffin would never believe she was innocent if Lauderdale let it be known he owned this painting. He'd never accept the truth. Who would believe any mother capable of perpetrating such a crime as Nerissa had tonight? Against her own daughter!

And if Lauderdale showed the painting to his friends, passed that provocative likeness from man to man . . . She shuddered. Ruination stared down at her from her own face.

Though the words stuck in her throat, she forced them out. "What do you want in exchange for that painting?"

* * *

Lydgate approached Griffin with a worried look on his face. "Have you seen Rosamund?"

Griffin shook his head and poured himself another drink from his brother-in-law's private stock. The library had been a haven until Lydgate arrived.

His friend frowned. "I saw her talking with her mother and Lauderdale. Then I lost sight of them and haven't seen them since."

Griffin slammed down his glass. "Good God, man! Why didn't you say so?"

It took them far too long to discover where the trio had gone. Griffin hoped Lady Steyne's presence would check any advances Lauderdale might make, but he wouldn't trust the woman as far as he could throw her.

Finally, a footman said he'd seen them go upstairs to the long gallery.

"This way," said Lydgate.

They took the steps two at a time. Griffin's heart pounded in his chest. If that bastard did anything to her, he'd rip his liver out.

The two men arrived in the gallery to find Rosamund quite alone.

"Christ!" said Griffin, and froze.

She stood precariously balanced on a spindle-legged chair with a great, shining sword held aloft. She'd lost one of her evening slippers and her hair was tumbling from its careful coiffure.

As Lydgate and Griffin stood there, transfixed, she gave a hoarse cry and hacked into one of the full-length portraits on the gallery wall. The portrait was of Rosamund, Griffin realized. She slashed at the image of her own face and body, while great, racking sobs burst from her chest.

Griffin strode forward, ducking as the rapier flashed dangerously close to his head.

He gripped the hilt where she held it and twisted it from her grasp. Handing the sword to Lydgate, he swung her down from the chair and folded her into his arms.

Between gasping, wrenching sobs, she related the entire tale. At the mention of Lauderdale's demands, Griffin exchanged a fierce glance with Lydgate over her head.

She shuddered. "I said I wanted to do it properly, at his rooms. I insisted we must go now. He went to order his carriage. I—I needed to get rid of him so I could do this." She gestured to the tattered remains of her portrait. She gave a broken, hysterical laugh. "The portrait is destroyed. He cannot touch me now."

White-hot rage burned through Griffin. A quick death was too good for that bastard. For taking this dastardly advantage of her, yes, but also for forcing her to annihilate her own beauty to escape him. Irrationally, the latter seemed far more disturbing than the captain's clumsy attempt at coercing Rosamund to his bed.

When Griffin had seen Rosamund slashing at her own features and body in that frenzied way, he'd felt sick inside, without knowing anything about the true cause for the destruction.

"I'll kill the bastard," said Griffin softly to Lydgate.

His friend's blue eyes held an unholy light of anticipation. Anticipation of committing violence on Lauderdale's person, if Griffin wasn't mistaken.

"He's mine," Griffin warned.

"Be my guest," murmured Lydgate. *Let's see how you do,* were Lydgate's unspoken words.

Then they turned their attention to the top of the staircase, where Lauderdale appeared.

To his meager credit, the captain didn't take to his heels or try to talk his way out of trouble. He squared up to Griffin, his head held at an arrogant tilt. Oh, good. He would take his punishment like a man.

Lauderdale raised his brows, looking haughty beneath that flopping fringe of golden hair. "Are you going to challenge me to a duel, my lord? How—"

He didn't get any farther. Griffin's fist stopped his mouth.

"No," said Griffin, advancing as Lauderdale crashed into the wall. "Dueling is for *gentlemen*. And you, my dear sir, are not one of those."

Lauderdale regained his footing and bore in, but Griffin was ready for him. Griffin drove a punch to the kidneys, then slammed his fist into Lauderdale's stomach and followed it lightning-fast with an uppercut that all but lifted the captain off his feet.

The man was tough, Griffin would say that for him. Lauderdale raised himself from the floor and slowly got to his feet. Staggering like a drunk, he squared up again.

"Finish it." Lydgate's clipped voice cut through the deadly atmosphere. "Finish it now, Tregarth, or I'll finish it for you."

Griffin shook his head like a dog. Fury pounded in his blood, roared in his ears. He'd finish it, all right. He'd be satisfied with nothing less than total annihilation. He was going to kill Lauderdale for the pain he'd forced on Rosamund.

He dealt Lauderdale a sickening punch on the temple that sent him reeling back. Baring his teeth, Griffin started after the captain. He wanted to pound that pretty face into a bloody bag of bones.

But somehow, Lydgate got mixed up in the fight. Or at least, his foot did. Lauderdale tripped over it, lost his footing completely, and tumbled back down the stairs.

Baulked of his prey, Griffin could only watch, bemused, as his enemy dropped from view.

There was a shocked gasp from below, and a calm speech from Lydgate, who had followed Lauderdale down in a more leisurely fashion. "Thank you, ladies and gentlemen.

Deepest regrets. Man ought to be able to hold his liquor, eh? Call the captain a carriage, will you, my good man? Tsk-tsk, ladies present, too."

Griffin ducked back out of sight of the guests downstairs. His fists were still clenched and his chest heaved. Curse Lydgate's interference! He'd fully intended to rid them of Lauderdale once and for all.

But as his bloodlust faded, he began to feel grateful. Lydgate's coolheaded thinking had saved him from an irrevocable act that would have embroiled Rosamund in scandal and perhaps seen him arrested or obliged to flee the country.

Satisfied that Lydgate had matters well in hand downstairs, Griffin turned again to Rosamund.

She was shaking, shaking hard. He led her to a sofa by the wall, where they sat down. He put his arm around her and murmured soothing nothings while he stroked her hair.

She shrank into his chest and clutched his coat lapel. "I never loved him. Never!"

"I know, sweetheart. I was a fool to believe otherwise. Indeed, I have not believed it for some time."

She seemed to accept that, and the relief of having Rosamund safe in his arms slowly sank in.

He looked down at the golden top of her head, at the curls that tumbled about it in disarray from her exertions with that sword. Where had she found it? Glancing around, he spied a collection of rapiers decorating the far wall of the gallery and had his answer.

Marveling at her courage and resourcefulness, he stroked her shoulder in a soothing motion.

She stirred then, disengaging herself. With a self-conscious smile that slipped a little, she put her hand to her hair. "I must look an awful fright."

"I don't care," he said.

"Yes, but *I* do," she said ruefully. "I doubt *that* aspect of my character will ever change."

She rose to stand straight-backed and elegant, her natural grace reasserting itself despite the disarray of her person. "I'll go to one of the upstairs chambers and ring for a maid to attend me and be with you directly."

"I'll come with you," he said, getting to his feet. He worried about her going alone.

Her smile lasted longer this time, but he saw what it cost her. "No, thank you. But if you would have the carriage brought, I should be grateful. I want to go as soon as I have tidied myself."

Before she left him, she laid a hand on his arm. "Thank you, Griffin," she said softly.

And she stood on tiptoe and pressed a soft kiss to his cheek.

CHAPTER TWENTY-FOUR

Griffin couldn't sleep, knowing Rosamund lay wakeful beside him, though she'd assured him she needed nothing more from him tonight.

She did need something, though. She needed to talk. That's what women liked, wasn't it? To talk about things.

The trouble was, he hadn't a clue what to say. He couldn't imagine anything worse than reliving such an unpleasant experience. Wouldn't talking about tonight make things worse? Wouldn't she be better off putting it out of her mind?

He didn't know. But he owed it to her to give her what she needed. He hated the thought of her suffering beside him.

Griffin rolled onto his side and spoke into the darkness. "I am awake. If you like, we could . . ."

In a strained voice, she said, "I'm terribly sorry, Griffin, but I'm not in the right frame of mind for making love tonight."

Appalled, he said, "No, I didn't mean—I meant, you know, if you wanted to, ah —" *Oh, Hell.* "—talk. About things."

He winced and waited for her to annihilate him with scorn.

She didn't, though. She didn't say anything at all.

He heard her swallow a couple of times. Loud, inelegant noises that sounded like a valiant attempt not to weep.

"Sweetheart." Gingerly, he took her into his arms.

She laid her head on his shoulder. In a quiet, trembling voice she tried desperately to control, she said, "If my mother had offered *you* that portrait, Griffin, would you have bought it?"

It was too dark to read her expression. She held herself rigid in the circle of his arms, however. He sensed a subtle withdrawal, though she did not move from his embrace.

"The portrait?" he repeated. His answer to this question was vitally important; that was clear. "Hmm. I hadn't thought about it."

"Oh, never mind. Forget I asked."

The temptation to take her at her word was one he nobly ignored. "Of course, I would have bought the painting to save you from embarrassment. . . ."

"But otherwise?" she asked. "Would you want that painting?"

He hadn't seen the painting—not intact, at all events. He'd scarcely glanced at the unfinished canvas when he'd arrived at her brother's house. But he'd seen her pose for it, hadn't he? And he'd certainly admired the way she appeared that day.

But there was something . . . not right about gawping at a portrait of her in semi-undress, particularly one that had been completed so as to identify her without her knowledge or consent. It was too much like a dirty old man leering at one of those bawdy cartoons in a print shop.

"I don't think so," he said finally. "Certainly not from your mother." He stroked the silken softness of her shoulder. "And, well, why would I need a picture of you when I have the flesh-and-blood woman right here?"

She made an inarticulate sound, throwing him into panic. Oh, God, he'd said it all wrong!

"Not that I don't want to look upon you all the time," he assured her hastily. "I do, but . . . I want *you,* not just your beauty. I want to talk with you, laugh with you. I want you to have your own mind, to make me lose my temper, to be your own self. I want you in my arms, in my bed." He hesitated, feeling his chest tighten with the well of emotion his own words had evoked. "That's it," he said gruffly. "I'm not good at explaining."

"I think I understand," she said. He nearly groaned with relief when he heard the smile in her voice.

She turned in his arms and kissed him on his crooked beak of a nose. "Thank you, Griffin."

He released the breath he'd been holding. "Was it a good answer?"

"It was the *perfect* answer. Better than perfect, in fact." She subsided into his embrace again, and he closed his arms about her and held her tight. He *should* have killed Lauderdale for bringing her to such a pass.

Rosamund tilted her head up to press her lips to his.

Perhaps she'd meant it as a chaste, brief expression of her gratitude. To Hell with that! Griffin lashed his arms around her and crushed his mouth down on hers and lost himself in Rosamund.

With a choked little cry, she responded, opening to him, tangling her tongue with his. Their kiss was raw and perhaps a little clumsy, too. But it shimmered with honest, true emotion. He'd never realized a kiss could communicate so much, reveal so much.

Griffin raised his head and stared down at her in wonder. Beneath all that tumbled beauty was an aching vulnerability that he had not seen before tonight.

He'd been willfully blind, had he not?

Had he ever truly seen her before? Had he been no better than Lauderdale? In love with the dazzling face and the heavenly body and not troubling to discover the heart and soul and mind behind them?

In that moment, his own heart shifted in his chest. She was neither perfect nor an angel, his countess. Despite her incomparable beauty, her good breeding, her wealth and her charm, even Lady Rosamund Westruther was not unassailable.

Rosamund experienced pain, betrayal, and loss, just as everyone did. Her beauty was no armor against them.

Why hadn't he seen it before? Perhaps he'd been too busy protecting himself from pain. He loathed his own looks and hated being judged by them. Yet he'd done the same to her, hadn't he, without even knowing it.

Her beauty had always staggered him; it still did. But he knew now that if some bad fairy took away Rosamund's stunning looks tomorrow, his feelings for her would not change.

And he knew now, without a shadow of a doubt, that he loved her.

She'd said she loved him. Indeed, she'd never shied from his looks, even when they first met, though his scarred, puckered face must have come as a shock.

Did she see past *his* exterior, too? He was beginning to believe that she did. The thought was frightening, exhilarating.

She entwined her arms around his neck and pulled him down to her once more. "Griffin, I've changed my mind. I need you. Make love to me. Please."

When Griffin finally thrust inside her, Rosamund released a long, soft sigh.

Griffin's lovemaking was slow and passionate and careful—as it often was—and immensely pleasurable, too. He did not do anything different, but everything had changed between them, nonetheless.

Tonight, he'd made her feel safe and loved and secure.

But it was more than that. Her love for him had deepened somehow. When he touched her, when he stroked her inside, it was as if her pleasure existed on two planes, spiritual and physical. Each heightened and informed the other until she lost touch with the difference between them and flew with him in a glittering transcendence of color and light.

There were no words to express what she felt. She only hoped he experienced some small fraction of that unparalleled bliss, too.

"I love you," Griffin whispered.

She squeezed her eyes shut as silent tears of thankfulness leaked from them. At last! She couldn't contain the happiness that flooded her. Her joy in hearing him say the words was so intense, it was almost painful.

"Oh, Griffin! Oh, my darling." She stroked the hard line of his jaw, laughing and crying at once. "I love you, too."

Griffin was waiting in the drawing room at Steyne House when Lady Steyne walked in.

He rose, more from the desire to intimidate than from politeness.

The lady had been unpinning her bonnet, but at the sight of him, her movements faltered and her hands fell to her sides.

Then she lifted her chin and stared up at him, cold lights sparking in her eyes. "How did you get in here?"

"Oh, it really was not so difficult."

She whipped around and saw her son lounging in the doorway. He pulled the doors shut behind him and leaned back, surveying her for a long, silent pause. Then he strolled toward her like a panther stalking prey.

Griffin grinned as his mother-in-law shrank perceptibly in stature and confidence.

"I—I thought you were out of town," stammered the marchioness. Her face hardened. "But perhaps you merely made that excuse to avoid my party."

"The absence was unavoidable, or I would have attended, I assure you. Perhaps then I might have saved my sister an intolerable insult. From her own mother, no less."

Lady Steyne drew herself up. "Oh! Is that what this is about? I assure you, the girl has far too much sensibility. There was no harm intended. If I'd known she had such strong objections . . ." With a smug curl of the lips, she lowered her gaze. "Well," she said softly, "she could hardly be expected to confide such things to her brother. Or to her husband, for that matter."

"That won't wash, ma'am, so don't waste your breath," said Griffin. He no longer felt a particle of jealousy toward Lauderdale. Clever of her to prey on that particular weakness. A few weeks ago, she might well have succeeded.

Icily, Xavier said, "I trust you do not mean to compound your villainy by implying that my sister willingly participated in your little scheme?"

Lady Steyne opened her mouth to speak, but he cut her off.

"Because if you are, indeed, implying such a thing, I shall have to think of a suitable punishment in addition to throwing you out of this house and cutting off the outrageously generous allowance I pay you."

Her eyes widened as the enormity of his words sank in. "What?" she screeched. "You selfish, ungrateful black-

guard! I should have aborted you when I had the chance."
She picked up the nearest object, which happened to be a
fine example of Chinese porcelain, and hurled it at Xavier's
head.

He caught it so deftly, he might have been playing in the
slips in a game of cricket. Turning, he set it on the mantel.

With an aristocratic sneer, Xavier said, "Take your
malice and your tantrums somewhere else, Mother. Like
every other man who has ever figured in your vain, shallow existence, I am done with you."

Xavier opened the door and spoke to a footman outside. "Have Her Ladyship's bags packed and the traveling
carriage brought around."

"You wouldn't dare!" sputtered Lady Steyne. "This is
outrageous! Preposterous! Xavier, you cannot do this to
your own mother. What will people say of you?"

"I do not doubt they will say a great deal," he agreed.
"But if you spread tales of that night or lies about Rosamund, you may be sure that I will hear of it. And I will
destroy you."

"I want what's rightfully mine! Two children I brought
up on my own when he left me. Do you think that wasn't
a sacrifice?"

He curled his lip. "We would have been safer with a
pack of wolves."

After a moment, Xavier shook his head. "No, my lady,
you frittered away your fortune on jewels and pretty gowns
and on your gaming, too, I have no doubt. You have your
jointure, however—"

"A pittance!"

"On the contrary, ma'am," returned her son. "It is far
more generous than you deserve."

She licked her lips and shifted her stance. "What
would you give for my silence about Rosamund?"

The look Steyne bent on her sent a shiver down Griffin's

spine. "Shall I tell you what I will do if you do not remain silent?" he purred. "The lives we lead in these modern times are so fraught with danger, are they not? Carriage accidents, a stray shot from a poacher in the woods, an inadvertently large dose of laudanum at night." He spread his hands. "So many possibilities."

Finally cowed, Lady Steyne began to weep. Even Griffin was a little shocked at that one.

Xavier sighed. "Oh, dear Lord, spare me." He opened the door again and said to the footman outside, "Take her away. Escort her to the carriage when all is ready for her departure. If she gives you trouble, you have my permission to throw her into the street."

The footman, definitely one of Xavier's men, received these orders with commendable impassivity.

The defeated marchioness swept from the room, her head held deliberately high. Xavier turned back to Griffin.

"That was immensely satisfying," he said. "I've been looking for an excuse to do it for years."

"I enjoyed it, too," Griffin admitted. He held out his hand. After only a moment's hesitation, Xavier shook it.

Xavier's face, Griffin noted, appeared slightly gray, and his eyes looked almost feverishly bright. Despite the vitriol that laced his dealings with Lady Steyne, it could be no easy thing to cut ties with one's sole living parent.

Gruffly, Griffin said, "If I had stopped her in the first place, none of this need have happened. If I'd known—"

Xavier's sleek brows twitched together. "It's not your fault. You could not have known what she was capable of. Truthfully, even I did not guess." His mouth set in a grim line. "I should have been there. I could have prevented it."

"You are not responsible for your mother's actions."

Xavier shrugged and turned away. Then he said, "I owe you an apology, it seems."

"What? Good God, no."

"You love my sister," said Xavier softly. "And she you. And I was wrong about both of you."

The feelings he had acknowledged to Rosamund were too new and raw to admit to anyone else. Griffin made no reply.

He glanced out the window to see Lady Steyne being firmly escorted to the traveling carriage. Her head was high, but a hectic spot of crimson bloomed in each cheek.

He hoped to God they'd all seen the last of her.

CHAPTER TWENTY-FIVE

I saw who killed Allbright.

The letter was written in the same hand as the previous one he'd received at Pendon Place. Only this time, the writer had troubled to send it to the London house.

Griffin stared hard at the note. He'd wondered whether there'd been any more point to this correspondence than simple malice, and now he had his answer.

Blackmail. Clearly, the writer wanted money and was leading up to a demand. Pay him once, however, and Griffin would be paying for the rest of his days. He had no intention of allowing himself to be bled dry over Allbright's death.

There must be a way to find out who was sending these notes. The same person who'd started the rumor around Pendon, no doubt. Someone literate . . . Someone with an ax to grind . . .

Suddenly Griffin realized he had a sample of Crane's writing at home at Pendon Place. He'd seen it a time or two when he looked up his grandfather's estate records, but he could remember nothing about it.

He'd immediately suspected his grandfather's former

steward when the first note came, then told himself his own prejudice led him to suspect Crane of everything from smuggling (of which Crane was doubtless guilty) to stolen cattle and failed crops.

Logically, it seemed pointless for Crane to write such an ineffectual note as the previous one. Crane was a man of action, not one to sit around writing poisoned-pen letters with no particular aim.

But what if the point were to keep Griffin on tenterhooks until he was so softened by fear, he'd pay any amount to silence the writer of that note?

That sounded too subtle for Crane, somehow. If he knew the truth, he would also know that he held Griffin's life in the palm of his hand. He wouldn't wait to use that information to his own best advantage.

"Griffin, Lord deVere called again this aft— Oh! I'm sorry." Rosamund pulled up short. Then she hurried toward him, concern pinching her features. "What is it? Griffin, what's wrong?"

"Wrong?" he said, tucking the note into his breast pocket. "Nothing. What did deVere have to say?"

She continued to stare at him with a worried frown in her eyes and something else, too.

Hurt, he realized. She knew he hid something from her, and she wanted to know what it was. The fact that he did not intend to tell her would continue to lie between them, keeping them that fraction of distance apart.

A sudden rush of remorse and frustration swept through him. He *wanted* to tell her, but he'd promised not to divulge the truth to anyone. It wasn't his secret to tell.

She was talking about a ball, he realized, rattling on as if she hadn't cared one way or the other about this secret he kept.

He scowled. "A ball? Here? You must be joking."

"We have been in Town for over a month, easing

Jacqueline into society," said Rosamund. "It is time to launch her in style. She now has the confidence to carry it off and sufficient acquaintances in London that it will not seem like we are throwing her into the shark pool without a raft."

She laughed. "An unfortunate metaphor! But ton parties can be very like shark-infested waters without the support of one's family and friends."

He nodded. He knew that from firsthand experience, did he not?

"And," she continued, "we will gather all of the prospective suitors on that odious list of Lord deVere's together in one place so that you can make your inspection."

She said it as if inspecting a load of callow youths were an enticement. He sighed. Well, he supposed it was, in a way. He needed to get Jacqueline riveted to someone by the end of the season. Since Rosamund's allegiance was firmly with Maddox, that left Griffin to play Cupid.

"Does it have to be a damned ball? Why not a soiree-type caper or one of those devilish musicales?"

"Oh, but there is *nothing* like a ball!" said Rosamund. "What could be more conducive to matrimony than dancing in a gentleman's arms?"

Suddenly those luminous eyes dimmed a little, and her gaze lowered.

With a pang, he realized she regretted never having danced with him.

"I suppose we could have a soiree," she said unenthusiastically.

Inwardly, he cursed. But when she'd looked so excited and happy about the damned ball, how could he gainsay her?

"Oh, very well," he grumbled. "But do not, under any circumstances, expect me to dance."

She flew to him and hugged as much of him as she

could and pulled him down to kiss him repeatedly on the lips. "Oh, thank you, Griffin! You will not be sorry. It is going to be the grandest ball London has ever seen! Everyone will be there."

Oh, Hell.

But how could he refuse her anything when the rewards of giving in were so great? He bent his head to hers.

After a pleasant interlude, she spoke into his ear in that husky, sensual voice she had. "I should so love to dance the waltz with you, my love. You have no notion how . . . exhilarating it can be." The warmth of her breath on his ear sent thrills down his spine. "In fact," she said, teasing delicately behind his ear with her tongue, "I do believe I should become quite crazed being so close to you in public and unable to . . . do . . . this. . . ."

He groaned as her clever, elegant hands did wicked things to his body.

"But there is always afterwards," she said softly. "Or even a moment or two during the ball when we might steal away . . ."

The blood in his brain packed its bags and headed south for the duration.

"You do know how to waltz, don't you, Griffin?" that siren's voice breathed.

He nodded.

"I would so *love* for you to waltz with me."

Damn it! There was only so much torture flesh and blood could stand. "All right. You win. One waltz."

Those sapphire eyes glinted up at him beneath half-lowered lids. "Promise?"

"Word of a gentleman," he growled, and lifted her onto the desk.

* * *

Jacqueline's eyes widened. "You actually persuaded him to agree to dance? How on earth did you do that?"

Rosamund had the grace to blush. Not only because the nature of the methods she'd employed had produced such sinful and utterly satisfying results, but because her tactics had been underhanded and she'd known it, even at the time.

Still, the end was a noble one. Why should Griffin hide himself away and miss out on all the joy that dancing could bring? She'd hoped that once he became more accustomed to wearing fine clothes and attending ton parties, his self-loathing would lessen.

The ton had become accustomed to seeing this big bear of a man among them. The Earl of Tregarth had been the talk of London for a time, but that was mostly due to his sudden marriage to her. She took care to sing his praises wherever she went, and she'd been gratified to see that he'd made a number of friends on his own account.

She said to Jacqueline, "Why should he not dance— and what's more, why should he not do it well? He is an excellent pugilist, or so Andy tells me, and for that, a man must be very light on his feet."

Cecily looked dubious. "As long as he doesn't forget himself and plant his partner a facer in the midst of the cotillion."

All three ladies contemplated this. Then they burst into peals of laughter.

"Oh," said Rosamund, wiping her eyes. "Can you imagine the scandal? But as he has stipulated that he will dance only one waltz, and that one with me, I must hope he does nothing so violent."

"Wear sturdy shoes," Jacqueline advised her.

Rosamund lifted her chin. "I certainly will not! I have more faith in him than that. You'll see."

"That's the power of love for you." Cecily rolled her eyes. "Women grow blinkers on the sides of their heads."

"Love?" Jacqueline and Rosamund chorused.

Jacqueline sat up straight and stared at Rosamund.

Rosamund blushed and bent over her embroidery. "How can you talk such nonsense, Cecily?"

"Really? *Is* she in love with Griffin?" said Jacqueline to Cecily. Rosamund noted that the question had not been directed to *her*.

"Of course she is," said Cecily. Then she adopted the pinched, nasal tones of a renowned naturalist whose lectures at the Royal Society they had often attended. "You will observe, my dear Jacqueline, that the specimen we have here has bent her head and will not meet our eyes. In an animal in the canine family, this would indicate submission to the superior beast. In the genus *Rosamundus,* however, the pose tends to indicate guilt or embarrassment."

Jacqueline giggled. Rosamund looked up and returned Cecily's gaze with a defiant lift of one eyebrow.

"Next," intoned Cecily, "we note that the skin of the creature has turned bright pink in hue. In a chameleon, we would conclude changing color in this manner was for the purpose of camouflage. But while our *Rosamundus* here might *wish* she could fade against the sofa cushions to escape our notice, sadly she does not have the capability. She also displays—and has for several weeks shown this trait, I might add—suspiciously bright eyes. A sign of health in canines, but in female *humans*—"

"Stop! Stop! I will admit it if only you will stop droning on in that awful voice," said Rosamund. "Yes, I love him. There! I said it."

Cecily pointed at her dramatically. "Traitor!"

"I beg your pardon?" said Rosamund.

"Isn't it obvious?" Cecily sighed. "Montford chose men

for each of us that we could not possibly fall in love with. And look what happened! Jane deserted us for the love of her life, and now you are enjoying *your* happily ever after with a man who should give you nightmares. I am the only one who will do the sensible thing, it seems. I shall *never* fall in love." She gave a naughty smile. "Well, not with my husband, anyway."

"Ha!" said Jacqueline. "Why should you not succumb, just as your cousins have? Perhaps your duke is a better Cupid than you give him credit for."

Rosamund and Cecily exchanged glances. Cecily sipped her tea. "If you knew my betrothed, you would not ask *that* question. Besides, Montford didn't choose him. My parents betrothed me to him before they died."

Jacqueline wrinkled her nose. "Is he a wicked, horrid man?"

"No," said Rosamund.

"Is he old and toothless like Lord Malby, then?"

Cecily shook her head. "No, none of those things. Although if he *were* wicked, he would be a great deal more interesting." She smiled. "My fiancé is one of the few single dukes under fifty in the kingdom. I have known him forever. He is quiet and mild, and I shall like being married to him very well."

"Because you will ride roughshod over him," said Rosamund.

Cecily showed her teeth. "Precisely."

Jacqueline frowned. "One never truly knows, though, does one? I was acquainted with a gentleman once who seemed so quiet and self-effacing. Almost awkward, you know. I thought him such a lamb!" Her brows drew together, and she gave a slight shudder. "But he turned out to be a great dirty *rat* in lamb's clothing instead."

Jacqueline's gaze turned inward, and it was clear that she intended to say no more. Rosamund put her hand on

Jacqueline's and pressed it. She wanted to talk about All-bright with Jacqueline, but not in front of Cecily.

Rosamund took a deep breath. "Well, Cecily, no doubt your duke will be at the ball and Jacqueline may judge for herself if there is any species of rodent beneath his woolly exterior."

Cecily laughed. "If there is, you may be sure that it is a mouse."

CHAPTER TWENTY-SIX

The ball would be magical, Rosamund thought as she surveyed the ballroom. She'd filled it with masses of spring flowers to create a soft bower against the pale green walls. Chandeliers glittered; the floor had been waxed to a deep, lustrous shine. The musicians were first-rate, as were the delicacies from her new French cook.

For the past three years, Rosamund had played hostess at Montford's balls and entertainments, so she knew precisely how such things should be done. But this night was special—her first ball as Countess of Tregarth, not to mention the event that would officially launch Jacqueline on the ton.

As Rosamund waited in the receiving line with Griffin and Jacqueline for the first guests to arrive, her nervousness grew.

They had held a dinner beforehand just for her family and the closest of her friends and one or two matrons who would be useful in smoothing Jacqueline's path.

She'd been tempted to invite Mr. Maddox to dine also, but she'd decided not to anger Griffin or upset Jacqueline by making such a pointed statement in Maddox's support. He'd be at the ball, however. It would have been rude not to invite him. At least that's what she intended to tell Griffin when he fumed about it.

The Duke of Montford moved to speak with her. "I have scarcely seen you these past weeks, my dear." He glanced at Griffin. "I wonder why."

Avoiding her former guardian had been a deliberate strategy on her part, and it seemed Montford knew it. Did he also suspect the reason? That she had been foolish enough to fall in love with her husband, of all things?

Well, of course he did. The duke always knew everything.

She laughed and gave a slight, helpless shrug. "We Westruther ladies are sad cases, are we not?"

The concern in those intelligent dark eyes made her take his hand in hers and press it. "I might look like a spun-sugar angel, but I am strong, Your Grace."

Montford's expression relaxed. "I never doubted that." He turned the subject, but he watched Griffin with a calculating light in his eyes until the earl happened to glance her way.

The tender glow in Griffin's expression was so palpable, it seemed to light up her heart. Rosamund could not help beaming back at him in a totally slavish and embarrassing way.

Montford sucked in a swift breath. Observing her flush, he said dryly, "I begin to feel faintly ill."

"Oh! I hope it wasn't anything you ate, Your Grace," Rosamund said with spurious sympathy. "My cook would be distraught to hear it."

A twitch of his thin lips acknowledged her sally, but he did not reply.

He surveyed the guests as they streamed between the double doors, pausing to be announced before proceeding toward the receiving line, where Rosamund and the duke stood.

"Did I hear correctly?" he murmured. "Cecily told me you invited your mama tonight."

"Yes," she said.

His lips tightened. "After what that woman did, you ought to cut the connection. You have my full support in this. That goes without saying, I hope." His lips spread in the thinnest of smiles. "I believe Steyne threw her out of his house."

She had heard that, of course, and regretted the necessity. She also knew Griffin had been there, but he hadn't spoken of it and she hadn't asked.

"I thought you would wish to have nothing more to do with her," pursued Montford. "Aren't you taking the precept of turning the other cheek a trifle too far?"

"Oh, no, Your Grace," she said. "With me, it is more another part of the Scripture. 'An eye for an eye,' is it not? Tonight I shall have my revenge."

Montford's brows drew together. He looked more concerned than before. "It is not like you to be vindictive."

"Oh, no!" she said. "I don't mean to waste time being *vindictive*. In fact, I shall scarcely notice Mama is here, I daresay. One is always so busy when one hosts an event of this nature, don't you find?"

He gazed at her a trifle blankly, and she hid a smile at having stymied him, if only temporarily. "My revenge is to show the marchioness how blissfully happy I am despite all her scheming. Perhaps even *because* of it." Thoughtfully, she added, "Wouldn't *that* make her green if she knew?"

Montford's shoulders shook with silent laughter. "Where on earth did you learn to be so devious?"

She offered him a glinting smile. "Oh, I learned from the very best."

* * *

Griffin was not as complacent over Lady Steyne's presence in his house as his wife seemed to be. The marchioness arrived a fraction too late for the receiving line, which was probably her intention. Fine by him, he thought.

Which was why he was startled and displeased when she detached herself from her fawning escort later in the evening and addressed him. "Lord Tregarth. You are surprised to see me here tonight, I daresay."

"Not at all." Rosamund had informed him she would invite her mother. That she had the gall to accept the invitation did not shock him. Xavier was quite correct: The woman was capable of anything.

"I came because I was invited," said the marchioness airily. "Do you think I am forgiven?"

"Forgiven?" he repeated, feigning puzzlement. "For the portrait incident or for the past twenty years or more?"

Her face whitened. "You know nothing of my family, my suffering, what I went through!"

"I don't particularly care to know what you think you went through," said Griffin. "I don't know if Rosamund has forgiven you, either. It seems like the sort of thing she might do. I only know that I never shall."

He bowed and bade her good evening. He would have left her then, but she took hold of his arm with both hands, and in such a tight grip, it would cause a scene if he tried to throw her off.

Her rouged lips curled back in a faint snarl. "How dare you treat me as if *I'm* the one who ruined her life. You ruined it the day you married her."

"I'm not going to listen to this."

"You will listen or I'll scream the house down," she hissed. "Do you want that? Do you want me to ruin Rosamund's first ball? Believe me, Lord Tregarth, I have very little to lose at this juncture!"

Griffin's hand clenched in a reflexive movement. He'd never wanted to hit a woman in his life. Until now.

Yet, something deep within him cringed away from this woman like a whipped cur. So slight in stature but so powerful in the weapons she could use to devastate those around her. The small boy inside him recognized that brand of cruelty, knew it all too well.

Jaw as hard as granite, he stayed where he was. As soon as she released him, he'd have her escorted from the house, no matter what his wife said.

Why couldn't Rosamund understand that there was no controlling or appeasing this woman? She was pure, un-adulterated poison. Rosamund needed to purge the marchioness from her system, once and for all.

He tried to block out Lady Steyne's vitriol, just as he had tried to shut out blow after blow from his grandfather. Oh, not the physical blows. Those brutal whippings were child's play compared to the harsh bludgeon of his verbal abuse.

"Look at her!" The marchioness swept a hand toward where Rosamund stood, resplendent as an angel in gold spangled silk. "My daughter has *everything* a young woman could wish for. Any man in the kingdom would have blessed himself to marry her, but Montford chose *you.*"

She narrowed her eyes to slits. "Do you think that dressing like a gentleman makes you any less the oaf you were when you first darkened my door? My daughter ought to have had a handsome, refined gentleman in her bed, not some uncouth, overgrown ape!"

Her voice rose to a pitch that was clearly audible to the guests nearby. A few heads turned. Snickers scattered through the crowd. Whispers and titters rippled around them both like eddies in a pond.

Suddenly, his entire body turned hot, then cold. The years spun away. He was back at another ball, a callow, lumbering seventeen-year-old with his grandfather ridiculing him to the world.

Griffin felt his face redden on a tide of humiliated fury. It took every ounce of the strength he possessed not to whip around and snarl at those who would mock him. He burned to call every last one of them to account.

Regardless of his contempt for her, Lady Steyne's cutting words slashed open a wound that had only recently begun to heal. Rosamund had done her utmost to make a silk purse out of a sow's ear. She'd even persuaded him to dance at a ball, for God's sake!

But his mother-in-law saw through all that. So did everyone else, it seemed. He had been fooling himself to suppose he would ever be part of this rarefied existence. And Rosamund . . . She had been fooling him, too.

Lady Steyne's face twisted with malice. "My God, my daughter must lie there at night with you sweating over her like some—some *beast*—and pray for you to be quick—"

Griffin cut her off. "You have said quite enough, ma'am, to show that your mind is as filthy as the gutter. I will not listen to any more. Make a fuss if you wish. Scream the house down, for all I care. Beast as I am, the racket of harpies will not injure me." He bent until their gazes were level. "On the other hand, they *would* hurt my wife. If you hurt *my wife,* I might take your neck between my beastly hands and snap it in two. Your choice, *Mother.*"

He wrenched from her grasp and strode away. The onlookers fell back as he cut a path through their midst.

He did not hear any screams behind him. But the first strains of the waltz made his guts roil and his steps falter.

Then he bowed his head and kept walking until he'd left the ballroom far behind.

* * *

Rosamund finally found Griffin in their bedchamber. Of all places to be in the middle of their ball!

Then she stopped as she took in the scene. Dearlove moved between the dressing room and an open trunk beside the bed, his arms laden with shirts. They were packing.

The valet put down the shirts. Without a word or a glance in her direction, he left the room and closed the door behind him.

"Griffin?" Her gown hushed on the Aubusson carpet as she moved toward him. "What is the matter? Is something wrong? Is it the estate?"

He turned to face her, and the look in his eyes was so bleak, so devoid of any spark of warmth or hope that she could not suppress a cry of alarm.

Hoarsely, he said, "Nothing is wrong. At least, not with Pendon Place. I'm going back. Rosamund, I don't belong here."

"But you . . . But we . . ." She passed a hand over her eyes, struck by the bizarreness of his leaving in the middle of the ball he was supposed to be hosting. "But you seemed happy tonight," she said. "You were talking and laughing with your friends. Miss Porter even tried to flirt with you. I saw her!"

Grim-faced, he bowed his head.

"Griffin, it is Jacqueline's special night," she said softly.

"And you have launched her in magnificent style." The words themselves were complimentary, but the voice in which he said them seemed stripped of any feeling. "I believe she can take her pick of suitors now, and I . . . I thank you for that."

Not the suitor she wants, thought Rosamund.

She did not say it. Nor did she inform Griffin that Maddox had beguiled Jacqueline into dancing the waltz with him tonight.

The waltz that she and Griffin should have danced together.

How she'd dreamed of whirling down the floor in his arms at their very first ball. She'd chosen the music so carefully, too. "The Angels' Waltz," a little joke between them. In her fantasies, that piece of music would be their very own. Even if Griffin never derived the same level of enjoyment from a ball as she did, when *their* waltz played, he would not refuse to dance it with her.

But she would never have pushed him to dance at this ball if she'd suspected he might leave her because of it.

He was leaving her.

Rosamund's knees wobbled. She had to grip the post of the bed to steady herself. She felt weak; as weak and powerless as the day she'd realized that her father had sent her and her brother and their mother away and was not ever going to fetch them back.

She made a sound that was half incredulous laugh, half sob. "This can't be about our waltz, can it?"

He sat down on the bed, his hands hanging loosely between his bent knees. "You say that as if a waltz is such a trivial thing." He looked up, his eyes like slate. "And it is to you, isn't it?"

Her voice shook. "No, actually. *That* waltz was far from trivial. In fact, it was very important to me, Griffin. I wanted *so much* to be held in your arms and dance, caught up in the romance of it all. I wanted to show the world that we belong together."

"No." His voice was so low, she had to strain to hear it. "You wanted me to be someone I am not and never can become."

He went on, ignoring her repudiating cry. "You are Lady Rosamund Westruther, top of the trees, a diamond of the first water. You are a creature of this world. You not only belong to it, you are its cynosure." His lips twisted. "They name *bonnets* after you, for God's sake! And hair ribbons! And God knows what else."

"That is scarcely my doing," she said.

"So effortless for you, isn't it?" he agreed. "When *you* look at that ballroom, you see only acceptance and adulation and pleasure."

She did not think he knew very much about her if he believed that. But she knew what he meant. She belonged. He didn't.

"And what do *you* see?" Rosamund asked quietly.

"Can't you guess?" He drew a deep breath. "I see the agony of being awkward, seventeen, a lumbering uncultivated giant in a ballroom full of elegant, cruel strangers. All of them tittering and curling their lips, pointing out my clumsiness. And my own grandfather leading them in their ridicule."

A humorless laugh dragged out of him. "That ball was in *my* honor, just as this one is in Jacqueline's. What an introduction, eh? Meet Griffin deVere, the laughingstock of the ton."

Rosamund felt his pain as if it were her own. Oh, she had never been humiliated in public, not even by her mother. But she knew the wounds spiteful mockery and contemptuous taunts could inflict. Particularly from someone close, someone who was meant to put the welfare of their child or grandchild above all else. Those barbed remarks chipped and chipped at one's confidence until it all but eroded away.

That was what had happened to Griffin. And he had not possessed an elder brother to protect him from the worst. Nor had the Duke of Montford swooped down to pluck him from that vicious environment before it irreparably damaged his soul. Only the earl's death had released

Griffin from that harsh existence. By then, she suspected, it was too late.

"I love you *as you are,* Griffin," she said. "I do not wish to turn you into someone else. Indeed, you will laugh at this. But when you cut your hair and wore your new clothes for the first time and looked so fine and gentlemanly, I was not pleased at all."

He looked up at that, and she was encouraged to see a glimmer of interest in his eyes.

"Oh, you looked splendid, of course. Too splendid, I thought! Now all the other ladies would see you as I had seen you from the start. I did *not* like that notion, Griffin. Indeed, I wanted to stick Miss Porter with one of my hairpins for daring to flirt with you tonight."

The smile he awarded to that sally was but a faint echo of hers.

She was trying too hard. She did not patronize him; every word she said was the truth. But to someone whose confidence had been brought so low, it must seem that she did patronize him, that she lied to make him feel better.

The truth of the matter began to break upon her like a snaking fissure that widened and lengthened beyond hope of containment. Griffin was so utterly demoralized that nothing she said now could make him change his mind.

"Very well," she managed. "I will go with you to Pendon Place."

"And leave your guests? No, don't do that, my dear. Besides, it is Jacks's ball. She will understand that I must go if you tell her it was an emergency. It would bewilder her and hurt her if you abandoned her, too."

"Perhaps I could bring her afterwards, just for a short stay." Desperation made her clutch at straws.

His hands gripped together. His expression turned hard. "I do not want Jacks to come back to Pendon Place."

"But—"

"Please, Rosamund." There was a note in his voice that silenced her objection.

Surely his determination to go back was not an insurmountable obstacle? Desperate, she said, "I shall ask another lady to chaperone Jacqueline for the rest of the season. I'll follow you in a few days. There is no reason we cannot be together in Cornwall if you dislike Town so much."

He was silent. Then he said, "You were made for this life, Rosamund. I could no more bury you in the country than I could trap a butterfly in a tea caddy."

A butterfly? That stung. "You think I am ephemeral, a frivolous creature made only for pleasure?"

"I think you are—" He sighed. "—too many delightful, good, honorable things to name. But you should be in London, not Pendon Place, this season."

"Not without you."

"You belong here, Rosamund."

"I belong with *you*! You stupid man! How could you dream that I'd choose all this—this flummery over you? Griffin, I *love* you! And you said that you loved me!"

Suddenly, she realized. She would choose him. But he would not choose her.

She sat down abruptly on the chair behind her. Thank God there *was* a chair or she would crumple to the floor.

"But it's not my choice at all," she whispered. "Is it?"

Slowly, he shook his head.

CHAPTER TWENTY-SEVEN

Despair was an emotion Rosamund had not felt for many years, not even when Griffin failed to come for her, year after year. Somehow, she got through the rest of the evening, though she could not have said whether she fooled anyone about the state of her mind and heart.

Control was so ingrained in her that she expected she'd made a good fist of it, however. She held her head up and gave the explanation Griffin had given her for his sudden absence.

Called away to an emergency. Such a pity. Yes, she believed she would remain in Town. She had a duty to chaperone her sister-in-law, and one could not interrupt the dear girl's pleasure in her first season.

She could have laughed to remember her words to Montford earlier that evening. That she would take her revenge on her mother by showing that lady how happy she was. She *could* have laughed, had she any laughter left in her soul.

Lowering to admit that the crowning misery of the evening had been walking into the library after everyone had gone to find Jacqueline locked in Anthony Maddox's embrace.

They'd been totally oblivious of her, of course. Shock had made her freeze as she watched Maddox's dark head angle over Jacqueline's. They made a striking couple, she thought with a hard wrench in her chest and a welling sob in her throat.

As Jacqueline's chaperone, she ought to put a stop to this at once. As Griffin's wife, she should demand to know what they meant by it.

On the other hand, Griffin was so adamant against the match that he would not wish her to make a scene that might force Maddox to declare himself.

Above all, her aching heart urged her to leave them be. True joy happened so rarely in life, and passion such as she witnessed between them was precious. They loved each other. Their love might never exist within the sanctity of marriage. Let them have tonight.

As she slipped from the library unnoticed, her mouth was set with determination. She would not let Jacqueline throw this love away out of a desire to please her guardian and brother's arbitrary notions of a good match.

She would present Maddox and Jacqueline's marriage to Griffin as a fait accompli. All she had to do was obtain deVere's consent. She suspected that if she enlisted Lady Arden's aid in that endeavor, the two of them could annihilate deVere's objections. Failing that, she would ask the Duke of Montford for help.

On that resolve, she climbed the stairs and took her weary self to a cold, lonely bed.

"But I cannot marry him! I *cannot*!" Jacqueline wrung her hands, looking as if she might burst into tears at any moment.

"You should have thought of that before you kissed

Mr. Maddox in the library," said Rosamund severely. She glanced at Maddox, who was white to the lips.

She'd summoned him here after breakfast, having no notion of when he'd left the house that morning and even less of a clue why she herself had been rash enough to allow him to remain. She trusted he had not crossed the line here last night, but knew that she ought to have seen to it personally that he did not.

What had she been thinking?

Maddox, of course, offered for Jacqueline at once, saving Rosamund the necessity of raising the subject. That made her think well of him, on the whole.

She was not so sanguine about Jacqueline's attitude. The girl could not possibly believe she'd escape marriage now that she'd been compromised.

Rosamund winced as another shard of pain lanced through her head. She felt as if she'd drunk too much champagne the night before, although in fact, she'd drunk very little.

"Why can you not marry him?" she demanded. "The truth now, Jacqueline. I think you owe it to both of us, don't you?"

"Oh! Oh, yes, but . . . but it is all such a mess, and I . . ." She turned stricken eyes on Maddox. "Oh, you will hate me when I tell you, Tony. I swore to Griffin I would not tell anyone. And now I've ruined everything!"

Jacqueline burst into long, noisy sobs.

His face like granite, Maddox put one arm around her and hugged her hard to his chest. "I cannot conceive of hating you, Jacqueline.

He looked down at her bent head with such tenderness, it made Rosamund want to join the weeping. "I think I know what this terrible secret is," he said softly. "Griffin killed my cousin Allbright, didn't he?"

Rosamund gasped and sat down abruptly. Her head swam with shock, but she kept her gaze fixed on her sister-in-law. "No," she whispered. "No. He didn't do it. He didn't."

A shudder ran through Jacqueline. Vehemently, she shook her head. "It was all my fault! If I'd simply told him I did not want music lessons anymore and left it at that, it would never have happened."

She dragged the back of her hand over her eyes.

Maddox led her to sit on the couch. "What happened?" he asked hoarsely. "What did my cousin do to you?"

"It was all very subtle at first. I didn't realize what he was about." She swallowed, lifting her tear-filled gaze to the ceiling. "A touch on the hand, you know, or on the arm, or a brush on my breast. All of them could have been accidental."

Maddox's arm dropped from Jacqueline's waist. His mouth had flattened to a grim line, and his up-cut nostrils flared. From the dangerous light in his eyes, Rosamund could not help thinking it a good thing for Allbright that he was already deceased.

"And then?" he prompted.

Jacqueline struggled for command over her voice. "One day, he kissed me. But it wasn't a nice kiss. He pawed at me and tore at my clothes and told me I'd been wanting this, I just didn't know it. And oh, I was so ashamed! That I'd somehow invited his attentions. He did not . . . have relations with me. Looking back, I think he was working toward that, but perhaps he sensed if he did it too soon, I might cry out or be impelled to tell Griffin. Oh, I used to *dread* going to my lesson each week."

Rosamund turned cold, listening to this speech. She wanted to put her arms around Jacqueline and hold her tight, and she wondered why Maddox kept a careful distance between them. Out of concern for the proprieties, or was he angry with her? Surely not angry. Perhaps he felt Jacqueline wouldn't welcome his touch when she spoke of another man's assault.

"And Griffin found you," Rosamund said softly.

"Yes, and he . . . he hauled Mr. Allbright off me and beat him to within an inch of his life. I was not supposed to be there, but I stayed." Her face darkened. "It helped to watch that, you know. I think if my lessons with Allbright had gone on much longer, I would have run mad."

"That was when Tregarth threatened my cousin's life," said Maddox.

Jacqueline nodded. "And Allbright made sure everyone in the county knew about it. He went away, we thought for good. But a week or so later, he came back."

She put a shaking hand up to her hair. "There was a place. A sort of cave on the cliff." She glanced at Rosamund. "Near where I showed you that day, Rosie. I used to go there alone to think."

She drew a deep breath, and finally, Maddox put his hand over hers and squeezed it.

"I was heading there one evening. H-he followed me and caught me on the top of the cliff, and told me he was going to . . . rape me. *That* would teach my brother, he said." She blinked rapidly. "And I fought him, tooth and nail. Oh, I was in a frenzy, as you can imagine! So furious at myself for never having the courage to fight back before."

Maddox frowned. "Where was Griffin?"

"He wasn't there. Somehow, in the struggle, Allbright lost his footing and lost his grip on me. I did not even look to see what had happened to him. I just ran."

Maddox squeezed his eyes shut. He opened them and dragged in a breath. "And you told Griffin, who searched for him and found him at the bottom of the cliff."

Jacqueline nodded. "He has been protecting *me* all

this time. He took the brunt of the gossip and shame. Our indoor servants deserted us. The neighbors reviled him. Only you and the vicar stood by us, Tony."

She made a valiant attempt to smile. Tentatively, she turned her hand in his to grip his fingers. He returned her clasp.

She looked up at him in wonder. "You are not angry with me? Allbright was your cousin. I thought—"

"*Angry* with you?" He shook his head. "God! No, darling. I'm livid with *him* and with myself for recommending him to you. If I'd had the least suspicion, I'd never have suggested it."

"Griffin forbade me to tell you. I think he wanted to believe you'd stand by us, but he was so very hurt at the reaction of everyone around us, I don't think he knew whom to trust. Allbright was so personable and charming. He had them all wrapped around his little finger."

Slowly, Rosamund said, "So all this time, Griffin has been content to let suspicion rest on him to deflect attention from you."

"Yes, and it has been killing me! But he would not let me put it right. The feeling against our family was so strong because of our grandfather's harshness, you see, that he was afraid of the outcome if I confessed. He was taken in for questioning, but there was no evidence he'd been anywhere near the cliff that night. It was only hearsay that Griffin had threatened Allbright's life. No one actually heard Griffin make those threats. The coroner found that the death was accidental, and it has been some time since anyone has questioned Griffin over it. But something has occurred lately to put him on edge again. I am sure of it."

Maddox straightened. "There was a rumor in the village of a witness. Good God, Jacqueline, if there was, he might be able to clear your name. What you have described was not murder, I am sure of it. The man was trying to rape you, and all you did was defend yourself. You did not even push him."

"But to a witness, it might have looked as if I *did,*" said Jacqueline. "And why come forward now? Besides, it is all rumor and conjecture. Whoever this witness is, he has not even made an official statement to the local justice of the peace. I think it is some idle, malicious person trying to hoax us."

Rosamund clutched the arm of her chair in alarm. "Do you think Griffin has discovered the nature of this witness's testimony? Do you think he is going to do something rash?"

"What, confess, you mean?" Maddox shook his head. "He'd be a fool to do that. If it were me, I'd wait until I knew Jacks was to be arrested for murder. I'd try every possible alternative before that."

Letting out a long breath, Rosamund said, "We must go down there. There is not a moment to lose! Or, no, Jacqueline, perhaps you ought to stay here. I shall send you to Montford House and—"

"You will not send me away this time," said Jacqueline with that stubborn set to her chin Rosamund knew only too well. "Besides, Tony will protect me, won't you, Tony? If things get hairy, we can escape justice on the next smugglers' boat to France."

Jacqueline's pathetic attempt at humor could not raise a smile from anyone.

"Smugglers?" said Rosamund. "Are there smugglers operating in the bay?"

"Oh, yes. It is rife in that area, led by a man named Crane," said Maddox. "Before the war, such practices were tolerated, even condoned. It is a different matter now, with information traveling those same channels and into the hands of the enemy. But Crane and his bullies intimidate the populace. No one will inform against them for fear of retribution. Even the local justice of the peace turns a blind eye."

Rosamund said, "Might it be one of the smugglers who saw what happened between you and Allbright, Jacqueline?"

"It was dusk. A little early for them, I should say. But I don't know. It's possible."

Rosamund stood, shaking out her skirts. "I'm afraid, my dears, your wedding must wait. I need to make arrangements for the journey. You will escort us, Mr. Maddox?"

He bowed. "Of course, my lady."

As she hurried from the room, she heard him say, "And now for that proposal, my love . . ."

Tired and anxious though she was, Rosamund gave a weary smile.

She did not even reach the stairs before she heard Maddox's distressed shout.

CHAPTER TWENTY-EIGHT

The breeze whipped off the ocean in cold gusts, and dark clouds blanketed the moon. A perfect night for smugglers to shift their cargo. Or so Griffin hoped.

He and Oliphant lay prone in a natural hollow in the cliff face, the perfect vantage point from which to spy illicit doings on the beach below. Each of them had a shotgun and two pistols. More men were stationed about the area. The vicar had been instrumental in rallying their neighbors to the cause. Since the justice of the peace would not intervene in the smugglers' nefarious activities, the people of Pendon would.

And Griffin would thereby be rid of Crane and his malicious blackmail forever.

"What if Crane isn't there?" said the vicar softly.

"Then we come back again and again until he is. I don't want the decent lads he's led astray, nor do I want the small fish. He's the one. Everyone knows it. And I'm going to take him."

The wait was a long one, but eventually, Griffin sighted movement. A large, dark figure led a trail of pack ponies slowly, quietly down the winding path along the cliff face.

If Griffin had not possessed field glasses as well as excellent night vision, he might have missed them.

"Let's move."

He and Oliphant picked their way silently down the rocky cliff.

Wet sand sucked at Griffin's boots as he finished the descent. The sea spray whipped into his face. He heard nothing above the low roar of the ocean, but he knew the direction the ponies were headed.

There was a cave on that side of the cliff, where he and Jacks and Timothy used to play.

The sole of his boot crunched on something—shells?

The next instant, a bird called. But it was not a bird, of course. It was a sentry.

"Damn," muttered Griffin.

A shot rang out from the direction of the cave.

"Come on!" he said to Oliphant. He whistled up his own signal, calling his men to action.

Shapes rose out of the gloom, coming at them from the direction of the cave.

His own men and Crane's clashed together on the beach like two opposing tides. Griffin needed to get to that cave on the other side of the cove. For that, he had to get past Crane's henchmen, but there was no way he could fire a shot in this melee. He didn't want to kill anyone, particularly his own men. He threw down his rifle and joined the fray.

They fought on wet, uneven sand in near silence. Only the ocean's roar and the grunts and cries of men as they attacked and fell could be heard.

Using his brute strength to his advantage, Griffin milled his way through the crowd. From the corner of his eye, he saw movement by the cave. In an instant, he registered that someone had used the cover of fighting to pack the ponies and escape.

Crane. It was exactly the kind of thing the blackguard would do.

Griffin yelled to Oliphant, then went after the ringleader, drawing the pistol from his pocket and releasing the hammer as he went.

As he drew closer, his suspicions were confirmed. He couldn't see well in the darkness, but he would know that hulking form anywhere. It was, indeed, the tormentor of his youth.

Griffin firmed his grip on his pistol. He didn't want to shoot Crane, but if Crane left him no choice . . .

Silently, he moved up the path toward Crane. The man was not alone. A woman struggled along beside him.

Bessie, from the inn. What was she doing there?

As Griffin hesitated in surprise, Crane swung around, shining his shuttered lantern directly into Griffin's eyes.

Blinded by the sudden flash of light, Griffin dropped to the ground and rolled to the side. At the same time, a pistol barked, missing him by inches, judging from the shower of rock splinters that fell on his head.

Before another shot fired, Griffin picked up a large rock and hurled it in Crane's direction. The second shot went wild.

Two shots. He gambled on Crane carrying only two pistols, maybe a knife.

He rose to a crouch, then launched himself at the bastard. Together, they fell off the path and went tumbling down onto the sand.

Crane came down on him with an elbow to the gut. The impact winded Griffin, but he drove through the pain, wrapped his hands around Crane's throat.

Then he saw the knife bearing down. He caught Crane's wrist with one hand, struggling to hold the knife at bay while simultaneously attempting to crush his enemy's windpipe with the other hand.

"Thought you didn't care about free trade," panted Crane.

"This is personal," grunted Griffin. With a surge of strength, he bore Crane's arm back, dashing the hand that held the knife against the rock.

The knife fell from his splayed fingers.

In a wrestling move, Griffin flipped Crane onto his back and punched him in the face. "You dare to threaten me with silly notes, and you think I'll just sit there meekly? Did you think I'd let you blackmail me for the rest of my life?"

Crane laughed silently, in spite of the bloody mess Griffin had made of his mouth. "I didn't write you notes. Why should I? Say it to your face if I have something to say, don't I?"

Griffin hit him again. "Who's the witness? The one who saw Allbright's murder?"

Crane's chest, which had been shaking with mirth, stilled. "Witness," he repeated. "No witness that I ever heard of. Someone pulling your leg."

"Liar." Griffin hit him again. And again. And once more, for all those lashings Crane had so enjoyed giving him as a boy. Another time for the scars Crane left. On Griffin's face and on his soul.

But he found no enjoyment from meting out this punishment. That was the difference between them. They were both big men and powerful with it, but Griffin simply had not the heart for cold, systematic violence.

Leering up at him, his face a bloody mask, Crane was defiant to the last. "Go on, then. Finish it," he said thickly. "They'll hang me anyway, won't they?" Disgust laced his tone, even as his voice grew faint. "Ah, you don't have the guts."

"You're right," said Griffin, getting to his feet. "I don't have the stomach for this."

Crane didn't move. For all his bravado, he must have been hovering on the edge of consciousness.

Griffin looked around to see bodies littering the beach—most of them moving still, many groaning. And a number of his men walking slowly toward him, led by the vicar.

Someone ran for the justice of the peace, who'd no doubt cowered in his house while all this went on without him. The constable was fetched to make the arrests and the contraband unloaded from the ponies and inspected.

Griffin took one long, last look at his nemesis, shook his head, and started for the path where the docile ponies still stood, and Bessie with them.

"Is he dead?" she asked.

"No. But he will be hanged," Griffin said. He took the reins and led the ponies behind him, not caring if she followed or not. Not caring much about anything.

They walked in silence all the way back to the village. It occurred to Griffin that he didn't know where the ponies belonged.

"Where shall I take these?"

"They belong at the inn," said Bessie. She put her hand on his arm. "Come into the taproom, my lord." She smiled up at him tremulously. "Drinks on the house."

He glanced toward the cheerful lights and sounds of the taproom and shook his head. "Thank you, but no."

"Well, then." She took the ponies' reins from him and bobbed a shaky curtsy.

He turned to go, but before he could, she caught her breath in a choking sob and grabbed his hand and kissed his broken, bloody knuckles. "Oh, my lord! Thank you! Oh, thank Heaven we are free."

"Free of Crane, you mean?"

"Yes." She was silent for a few moments. "My lord? Those notes," she said in a low voice. "They were from me."

He halted and stared at her in the darkness. "From *you*?"

She glanced over her shoulder, as if she could not truly believe she was safe from Crane now. "Your sister did not cause Allbright's death. It was Crane."

"What?"

She flinched at his tone. He cleared his throat and said more softly, "Crane killed Allbright? How can that be?"

Bessie swallowed. "I—I saw your sister struggle with Mr. Allbright. I wanted to cry out, to put a stop to it, but I was with Crane and he wouldn't let me. I was so thankful when Lady Jacqueline got away. She—she'd pushed Allbright and he staggered and wrenched his ankle, I think, and fell down. He struck his head and rolled a little way, but he was nowhere near the true edge of the cliff. And he was breathing, I know, because we went over to check on him. I said I'd run for a doctor."

She covered her face with her hands. "I don't know what made me do it. But I looked back to see Crane put his foot out and—and roll Mr. Allbright off the cliff with the toe of his boot."

She was sobbing now, but he took her by the shoulders, willing her to steady herself. "Do you mean to say Crane killed Allbright? And you knew this all along?"

She raised stricken eyes to his. "I was so frightened! He said he'd kill me if I said anything to anyone. And he *would* have killed me, my lord. You know he would."

Yes, he knew it. He couldn't blame her for keeping quiet, but what a nightmare! He could scarcely comprehend the enormity of what Crane had done, both to Jacqueline and to him. And to Bessie as well.

"Will you be prepared to sign a statement to that effect?" said Griffin. "I will use it only if absolutely necessary, I swear. It is likely that it won't be necessary. Crane is going to be hanged anyway, and without further evidence against me, I do not think this murder investigation will reopen."

"Yes," she whispered; then in a stronger voice, she said, "Yes. I will do that, my lord."

A big hand clapped him on the shoulder. "Come for a pint!" said the vicar. "Or something stronger, eh?" He peered at Griffin's companion. "You here, Bessie? Come along, come along, you have a horde of thirsty men about to descend on you, and it will be all hands on deck, I expect!"

Somehow, Griffin was swept up with the crowd. He found himself crossing the threshold of the taproom before he could object.

Bracing himself for the cold shoulders and dirty looks he always received when he came here, Griffin stuck his chin out and walked in.

To be met by a deafening cheer.

The news of their raid on the smugglers as well as his own bloody battle with Crane had traveled fast. The villagers' hatred and fear of Crane and his men far surpassed their fear of the resident ogre, it seemed.

Bewildered, Griffin received pats on the back and congratulations from the same people who had looked at him askance before. Tankard after tankard of ale was pressed into his hands by men he knew and others he'd never even met or spoken with. Smiling faces met him everywhere.

That night, in spite of his efforts to resist, the hard layer that resentment and anger had formed about his heart crumbled into dust.

"Don't let all the adulation get to your head," recommended the vicar with a fond smile for his parishioners. "Tomorrow, they'll be grumbling about the rents."

Griffin grinned and raised his tankard to his lips. Perhaps they would, at that.

As he walked a trifle unsteadily back from the village,

he felt disoriented, light-headed with drink—and with relief.

Everything was going to be all right.

For Jacqueline, at least.

"I cannot leave her." Rosamund turned to Maddox, who hovered on the threshold of Jacqueline's sickroom, a cheerful bunch of daisies in his hand.

Jacqueline had no sooner received Maddox's proposal than fainted in his arms. Certainly, a dramatic and memorable reaction to a gentleman's addresses if Jacqueline had been at all romantically inclined. Unfortunately, her swoon had been no missish piece of amateur dramatics, but rather a total collapse.

Rosamund took the flowers from Maddox and put them in the vase beside the bed where Jacqueline fitfully slept. She laid a finger to her lips and moved past him and out into the corridor.

"The doctor says it is a fever. She must have complete bed rest." Rosamund gripped her hands together. "He says the strain of the season has knocked her up, but I believe you and I know the cause."

She pursed her lips, feeling traitorous but so impatient to know what was happening in Cornwall that she felt as if she were permanently on the verge of screaming. "I cannot leave her. But perhaps you could post down to Cornwall, sir."

His concerned gaze slid to the open door of Jacqueline's bedchamber. Then his lips twisted in a wry smile. "I am not the least use here, am I? Not until she is a little better and can perhaps sit up and play cards and the like."

He blew out a breath. "I'll go. But I do not expect Griffin will confide in me."

"I think he will when you offer him your friendship

and support." She didn't know that, though, did she? Griffin was a very stubborn man.

Oh, how she missed him! Feared for him, too.

Maddox voiced her unspoken fear. "What if he *has* been foolish enough to make a false confession? I could just see him doing something so deuced noble and ridiculous."

"See that he doesn't, Mr. Maddox. I am quite depending on you."

She glanced away. "And tell him—"

Tell him I love him. Make him come back to me.

She forced a smile. "Tell him Jacqueline is in no real danger. There is no need for him to hurry back to Town if he does not wish."

CHAPTER TWENTY-NINE

Griffin inwardly groaned when he heard Oliphant's cheerful voice greet Mrs. Faithful. Firm steps approached the library door.

The vicar had made it his mission to stop Griffin from going directly to the Devil. Why he must take it upon himself to interfere in that worthy enterprise, Griffin didn't know, except that vicars tended to do that sort of thing.

Of course, thought Griffin, eyeing his empty glass, Oliphant might just be here for the brandy.

After the euphoria of the night he'd almost killed Crane with his bare hands, Griffin had returned to an empty house. Oh, it was full as it could hold with servants, but it felt empty without Rosamund.

He was a maudlin, besotted idiot, and he wanted her back so badly, he could taste it. But nothing had changed since the night of Jacqueline's ball. He couldn't pretend to himself that it had.

Maddox had tried to see him but been denied. Only Oliphant had the courage to come despite the increasing rudeness with which Griffin spurned his attempts to cheer him up.

"Rise and shine!" The vicar went over to haul the heavy

curtains back from the French windows, flooding the room with light.

Griffin winced as the combination of a persistent headache and nausea rolled over him with a vengeance. He shot the vicar a crude and anatomically impossible insult that ought to have seen him excommunicated on the spot.

Ignoring him, Oliphant said, "Did you sleep in that chair last night? Are those yesterday's clothes? Dearlove will have a fit."

"I'm surprised he's still with me, to tell you the truth," said Griffin. "There is nothing for him to do here." He scratched his chin, which he had not allowed Dearlove the privilege of shaving in the past week. "Do you know, Olly, having a sensitive manservant is the very Devil? He is forever in a snit about something. It's like living with a damned female, only without any of the privileges."

The vicar poured himself a drink and disposed his long-legged body in a chair. "Surely not," said Oliphant.

Griffin flung out a hand. "Take yesterday, for example. 'Dearlove,' I said, 'hand me that green coat.' 'But my lord!' says he. 'That thing cannot be dignified with the name of *coat*. It is a rag, not fit for polishing Your Lordship's boots with. I cannot allow you to wear it.' '*Allow* me?' says I. 'Just who is master here?' *He* bleated on about his reputation; *I* put on the coat. And do you know what he did?"

Oliphant regarded him with a twinkle in his eye. "I couldn't guess."

"He burst into tears. *Tears!*" The horror of it was nearly unspeakable.

"Good God!" said the vicar.

"Precisely." Griffin gave his brandy glass a fulminating glare.

There was a pause. Then Oliphant said, "I see you are not wearing your green coat."

Griffin rolled his eyes heavenward. "What was I to do?

When a woman cries, it's bad enough. But a man!" He shuddered.

"Regardless, you must dress and come riding with me this morning. No, I insist," said Oliphant, raising a hand to silence his objection.

Griffin repeated his earlier, vulgar recommendation and sank deeper into his chair.

He couldn't eat, couldn't sleep. He certainly couldn't ride. Everything, everywhere reminded him of her, even the places she'd never been.

The agony of living without Rosamund drained him until he scarcely had the will to move beyond lifting the brandy glass to his lips. He couldn't even get thoroughly drunk, for some reason. At least, not drunk enough to numb the pain.

And now Oliphant thought a hack around the estate would restore him?

Oh, Griffin knew he had responsibilities. He'd get around to recovering eventually. Now, he wanted to wallow, and anyone who tried to stop him could go to Hell, including the bloody vicar.

Before their argument could become more heated, Mrs. Faithful tapped on the door and walked in, beaming with delight. "One of the maids found Lady Rosamund's locket, my lord. It had fallen down behind a sofa. I'm so pleased, for Her Ladyship wore it often and was distressed to have lost it."

Feeling as if she'd planted him a facer rather than dropped a piece of jewelry into his outstretched hand, Griffin could barely find his voice to thank the housekeeper. His fingers trembled as they closed around the locket.

He shut his eyes, remembering the argument they'd had over this piece, the way he'd ripped it from about her slender throat. The earth-shattering love they'd made against the wall.

She'd implored him not to open it. But what did it matter now?

He gazed down at the small gold oval with intense focus, as if by concentrating very hard, he might see through the metal to the portrait or keepsake within. His fingers moved over its surface, rubbed the ridge of its clasp.

He shouldn't. It was a violation of her privacy. An honorable man would not open that locket.

She'd begged him not to look inside it that day in the music room. He'd taken it from her anyway, and no consideration of honor would have stopped him opening it then. In the end, only his desperate need for her had eclipsed his jealousy.

Then, he'd *known* that if he opened that locket, he'd see Lauderdale's face or perhaps a lock of guinea-gold hair or some such keepsake that told of her love for the glittering captain. Griffin was equally certain now that the locket did not contain a memento of Lauderdale and never had.

His fingers fumbled with the small catch. Then he stopped and closed them again around the cool gleaming metal.

Suddenly, he didn't need to open it. He *knew* whose face he would see.

And like tumblers clicking over in a lock when a key turned it, everything suddenly fell into place.

Rosamund hadn't tried to change him at all. She'd tried to give him the life he ought to have had. If his grandfather had been a decent man instead of a vitriolic tyrant, if his parents had not died far too young—he would have been as comfortable in London society as she.

Rosamund had not tried to model him into the perfect husband. She'd tried every way she knew to restore his confidence. To take away his fear.

Fear. A big, strong beast like him, afraid? But she'd

sensed it from the first, hadn't she? He'd been terrified of that exquisite slip of a girl who stood up to him and saw through his snarls and his bluster.

His fear had prevented him from accepting her love. It had stopped him from taking his role in the community and stamping out the tyranny of Crane and his cohorts, once and for all.

Fear had made him shun his neighbors before they had the opportunity to reject him. He had shut himself away, resenting them and their prejudice instead of showing them he was not the monster his grandfather had always made him out to be. And it was his isolation that had made popular opinion turn against him when he stood accused of Allbright's murder.

All of it because he had been too afraid to reach out to anyone, in case they ridiculed him as his grandfather had.

Rosamund had seen it all, hadn't she? And she'd tried so very hard to make it all better. She'd very nearly succeeded. But no one could take that final leap for him. He had to do it himself.

"Will you send it to her?" Oliphant broke the long silence.

"Hm?"

"The locket."

"No," said Griffin, launching to his feet. "I'm going to take it to her myself."

Possibly the last place on earth Rosamund wanted to be after a fortnight in the sickroom was at the Duke of Montford's annual ball.

Cecily had insisted, however. "You simply must get out of that house! Take me to your dressing room this instant and show me what you will wear."

So between Cecily's scolding and Rosamund's own

desire not to appear to wear the willow for her absent husband, she made up her mind to go.

Deliberately, she chose a gown with a demi-train so that she would have an excuse for refusing to dance. She was not ready to dance yet. She could barely contemplate listening to music at this juncture, much less taking part in a waltz or jigging about in a lively reel.

At the ball, Rosamund was glad of her forethought when Andrew offered to lead her into the first set.

She declined, making him eye her suspiciously. "You're not increasing, are you? Never known you to knock back a dance."

She flushed and turned her head, tears starting to her eyes. "Don't be vulgar, Andy. Of course I'm not increasing. If I look peaky, it is true that I am a little weary from tending to Jacqueline. I do not feel equal to dancing tonight."

"Tregarth not back yet?" he said in a casual tone.

"Not yet, no."

"Any idea when he'll return? Only, I had an appointment with him at Jackson's next week."

"I have no idea, Andy," Rosamund said with something close to a snap. "I should not count on him."

"Deuced shame, that. I was looking forward to rearranging that ugly face of his."

The steel in his voice made her glance sharply at him. One ought never to underestimate Andy's perceptiveness.

"He has hurt you." He sighed. "I'd suspected as much."

She did not want to talk about it. She pasted a brilliant smile on her face. "Pray, excuse me, my dear. I see someone I *must* speak with."

With an ironic bow, he let her go.

She escaped and moved through the ballroom, greeting various acquaintances but taking care not to stay long enough to be quizzed about Griffin's failure to appear. Finally, she joined the Duke of Montford and Lady Arden.

After a few minutes of small talk, Rosamund wound around to the topic she wished to broach with Her Ladyship: Jacqueline and Mr. Maddox.

With a flick of her fan, Lady Arden said, "My dear, do not concern yourself. All is in hand. Mr. Maddox was before you in asking for my help, and I have arranged it all with deVere. He is sulky as a lion with a thorn in his foot, poor man, but I have promised him certain concessions if he lets Maddox have Jacqueline." She turned to the duke. "Do you know Anthony Maddox of Trenoweth Hall, Your Grace? He is *quite* a favorite with me."

"I believe we've met," murmured the duke. To Rosamund, he added, "I am relieved to hear that your sister-in-law has found a palatable alternative to either a decrepit old man her grandfather chose for her or her henpecked cousin."

"Yes, indeed," said Rosamund. "And they are in love, which is the very best part, of course."

Montford's expression said, *You are in love, and look what it has done to you.* But he didn't put that sentiment into words, of course.

"How is Lady Jacqueline?" said Lady Arden. "Such a dreadfully daunting thing to have the girl faint before she answers your proposal, don't you think? One would wonder, did she faint from happy surprise? Or horror? Terribly unsettling for the poor boy."

"I believe that when Jacqueline finally came to her senses, it was an enthusiastic yes, my lady," said Rosamund, smiling. "She is well now, if a little low in spirits. She detests being cooped up indoors."

The relief of unburdening herself of her secret had been the catalyst for Jacqueline's collapse, Rosamund did not doubt.

The reminder made her think again of Griffin and the difficulties he faced alone down in Cornwall. The agony of knowing nothing of what went on there wrenched at her chest until she could scarcely breathe, much less smile and engage in witty repartee.

Rosamund did not know how much longer she could bear to remain at this ball. Every encounter stung her with reminders of Griffin, of what she'd lost. As the orchestra struck up a waltz, she made her excuses and left the duke and Lady Arden. She hurried away to find a quiet place where she might curl up for a good bout of weeping.

As she threaded through the crowd, she stopped and squeezed her eyes shut. That melody. It was "The Angels' Waltz." The one she'd wanted so desperately to dance with Griffin.

Hurrying now as tears welled in her eyes and dripped down her cheeks, she left the ballroom and dashed up the servants' stair to Cecily's bedchamber.

Cecily wasn't there, but Ophelia was. Rosamund plunked down on the rug beside the big old dog, flung her arms about her, and wept into her graying old coat.

At least half an hour passed before Rosamund lifted her head and dragged herself to Cecily's looking glass. She shuddered at the sight and rang for a maid.

Perhaps, she thought, as she descended the stairs again some time later, she might go to the card room and avoid the dancing altogether. Andy would play with her, she was sure.

She went to the ballroom to find him, but ran into Xavier instead.

"There you are." There was a gleam in his eye she found difficult to interpret. "I've looked everywhere for you."

And there it was *again,* that confounded "Angels'

Waltz"! Would it haunt her for the rest of her days? She clutched Xavier's arm. "Take me to the card room. Please, Xavier. I—I can't stay here."

"But I don't want to play cards," he said, glancing beyond her. "And neither do you."

"No, you are perfectly right. I want to go h—"

"I believe," a deep voice rumbled behind her, "that this is our waltz."

She froze. She knew that voice.

Glancing up, she saw Xavier quirk an eyebrow at her, then melt away into the crowd. Traitor!

She took a deep breath, steeled herself, and turned. Her first sight of Griffin after so very long—too long— made her heart rap against her rib cage and her mouth turn dry.

But *he had left her,* and she was not going to let him get away with it so easily.

She raised her eyebrows with her best attempt at cool disdain. "A *gentleman* would surely notice that I wear a train and do not dance this evening."

"Would he, indeed?" Griffin looked remarkably composed for a man who had just received such a cold rebuff. "But as you have so often remarked, my lady, I am *not* a gentleman."

She inspected him slowly, from the top of his dark, tamed curls to the soles of his evening pumps. She did not linger at his jaw, so manly and strong, or at his shoulders, gloriously molded by skintight black superfine. Nor at the diamond pin in his exquisitely tied cravat nor even at the sliver of pearly waistcoat that showed beneath his coat.

His white silk knee breeches encased legs that were powerful and muscular, but she did not stop to admire them, either.

Upon completing her inspection, she indicated her train with her fan. "I regret I cannot dance, even if I wished to. My train would trip us up and send us sprawling. We would not wish to create such a spectacle of ourselves. We would hate for people to laugh at us, wouldn't we?"

"The train is the problem?" he said.

"Yes. Insurmountable, as you see."

He grinned slowly. "Oh, not *insurmountable*."

Before she could guess what he was about, he bent down, gripped the fabric of her gown, and ripped the train clean away. As he straightened, he tossed the scrap of satin and lace to the floor.

She gave an appalled laugh that held a good dose of delight. People were staring. A number of shocked gasps rang out. She didn't care in the least.

Griffin held out his hand to her. Still laughing, giddy with relief and joy, she let him lead her to the floor.

Technically speaking, he was not the best dancer she'd ever waltzed with, but he was certainly not the worst.

But this dance. *This!* Oh, it was Heaven to be back in his arms, where she belonged. Heaven to feel his hand clasping hers, his big shoulder hard and muscular beneath her other hand.

The intoxicating delight of twirling with him down the room in her ragged, disreputable gown nearly overwhelmed her senses. Most of all, she savored the delicious and nigh unbearable temptation of having him so close to her while the public arena prevented them from giving in to their longings.

They talked sparingly at first, and then the words just seemed to flow like music. She told him about Jacqueline's confession. He told her about Crane and about Bessie, too.

"So it was not Jacqueline, after all!" she exclaimed. "How utterly thankful she'll be to hear it."

He nodded. "I have Bessie's affidavit, should it ever become necessary to use it. I doubt it will, though."

She narrowed her eyes at him. "I happen to know that you, at least, have an alibi for that night."

He sent her a startled look.

"Thursday nights at the vicar's," she said, unable to conceal her triumph. "When Jacqueline mentioned Allbright died on a Thursday, I thought of it immediately."

"Clever of you." He nodded. "Yes, I had that. But I couldn't use it. Not when suspicion might have fallen on Jacks."

She smiled up at him, a little misty-eyed. "You are a noble beast, dear bear," she said. "I am so very glad you came back to me."

"Not as glad as I am." His expression grew intent. "Rosamund, this is not the time, but I—"

She shook her head, blinking back tears. "No, this is not the time. But I understand, Griffin. There's no need to say any more."

She turned her head to see the Duke of Montford watching them. She gave him a brilliant smile, the first genuine smile she'd given him that night. Full of joy and some tears, too.

As if acknowledging defeat in a bout of swordplay, he bowed to her with a rueful quirk of the lips. Then he gave Griffin a quick, hard stare and turned to resume his conversation with Lady Arden.

"What was that about?" said Griffin.

"Oh, His Grace does not believe in love—or at least, he does not condone love matches among the ton. Yet, his charges keep falling in love anyway." She sighed. "I wonder if the duke will ever be struck by Cupid's dart."

"Him?" Griffin snorted. "Not likely."

She sent him a saucy glance. "I can think of equally unlikely candidates."

"Keep looking at me like that, woman, and I shall forget that I'm a gentleman." He leaned in to rumble in her ear, "And that we are in public."

She looked up at him through her lashes in blatant provocation.

With a suppressed groan, he took her by the arm and steered her out of the ballroom and down the terrace steps. Then, because she did not move fast enough for him, he picked her up and ran with her into the garden through the rain. She gave a peal of laughter, kicking her slippered feet and turning her face up to feel the rain upon it. He did not stop until they were back in the summerhouse, the scene of their very first tryst.

"So masterful," she murmured, sinking down with him into the wide banquette.

But his face had turned serious. "My God, Rosamund, I love you."

He kissed the raindrops from her face, hot lips on shivering wet skin. She sighed and he captured that sigh with his own mouth in a deep, soul-stealing kiss.

Everything Rosamund loved about him was contained in that embrace. The wildness, the tenderness, and the passion. She'd found wonder and joy in his lovemaking before, but this surpassed anything she'd dreamed of. Finally, she could give herself to him, secure and free in the knowledge that he loved her. That he accepted her love in return.

Griffin slid his hand beneath her skirts, and she gasped against his mouth. "Someone will see us!"

"It's raining," he said, moving his hand higher. "They won't come down here."

"Griffin!"

But he wouldn't be dissuaded, and the truth was she

didn't try very hard. She lost herself in the heat and strength and size of him, plunged with him into the depths of desire, soared to the heights of passion and delight.

Afterwards, they lay panting and spent, side by side. Rosamund gazed at the stars through the panes of glass overhead and felt a sense of wholeness and peace she'd never experienced before.

"Oh, here's something I forgot." Griffin shifted his weight, fished something out of his pocket, and handed it to her.

"Oh!" she breathed. "My locket!"

She raised herself on one elbow and smoothed her fingertips over its surface, inspecting it for scratches by touch, for she could see little detail in the darkness. There was no damage that she could feel.

Then she checked the links on the chain itself. "Yes, that was shoddy repair work on my part," she murmured. "The same links broke again."

She closed her fingers around the locket and looked down at Griffin. What had he thought when he saw his own portrait there? He'd have been pleased, wouldn't he? Was that why he'd come back?

"I didn't open it," he said, as if he read her mind.

"Oh," she said, torn between pleasure that he'd respected her wishes and concern that his lack of curiosity argued a lack of . . . interest, perhaps? But how could she believe that after the passion they'd shared tonight?

"Were you not tempted?" she said.

"No."

"Not even a little bit?" She was starting to feel put out by this.

With a peculiarly boyish smile, he shook his head. "But that's because I know what is inside."

"How do you know it?" she asked, a little archly.

"Because you love me," he said, kissing her on the nose. "And you always have."

"Just as you are madly in love with me," she retorted.

"And always will be," he said. And with a wolfish grin, he drew her into his arms once more.

EPILOGUE

It had become something of a tradition for the Duke of Montford to end the evening of his annual ball by drinking a quiet glass of wine in his library with Lady Arden.

It would go no further than that. They were not lovers, of course. *Not yet.*

He was fond of adding that last part—a delightfully tantalizing notion. But in truth, he'd qualified their association thus for the past fifteen years or more. The companionship they enjoyed and the challenge Lady Arden presented to his wits and his ingenuity were things he would not willingly trade for something so transient as an *affaire,* no matter how desirable the lady.

And she *was* infinitely desirable, with her brandy-colored eyes and luxuriant honey-brown hair. Her nose was noble, her chin feminine but determined, and those aristocratic cheekbones could slice butter. Not to mention the delectable body that curved lushly beneath the bronze silk gown she wore.

She bent her clear gaze on his. "I hear that your little Rosebud's mama, Lady Steyne, has married. To a diplomat, no less."

"Ah," said Montford, crossing his legs at the ankles in a relaxed pose. "I, too, had heard something of the sort."

"Then, immediately after the wedding, what must happen but the poor fellow is posted to the steppes of Siberia or some such place!"

His lips twitched. "Oh? I heard it was St. Petersburg." In fact, he *knew* it was St. Petersburg. "Perhaps Lady Steyne does not understand the difference."

"Quite possibly," Lady Arden agreed. "In any event, she will be far enough away that she will cause Rosamund no trouble. Yet the diversions open to a woman of her, ah, tastes in the court at St. Petersburg will induce her to stay there. One would not wish the lady's exile to be *too* unpleasant, or she would simply run back to London again."

"Remarkable," observed Montford, "the way your mind works."

"Isn't it?" she agreed with an ironic smile. "At present, my mind is exercising its considerable powers in favor of your Lady Cecily."

He shifted in his chair. "She's already spoken for. Don't waste your time."

"I have told you, I cannot like that match."

"You do not like it because you had no hand in arranging it. Nor had I, as it happens. Lady Cecily's parents secured the duke for her." A bare month later, they'd been killed in a carriage accident. A very great tragedy, indeed.

"I see," said Lady Arden, a furrow between her brows. "Was there any formal betrothal, or is it merely an understanding?"

"What it is, my lady, is none of your concern." He regarded her narrowly. "Be satisfied that you've managed to gain deVere's consent to Maddox and Lady Jacqueline's marriage—a major coup. How *did* you manage it, by the way?"

She waved an airy hand. "I have my methods."

The silence lay thick between them as he wondered what those methods had been. Then a movement in the garden caught his eye.

Rising, he crossed to the French doors and peered out, into the rain.

He saw two figures, both disheveled and sodden, running together toward the back gate. Montford raised his brows.

"Do they intend to walk all the way home, do you think?" Lady Arden's breath tickled his ear.

"They?" said Montford, raising his brows. He slanted a glance at her. "I didn't see anyone. Did you?"

"No, no one at all," said Her Ladyship on a low, delighted laugh.

In spite of himself, Montford smiled, too. An unaccountable sense of satisfaction warmed his chest.

Then he closed the curtains to shut out the night.

A Duchess to Remember

Cecily froze. Confound that blasted footman! He'd betrayed her.

It had all been too easy, hadn't it? But good God, how could she have guessed he'd tell the duke of her plans? How many servants would remain loyal to their masters when offered the kind of bribe she'd intended to pay?

Or perhaps the footman hadn't informed on her and the rumors were true. Perhaps the Duke of Ashcombe *was* omniscient.

He was certainly exceedingly strong.

All of this passed through her mind in an instant. She fought him, twisting ineffectually in his iron grip, jabbing with her elbows, kicking back with her heels. If she could get free, she'd make a dash for it. She was fast when she needed to be and tonight she didn't have skirts to hamper her.

His hold was not vicious, but it was implacable. Seeming not to notice her struggles, her captor swept her into a room that was not a vestibule as the footman had informed her, but a library. Not filled with members of the Promethean Club, but empty of anyone save her and the man who held her captive.

Once inside, he released her.

He was very dark and very tall and he had the most uncompromising mouth she had ever seen. His strange eyes regarded her intently for a moment, sending an unwelcome chill through her body. Then he moved to close the door and lock it.

When he turned back to face her again, she refused to show him fear. Instead of quaking or begging, she folded her arms across her chest and lifted her brows.

His grim lips relaxed slightly. Holding up the ornate brass key, he said, "A precautionary measure," and slipped the key into his pocket.

That almost imperceptible change in the forbidding coldness of his expression made her less apprehensive of physical harm. But the preternaturally acute way his eyes assessed her was far from reassuring.

He was hard and lean and broad-shouldered. Not an ounce of frivolity or decoration softened the harshness of his aspect. Dressed soberly in a black coat and gray trousers and waistcoat, white shirt and cravat, he wore no adjuncts to fashion save a heavy gold signet ring on the third finger of his right hand. His close-cropped black hair seemed to emphasize the hawkish lines of his nose and the sharp, almost Slavic contours of his cheekbones.

And his eyes. They were a stunning golden-hazel with dark brown flecks, framed by thick, black lashes. Amber ringed with onyx.

Unsettling, almost feline, those eyes. She wondered if they glowed in the dark.

"Take off your wig," he drawled.

The instruction was not quite a command, but it was not a request, either. More a suggestion with overtones of intimidation.

He knew she wasn't a footman. The disguise was never meant to fool anyone except at a distance and in the dark of night. Besides, his manhandling had brought him into contact with the softer parts of her person. The notion sent a hot spear of . . . *something* through her body. She wouldn't let him see it, however.

Forcing herself to give a casual shrug, Cecily lifted the perruque from her head and set it on a piecrust table nearby.

His brilliant gaze flicked over her.

She'd worn breeches enough times to feel neither shame nor embarrassment that he'd caught her in them. But somehow his impassive regard made her want to leap to the defensive, to justify her actions to him.

As the Duke of Montford's ward, she'd long since mastered control over such inclinations. Instead, she forced herself to study the Duke of Ashcombe as dispassionately as he studied her.

He was far younger than she'd supposed when she'd seen him at a distance. The harshness of his features, his arrogant air of authority, and the deference more senior members of the ton paid him had deceived her.

She resented that illusion, as if it had been a deliberate ruse on his part. Older gentlemen were so much easier to handle.

The silence lengthened between them until it became an object with her not to be the first to break it. She let her gaze wander around the room, over bookshelves and tables, globes and maps. As if she'd appraised him, found him tedious, and now looked for some other source of amusement.

"Your accomplice betrayed you," he said at last.

"I'd rather gathered that at the start of our acquaintance." She tried to make her tone cordial but it came out with something of a snap. Now that her initial fear had abated, chagrin at her failure took its place.

Though perhaps she'd not failed entirely. She turned a speculative gaze to Ashcombe. Might she discover what she wished to know from him? If she was clever about it, then perhaps . . .

Drawing herself up, she donned her most regal air and waved a careless hand. "But I am keeping you from your guests, Your Grace. Do go ahead. I shall find my own way out."

Rand, Duke of Ashcombe, nearly laughed aloud at this summary dismissal. Who the devil did the chit think she was? She couldn't be more than twenty, but she waved him away with the careless aplomb of a dowager duchess.

"My guests go on most happily without me," he said, leaning one shoulder against the door. "Besides, you interest me far more than a meeting of the Promethean Club."

"I'm so happy to provide you with entertainment," she quipped.

Better and better.

He allowed his gaze to drift over his captive's person, lingering at the lush bosom that jutted unmistakably from her blue velvet coat, pausing again at the womanly flare of hips that made her knee-breeches tauten a shade too much across her thighs. He imagined her bottom would be as round and female as the rest of her and experienced a sharp tug of curiosity on that account.

It really was a very poor disguise.

He regarded her face. Wide brown eyes with a slight tilt at the corners, a sweet, pert little nose, and the rosiest bud of a mouth he'd ever seen. Her lips reminded him of the dimpled lushness of a cherry when the stalk is plucked. Ripe and sweet, begging him to bite.

"What is your name?" he said.

She watched him for a few moments; it occurred to him that she scrutinized him quite as critically as he ex-

A DUCHESS TO REMEMBER

amined her. A new experience. A not altogether comfortable one.

Breaking off her inspection, she wandered over to a set of globes that stood by the desk. Tracing the arcing frame of the celestial globe beside her with a fingertip, she said, "If I tell you who I am, will you let me go?"

"I'm more likely to convey you home to your papa so he can beat you," said Rand.

"But I don't have a papa," she said on a note of false mournfulness. "I am quite alone in the world, you see."

Quite alone. He suppressed a pang of predatory opportunism that was entirely out of character for him.

Ah, but she was lying, of course. And even if she wasn't . . . He'd never been the sort of evil lecher who took advantage of helpless, friendless maidens. He'd never ruined a woman in his life.

But he wanted her. And what the Duke of Ashcombe wanted, he would have.

One way or another.

"If you won't give me your name, at least give me your direction and I'll take you home." He did not intend to take her anywhere, at least not before they became rather better acquainted. "You'll not walk the London streets alone at this hour."

"If I tell you," she said, "will *you* tell *me* something in return?"

Her effrontery knew no bounds, it seemed. She didn't even seem to register that he had her at his mercy. That he had not even asked her what she was doing stealing into his house.

Rand angled his head and said in a soft, menacing voice, "I don't think you're in a position to bargain with me."

He wished she'd take down her hair. It looked dark and

rich as mahogany, thick and soft and luxuriant. The kind of hair a man dreamed about trailing over his naked body, following the path of those cherry-sweet lips . . .

But she'd scraped her shining tresses back from her face and twisted and pinned them in a fat knot at the crown of her head. Little curling tendrils had fallen free, however, gleaming darkly against the pale, delicate skin at her forehead and temples. He wanted to reach out and twist one of those mad little springs around his finger.

Seeming oblivious to the intensity of his regard, she strolled toward him. "Well, that depends. If you were an ordinary man, perhaps I wouldn't dare. But you, my lord duke, suffer from the eternal ennui of the pampered aristocrat. You're intelligent enough to perceive that I am no common housebreaker. *I,* in fact, am a novelty."

"You, in fact, are a criminal," he corrected.

"But you are curious about me," she murmured, staring up at him with those big, pansy-brown eyes. "Admit it."

She was wrong. His interests were wide-ranging and intensive. He was never bored. But . . . he failed to remember a time when he'd felt so *enlivened* by a woman's presence. Furthermore, his curiosity about her nearly consumed him.

He could have her hanged twice over for attempting to bribe his servant and breaking into his house. Quite apart from that, he had her here, alone, in circumstances that were entirely to his advantage. Who was this girl that she wasn't even slightly afraid?

"You are very sure of yourself," he commented.

She spread her hands. "Why go through all of this if you intend to hand me over to the law? Why not simply order one of your minions to deal with me? You do have minions, don't you, Your Grace? You look like the sort of man who has minions."

He favored her with an unpleasant smile. "Perhaps I

merely seek to toy with my prey before I devour it—or in this case, hand it over to the law."

She shook her head decisively. "No, I don't believe that. You are intrigued."

"I am," he admitted. "Most intrigued. But you do yourself an injustice if you think it is your novelty that excites my interest."

He stepped closer to her and had the satisfaction of hearing her breathing hitch. One side of his mouth curled upward. He let his gaze sweep down her curvaceous little body in a manner calculated to intimidate and confuse a virginal, gently bred female. Or excite an experienced one.

She gave a sudden gurgle of laughter, startling him so much that his gaze shot back to her face.

"Oh, dear," she said, her brown eyes dancing with mirth. Her teeth were very white, framed by those deep red lips. "Pray, do not *smolder* at me so! You will set me off into whoops."

Disconcerted in spite of himself, he said, "I beg your pardon?"

"Oh, you needn't do that," she replied generously. "Though it *is* quite improper for you to stare at me in that odious way, of course."

Now the predator in him awoke, stretched, unsheathed its claws. "My attentions would not be welcome to you?" he murmured. Reaching out, he stroked one fingertip down her cheek. "Somehow, I don't believe that."

Her skin was satin-soft, and he let his fingertip linger at the hinge of her jaw.

Something in her eyes gave him pause. For a strange, heart-stopping moment, time seemed to hold its breath . . .

As if something snapped inside her, his fair intruder blinked and shook her head slightly. Then she put up her hand to lightly bat his away. "*I* am not one of your high-fliers, Your Grace. Keep your hands to yourself."

Already, he missed the satin warmth of her skin. A singular and unprecedented need filled him. He folded his fingers into a fist to stop himself giving in to it.

Most men in his position wouldn't hesitate. She was dressed scandalously in a footman's garb. She was alone, unchaperoned in his house at night. Entirely at his mercy. He affected her on a visceral level. Though she did her best to conceal it, he knew the signs. He could easily give in to his inclinations and make his best effort to seduce her.

What stopped him? Not her clipped aristocratic accent nor her air of gentility. She might speak like a duchess, but he'd known—and enjoyed—duchesses who had the morals and inclinations of alley cats.

No, there was some quality about this girl, some innate core of resilience, of feminine strength, that intrigued him. He responded to it in a way that ranged beyond his physical reaction to her, even as it seemed to heighten his desire.

And for some strange reason, it held her inviolate. At least for tonight.

"Why are you here?" he murmured. And why hadn't he asked that question sooner?

He could almost see the cogs whirring in her brain as she decided how much information to give him. "I wasn't burgling the place, if that's what you're thinking."

"I think you came to find out about the Promethean Club," he said. "Unless you have designs on me," he amended, giving her a flashing grin. "In which case, I'd be most happy to oblige."

She gazed at him wonderingly. "Do you know, you are quite the most conceited man I've ever met? And that's saying something when you consider my family."

"Ah. Yes. Your family," he said. "And who might they be? I thought you were all alone in the world."

Challenge sparked in her eye. "No, you didn't, and my

family is every bit as powerful as yours, so I think you should let me go now."

Was it his imagination, or did he detect a slight squaring of her shoulders, a renewed courage when she mentioned her family? She was proud of her origins, then.

"You interest me exceedingly," he said, mentally sorting through any dukes he knew with daughters around Cecily's age. He couldn't immediately think of any. "And will you not tell me who this so-powerful family of yours is? I shall discover the answer whether you do or not, you know."

She looked for an instant as if she was debating whether to trust him. Then her chin lifted. "I daresay you will. My name is Lady Cecily Westruther."

Well, now. This was a surprise. And she was correct. The Westruthers were every bit as old and powerful as his family. But surely she was one of the Duke of Montford's wards. Why, then . . . ?

His stomach clenched. Suddenly it all made sense.

Slowly, he said, "I knew your brother." He blew a long, unsteady breath. "He was brilliant. Some called him a genius."

"He would have scoffed at that notion," said Lady Cecily. Her voice was steady, her eyes dry. Only the convulsive movement of her throat betrayed any hint of grief.

"Yes," said Ashcombe. "He could never be satisfied with the boundaries of his knowledge. There was always more to discover."

Her expression held a mixture of pride, sadness, and a hint of surprise.

"He belonged to the Promethean Club, didn't he?" she said. "He was here, in this house, the night he died."

Where was she heading with this? "He attended a meeting here, yes. But those footpads set upon him quite a distance from this house." Gentling his tone, he added,

"I am sorry. More sorry than I can express. But it was a senseless, random killing. Nothing at all to do with his activities here."

His assurance didn't seem to make an impression on her. What did she know to the contrary? Or think she knew?

She licked her lips. "Your Grace, you must tell me everything you can about this club."

Deliberately, Rand said, "I am surprised that your brother should have mentioned the Prometheans to you."

"He didn't. I found his diary a few weeks ago, and I—I read it." She colored faintly, as if the admission embarrassed her.

He experienced a hot flash of irritation. "If that's the case and if you suspect someone in the club was involved in his murder, what possessed you to come here yourself? You had no way of knowing what trouble you might stir up."

She regarded him with the alert inquisitiveness of a robin. "Is it a secret organization, then?"

"Not especially." Only some aspects of it were.

He spread his hands as if he were laying all his cards on the table. "I'm afraid if you were expecting cloaks and daggers, you'll be disappointed. The Promethean Club is no more than a group of scientists, inventors, philosophers, and the like who meet once a month to debate and exchange ideas."

Lady Cecily regarded him in silence for a few moments, during which he had the odd, disconcerting sensation that she saw far more than he wished to reveal to her.

"It *sounds* innocuous," she said. "Given what I know about my brother and my . . . another member of the club, your explanation makes sense." She narrowed her eyes. "But there's something you're not telling me, isn't there?"

"Perhaps there is," he said, refusing to show any hint

of his unease. "But you will not hear any more from me tonight. Repay me for the information I've given you by letting me take you home."

Now that he knew who she was, for some reason her continued presence in his house and in that costume annoyed him. "We will discuss this in a more appropriate time and place."

She took a deep breath and let it out slowly. "Very well, then."

What? No argument? The quick about-face surprised him. Was she truly so mercurial, or had she accomplished her real purpose in coming here without his realizing it?

As he rang for a servant, she replaced the perruque on her head. Gazing up at him with an impish gleam, she said, "Are you going to be like Scheherazade and spin out your tale over successive meetings?"

His lips twitched. "Something like that," he replied. With a wolfish smile, he added, "But my motives are not nearly as pure."

He had the dubious satisfaction of seeing her eyes flare with alarm. At last, he'd frightened her.

That vague sense of irritation flared to annoyance. What sort of woman was this? He was not pleased to discover that while his physical intimidation had not scared her, the allusion to more amorous intent made her quake. A salutary notion, indeed.

While his fair intruder wrapped herself in a cloak he found for her, Rand disposed of the perruque wig and gave orders for the carriage to be brought around.

As he did so, he continued to question her, but she didn't give him any more information about herself. He suspected she would withhold personal details just as he withheld information about the Promethean Club.

Lowering to reflect that he needed to resort to trading information for a lady's company. The most effort he ever expended over a woman was in calculating how best to extricate himself from her arms at the end of an affair.

This one, however . . . Lady Cecily Westruther was neither intimidated by his manner nor impressed by his rank. She *was* novel, but not quite in the way she meant. And his immediate, powerful response to her . . . Well, that was unprecedented.

When he wanted something, Rand approached getting it with a single-minded drive and implacable determination. Lady Cecily Westruther was no exception.

As he escorted her to his carriage, Rand began to plan.

Don't miss the first Ministry of Marriage novel from

Christina Brooke

Heiress in Love
ISBN: 978-0-312-53412-7

"[An] enchanting read."—*Romantic Times*

Available from St. Martin's Paperbacks